NEITHER HERE

NOR THERE

NEITHER

HERE

NOR

THERE

BY NIKKI HARMON

www.mt.airygirlpress.com

NEITHER HERE NOR THERE
Copyright © 2019 Nikki Harmon
All Rights Reserved
ISBN: 978-0-9965373-4-6 (paperback)
ISBN: 978-0-9965373-5-3 (ebook)

Cover art from the original painting *Foxy* by
Art87JR a.k.a. Jason Rodriguez
Jason.art87@gmail.com

Dedicated to my mother, Carole Harmon,
a wonderful woman whose love, support,
and inspiration continue to keep me aloft.

Thank you for instilling in me a love of reading,
keeping a wonderful collection of books in the house,
encouraging me to make good use of our local library,
and providing me with the title of this book.

IT HAPPENED AGAIN. I JUST CAN'T UNDERSTAND HOW. NOT TO MENTION WHY. WHY DO I FEEL SO LOOSE IN MYSELF? IT'S AS IF "MY SELF", MY BODY, MY "KIM-NESS" IS A COSTUME. A LOOSE-FITTING COSTUME THAT I AM ROLLING AROUND IN. I CAN SPIN ALL THE WAY AROUND IN IT WITHOUT ANYONE NOTICING. I CAN DUCK MY HEAD INSIDE THE COLLAR OF IT AND HAVE A TEA PARTY. BUT AS LONG AS THE COSTUME SHOWS UP. IT'S ALL GOOD. I'M THERE ENOUGH FOR EVERYTHING TO CARRY ON. BUT ME? I'M JUST A TINY THING WEARING MAMA'S FANCY DRESS AND FUR COAT AND SPARKLY RED HIGH HEEL SHOES.

I WAS JUST COMING FROM CLASS WHEN I RAN INTO SOME OLD FRIENDS OF MINE AND I FORGOT WHO THEY NEEDED ME TO BE. WHO I NEEDED TO BE FOR THEM. I MESSED UP AND I THINK I MAY HAVE LOST THEM. NO. THEY WON'T TURN THEIR BACKS ON ME BUT THEY WILL WONDER ... AND FEEL THE GULF BETWEEN US. AND IT WILL MAKE THEM UNCOMFORTABLE. OH. THEY WILL STILL GREET ME AND JOKE WITH ME BUT IN TIME. THEY WILL KNOW IT FOR ACTING AND THEY WILL DRIFT AWAY FROM ME AND I FROM THEM. AND JUST LIKE QUANTUM PARTICLES. UNOBSERVED, WE WILL CEASE TO EXIST FOR EACH OTHER.

Chapter 1

I shut my eyes to block out the reflections of my fellow passengers but I'm not stupid. I keep them eyes closed for just a few seconds of peace. I'm on the subway, the Broad Street Line heading home to West Oak Lane and a lapse in vigilance could be a costly mistake. I stare back out the windows, which look onto nothing but the blurred walls of the tunnel we are rushing through. The train stops with a jerk every 3 minutes or so to let a few people on or off, varying the composition of the car but not the mood. Most of the passengers exude the same public transit vibe: a mix of weariness, wariness and detachment. The subway is like purgatory. You are neither here nor there. It's too loud for conversation, too jarring for reading, and too busy for quiet meditation. So, you just pause, wait for your stop to get off, and get back to living.

At my stop, I get up careful not to bump anyone, sway to the door as it opens, cross the gap onto the platform, and exhale as the door swishes to a close behind me. Climbing up the grimy station steps, I resume my life as a commuter college student headed home after classes, praying that someone has made dinner because I am starving!

It's the middle of October and the leaves are just starting to get serious about turning color. The air has lost its humidity and Halloween decorations are popping up here and there. During the two block walk to my house I alternate between admiring the work some have put into their houses and scowling over the equal number of boarded up windows and run-down apartment buildings. My neighborhood has always had these extreme contrasts. Mrs. Harbison's porch would rival any horticultural display at the Flower Show. Mums and pansies and zinnias, wind chimes and bird feeders and beautiful small statues of the Virgin Mary accompany ferns and palms. There is even a small waterfall over Zen rocks. It should just be a lovely garden, but instead it seems bizarre because right next door to her row home is a house that was owned by a hoarder. It was condemned a month ago, but through the windows, you can see piles of boxes, stacks of chairs, and rows upon rows of thrift store tchotchkes that have not been touched. You can still smell the 37 cats. On the other side, there is no house at all. It collapsed four years ago, the city finally demolished it two years ago and now it's a vacant lot overrun with scraggly weeds growing among the abandoned slabs of concrete. Too little on one side, too much on the other and Mrs. Harbison in the middle doing her best to incite beauty in her little patch of the world.

I know Mrs. Harbison because she goes to my church. Or, at least, what used to be my church. I went there my whole life, but my mother got married there seven years ago. Now it's my mother's church that she goes to with her new husband. In junior high school, I used to go with them even though I felt like a third wheel. I didn't care. Going made me feel rebellious. Having discovered my affinity for girls in 8th grade, I knew myself for an outlaw and I knew most sermons to be bullshit. I went anyway, with all my secrets, determined to be seen if not heard. It didn't last long. My mother could not countenance hypocrisy; consequently, she just stopped reminding me to get dressed, stopped waiting for me, and then stopped mentioning it at all. They would just be gone early on Sundays and I learned how to make a mean French toast and drink coffee in their absence.

Walking up to my front door, I can see the lights are on and I hear a saxophone solo, Charlie Parker, I think. I imagine the scene inside. My younger brother and sister are sitting at the dining room table, practicing their letters or coloring. My mother is bustling about in the kitchen making some kind of healthy chicken dinner. Her husband is not home yet but eagerly expected any minute. The scene is warm and cozy, a veritable Cosby show episode and here I come, rings cascading down my ears, nose stud sparkling, tattoos peeking out when it gets warm. I mess up the whole picture. I know it and I don't care. I am an outsider here and yet a small part of me is happy about that.

My locks are braided back today, but they, too, have been remained a source of irritation to my mother, who remains scarred by the memory of a close call. MOVE was a back to nature group in Philadelphia in the eighties. Easy to spot by their then unusual dreadlocks, my mother, young and curious, met and made friends with a few of the members and even thought about joining them. A few months later, they were bombed by the city of Philadelphia. Children died. My mother's friends died. The city was traumatized and my mother was racked with guilt. Apparently, my dreadlocks remind her of the loss. I'm sorry about her friends; I am. But I like my locks and I'm not giving them up, bomb or no bomb.

I reach in my coat pocket for my keys just as I hear bass coming down the street, followed by what sounds like a song, then finally, a car engine. Squinting through the dusk, I recognize the driver. It's Meer.

She was Amira until 7th grade, when she cut her hair, took up basketball, gave up wearing anything "girly" and challenged anybody to say anything to her. She went full-fledged hard-core dyke in 10th grade but by then, everybody knew and accepted her and nobody much cared. I also came out in high school, though, I did it in dribs and drabs, parsing out my secrets to a few close friends who I trusted and to the one girl I liked. And that didn't go well. In my mind, Amira and I have always had a complicated relationship, even though we were not friends. She was tall, loud, funny, and bold, while I, though a rebel in my own mind, kept myself amused with academics, science fiction and sarcasm. We didn't have much in common, but I was always curious about her.

Meer. She's creeping down the street, her neck craning around. A weird hum starts in the back of my skull, like an overloaded electrical circuit. I give a shake to clear it, but then my vision starts to blur. I blink and squint to try and focus, but it feels like time has slowed down, the world feels underwater, but I am buzzing with energy. When I tilt my head left, I have a vision of myself flagging her down, walking up to the car and saying, "Hey Meer!" When I tilt my head right I get a glimpse of myself turning back to the door, inserting the key, and continuing into the house. When the car reaches my house, I decide to raise my hand and take a step down the stoop. She notices me. The buzzing and blurring recede as I exhale and focus on her. She rolls to a stop as I walk down the steps towards her. I glance back up at the front door and see a brief outline of where I used to be, a shimmer, a wink of light, and then nothing.

She rolls down the window. I lean down and say, "Hey Meer!" She peers at me, trying to place me.

"Heyyyy ….". I decide to help her out.

"It's Kim, Kim Thornton from Central. We graduated together…from high school, like last year?" I'm starting to feel like the biggest loser ever when she says, "Oh yeah! Kim! Yeah, I remember you! How are you? You live around here?"

"Yeah," I reply. "I live right there," I say jerking my head to indicate the house behind me.

"Hey, I like your locks! They're so long! Look, I'm just starting to grow mine." She rubs her hand over her head full of baby locks. "Hey, I'm supposed to be picking up a friend to go play ball. She said she lives at 136 but I don't see any address like that."

"Hmmm, these number start at the 1400, are you sure you have the right address?"

"I thought so. She said she'd be outside but her phone is broken. I guess I'll just look for her. Hey, you want to come and help me? It's getting dark and I'm already late." I look up at my house and back to Meer, who is grinning at me with her hands pressed in mock prayer.

"Please, pretty, pretty please," she begs. She seems just the same: friendly, loud, and confident. I can't think of anything important that I have to do. I shrug and reply, "Sure, I'll come along."

"But you have to come to the game, too, ok? I'm already late. I'll bring you back home though, I promise." I shrug and say, "ok". I get in the car. It's an old dark blue Lincoln – wide and long with leather seats. I suppose it fits her fine since she's almost 6' tall, but I am pretty small in that big seat. She smiled as I slid in, and then peered at me a little closer. She reached out and touched my ear and smiled. I knew that she had spotted my double woman sign earring, which pretty much announces that I'm a lesbian. I raise my eyebrows at her and smile.

"You? You're fam?" she asks incredulously.

"Yup." I say. She laughs out loud.

"Since when?"

"Tenth grade."

She grunts approval and nods.

"Well, this day is just getting better and better!" She looks at the clock on the dash. "Shit! We gotta go! You look right, I'll look left. She's holding a basketball. It shouldn't be too hard to find her."

꩜ ꩜ ꩜

After four blocks of staring out the windows, we find her friend Tamika, and she climbs in the back huffing and puffing about Meer always being late. We take off and drive to a huge rec center in Germantown and park right in the front. Meer and Tamika jump out and sprint across the parking lot to the entrance. Laden with my books, purse and big puffy coat, I trot behind them and tell them not to wait for me. When I find the right gym, I make my way up to the bleachers and arrange all my stuff around me. I look around and wonder what the hell am I doing here? I don't know anybody, I'm sitting alone on hard, cold bleachers and I'm starving. I look out on the court and see a dozen black and brown women with Meer in the center, laughing and apologizing and making jokes to what appear to be her teammates. The girls towards the left side are looking at her a little pissed, but I don't think you can hold a grudge towards someone who crawls on her knees begging forgiveness and then gets up, and slaps you on the butt.

After a few minutes, they settle down as two women head to the center of court. The ref throws up the ball and they jump up to tap it. As they begin the game, I start to feel stupid. No, maybe not stupid. Ignorant. The players are talking, laughing, grunting, running, pushing, jumping, defending, and shooting the ball. They are at ease with themselves and their game.

Besides the obligatory rooting for the local Philly teams and attending the occasional high school football game, sports have always seemed kind of pointless to me. But now, it dawns on me that I have been oblivious to the obvious appeal of sports for women. Nobody cares about looking cute or being cool. Nobody is asking permission or being nice. And no one is apologizing for wanting to win. These women are free, at least during the game. How did I miss this? Some feminist I am!

I turn my attention to Meer. The last time I saw her was graduation. Everyone was hugging everyone else, making promises for the summer, plans for the night. I had stumbled in her path of hugs and she smiled and reached out for me. I went right in there and hugged her. She felt muscular but soft at the same time and smelled like sandlewood. It stirred something in me, but people were calling her name and she moved on to the next girl eager to have an excuse to hug the big gay basketball star. I shook it off and looked for my parents at the far end of the auditorium. But right now, Meer is focused on the ball. She moves to the right and blocks another woman, looking for the ball. Her hands up, she catches the pass and dribbles left towards the basket. She pulls up and shoots, but misses. She chases the loose ball, gets it back, and passes it to Tamika, who shoots and sinks it. They high-five and jog down the court to defend on the other side.

Stomach growling, I find a smashed granola bar in the bottom of my book bag and devour it as I sit back to watch the game. To be honest, I just watch Meer. At half time, the teams return to their benches, pull out water bottles and towels and discuss strategy. I walk down to say hi and ask directions to the bathroom.

"There you are!" exclaims Meer. "I didn't see you and thought maybe you'd left or something. Why are you sitting all the way up there? You should be sitting down here where I can see you. I need someone to cheer me on!"

"Oh, I ...ok... I just didn't want to be in the way," I stutter. She is sweaty and happy. I smile back at her and ask for the bathroom.

She points left and says, "You can leave your stuff here. I'll watch it." I do just that and make my way to the ladies' room. When I return, the game has resumed and my stuff is right there on the floor, courtside. I move back a couple of rows so I can get a better perspective. Meer glances over at me a few times and smiles. I wave back and try to concentrate on the game.

Meer is not my type. I'm clear on that. Though to be honest, I'm not sure I have a type; romance has never been my forte. In high school, I had a crush on one girl, Amber. She was very funny and sarcastic, but confident, too. And she was pretty, one of the prettiest girls in the school. I know I should not have said anything to her. I should have just kept it to myself, but I was having a moment and I boldly told her I liked her. To my surprise, she replied that she liked me, too. But then she looked at me, and something must have been on my face because she continued, "I mean, I like you as a friend. Isn't that what you mean? Right, Kim?" I guess I didn't answer right away. I was trying to choose my words carefully but that hesitation was enough to send her backing out the room, apologizing for not being interested. She was awfully *nice* about it. We talked just one time after that. Out of the blue one day, she invited me to a party after school. I almost went, but my best friend, Jen, begged me to help her with biology so I went to the library with her instead. I saw Amber in the hallway the next day and tried to apologize to her, but she didn't seem to hear me. I was just glad she didn't embarrass me at school or snicker behind my back. She didn't do anything at all except ignore me for the next two years. I stuffed my "like" for her back, way, way back until I forgot all about it and I focused on school. There were a few other "special" friendships that might have become something more, but I didn't pursue it. I was not willing to risk another rejection at school. I had set my sights a little higher elsewhere.

Meer. She's coming right towards me. She leans on the bleachers and grins up at me.

"I guess you like being a little higher up huh?"

"I can see better from up here," I reply.

"Uh huh," she says. She turns to sit down and drinks some water. I look at the back of her neck and the little droplets of sweat rolling down it. She stretches her arms out and bends them back to lace her fingers behind her head. I watch her biceps lengthen out and tighten back into hard rocks. Her fingers are long, her nails short. A whistle blows and she runs back out onto the court as another player trots to the bench. I get caught up watching her and have to distract myself. Swallowing hard, I try to think of other things like basketball and physics, the socio-economic reasons that most of the women here are African-American, the paper I have to start writing for my organic chemistry class. After a while, older guys start drifting in one by one until the bleachers are loud and crowded. I look at my phone; it's almost 8:00pm. The whistle blows. It's hard to tell who won because Meer is hugging everybody goodbye. She comes over to me, pulling on her hoodie and popping on a baseball cap.

"Want to get a bite to eat before I take you home? I'm starving."

"Um, sure. Is Tamika coming?" I ask.

"Naw," she says, "Tamika is going home with her new girlfriend." Tamika, hearing her name, looks over and waves before she walks out, arm around a woman from the other team.

"It'll be just you and me. I think we have a lot of catching up to do, don't you?" She is almost yelling now because the guys are loud and boisterous and just about to start their game. I smile and nod and follow her out the door.

卐 卐 卐

At a small bar around the corner, which apparently, Meer goes to after every game, we catch up. Meer inhales the hot wings, fries and a Bud special. I, however, am unsuccessful in my attempt to be neat and dignified while eating my favorite sandwich.

"What is that called again? A Turkey Reuben?!" she asks.

"Yeah," I mumble trying not to spill out the contents of my sandwich, "It's messy but it's my favorite. Mmm … delicious!" She laughs and shakes her head at me.

After the waitress has cleared our plates, I tell her about my scholarship at Temple. She responds with tales of her one year on scholarship at Lincoln University. She played varsity ball, but she couldn't keep up her grades and had to drop out.

"So what's your plan?" I ask her.

"My plan? I think I would be good in sales. You know, I like talking to people, and I can be pretty convincing when I want to be. I have some leads I'm working on but you know…" She trails off.

"But what?" I ask her.

"But right now, I'm not thinking about work. I'm kind of thinking about you. I wish I had known you were gay in high school. We could have gone to prom!" She laughs.

"I doubt it, even if you knew about me, you were way too out there for me. I like to be a little more low-key."

"Aahh", she replied, nodding her head. "Keep it on the down low, I got you shortie. Is that how you roll now? You got a boyfriend somewhere you keep for special occasions?" she asks.

"No, that was then. I'm grown now and don't care what anybody thinks!" I say.

"Is that right? You out and proud, huh? Good for you! I bet you wouldn't mind kissing me right here, right now, in front of all these folks, right?"

She waves her arm indicating our fellow patrons. I look around. The bar is half full with older men enjoying a drink and watching basketball on the TVs mounted above the bar, but there are some couples and a few women alone with their wine. They all look like they could be friends of my parents. I swallow my doubt and say, "No, I'm not afraid to kiss you here in this bar but I don't go kissing every girl I hang out with. You're cute and all but my kisses ain't cheap."

"You think I'm cute?" she says smiling. "I knew it. I knew you were checking me out this whole time!"

"Oh you are too much! I'm sure you have a girlfriend too! I know your type, player!" I tease.

"Ooohh, now you want to know if I have a girlfriend! This is getting better and better," she laughs, stroking her chin and grinning at me.

I laugh but I am blushing. I say, "Look, I have got to go. I have things to do. Papers to write. My mom is probably wondering where I am. Seriously, we should go."

She looks a bit taken aback. "Yo, chill. I was just messing with you, Kim. Don't worry, I won't make you kiss me. I see you have not changed. So serious all the time!"

"Meer, I am chill, I just have to get back home. I don't even know what possessed me to come out here. I had fun, though. I really did. It was good to see you again," I say trying to soften my earlier words.

Meer says, "Ok let's pay up, I have to hit the bathroom and then we can go."

I watch her stride away. I wonder if she does have a girlfriend. My guess is that she probably has a few. I reflect on how confident she looked playing ball, how at ease she was hanging out with her friends. Even as I admire her, I'm a little jealous. I can hear her laughing and joking with some guy before I see her turn the corner. I catch my breath and smile to myself. I start to stand up as she approaches the table. I hear a buzzing in the space behind my ears, time slows, my vision blurs. I tilt left and I see me slide up into an unexpected but welcome kiss. I tilt my head right and I see us walking out the door laughing and joking. She's looking at me with a raised eyebrow. I shake it off, hand her my bag, which she takes laughing, and we walk through the bar to the door. I look back towards our table and see the faint outline of us kissing, long and hard. I think I hear hoots and clapping. I pause. I want to go back there, but the moment is gone, the outline fades and she's holding the door for me. I go through it.

She drives me home. We listen to Beyoncé and sing along with the music. When we get to my block, I show her the house and we slide to a stop.

"Hey", she says, "give me your phone. I'm gonna give you my number in case you ever want to hang out again."

I give it to her and she taps in her info and then makes a call. I'm about to protest when I hear her phone ring. Ahhh… She grins at me.

"It was really nice hanging out with you Kim. I don't know how I got so lucky but if you ever want to do it again, just give me a call. Maybe a movie, whatever …"

"Ok", I say, "I'll do that. Good luck with the sales thing," I add on and immediately cringe. Why did I say that?

"Yeah, and you too, have fun at Temple!" she says as I drag my bags out the car behind me. I close the door and look back to wave, but she is already putting the car in gear and pulling off. I climb the steps feeling like I just lost something important. I want to yell for her to come back. I want to call her and apologize for being an ass. I want to go back and get that kiss. But I don't do any of those things. I fish my keys out, put them in the door and go in.

Chapter 2

My mom and step-dad are in the living room when I come through the door. My mom is reading a magazine; Walter is listening to Miles Davis and flicking through TV channels. They look up, glance at the clock on the wall and greet me.

"You're kind of late today, Kim. I thought you would be home for dinner," my mom says, trying to keep it light, though I can tell she's annoyed.

"It's a long story, but I ended up running into an old friend and we hung out for a while. Sorry I didn't call but I didn't think I'd be out too long," I explain as I hang up my coat.

"Ok, Kim, but a phone call would have been nice. I left you a plate in the fridge," she replies.

"Thanks, but I ate out. I'll eat it tomorrow for lunch, I promise." I lug my bags upstairs and deposit them there. I poke my head in both of the kids' rooms, but they are fast asleep. Oh well. When I come back down, they have turned off the music and are watching a crime drama on TV. I grab myself some water and cookies and sit down to watch with them.

"Hey, something weir ...." I start to say.

"Shhhhhhhh!" they both hiss at me. Man! People are intense about CSI.

I close my mouth, sit back, munch my cookies and look at my parents. Even though he's my step-dad, I've known Walter most of my life. He and my mom were friends even before she met my biological father. And yes, that is what we call him, he was such a dirty dog he gets "adjectified". He and my mother were together for about five years, only two after I was born. Apparently as soon as I became verbal and prone to tantrums, he had had enough. My mother says it wasn't me. She said that they were on their way out the day they began but I can't help but wonder. They looked happy in their pictures before I was born, afterwards though, they look stiff. But I'll never know because he up and left for Alaska to work on the oil drills and we haven't heard from him since. It was just my mom and I for eight years after that. We didn't have much but we had fun. I spent a lot of time with family while she worked but I was a pretty happy kid growing up, oblivious to most of the world around me.

Walter started coming around as I left childhood and entered puberty. I hated him and everything about him. My mom fell head over heels for him. I was disgusted. They dated. I grew bitter and jealous. They got engaged. I was furious. They got married. I withdrew into myself. They got pregnant and I resigned myself to being alone. To be honest, Walter was always good and fair to me, but I was an asshole to him and my mother stayed angry with me. She tried to be understanding and empathetic in the beginning, but by the second year, she'd had enough and grew cold to me. I think she thought I was trying to ruin her happiness. I was only trying to preserve mine but neither of us could have said those things then. Her love was my tragedy and over time we grew distant and became polite to mask the cold between us.

She was preoccupied with her newborn son when I inconveniently came out at thirteen. I spent months agonizing and trying to understand "gayness" and what it all meant for me and my "identity". I had my short-lived tomboy phase, my granola crunchy activist phase, my fag-hag phase ... it was all just too much for my mother and she left me to my own devices to figure it out. She had a baby and then a toddler to care for and when I came home with the tongue piercing, she just looked and walked out the room, shutting the door behind her. I became the babysitter and later, just a ghost drifting through the rooms. The years came and went and we became accustomed to the chill. We used good grades and school activities to stand in for approval and affection. We've come a long way since then, but even now she tolerates me and I fend off the pain of it. I need her and she knows it. Walter is smart. He stays out of it.

It's late and I'm tired. I head on up to bed.

"Good-night," I say to them.

"Good-night," they chime back, eyes never leaving the screen.

愁 愁 愁

It's Wednesday and I don't have a class until 4:40pm. I spend the day reading assignments and writing a paper on phages, looking at my phone, and Instagramming my cat, Chuckles. My mom and step-dad are at work, my brother and sister are at school, and I am here alone (with Chuckles). We are two peas in a pod. We like to appear very aloof and self-sufficient, but we are one good belly rub from rolling over and throwing our legs in the air begging for more. And we purr. It's true.

I think about calling Meer but it already feels over. It felt like trying to wave to someone on a ride, by the time I lifted my hand, I was feeling the breeze of her rushing by, watching the blurred back of her head. I decide to write my paper and watch the astronauts on NASA.tv. That's probably weird but it helps me stay focused. I have wanted to be involved in space flight since I was 12 years old. I got into science fiction first by reading Octavia Butler's *Xenogenesis* trilogy. Then for a science fair, I did a presentation on gravity and the effects of zero gravity on mice temperaments and temperatures. I decided then I wanted to work for NASA. When I began high school, I joined the afterschool STEM program. I thought I was in heaven. Robotics and engineering with other kids like me, from all over the city. The program was intense. We met after school, over the summer and sometimes on the weekends. Most of the kids were boys. As a matter of fact, all but five out of 50 were boys. But we girls hung tough and bonded into our own little crew. Until she came.

She was Savvy. Savvy Montana. There was never a more perfect girl than she. Smart, kind, generous, compassionate and gorgeous. She was half Dominican and half Filipino but grew up in Brooklyn and had just moved to Philly where we were just not used to such exotic loveliness accompanied by keen intelligence and a Brooklyn accent. Bronzed-skinned, lithe but curvy around the hips, all fifty of us wanted to be her best friend and fights would break out over who got to sit next to her, who got to be her partner for an assignment and who got to walk out the door with her when the day was done. Even the teachers were in her thrall, calling on her all the time, giving her extra help and consideration for assignments. None of us minded though, she was unabashedly beloved.

I, too, coveted her but I was patient and bided my time. And it came. She was a senior, and I was a junior and we were paired up for her last assignment in the program. It was the beginning of May, the flowers were blooming, the air was warming up, the days were longer and we were given the task of building a mini solar car for a competition with our fellow STEM nerds. Because we wanted to keep our designs secret, we decided to build it at her house. She and her dad had converted their detached garage into a workshop and its dusty greasiness was perfect for our project. I took the bus there just about every day after school that May. We became friends and I realized that for all her popularity, she was lonely. Her parents were strict and kept a close eye on her. She wasn't allowed any male friends and few girls could stand to be around her for too long as her perfection threw their imperfections into sharp relief. But not me. I wasn't interested in comparisons; I was infatuated and only interested in being with her, whenever I could. She was graduating and going to MIT in the fall. I wasn't going to squander my time.

Every day we worked on the car, talked, complained, solved problems and became friends. Even though she had to know I was smitten with her, she allowed it and, I'm sure, she enjoyed the attention. I was aware of how fragile my position was so I did nothing to jeopardize it. But she, I think, wanted to be kind to me and began to bestow gifts – a hug, a brief hand hold, a kiss on the cheek. My blushing and stammering must have pointed out the obvious – that she had all the power in this relationship and she used it. She would ask me to bring her things, or fetch something from her house or do more than my fair share of the work and I would do it with adoration. She began to run her fingers up my arms and to find reasons to touch my clothes incidentally caressing the skin underneath. She liked to see me squirm. She would look over my shoulder and breathe on my neck or whisper something in my ear and I would swoon. She would pass by me too close and her breasts would brush my arm or my hand and I would nearly faint. Oh, it continued like this for weeks until one day she asked me if I had ever kissed a boy. I said I had, but I had not been impressed as he had been a very wet and sloppy kisser. She confided that she had not kissed any boy except her cousin and she didn't think that counted.

She took a step towards me, I took a step towards her and she kissed me. I had never felt passion before, but I felt it that day. That kiss was like a dam bursting. I had been walking on eggshells for so long that the relief of being able to touch her, to hold her, to kiss and caress her was overwhelming. I devoured her as I had in my daydreams many times before. I think even she was surprised by the intensity of my desire, but she didn't back down. I went up her t-shirt and cupped her breast through her bra running my thumb over her nipple until she unbuttoned her bra and offered her flesh. She sighed in my ear and whimpered when I lowered my head and put it in my mouth, running my tongue all over and around it. She brought my head back up and kissed me while running her hands all over my body, grinding her hips against mine. I started to reach around to the front of her jeans when we heard the back door of her house open and her dog run out into the yard. We both knew her 10-year-old brother would not be far behind. We quickly straightened our clothes out, putting her bra back on but sneaking kisses all the while.

Her brother busted in as expected. We showed him the progress on our car and hurried him out to get back to kissing. We had two more weeks left to work on the car and, although we completed it and raced to a second-place finish, it didn't come out as perfectly as we would have liked. I didn't mind though. I had two weeks of all consuming passionate making out with the most perfect girl in the world. And as it turns out, she was kind of into me, too, at least for a while. She wrote me every week that summer from her pre-freshman program at MIT. But once school started, I didn't hear from her again. I wasn't able to afford going straight to MIT from high school, but my plan is to go there for my junior and senior years. If I work hard, get the grades and win the scholarship I want, then I will be able to transfer. And maybe I'll get to be with Savvy again, maybe I won't (but God, I hope I do). Either way, I'll be one step closer to NASA.

Chapter **3**

It's Thursday night and instead of drinking with my fellow students, I am sitting in the lab doing the most boring but well paid work-study research ever. Professor Patel, my advisor, is doing some really interesting work regarding the intentional movements of plants. Everyone knows plants can move grow, shrink, send out pheromones, and emit electrical charges. But nobody knows how the stimuli they receive are processed and interpreted. That's the objective of our experiment. Every 30 minutes I test a stimulus on this lovely sweet potato vine that I have named Mable, and we monitor its electrical output and then I take a cell sample, label it and file it for the grad students to analyze. Tonight, it's army ant pheromones, increasing distance in small increments. Professor Patel has very interesting ideas to ponder but very boring experiments to conduct. Hence, work-study students in the department do the grunt work, grad students do the analysis, and Professor Patel will take the credit. This is my second semester at this position, but I'm not complaining. It's an easy gig except for having to sit in this "isolation" room. It's sterile and self-contained to keep out any other influences, but it's creepy to be here alone at night. I can't use a computer (electromagnetic frequencies) and I can't play music (plants respond to music). I can only read ... on paper.

Biophysics. That's my major. I usually don't even tell people that. When people ask if I am in school and am I doing well, they just want to hear "yes!" So I say, "yes!" and smile. Once or twice I tried to tell a neighbor or an old friend about what I'm studying and after about the second sentence, their eyes glazed over. I stopped myself mid-thought and just said, "Yes, I love it!" Relieved, they smiled at me and said, "good for you, Kim!" Then I slipped back into whatever everyone else was talking about – Jay-Z or the upcoming election or whatever. I've learned that science is only interesting to other scientists and even then, if you're not into the same scientific field, they could blow you off in a heartbeat.

Bzzzzzz….Bzzzzzzz….Bzzzzzzz… time to take a sample, then I'm done for the night. Mindful of the blade, I pick up my X-ACTO knife and slice off a section of the stem near the base of the leaf. Then I press it between two tiny pieces of glass, label it and file it in the box of samples for examination in the morning. Next, I snip off a leaf and drop it into a preservative solution for chemical analysis. Then I make my comments in the log book, pack up my textbook, whisper good-night to Mabel and head out.

It's already 10pm and not the safest time to take the subway, but it's usually pretty empty and I always go to the first car, right behind the conductor. As I walk down into the station I see a young woman sitting by herself on the steps. She's alone with her head down on her knees. She has a plastic bag next to her that looks like it has some clothes and cans in it. I'm wondering if she needs help or if she's just waiting for the train and I slow down. I think I can hear my train coming, but it sounds very loud and it's not in front of me but in the back of my head. An older man with a long dirty beard is eyeing us from further down the platform; he has his hands in his pants and I can almost smell him from where I stand. Then my eyes start to blur, I feel heavy and underwater. I tilt left and I see me stopping and talking to the woman. I tilt right and I see me walking over to talk to the man. The sound gets louder and louder. It's the train. I glance at the man, then turn and stoop down next to the woman. My vision clears and the train screeches to a stop.

"Hi," I say to the woman. She doesn't look up, doesn't budge. I watch the man stumble onto the train. Through the smeary Plexiglas, I can see two teenage boys on the train; they are bobbing their heads to a beat on their earbuds. They are amped up and fidgety like they are looking for trouble. The man hesitates, but he's already on. He heads away from the boys, but they turn towards him. The door closes and he looks up at me. Our eyes lock and his face is somber, eyes hard with fear and resignation. I mouth "sorry" and close my eyes praying that he'll be all right. The train pulls off. I look back at the platform and see a shadow of two people making their way down the platform: an old stooped man and a young woman. I squint but they fade away. I hear quiet snoring. I look down at the woman again.

"Hey," I say, "hey, are you ok? Do you need some help?"

"Leave me alone! Can't you see I'm fucking sleeping! Fucking cunt!" she slurs but she means what she's saying and I back away, confused.

What just happened? I slide my card through the turnstile and stand on the platform. I keep looking for the people I think I saw but there is nothing there. I look back at the woman. She has slumped over her knees again, her bag sliding down a step. The station is empty. I squeeze my pepper spray bottle in my pocket and feel panicked. I'm worried about the old man. I keep thinking about that shadow of the couple, where did they go? Why did I think it looked like the old man and me? That's crazy. I try to shake it off. The train finally comes and I get on it. A SEPTA cop gets off my car and heads over to the woman. I see him shaking her shoulder as the train pulls away.

As soon as I get off at my stop and get up to the street, I call Jenny.

"Hullo?" She answers on the first ring.

"Hey Jen," I say but then I hesitate. I try to think of the right words ... 'look, something weird is going on' ... 'I think I'm seeing things' ... But they all sound straight from a science-fiction movie ... So I settle on keeping it simple, "Are you doing anything? Can I stop by for a minute?"

"Yeah, I just got in but hurry up. Mom and Britt are asleep and I'm tired." She sounds it.

"I'll be there in five minutes," I say and I hurry down the street, looking over my shoulder for the tenth time.

Jennifer and I have known each other since we were toddlers in Miss Jackie's Lil' Scholars' Daycare. She lives three houses down from me, across the street and we've been best friends since we fought over the last candy apple at the kindergarten open house. Growing up, Jennifer had the unfortunate reputation of being a good girl. Sweet tempered and well-mannered with dimples in both cheeks, her mother never let her go out the house with a hair out of place. Adults loved her. She was always the teacher's pet, and, except for our kindergarten tussle, she never got in trouble. Jen and I became like sisters. We went to the YMCA camp together, took dance classes together and her mother taught both of us how to drive a stick in her beat-up red Toyota. Some years we talked every day and other years, we hardly saw each other at all. But if I ever had a problem, or needed a favor, I could always count on her and she on me. Even when I came out, even when she got pregnant, even when I ran away, even when she became a stripper.

I climb up her front steps and text her that I've arrived. She opens the door and beckons me in. I have to squint to follow her. Her mom always kept the house dark – doors closed, thick plastic shades pulled down beneath the billowy gauze curtains, lights always low or off, with just the TV on and its constant blue shadows. I always wondered how they could find things or read, or even just be happy, living in what felt like a cave to me. Jenny never seemed to mind then and I guess doesn't mind now. She leads me through the house to her old room. Like mine, it hasn't changed much since high school. Tattered posters from school plays remain on the wall, friend's school portraits still border her mirror and the bookshelf holds her entire Judy Blume collection. There is even her junior prom picture with her second cousin James, six months pregnant and all. She doesn't look happy in the picture, though. She looks heartbroken. Like someone had stomped all over her heart and left it for trash.

Solicitous to a fault her entire life, Jenny's composure and wholesomeness crumbled and vanished when she met Alonso Belafonte Malfis. He was handsome, charming, attentive, older and bad to the core. He took her to a strip club when we were just juniors in high school and even though I'm certain she was on birth control, she became pregnant and he dumped her shortly thereafter. But she didn't know it that day. She found out over the course of the week when he never returned her calls, when none of his friends returned her calls, when he moved away from Philly and she never heard from him again. She looked for him after she had the baby, thinking the sight of her beautiful little face would bring him back. But she never found him. She did find herself a job though. She's been working at a strip club for two years now.

Tonight, she is sitting down across the bed from me and waiting for me to tell my story. I can see she is tired. She's probably been dancing since 3pm. I gauge her face and decide to tell her only about the old man, how scared and vulnerable he looked and about how I could have helped him but didn't.

"Damn, Kimmie, that is messed up. But I don't think you should feel responsible for that, I mean you tried to help someone, right?" Jennifer said.

"Yeah, but I know something bad happened to him. I picked the wrong person to help." I don't know what else to say. I don't even know how I would tell her about the other thing. Sigh.

"Jen, sorry I bothered you, I know you have a lot going one, I just, I've just been busy with school but I've missed you." I say. I shrug and smile at her. She smiles back at me and reaches over for a hug. She holds on to me and I think she needs it even more than I do. We separate and lounge back on the bed. She starts taking off her toenail polish. It was cherry red.

"It's good to see you, too, Kim. How's Temple treating you? I bet you still get straight A's right?" she asks looking up from her task.

"School is great," I reply. "I like my courses, the other students are ok, I'm not getting straight A's but I'm doing ok."

"You're still at your mom's, right?" she asks. "You two doing ok or do I need to set her straight again?" she laughs.

"Naw, we're good. We don't talk but we don't fight either so whatever," I say. "I'm trying to transfer to MIT next year though, if I can get this fellowship."

"Still want to be an astronaut? That is so crazy Kim! What if I know somebody who actually goes into space!??! That would be so freaking crazy! I hope you do it Kim, I really do. And when you do, I want to be there. I want to see you go up in a rocket!"

"Jen, calm down! I want to work for NASA, not necessarily go up in space. I just want to work on the projects that send people into space. It's not going to be me in the spaceship."

"Awwwww .... Please!?"

"Oh for God's sake ... can we talk about something else, here on Earth. How is your mom?" I say.

Jen caps the nail polish remover and starts rubbing her feet with lotion. "Well, she can walk, bathe, cook and take care of Brittney, but that's about it. She's in constant pain. It's hard to watch. She's always trying some new mix of drugs and diets and weird smoothie drinks, but nothing ever works."

"Sorry Jen. That sucks." She nods and inspects her feet. She leans over and pulls out a pumice stone and starts to work on her feet. I turn away.

"Yeah, I wish I could help her more, but I have to work so we can eat and keep the lights on. At least Brittany will be four soon and we can put her in Head Start. That should give mom a break."

"So, how is work?" I ask trying not to sound judgmental. It doesn't work because she looks up and glares at me.

"Kim, I know you don't approve of my work but it's what I do, what I can do, and what pays my bills. Let it be."

"Don't jump on me! I didn't say anything. I just asked how you were doing, that's all. You've always been a good dancer, glad you're making it work for you."

"Are you being fucking sarcastic? Because that is not funny," she growls at me.

"Let's just fucking drop it, ok? Forget I asked. Jeez. What *can* I ask about?" I say. I'm starting to regret calling her.

"No, I'm sorry, I'm PMSing. My bad. I'm crampy. My boobs are killing me and I've been bouncing them around for 6 hours straight. I'm just … tired and I have to be up at 7 because Britt will be up and my mom takes 2 hours to get herself together. I'm glad you're here. Sorry I snapped. I just … I had a bad night but I am really glad you're here." She slathers Vaseline on her feet and put on fuzzy socks. "Aahhh …"

"What's with the feet, Jen?"

"Just some asshole and his rude ass comments. He had the fucking nerve to complain to my boss!!! About my feet! He's supposed to be looking at my ass, not my feet … asshole. Anyway, want to play spit?" She pulls some cards from her nightstand and grins at me. I grin back.

"Yup! That's exactly what I want to do. Got any chips?" I shake off my coat and settle in. We play cards until midnight when I creep home and go right to bed wrapped in the comfort of friendship. Too bad it didn't last long.

Nikki Harmon

Chapter 4

"It's time for the percolator! It's time for the percolator! Breeeeeerrrrr!" That's my alarm going off at 7:30 am. Nothing like old school house music to get you pumped in the morning. My mother hates it, though, but at least it's just on my phone now and not blasting through the house. I can hear everyone is already up and downstairs eating and getting ready to start their day. I contemplate going to chat with them, but I know that it will be more trouble than it's worth. Maybe I'll hang out with the kids this afternoon. I haven't spent much time with them since school started. I'm a terrible older sister.

I step into the shower and relax as the warm water gently kneads me awake. I think back to last night and the subway, the old man, the woman asleep on the steps and the shadow. What was that? Uneasy, I turn my thoughts to Jennifer. I love how once we cut through the distance of time, we fall right back into our friendship. It's always been that way. When she was gone for two years and came back to take care of her mom and daughter, it took us a day or two to be ourselves again. It was like our friendship had formed a hard crust on it like a scab on a knee. We just had to soften it and scratch at it bit by bit until we could chip it away and get to the raw but resilient friendship underneath. I'd grown up jumping rope, playing Spit and Spades, piercing ears and discussing boys with her for hours. Me, her and another girl on the block,

Kendra, had been thick as thieves from 3rd grade, when Kendra moved in, to the end of high school when we all went our separate ways.

Kendra came later, but she always managed to be the center of attention of our little trio. Jen was the "good girl", I was the "smart girl" and Kendra was the spitfire who couldn't keep out of trouble. I wonder where she is now.

I get out of the shower and plan my day. Breakfast. Class. Studying. Class. Then home for pizza and movie night with the family. Before I can even get dressed though, my cell phone rings. It's Peter, the only other student worker for Professor Patel. He can't make his 6-10pm shift and wants to know if I can cover for him. It blows my plans up, but extra money is extra money and I agree to do it.

చ చ చ

After classes I grab a steak sandwich and Coke from Zo's food truck, wolf it down in the student lounge and head over to work. When I get there, I tell the lab monitor that I'm there to cover Peter's shift and he walks me down the hall to lab room 12. I explain to him that Peter and I do the same work and that I usually work in lab room 19. He says that Peter always works in lab 12 and that's all he knows. As soon as I walk in, I'm confused. The sweet potato vine is there with all the microscope slides and the testing kits. But it is not enclosed. It's in a regular classroom lab with 5 other students either starting or ending their shifts. They are eating, listening to music through earbuds, opening or closing laptops and just being normal. I see a couple of kids who look familiar, but I don't know the rest. Weird. I turn to comment to the monitor, but he's walking away, talking to another student. I look at my instructions for the evening ticked into the lab kit – hornet pheromones, increasing dosage, directly on the buds. No problem there, but why isn't the plant isolated? I chalk it off to experiment protocol, maybe it's just another part of the experiment. I decide to enjoy the company and access to music while I can. By the end of my shift, I've debated the consciousness and psychology of plants, argued for the superiority of cats over dogs, explained how I plan to get to Mars in the next two decades, met two other Biophysics majors and arranged a study date with a math major. I could use some help in linear algebra.

Light-hearted, I bop out of there and head towards the train stop when I get a text from Jennifer. She asks me if I can meet her at Silk City. I have a bag full of books and I'm dog-tired, but it's Friday night and I have nowhere to be in the morning. I tell her yes, and catch the train Southbound. Clutching my pepper spray and looking past strangers, I transfer to the El at City Hall and then walk three blocks from the Spring Garden stop to the diner. By the time I get there, I'm absorbed in trying to work out how much a cab will cost me to get home. I almost miss her as I enter the front door.

"Hey Kim!!!" I look around and see Kendra, with Jen smiling ear to ear behind her.

"Kendra!!" I shout and run over to give her a big hug, awkward for all my books but genuine all the same.

"Since I saw you yesterday, I thought it was time for the three of us to get together, just like old times! I miss my girls!" exclaimed Jen.

"Let's get something to eat, I'm hungry as shit!" says Kendra. I concur and we head into the diner. We get lucky and score a booth. I need space for all my books, so they sit on one side and I sit on the opposite. We order rum and cokes (thank god no one asks me for ID!) and some food and get to catching up. As usual, Kendra dominates the conversation, but I don't mind. I'm just happy to see her again. It's been two years already.

"So, I know you bitches want to know what I've been up to … well, don't choke but I'm a personal trainer …" I choke on my drink. "…and a real estate agent…" Jen frowns and gapes. "…and I'm getting married …" Jen and I both yell, "what?!?!?" "… to a white boy." We lose it. I knock over my drink, Jen throws her hands up in the air, we both start blabbering and the other customers turn to stare. Kendra tries to shush us but it's just too much. The waitress comes over to clean up my drink and I can't even think to thank her, I can't even close my mouth.

After an hour of explaining and re-explaining, two more drinks and constant head shaking, I'm wrapping my head around the idea that Kendra has changed. I cannot believe somebody could make this kind of 180-degree turn. Kendra was the bad ass of the whole neighborhood. She had a quick temper and would lose it if she felt she was being disrespected. I can't begin to count the number of fights I pulled her out of nor the number of felonies I have personally seen her commit. She had been a decent rapper and was training to be a boxer before she became a dealer's girlfriend. That was right before we graduated. I distanced myself from her when she got with Tyrell. I can't mess with drug dealers. I have plans. But somehow, she left Tyrell (with a broken finger, mind you), went back to the gym, started training someone else, then another, then another (turns out lots of women like tough love), then got hired, trained a real estate agent who talked her into taking the test, became an agent and fell in love with the first divorcé she met trying to buy a condo. Unbelievable.

Spinning from Kendra's news and tipsy from the Captain Morgan's, we decide to go into the club half of Silk and dance. They are playing some Emo and I could use a good sweat. We head in, it's hot, it's thick and funky and full of people dancing their asses off. It's exactly where I want to be. We tuck our coats and my bag into a corner and turn to check out the dance floor. Some gay boys are tearing it up in one corner, some breakdancers are battling it out in another, some couples are getting their freak on and a group of girls are under the disco ball letting go their work week stress. We bob our way into the fray when the DJ throws on "Break for Love". My jam. I close my eyes and lose myself in the music. When I open my eyes, I see Kendra drifting towards this tall brother with long locks and a generous smile. Jen is grooving in her own little world, keeping her circle tight around her and smiling to herself. I spin around and see a girl smiling at me. I smile back. She looks towards Jen and raises her eyebrows. I shake my head and she starts to dance towards me. Suddenly I hear the roar in the back of my head and my vision starts to blur. It takes me a second to realize it is not the music or the drink but the thing is happening again. I tilt my head left and see Jen dancing alone when a drunk and angry man grabs her and forces her to her knees. I tilt right and see Jen and I heading out the door together. I try to look around to see more, but it blurs and the roaring gets louder. I shake my head to clear it and I start making my way towards Jen. The cute girl is watching me. She shrugs, then dances over to another corner of the room. I stop dancing and just stand there. Jen opens her eyes.

"What's wrong Kim?" she asks. "Are you feeling ok? You look like you're going to throw up. You're not going to throw up, are you?" Jen asks looking disgusted.

"No, but I ... I have to tell you something. Come here." I pull her towards an empty spot on the wall.

"What's the matter, Kim?" She looks concerned but distracted by the music.

"Something weird is happening to me. I think I can see choices?"

"What? What are you talking about?"

"Sometimes, I get a rumbling in my head ... this sounds crazy, I know, but it's just in the last few days ... my vision blurs and I see two pictures?" Jen is looking at me like I'm crazy. "It feels like I'm seeing what would happen if I chose one thing, but I also see the other choice ... it's so weird, I know." I stop because I see the man, the drunk and angry man come through the door. He weaves around people and starts dancing right in the middle of the floor. I stare at him. Jen turns to see what I'm looking at and spots him right away. She sucks in her breath and says, "That asshole! What is he doing here? He kept bugging me for a blowjob all day long, asshole!" I just turn and stare at her. She looks back.

"Now what were you saying? You're having double vision? Maybe you should go to a doctor, Kim. Maybe something is wrong with your brain. Oh look, here comes Kendra." Kendra slips over giggling.

"Whoooo girl. He is sexy!!!! But I have to remember, I love Rob. I love Rob. I. Love. Rob! But good lawd, he is sexy," she says tucking a slip of paper into her back pocket.

Jen balks. "You did not just take his number!"

Kendra replies, "He says he's looking to buy a house and maybe I could help him. It's business Jen. Strictly business. I love Rob." But the last part just fades away as she waves again at him and then watches him walk away.

"Y'all ready to go?" asks Jen. "I have to get some sleep before Brittney is up in the morning." "Yeah, I'm ready." I reply. "Me too," says Kendra. "And I'm driving. Rob loaned me his car." She shakes the keys and leads us out the club. I smile at my good fortune and we go.

Chapter 5

Tired as I am, the sound of Saturday morning cartoons always wakes me up. I throw on a robe and stumble down to the family room where Maya and Lil' Walt are watching SpongeBob and cracking up. My mom and Walter are still sleeping, so I get us all some dry Corn Pops and settle down to watch. I remember this episode. Maya snuggles against my legs and Walt sits on my feet. At the commercial, I ask them if they would like to go to the playground today. They scream "yes" and jump on me. All my Corn Pops spill on the ground and we roll around as I tickle them. We are interrupted by a loud gasp and we look up at my mother's pissed off face. I look around. Smashed Corn Pops everywhere.

"I'll clean it up, Mom. I'm sorry. We just got carried away," I say trying to extricate myself from the kids who have gone back to staring at the TV.

"Of course you are going to clean it up, Kim," huffs my mom as she stalks off and goes into the kitchen. I hear lots of banging around. I wait until the banging subsides before I duck in to get the dust buster. Coffee is brewing and my mom is leaning against the sink looking out the window. Without looking at me, she sighs, "Should I bother cooking eggs and sausage or are they all full of sugar cereal?"

"It was just a snack until you got up. I'm sure they're still hungry," I say trying to unplug the duster from the charger.

"Hey, can I take them to the playground today? I know I've been busy with school, but I have some time this morning."

"That's a nice idea, but we have plans today Kim. We're going to the, uh, aquarium. Walt's been wanting to see the jellyfish exhibit and this is the last weekend. Sorry."

"Oh, ok, they'll love that." I leave to go clean up my mess, but have to wait until the commercial comes on.

"Hey guys, we'll have to do the playground another day. You guys didn't tell me you already have plans!" I say.

"What plans?" asks Maya. "I thought today was a free day?" My mom comes in with a cup of coffee and sits down on the couch.

"Oh, I didn't want to tell you about until we were sure, honey. But yeah, we're going to the aquarium today. Won't that be exciting?" She pats the seat next to her and Maya climbs up and snuggles in. Lil' Walt looks up and says, "Can you come, Kim?" I open my mouth to reply, but my mom answers for me. "I'm sure Kim has a lot of studying to do for school. I think the aquarium would be boring for her." Actually, I think that I can't remember the last time I went to the aquarium and that it might be fun but I get it, so I say nothing.

She would never say it out loud, but while she is very proud of my academics, she's not comfortable with my "lifestyle". She thinks it might rub off on the kids or that they may think it is ok. It doesn't matter that my lifestyle mostly consists of going to class and studying. It doesn't matter that I have not been out on a date in a year. It doesn't matter that they are my brother and sister and I have taken care of them since they were born. She doesn't want me with them even though she lets me live here. It hurts but I'm used to this pain, so I bear it and try not to be bitter about it. I get up, pat the kids on the head and go to the kitchen to get a cup of coffee. It's a warm fall day. It looks beautiful outside and I want to go out, but I have a reputation to uphold. So, I decide to study until they leave so that no matter what my mom might think about me, she can't accuse me of wasting my time or being lazy or not being serious about school. I throw on some sweats and settle down in the living room. I spread out my textbooks and flip open my laptop. Oh, I am going to look serious. I read, take notes, drink coffee and even get ahead in my Evolution class. All around me the kids eat, play, argue, get dressed, pack snacks and books for the ride over. All around me Walter Sr. is pleasant and playful with everyone, even reading over my shoulder then patting me on it. All around me my mother is a good mother, a kind mother, patient, caring and attentive. I study why and how lemurs evolved. I study natural selection and how whatever creature thrives in their environment gets to pass down their genes and influence generations to come. I look around me and wonder how many mothers influence natural selection through intent or neglect. I wonder how many creatures fight for existence despite their poor adaptations, despite their inability to best exploit the world they were born into.

They leave and I sigh a big sigh of relief. I close my eyes because I feel like crying and I will not. Absolutely not cry. I am strong, this shit is old and does not faze me. I am getting out of here in less than a year come hell or high water and I will not break. I open my eyes. I think I'm going to call Skylar.

Skylar would be a great girlfriend for me – smart, healthy, doesn't like science but likes science fiction, cute in a Tracy Chapman kind of way, out, and a really nice person. The problem? We just aren't attracted to each other. Oh, we tried but it felt like dating my sister; there was just no excitement whatsoever, so we became friends instead. She goes to Bryn Mawr, a small college just outside of Philadelphia, where she has her pick of politically curious white girls and quietly experimenting brown girls. Despite her crunchiness, she's a pragmatist and a Political Science major and will probably go on to law school.

I text her and we decide to meet at Tiny Bubbles, a café in the gayborhood. Walking from Jefferson Station to 12th and Lombard is a study in contrasts. Big retail stores at the Gallery give way to small storefronts selling jewelry and phones, which switches to coffee shops to cafes to cute expensive restaurants filled with handsome young men smiling at each other. Tiny Bubbles is one of the few women owned café's in the area so sometimes there are more than a couple of women, but it's still primarily filled with guys. Its décor is ethereal in an underwater kind of way. Big murals on the walls fade from pale blue to midnight featuring galaxies and mermaids and creatures of all sorts floating among them. It's relaxing and disconcerting at the same time. On the ceiling are scattered portraits of various people – movie stars, famous authors, and the waiters and waitresses. Skylar is already there when I arrive. She is sitting at the table in the front window. I know she does this on purpose. Visibility is part of her personal mission. She is knee deep in a book and doesn't notice me until I pull out my chair. She reluctantly looks up, smiles and stands up to greet me. I put down my bag and we hug hello. I know it's another part of her mission but I don't mind, I could use a hug today.

"Kim, you have to read this book. It's so deep and so sad and so infuriating! Honestly, I should not read this stuff. It's for a class so I have to read it, but how in the world am I going to be able to write an essay about it without cursing??? I don't know. Honestly, how does this shit go on, why do we allow it? People just suck. I mean it. Except for you, Kim. People just suck… and like in a bad way." She laughs. "So hi, how are you?" Skylar is a big talker.

"Hi," I say laughing. "Right now, I'm scared to ask what you are reading."

"Michelle Alexander's *The New Jim Crow*. It's a fucking disgrace, a fucking disgrace …"

Just then the waitress comes over. She's a beautiful light skinned woman sprinkled with brown freckles. I don't know what it is but I've always thought freckles are so cute. Her hair is pulled back in a scarf, but her braids reached all the way down her back. She pulls out her little notebook and says politely, "What can I get you ladies?' She smiles at Skylar who orders a pumpkin spice muffin and a chai tea. I'm a little distracted by her dimple.

"I'll just have a latte," I say.

"Are you sure you don't want a muffin too? They are really good today."

"Um … no thanks, I'm ok," I say and blush.

"Ok," she says and drifts away to clear a table before giving our order to the barista.

"So, how's Temple?" asks Skylar.

"Oh, it's fine. I like most of my courses this semester except this math class, which is kicking my ass." I sigh. "How about you?"

"Oh, it's all good. Politics of Public Education, 19th Century European Politics, Feminist Reading of Shakespeare, Microeconomics and I'm taking a pottery class."

"Pottery?"

"It was either that or Yoga and the yoga is at 6am, so yup, pottery and I like it, it feels so cool to get messy. I've already made a bowl." We laugh. The waitress returns with my latte and Skylar's tea. She sets down the mugs and cream and sugar. All the dishes are pale blue, rounded and delicate looking. She leaves and returns a minute later with Skylar's muffin on a beautiful blue plate covered in swirls. The muffin is a thing of beauty. Large and fluffy, with a crumbled sugar top, I can smell the pumpkin and spices from where I am sitting. Skylar smiles wide and thanks the waitress who nods and leaves.

"Man," I sigh, "I wish I had gotten one. That looks delicious!"

"I know," says Skylar and she says something else, but I don't really hear her because the roar starts up in the back of my head. It fills up my brain. I'm looking at Skylar and she's talking, but I can't hear her. As I look down, my vision blurs. I look back at her and take a brief second to marvel at that muffin again, wishing I had ordered one. I clamp my eyes shut trying to will out the roar. I shake my head and it stops. It clears. I open my eyes. Skylar is looking at me.

"What's wrong, Kim? Are you ok?" she asks.

"Yeah, I'm ok but ...." I stop talking. Next to my coffee is a plate with a muffin. Kim still has hers in front of her. I look at my muffin and back up to Kim.

"What?" she asks, "Is something wrong with it? Mine looks delicious." She picks up her muffin and takes a bite. I poke mine. I look around the café. Everything seems the same.

"How did I get a muffin?" I ask Skylar.

"Um, you ordered it and the waitress brought it," she replies talking slowly and rolling her eyes.

"I didn't order a muffin," I say.

"Yes, you did," she replies. "But if you don't want it, I'm sure you can send it back."

"No," I say slowly. "I want it, but I'm pretty sure I didn't order it. I don't remember ..." As I'm saying I don't remember, it's not true. I do remember.

The waitress said, "Are you sure you don't want a muffin, too? They are really good today."

"Um ... ok, thanks." I had said and blushed.

Skylar starts talking about the book she was reading and I pretend to listen, nodding and making noises of agreement and disgust as necessary, but in another part of my mind, I'm mulling over what happened. I did not order a muffin. I did order a muffin. The muffin appeared. The roar ... what is happening to me?

We finish paying for our food, leaving a generous tip for the waitress and walk out in to the street.

"Listen," Skylar says. "You seem a little distracted so I'm going to get going. I have to finish this reading and then I have the pottery wheel reserved from 5-7 tonight. There's a girl party on campus tonight if you want to come. It's a costume party, though. I'm going as Angela Basset."

"Angela as Tina Turner?"

"No, Angela as Marie LeVeau in American Horror Story." I give her a blank stare.

"Voodoo priestess from New Orleans?" She looks at me like I'm an idiot.

"Oh, sounds fun, I think, but I don't know if I'm up for that."

"Well, let me know, should be fun, you know people are less inhibited in costume. Even you might get laid."

"Ha." I reply but it caught my attention. "I'll let you know." We hug goodbye and she set off down the street. I stood there, enjoying the sun on my face and wondering who I could talk to about, I don't even know what to call it. This shift?? I decide to go to Temple, maybe I'll find someone to talk to in the science library. I head back to the train station.

꽃꽃꽃

At the library, I wander around looking for anyone I might know, but I don't find anybody. I walk through the stacks perusing book titles. I look in all the carousels, along the banks of computers, and into the private study rooms. There are mostly white men, some Asian men, a few white and Asian women and me. Nobody even looked up. I thought for a while that I might be invisible. I used to think that a lot when I was growing up. I would speak in school and no one would hear or if they heard, no one would answer. I could move through crowds at school, or in the streets and no one would catch my eye. No smiles, no frowns, no nothing. I used to imagine that I had the super power of invisibility and that I could and should use it for the betterment of humankind but I never figured out any way to make use of it. I would much rather have liked the ability to fly. At least it would be practical and save me transportation money. I knock over a book. People look up and for a moment they see me. Satisfied, I walk out. The air is crisp, but the sun is warm. The leaves scurry about. I decide to go to the lab.

꽃꽃꽃

Temple's campus is bustling and crowded all week long, but on the weekends, you rarely see professors. I suppose they must have real lives elsewhere. So, when I walk into the Science building, I'm expecting it to be quiet with maybe a student or two trying to catch up on research or an assignment. What I hear is an argument, a loud one-sided argument, so I surmise the other party is on the phone. It takes me a minute to realize that it's Professor Patel. I've never heard him speak in anything more than an elevated whisper. I stop walking and pay attention.

"No, you have the wrong person, the wrong Patel." Silence. Then, "I have told you sir, you can threaten me all you like but I do not do that kind of research. I study plant biology. My expertise is in plant kinesiology. I don't dabble in other fields. You have the wrong man." Silence. Then, "I cannot spend any more time arguing about this. You have incorrect information. Now, I must go!" I hear a quiet beep, then a moment of silence before frantic paper rustling and drawers slamming open and close. I have no idea what to do. I probably should just leave. It was definitely not something meant for me to hear but I am intrigued. Who would threaten a biology professor? I mean really, he studies plants. I decide to stay.

Just as I fake open the main door again, he comes out of his office and sees me.

"Kim!" he says kind of loudly and accusingly. A robust man around sixty, with warm brown skin that compliments his silvery hair, he usually glows with friendliness and enthusiasm. Today he looks shriveled and ashen and tense.

"Oh hi, Professor Patel! I was just coming in to see you. It's a beautiful day, isn't it?" I sound as false as I feel. He looks guilty as sin for a second, then composes his face as he re-adjusts his bulging briefcase.

"Yes, it is beautiful outside. I just popped in to get some work to look over this weekend. And you? Are you here for work too? Or just for fun?" He smiles, but his eyes are studying me.

"I was just coming from the Science Library. I was hoping to find a study buddy for the afternoon, but it seems like no one is around today."

"Oh, ok, well I'm going to get going." He turns to close and lock his office door.

"Professor, I do have a question for you. Last night, I covered a shift for Peter Clark. How come his lab is not isolated like mine? His workstation was in a lab with at least eight other stations and there was Wi-Fi and electricity. I thought it was important to isolate from all variables."

Professor Patel clears his throat and switches his briefcase from his right hand to his left. "Oh, I didn't know you covered for Peter. I don't remember seeing that on the log."

"Oh yeah, well it was last minute, maybe they haven't been corrected yet." He looks thoughtful, but is silent.

"So, Professor, is it important, the isolation? Because I seemed to be doing the same kind of tests on the plants ..." I trail off waiting for some clarification.

"Oh yes, Kim. Well ... it's all part of the experiment. You and Peter are conducting the same test, but in different environments so that factors into the results as well. You'll see when you read the results; it will all make sense then." I'm not sure I believe him, but I want to.

"Professor?"

"Yes Kim, I really must get going. My wife is waiting for me."

"Oh, ok, it's nothing, I don't want to keep you ... "I glance at his briefcase. He follows my look, starts to edge past me and head to the main door but then he turns, studies me for a few seconds and asks, "How are you feeling Kim? Are you ok?"

"Yeah, just not quite feeling myself lately. Maybe I'm coming down with something."

"Hmmm ... well you can always visit the Health Center if you have a medical need," he offers.

"Yeah, I don't know what it is ... I'm sure it's nothing," I reply.

He jumps when his cell phone starts to buzz.

"Ok, that's the wife. I have to go Kim. Why don't you come and see me Tuesday during my office hours? We can talk more then."

"Ok, Professor. Have a good day."

"Thanks, you too!" and with that he slams open the door and hurries through it. I watch him through the glass door until he turns the corner.

I walk down the hall to his office and try the door. It's locked. I continue down the hallway to the labs and see that further down the hall, there are some students working. But my lab is up here, closer to the offices, lab number 19. It's also locked, but through the window, I can see that there is a lamp left on for Mabel. I know it's stupid, but I feel sorry for her. I turn to go when I notice a hole in the ceiling tile in the corner of the lab. It's small but there's a white tube just poking out of the hole. Maybe it's some kind of ventilation fix. I squint at it through the glass and think I see a tiny red light. I blink, but I can't be sure if it's there or a reflection of some sort. I take a mental note to check it out on Monday when I come back for class. I wave goodbye to Mabel and head back out into the sunshine.

I am lonely as I walk through campus. I sit on a bench and watch the squirrels with their acorns. They are so fat this time of year. I try to identify some nests in the trees and guess how many live in just this part of the campus. I think at least fifty. Looking at my phone, I see it's almost five o'clock. Maya and Lil' Walt will probably be home soon, and my mother. I text Jen to see what's up with her. She texts back that she's working tonight. I text Kendra, she replies that she is hanging with Rob tonight. It looks like I have few options but to go ahead and get myself a costume. Might be fun anyway. I stand up and head for the train.

Chapter 6

Getting from West Oak Lane to Bryn Mawr would take about two hours on public transportation but Big Walter is nice enough to offer me his car for the night. If it were any other kind of party, I would hold fast to my independence and suck up the two-hour journey but since I'm dressed like an alien – gray mask, big bulbous black eyes, long black cloak and knee high leather boots, I accept with grace and promise to bring it back intact.

After finding the LGBT house on campus, I park and steel myself. I adore Skylar but these girls at Bryn Mawr are very, very white, and it takes a bit to get used to them. They can be nice, but they can be just so … different. I pour a little Jack Daniels into my trusty flask and knock it back before I get out the car. When I step out, I pull on my mask. It's hot and sweaty but the mask gives me a certain anonymity that I like. I have on black jeans and a tight black t-shirt underneath my cloak, but my boots have ass-kicking heels, and I feel powerful. Of course, it could be the Jack talking but I'm ready to have some fun.

I walk up to the three-story house. It is decked out in a weird mixture of gay pride and Halloween decorations; zombies with rainbow handkerchiefs in their pockets, drag queen Draculas, purple spider webbing. The music, classic disco, is blasting out the windows and despite the strobe lights,

I can see lots of people inside. I go in to search for Skylar. Despite the feminist mission statement, I guess college girls feel just fine dressing in ways that objectify themselves as long as it's for other girls. I see lots of "sexy" vampires, "sexy" nurses, even a "sexy" maid, which I find surprising. Most of the women are white, but there are a few Latinas and Asian girls. I look for other brown faces and find just one, Skylar. She is surrounded by Gloria Steinem, Frida Kahlo and Wonder Woman. Of course, they are debating who is the most important of the four. I make my way through the crowd and stop just behind Skylar who is on a rant about the Christian oppression of women. I wait until they notice me. One by one, the others grow quiet.

"Can we help you?" asked Frida.

"Only the one who speaks to the dead can help me. She is the leader I seek," I intone in a gravelly voice.

Skylar turns and points an accusing finger at me and says in her best Angela Basset voice, "Who is it that wants to speak with the powerful voodoo priestess Marie LaVeau?" The whole room seems to turns towards us and watch.

I kneel before her and take off my mask. We break out laughing.

"You so crazy!" she says, hauling me up. The party resumes around us and she introduces me to her friends. They seem a bit thrown off by our theatrics. The feminist one-uppance disappears when Thelma and Louis come around with a tray of tequila shots. We all have a few, then the DJ plays Donna Summer's "Bad Girls" and everyone gets up to dance.

Frida and Wonder Woman both come over to dance with me. I feel like quite the belle of the ball as I try to accommodate them. Frida starts to get more insistent though, reaching out to grab my hands, whereas Wonder Woman starts looking around and fingering her lasso as soon as we make it out on the "floor". So I turn my attentions to Frida and to the music. I'm beginning to feel my drinks, so I just let go and dance. I love the idea of dancing with the artist, Frida

Kahlo, but after few minutes, I am not so sure about this girl. She keeps doing this weird snake-like dance and when she gets close to me, she grabs my hips. And I can smell her breath, and it does not smell good. Her grabbing is throwing me off my rhythm. I look over the crowd and see Skylar in a heated discussion with a witch, or is it a Wiccan? To my right, I can see Wonder Woman dancing her ass off with a "sexy" nurse. I can't take my eyes off her ample cleavage. I wish I had danced with her instead. In my drunken state, I realize that it is just like the muffin. I wish I had made a different choice and I think it again, hard. Then swaying with the music, I close my eyes and imagine the roar in my head. I visualize Wonder Woman in front of me with that cleavage. I wish ... I see her in my mind and I *push*. I push with my mind like I am pushing something heavy through a glass wall. I push hard enough to break through it. I open my eyes. Wonder Woman.

She smiles and dances up close to me, teasing me with her hands and thighs. I'm drunk, but I realize what I just did. I look over the crowd. I see Frida getting freaky with a tall girl in a jumpsuit. Wow. I did it. And I am glad I did it. I take a liking to Wonder Woman and her curly black hair, and we dance most of the night.

Her real name is Diana, no really, and she lives there at the house. At the end of the night, she invites me up to her room, which she happens to share with Frida. By the time we get up there, Frida is already busy with an inmate from Orange is the New Black. Diana and I make out until we pass out. I wake up about 3am and spend 20 minutes trying to find my clothes. The inmate opens her eyes and winks at me. I wink back, grab my mask and tip out of there.

幾 幾 幾

Not much happens on Sunday. I sleep late, loll in bed "studying" until 4pm, take a shower, play UNO with the kids, eat dinner, check in with Skylar, who is mighty impressed with my antics, and go back to bed. I had a typical lazy hung-over

Sunday except one thing. I remember what I did. The memory of choosing to dance with Frida was very faint, like a blurry childhood photo – out of focus, with faded colors and weird angles but it was there.

I remembered pushing to change my choice, but I also remembered choosing Wonder Woman from the beginning. Frida was pulling on me, but I turned to Wonder Woman and suggested I was a threat to the human race. She took the challenge, "caught" me with her lasso and pulled me onto the floor. That memory is very clear. I go to sleep feeling proud, scared, worried and cautious. I want to talk to someone about it but it's too crazy. Maybe I'm crazy. Maybe Jen is right, and there is something wrong with my brain. I try to think about it rationally and decide I will have to experiment. Tomorrow.

Chapter **7**

Monday morning and I wait for everyone to leave before I head down for coffee. I don't have anything to do until my lab session at 1:40pm. Well, I do have reading and a short paper due on Friday, and I have to work on my Honors scholarship application essay, but that's not due until December 1, so I have time. I grab a composition book from the kids' school supply drawer and settle down to write.

JOURNAL ENTRY #1
OCTOBER 25

HISTORY OF THE PROBLEM

DAY 1 – I FIRST NOTICED STRANGENESS LAST TUESDAY NIGHT (OCT 19). I HEARD A LOUD BUZZING IN MY HEAD. MY EYES GOT BLURRY AND I SAW A SHADOW ON MY DOORSTEP.

THEN SAME NIGHT, AT THE BAR, I HEARD THE BUZZING, FELT LIGHT-HEADED AND SAW A "VISION" OF MYSELF KISSING MEER IN THE BAR.

DAY 2 – WEDNESDAY, NOTHING WEIRD.

DAY 3 — THURSDAY. IN THE SUBWAY. I HEARD THE BUZZING. FELT MY EYES GET BLURRY AND SAW A SHADOW OF MYSELF WITH AN OLD MAN. WHO I HAD JUST SEEN ON THE PLATFORM.

DAY 4 — FRIDAY. SAME THING. BUZZING AND DISORIENTATION AT SILK CITY AND WHEN I SAW JEN AND SOME DRUNK GUY WAS HARASSING HER. I SAW IT BUT IT DIDN'T HAPPEN BUT I SAW THE SAME GUY LATER AND SHE KNEW HIM FROM WORK. HE HAD BOTHERED HER EARLIER THAT DAY.

DAY 5 — SATURDAY. PUMPKIN SPICE MUFFIN INCIDENT. SAME PHYSICAL SYMPTOMS EXCEPT I DIDN'T/BUT DID ORDER IT. I WANTED IT /WISHED FOR IT AND IT APPEARED. SKYLAR WAS THERE BUT DIDN'T SEEM TO NOTICE A THING.

SATURDAY NIGHT. I CHANGED MY MIND ABOUT WHO I WANTED TO DANCE WITH AND I WAS ABLE TO CHANGE MY REALITY. NO. IT WAS LIKE I WAS ABLE TO CHOOSE MY REALITY BECAUSE I DEFINITELY REMEMBER CHOOSING DIANA EVEN THOUGH I KIND OF REMEMBER FIRST ASKING FRIDA. NOT FIRST BUT ALSO? BUT THIS TIME. I DID IT. I MADE IT HAPPEN. I WILLED IT TO HAPPEN.

DAY 6 — SUNDAY. NOTHING WEIRD HAPPENED.

DAY 7 — MONDAY. I WILL BEGIN EXPERIMENTS.

Nikki Harmon

<u>PRELIMINARY OBSERVATIONS</u>

1. IT STARTED WITH AMIRA. MAYBE SHE IS THE CAUSE/CATALYST?
2. ONLY HAPPENS ONCE OR TWICE A DAY. SOME DAYS NOT AT ALL SO IT'S NOT ON SOME KIND OF SCHEDULE.
3. HAPPENS NEAR FOOD OR DRINKS. MAYBE MUSIC? BAR. RESTAURANT. CAFE. PARTY. MAYBE ONLY HAPPENS IN SOCIAL SITUATIONS?
4. MAYBE HAS SOMETHING TO DO WITH CHOICES – MUFFIN? GIRL AT PARTY?

<u>10:00AM EXPERIMENT #1</u> – I WILL TRY TO CHANGE A FOOD I AM EATING. I WILL MAKE EGGS AND A BAGEL. PICK ONE. THEN WISH FOR THE OTHER AND SEE IF I CAN MAKE IT HAPPEN.

<u>10:30AM RESULT #1</u> – I FIRST PICKED THE EGGS. BEGAN TO EAT. THEN TRIED TO SWITCH TO THE BAGEL BUT NOTHING HAPPENED. I COULDN'T GENERATE THE BUZZING AND NOTHING HAPPENED. EGGS AND BAGEL GOT COLD THOUGH AND ENDED UP MAKING BAGEL AND EGG SANDWICH.

<u>10:45AM EXPERIMENT #2</u> – I WILL TRY TO CHANGE MY CLOTHES BY GETTING DRESSED AND THEN WANTING TO WEAR SOMETHING ELSE. PROBABLY JEANS.

<u>11:00AM RESULT #2</u> – I GOT DRESSED IN MY SWEATS BUT THEN WAS DISTRACTED BY A TEXT FROM JEN. SOMETHING ABOUT HER BOYFRIEND. I COULD NOT GENERATE THE BUZZ AND NOTHING HAPPENED. I TURNED ON SOME MUSIC AND TRIED AGAIN BUT NOTHING HAPPENED.

11:30AM EXPERIMENT #3 – I WILL TRY TO CHANGE AN EARLIER DECISION. THIS PAST SUMMER, WHEN WE FOUND OUT I WAS GOING TO LIVE HERE FOR ONE MORE YEAR, I ASKED MY MOM IF WE COULD PAINT THE WALLS IN MY ROOM BECAUSE THEY'VE BEEN LAVENDER SINCE 7TH GRADE WHEN I WAS GOING THROUGH MY PURPLE RAIN STAGE. SHE AGREED BUT ONLY IF I PICKED WHITE OR IVORY. I AGREED. WE PAINTED. I HATED IT. I STILL HATE IT. I WISH I HAD NEVER CHANGED IT.

12:00PM RESULT #3 – I DID IT!!!!! I PUT ON PURPLE RAIN. I SAT ON MY BED AND REMEMBERED ALL THE GREAT TIMES I HAD IN THIS ROOM. I VISUALIZED ME IN THIS ROOM. SLEEPING. STUDYING. LISTENING TO MUSIC. READING. MAKING MY ROBOTS. I WISHED. I MADE THE BUZZING AND THEN THE BUZZING JUST HAPPENED ON ITS OWN AND I PUSHED. I SHOVED INTO A PURPLE ROOM. I OPENED MY EYES AND IT'S PURPLE!!!!! IT'S PURPLE. IT'S PURPLE. WOW.

BUT IT'S WEIRD BECAUSE I HAVE A MEMORY OF JUST TELLING MY MOM. NEVERMIND IF IT HAD TO BE SO PLAIN. I REMEMBER THAT. AND I REMEMBER HER SHRUG AND SAYING SHE LIKED THE PURPLE. I SHOULD KEEP IT. AND I LOOKED AROUND AND LIKED IT TOO. SO I KEPT IT. EXCEPT I DIDN'T. NOT REALLY. BUT MY EYES ARE OPEN NOW AND IT'S BACK HOW IT USED TO BE. I DID IT. WOW.

❀ ❀ ❀

I hustle off to school filled with wonder and anxiety. What have I done? How can this be? But I have to put all that aside and focus. I need all A's in my classes this semester to even have a chance at this scholarship. I messed up last semester in Chemistry and it tanked my GPA. Strange happenings or no, I have to keep my eyes on the prize and beast these classes. So, for 5 hours, I'm at org chemistry lab, then linear algebra, then I eat some Chinese food off a truck – love those crispy dumplings and then it's time to go to work. At lab 19.

As I enter the building, I look at Professor Patel's office door, but it's locked tight, frosted windows dark. I walk down the hall, sign in the log, close the door behind me and take my seat. Mabel looks a bit droopy today so I croon to her and ask her how she's doing. I inspect my lab kit and read that we are using a particular kind of manure that is supposed to be a very potent growth agent. It's interesting until I take the cap off. Seriously, I'm stuck here with this smell??? I'm so disgusted I almost forget to check out the hole in the ceiling. Luckily, I roll my eyes enough times that I happen to catch a glimpse of it … and the little red light. From my vantage point, it's almost perfectly camouflaged by ductwork and the fluorescent light casings. I have to get up, stand on my chair and crane my neck to get a decent peek at it. I expend all that effort, but I don't really learn much more than when I was outside in the hall. There's a small tube, about ½ inch in diameter. I think I can make out a mere hint of airflow (or some kind of flow) coming from it. The dot of red light is barely discernible from my angle and looks to be nowhere near the opening. It looks like the opening reaches far back into the ceiling cavity. Oh well.

I drop back down to the floor and check out Mabel. She looks sickly. I check her soil; it's perfectly moist but not wet. The pH monitor reads 5.7, also perfect for her. I look at the thermometer on the wall – a comfortable 72 degrees. Near the thermometer I notice something strange. Peeking out from under the wallpaper, is a sliver of metallic. I try to pull up the wallpaper, but I can't without it being obvious. I check all around the thermometer and don't see anything else. Then I roam the room and look around all the embedded plates and the trim. I see four more teeny slivers of metal but cannot pull up the wallpaper any further. I inspect the corners of the room and try to squeeze behind some of the heavy desks. Jackpot! I moved a desk and found a small tear in the wallpaper, probably caused by the edge of the desk rubbing up on it. I can put my pencil tip in the nick and pull out the edge so I can see. I shine my iPhone flashlight down there and am dazzled by the light reflected back at me. Metal, all metal. This room is lined with metal. My heart starts thumping, and I get a sick feeling in the pit of my stomach. I extract the pencil, turn off the flashlight, nudge the desk back into position and sit down.

The alarm startles me. Time to hit Mabel with more manure. When I'm done with the spray, I go back to wondering what the hell is going on. Why would this room be lined with metal? I mean, I've heard of metal lined rooms like faraday cages, but they are basically used to block out radiation. We're doing experiments on a sweet potato vine. I hardly think we would need that kind of protection for Mabel. Maybe it just happens to be lined and is incidental to the experiment. But then I think about how far away this lab is from all the other labs where the student workers spend most of their time. They are halfway across the building. I am here. I consider various explanations for a long time but don't come to any conclusions. I try to read my textbook, but end up just staring at the words, not comprehending anything. The alarm keeps me on task, but I am utterly discomfited. When my shift is over, I decide to ask Professor Patel about it tomorrow. I struggle home to bed and fall into a deep sleep.

Chapter 8

After my classes on Tuesday, I head over to Dr. Patel's office. The room is dark and the door is locked. I double-check his schedule on the door and confirm that these are his office hours. I sit on a bench down the hall to wait in case he's running late. I need to talk to him. As soon as I get absorbed in my reading assignment, the main door is jerked open and a huge guy comes strolling in. He's at least 6'5" tall and almost as wide with a distinct bouncer look to him. He looks Russian or maybe Eastern European. He strides down the hall, scanning the names on the doors and stops at Dr. Patel's office. He peers in the little window, tries the door to no success, then bangs on it for good measure. He makes a sound of disgust. Then, turning to leave, he sees me watching him. He walks over to me.

"Have you seen Dr. Patel?" he asks. Yup, he's definitely foreign with that thick accent.

"No, I was waiting to see him myself. I haven't seen him all day," I reply with a shrug.

"Humph" he snorts and then stalks off and slams out the front door.

What was that all about? No longer feeling comfortable, I gather my things and start to head out. I hesitate when I think I hear something in Patel's office. After a minute, I decide I'm hearing things and I get out of there. It's been a long day, and I just want to go home.

❀ ❀ ❀

Twenty minutes later, I'm walking down my block when I hear a car horn. I turn to see a familiar old Lincoln. Meer. She stops and rolls down the window.

"Hey Meer!"

"Hey Kim! I'm on my way to pick up Tamika. You want to come again?" she asks smiling in that easy way of hers. After today, I could use a little fun but … I look up at the house and sigh.

"Hmmm … I have some work to do but what about picking me up after the game? Maybe we can get something to eat?" I say.

"Something to eat, hmmm … sounds almost like a date …" she drawls.

"Maybe it is," I retort. "So, yes or no?" She laughs.

"Definitely yes. I'll be here about 8:30, ok?"

"Ok. I'm at this house," I say pointing. "Text me when you get here, ok?"

"I can come to the door …"

"No," I cut her off, "It'll be better if I just come out."

"Ok, no problem. See ya then." She pulls off cursing about the time.

❀ ❀ ❀

I walk in the door just as my family is finishing dinner. After I decline a plate, my mom asks if I will get the kids bathed and ready for bed while she cleans up the kitchen. Happy for the distraction, I do. It's more work than I remembered, but I haven't done it for so long that I really enjoy it. Lil' Walt's naked booty dance makes me forget all about metal walls and thick accents. As I settle them down to read one of the Magic Tree House books, my phone buzzes with a text. I jump up and apologize to the kids telling them the truth – I had forgotten all about meeting my friend. I kiss them good night and run into my room to put on something … nicer. My mom hears the commotion and comes up stairs. When she passes me in the hall, she just shakes her head and takes my place on the bed. Texting Meer that I am on my way, I flick through my closet, pulling out a low-cut V-neck shirt and change into my "going out" jeans. I slip on my leather boots from the other night, have a brief flashback of Saturday night's adventure with Wonder Woman, spritz on some Lady Gaga perfume and am out the door.

I don't know why I rushed because when I get to the car, Meer is laid back in the seat, relaxing and listening to The Roots. I get her attention, open the door, and slide in.

"Hi! … Where are we going?"

Grinning, she says, "I know you enjoy a messy sandwich so I thought we could go to this little spot near my house. They have really good sandwiches and a pool table."

"Around your house? Hmm … Ok, let's go," I say. We head up Broad Street, past Temple and turn right onto Fairmount.

"I didn't know you lived all the way up here," I say.

"Yup. It used to be just North Philly but now it's "Fairmount'," she says, making air quotes. We make a few turns, then park next to The Tumble-Down Lounge.

"It used to be called "Juanita's" but you know, new ownership." I nod. We go in and get a booth towards the back. It's a decent sized place with a large bar in the middle, a couple of tables in the front, a few booths on the side and a pool table in the back, a little something for everyone. Meer knows the bartender, the waitress and a couple of people at the bar. She greets them and they nod and smile back at her. We sit and I pick up the menu. The sandwich menu is several pages long, and I have a hard time deciding. She recommends the pulled pork sandwich, so I go with that while she orders some grilled salmon and sweet potato fries. She orders a beer; I ask for a Sprite.

"So, how was your week?" she asks leaning forward on her elbows. I think back on my week and sigh. I can't even begin to explain it to myself much less approach it with her.

"My week was quite insane and complicated. Let's talk about you. How was your week? Oh, wait, how was your game? Did you make it on time tonight?"

She laughs and shakes her head, "No, but it wasn't my fault this time, there was traffic…." She tells me about the game including her last second shot which won it. I'm skeptical about this, but she assures me that it's true. She tells me about her week working for her Uncle Teddy, a kitchen supply wholesaler with a bootlegging side hustle. As she starts to explain how she got tricked into recording a kids' movie with her little cousins, she stops, sits back, crosses her arms and looks at me.

"I hope you don't take this the wrong way, but in high school, I never noticed how pretty you were. Was I blind? How did I not see you?"

I'm not sure how to feel about this confession, so I just laugh and say, "Thank you? I think. Maybe you were just too busy with all those other girls to see me."

"What other girls? I had like one girlfriend in high school, and she didn't even go to our school. She went to Girls High."

"Oh really? I seem to remember you being surrounded by girls all the time."

"Maybe my teammates and some friends. But no *girl* girls, I might have been out but I was definitely solo most of the time." Our food comes and it smells divine. Before I get a chance to take a bite she asks, "What about you? Did you have a girlfriend in high school?" I take my bite and think about how to answer that while I chew. Oh my god, it tastes as good as it smells. I must have moaned out loud because all the sudden she is looking at me like I've grown a second head.

"What?" I ask, covering my mouth.

"Are you always that … expressive? Damn, I know it's a good sandwich, but you are enjoying that a little too much.

I'm getting fired up over here just watching you." She laughs but she looks a little … intense.

"I'm pretty good at expressing myself when the mood strikes me," I say and take another big bite. This time I close my eyes and moan on purpose. She laughs and begins to eat her sandwich.

"It's probably a good thing we didn't meet in high school. I think you would have been too much for me!"

"Ha! I think you would have been too much for me! I don't know how you could be so brave. Gay/straight alliance or not, it was terrifying to come out to the few friends I trusted, and even then, I was sure they were going to reject me."

"Did they?" she asks.

"No, not my friends. They were cool."

"I didn't have a choice in coming out. I mean, look at me. I was born dykey. People have been calling me gay since I was six or seven. I didn't know what it meant but I didn't argue. I just played ball, made friends and tried to just be me."

"Still, I thought you were brave."

"Oh yeah? What do you think now?" she asks.

"Now? Now, I think you're kind of cute," I say. She blushes. I laugh and eat my sandwich.

After we finish eating and pay the bill, we get up to play pool. There is a couple playing ahead of us, so we just hang out by the jukebox while we wait. At one point, she holds my hand. At another, I kiss her cheek. When it's our turn, I confess that I can't play at all and everything I know about pool has to do with how I learned physics in high school.

"I'm a good teacher," she says. She sets up the balls and breaks. The balls scatter. I'm already intimidated, but I'm a good sport.

"Ooh, I should have known you would be a good player. You got two down the holes!"

"Number one, you don't "play" pool, you "shoot" pool. Number two, they are called "pockets", not holes. Number three, I got two solids down the pockets so I'm solids, and you are stripes. Grab a stick and let's line you up behind the cue ball."

I do as I'm told and try to look dignified as I lean down towards the cue.

"Oh Jesus, let me help you out," she laughs. Meer comes up behind me and arranges my hands on the stick, shows me how to line up the balls with a pocket and how to shoot, not just tap or push the cue ball. All the close contact is getting to me and I purposely lean over and give her a peek of my cleavage as often as I can. I can see she's interested, so I start brushing past her for purely invented reasons like brushing lint off the able; she starts putting her hands on my hips to "help" me get in position. When I finally sink my final ball, I jump up and give her a big hug. She doesn't let go. I pull my head back and she's looking down at me smiling. I think she is about to kiss me when I hear a big commotion up towards the front of the bar.

"Oh no! Oh no you didn't! Oh no you didn't come back here and bring one of your bitches! Are you fucking kidding me!!?" And up strides this young, sassy but pissed off woman. She looks like she just came from the salon — hair is fresh, nails are shining, make-up is flawless. She walks up to Meer and stands right under her chin and whispers, "Why? How could you come back here? And with her? Are you trying to make me crazy?" The woman glares at me, and I take two steps back and look for my coat. This is not my drama and I am so out of here. Meer turns to me and says, "Wait. I'm sorry. I'll take you home."

The woman spins Meer around to face her. "Sorry? You are apologizing to her? What about me? Where is my apology? Where is my money?" And with that, she pushes Meer backwards. Instinctively, I take a step towards Meer, but the woman turns her head to me and says, "You don't want any of this, trust me." Meer is trying to calm the woman down, backing up and around the pool table, but I can see that it's not going to work.

"Keisha, please calm down. I'm sorry, I can explain. Let's just take a minute here. Keisha, come on, let's not do this baby."

"Oh I'm going to do this. I've put up with your broke ass for months and then you have the nerve to break-up with me and leave. Where is the rent you owe me? Who do you think had to pay that??" She picks up one of the pool sticks and starts hitting Meer with it. The other patrons, who were already staring, scatter while the bartender calls the police. Meer ducks and tries to run out but the woman starts grabbing the balls from the tray and throwing them at Meer. I tuck into a corner and try to sidle my way to the door. Meer turns and runs back at the woman, tackling her. I think she is trying to stop her from throwing the balls that are crashing everywhere breaking glass and narrowly missing the other customers. I hear police sirens in the distance getting closer and closer. I close my eyes. I wish I had just stayed home and read the stupid book. I wish I hadn't gone out tonight, I wish I had just stayed home. The roar starts up in the back of my head. Yes! I welcome it. I bring it on. I think about home and the kids and getting away from this craziness and I push hard, harder. I throw myself into it, a desperate jump ... silence.

卐 卐 卐

Darkness, my pillow, my room, I see the clock; it's only 11:00pm. I stretch. It feels like I fell asleep a couple of hours ago. I'm tired, but I have to use the bathroom. I get up and see I'm still in my clothes from earlier in the day. As I walk to the bathroom, I remember that I have a date with Meer tomorrow. As I start to smile with anticipation, a different thought intrudes. A pool table, a woman, dinner, pulled pork, learning to shoot, the closeness of her body, the yelling, me hiding. What the ... did I dream it? I must have dreamed it because I remember when she texted me, I made up a lame excuse about schoolwork when truthfully it was the kids I couldn't leave. I made another date with her, for tomorrow.

Lunch. But what about the pool table, that woman, that sandwich (that sandwich!)? And I remember changing clothes and leaving the house. I remember the look on my mother's face as I passed her by.

I believe I did it again. I changed my mind, I changed ... I jumped into another reality? Another choice? Oh my God. I did it way past the choice though, hours after ... I think this has to do with something in quantum physics, the one branch of science I don't know much about. But I do know they talk of alternate realties and multiverses but what does it mean and how am I able to jump? I'm tired but decide to write another journal entry while it is fresh. I leave the bathroom and head downstairs to find my book. I find it in the kitchen. I should probably try to be more careful with it.

Nikki Harmon

JOURNAL ENTRY #2
OCTOBER 26

*DAY 8 — TUESDAY I BELIEVE THAT TODAY.
TONIGHT SOMETHING SOMEWHAT BIGGER
HAPPENED. I THINK I WENT OUT WITH MEER. KIND
OF ON A DATE. I HAD A SANDWICH AND I THINK WE
PLAYED POOL. A WOMAN. HER EX??? THERE WAS A
FIGHT AND I TRIED TO GET AWAY. I CLOSED MY
EYES AND WISHED I HAD JUST STAYED HOME. I
PUSHED AND SOMEHOW ENDED UP IN MY BED.
SAME TIME OF DAY. I THINK. BUT IN A TOTALLY
DIFFERENT LOCATION. THE PUSH WAS A
DESPERATE ATTEMPT AT ESCAPE. I DIDN'T PLAN
IT. I JUST WANTED TO GET AWAY FROM THAT
SITUATION. WHAT IF I DREAMED IT? I CAN ASK
HER ABOUT THE RESTAURANT. I'VE NEVER BEEN
THERE BEFORE BUT SHE SEEMED TO BE A
REGULAR. THERE WAS FOOD, MUSIC AND MEER. ALL
THE ELEMENTS FROM PREVIOUS "SWITCHES?
PUSHES? JUMPS?" WHAT AM I GOING TO CALL
THIS?*

*PLAN — CHECK MEER'S MEMORY OF THE NIGHT.
ASK ABOUT THE RESTAURANT. ASK ABOUT AN EX
WHO MIGHT BE CRAZY — THAT'S ALWAYS GOOD TO
KNOW!*

*READ UP ON QUANTUM PHYSICS!!! WHAT THE HELL
IS IT??*

Chapter 9

I wake up just as everyone is leaving. I don't get a chance to say good-bye and they don't seem to notice my absence. I come down to an empty kitchen but at least there is coffee in the pot. I pour some and plan out my day. I'm going to meet Meer at noon at Victoria's Kitchen, a soul food restaurant on Ogontz Avenue. I have all morning to work on my application for the scholarship. I find myself drifting back to last night but I have to brush it off. I have to get this scholarship. I have to get to MIT. All the great research comes out of MIT and Cal Tech. So, I spend the morning writing and rewriting my personal essay. I also send out my emails to my professors to get recommendation letters. I abandon the idea of asking Dr. Patel and but go with my old STEM supervisor instead. Something tells me Patel will not have time to write anything in the near future. I'm nervous about work tonight. The guy with the accent was huge and I don't think he cares at all about academics or students or scientific research. I wonder if Patel owes him money, maybe he's a gambler or something.

I re-read my essay. I'm satisfied with it and decide to do some quick research on quantum physics. I never had an interest in it before. I've always been more interested in classic biology, chemistry and Newtonian physics. Quantum physics just seemed like the fantastical ramblings of scientists looking for magic or God. I read a bit about it when the Stephen Hawkins film came out but I thought there was too much conjecture and not enough hard science for me. I like to be able to observe and measure and experiment.

After a Google search and scanning a few websites, I still don't understand it. There's a theory called *many world theory* or *multiverses,* but it suggests that there are an infinite number of universes existing parallel to ours with new ones being endlessly created. I don't know if that has anything to do with me. Maybe. I think I need to talk to an expert, but how without seeming crazy? 11:45 am. Time to go.

࿊ ࿊ ࿊

Meer is outside the restaurant when I arrive just a few minutes late. We exchange an awkward hug and walk inside. The hostess seats us and we pore over the menu for a few minutes. I am nervous and I think she is too. Maybe it's the daylight, maybe it's the formality of sitting down to eat together, maybe it's because I have a vague memory of a date we had last night ... but didn't. I order the turkey chops and collard greens platter. She orders grilled salmon with a macaroni and cheese side. I look up at her and try to sound casual.

"So, sorry about last night. I just haven't been able to spend as much time with my brother and sister as I used to. What did you end up doing?"

She looks a little guilty as she says, "I ran into a friend at a bar." We hung out."

"Oh, yeah? Did you have fun with your *friend?*" I ask raising my eyebrows.

"Not really. We used to be ... something but now we're not and she's not taking it too well." She takes a sip of the water the waitress just brought.

"Oh, sorry to hear it. So ... I'm a bounce back then?" I put my chin in my hand and smile at her.

"You? No! I don't know what you are. I just know I couldn't stop thinking about you last week and last night. I feel like we have a connection, like I know you or something. It's weird."

I study her face. Under all that bluster and confidence, she's just as unsure as I am, maybe more. She looks away, uncomfortable under my gaze but I don't let up. I memorize the shape of her eyes, the length of her lashes, the way her eyebrows hint at a curve but never quite get there. I observe the way her mouth is never still but always ready to smile, or talk or twist. I notice the flare of her nostrils, the mole near her ear, the coils of hair escaped from her baby locks. She looks back at me and into my eyes. My vision starts to blur and the roar starts in the back of my head, but I don't want to leave. I try to shake it off but the roar becomes unbearable. I can't hold on and I am pulled through and back, back, back …

卍 卍 卍

My head is aching, but I open my eyes. I'm sitting on a broken-down lounge chair not sure of what to do. I am at a party at my friend Jamal's house. There are a few kids I know from school dancing to some underground rapper and drinking cheap vodka out of Dixie cups. I don't know why I'm here. I was invited by Amber, a girl from school who I think is really cute. I came out to her the other day hoping that she might be interested but I don't think she is. She brought me here then she disappeared with some boy.

I look around wondering if Amber will ever come back. Some random boy comes and sits next to me. He asks me to dance, but I say "no". He walks to the corner of the room and comes back with a cup of "juice" for me. I drink it. It burns. He says Amber sent him, and she wants to talk to me in the other room. Confused but encouraged, I follow him down a hallway, into a small den. Amber is there, but so are two other boys. "So, we heard you are a dyke. We can cure that," the fat one says. As I turn to run out, I see Amber's face. She looks dangerous and wolfish. I almost make it to the door when the short one grabs my arm and pulls me back. I try to shake him off, but the fat one grabs my other arm. I hear Amber say, "Pull her down, get her!" There are hands on my jeans; I feel them yanked down over my hips. I yell out, "No!!!!!!" I kick my feet; somebody punches me in the head. I fight them, but they fight me back. Somebody grabs my arms and pulls them behind me. I keep kicking. Somebody is pulling my panties off, I look and it's Amber. I roar, "NO!!!!! Get off of me!!!" I hear somebody else come in, and another and another. I think I am doomed, but there is more fighting, people yelling. I have been set loose. I drop to the floor and try to pull up my underwear. Somebody comes over to me, puts their arm around me, hands me my pants. I am crying. I look up. Meer. Meer with a bloody lip and a swelling eye. She shoves our way through the crowd who has stopped fighting. They jeer, they laugh, they call us names. They kick at us as we pass. But we pass. She gets me dressed. Someone helps me into a car and we drive off. I am at once aching but also numb. I stare out the window seeing nothing but my own eyes staring back at me. When we stop, Meer helps me out the car and into her house. She cleans me up with an old blue washcloth. She cleans herself up. I can't talk. She seems to understand. We go down into her basement and sit on a lumpy, stained couch. There is a small floor lamp with only one dim bulb. I stare at the black screen of the TV. I hear her sigh and say, "It's ok now, you are safe here." I let go the breath I did not know I was holding and she holds me while I cry. When I'm done, she just holds me. I find my voice to speak.

"Thank you. Thank you for saving me." She looks down at me concerned and then smiles.

"You're welcome. What's your name?"

"Kim. I'm Kim."

"I'm Amira but you can call me Meer."

"I already know who you are, Meer."

"Oh yeah. Are you alright, did they …?"

"No, they didn't get me." I cry again. She holds me again.

"How did you … why did you help me?" I ask.

"I came by for the party but we heard screaming. So, we went to see what was going on."

"Who?"

"Me, my brother and a couple of his friends."

"Thank you."

"You said that already."

"Thank them."

"Ok, I will," she says. "It's getting late. I should get you home."

"I heard you were gay," I say.

"Is that what you heard?" she says.

"Yeah, are you?" I ask.

"Yes" she replies.

"Me too," I say.

"Oh yeah?" She smiles at me. I smile back and reach for her hand. We lace fingers and look into each other's eyes. My vision blurs, the roaring comes and there is a lurching in my stomach. I close my eyes and feel pulled through and forward. It stops. I open my eyes.

I'm back at the table at lunch, with Meer. She's looking at me and saying something. I'm clutching my glass of water. I shake my head.

"Are you ok?" she says. She sounds a little freaked out. "Yo, for a second, you seemed to blink."

"What?" I say.

"You blinked, you flashed, you blipped. Like ... like a flashbulb or something. Yo, that was weird." She sits back in her chair. I take a long drink of water. I remember everything that happened, but it feels like I watched it on TV, as if I watched it happen to someone else, but I felt the feelings. I was terrified and hurt and angry and so, so, very sad. And thankful, so, so very thankful.

"Oh," is all I can manage. The food comes, but I don't think I can eat. I sit back and look at her. She looks at me with suspicion.

"What the fuck is going on?" she says.

"Hell if I know," I reply.

"Look, I'm not hungry anymore. I'm going to get this wrapped up." She looks around for the waitress, and flags her down.

"Wait," I say. "I can't explain what you saw but I'm just as scared about it. I need to know something, though, it's going to sound crazy …"

She is handing her plate to the waitress along with 2 twenty-dollar bills. The waitress rushes off.

"You said you went out last night. Where? Where did you go?" I ask.

She eyes me. "Why?"

"Please just tell me. I have to … it's hard to explain but I need to know." I'm pleading; I sound desperate and crazy to my own ears. "Meer, it's not a big deal, I just want to know to check something, something I heard about."

"I went to the Tumble-Down Lounge on Girard Avenue," she concedes. "It used to be …"

"Juanita's." I finish the sentence for her. The waitress comes back with a brown paper bag and some change. Meer takes the bag, but pushes the change back to the waitress. "That's yours, sweetheart," she says. The waitress nods, drops it in her pocket and moves on.

Meer turns to me and says, "I like you, Kim, but honestly, I have enough drama. I don't know what just happened here, but I, I just can't, not now." She leans forward and kisses me on the forehead. As she pulls away, I see she has a small tattoo on her forearm. It says, "Keisha". I sigh. She nods at me, and walks away. I stay. I eat without tasting my food. I don't think. I don't know what to think. I just know I have class in two hours, and work after that, so I had better eat. I try to pay but the waitress waves me away. It's already paid for. I sit for another hour just staring through the glass. I see my reflection, but I don't recognize myself. It starts to rain. I watch that instead. Sometime later, I get up and get wet as I wander and wonder what is happening to me.

Chapter 10

After math class, I grab a bite to eat at the Student Center and head over to work-study at the lab. I enter the building and look around. There are students at the far end of the lobby studying in the lounge chairs. The administrative offices are closed and most lights are off. I think I see a light on in Dr. Patel's office, but as I walk past it, the office is dark. I approach lab #19 with more than a little trepidation. I don't want to be here anymore, but it's part of my financial aid package, so I don't really have a choice. I notice a change as soon as I walk in. Mabel has been replaced. Instead a new, healthier looking plant is on the table, and Mabel is about two feet away on a little stool. But poor Mabel! Her leaves are beginning to yellow and furl, her stems in a half-wilt. I walk in and croon to her; she perks up a bit. I check the lab kit. It is stocked a bit more than usual, and today it's flea beetle saliva. Additional instructions tell me that Mabel is now the "remote receiver" plant, and that I should take samples from both plants. Maybe Mabel was getting worn out with all the direct pheromones, or maybe this is just a new phase of the experiment. There is nobody here to explain anything to me. I'm just the grunt.

I read for bioethics between spritzes and slices. I can't stop myself from looking at all the places in the room where I know there are tiny bits of metal peeking through. I do stop myself from looking up into the hole in the corner. It occurs to me that the red light might be a camera or recorder of some sort. I wish there was someone else to talk to about this, but with the ban on cell phones and my weird hours, I am feeling well and truly alone. At 10pm, I pack up, give Mabel a caress good-bye, turn off the light and lock the door behind me.

As I head towards the subway, the turmoil and stress of the day starts to weigh on me. I need someone to talk to and think of Jen. I pull out my phone to see if I can stop by on my way home when I am yanked from behind. A hand covers my mouth, and I hear a click behind my ear.

The accent is thick and familiar. "Don't even think about trying to fight. You are nothing to me, and I will kill you like nothing if you give me any trouble. Get in and you might not get killed." My phone tumbles from my hand and lands in the sparse patch of grass by the curb. The solid wall of a man pushes me towards a dark green van with an open door. I hesitate, trying to think of an escape, but he is too strong and too fast and he propels me into the van where another hand reaches over my face and covers it with a thick, sweet smell. I lose consciousness.

೫ ೫ ೫

I wake up cold and nauseous. I am lying on a floor … of a van. It's moving. I open my eyes, but don't see anything but the floor rug and the feet of the person in the seat in front of me. I try not to move or breathe too hard. I feel the leg of someone next to me. They must be sitting in the seat. I can hear them breathing over the rumble of the engine. It's dark in the van, so it's still nighttime. I am starting to feel my body again, and I am stiff and uncomfortable. My legs are twisted up and bent pressing against the metal bottom of the seat. My arm is contorted beneath my body, and I have an irresistible urge to straighten myself out. I listen. I think the breathing person is asleep. Ever so slightly I lift up to try and free my arm. I manage to untwist my shoulder before I hear the breathing change, and I force myself to stillness.

"Are we almost there?" asks the man who abducted me in his thick, slow speech.

"What are you, my kids?" retorts the driver. He also has an accent but it is not as thick as the big guy. He sounds smaller, nasally and quick. The big guy grunts, "Fuck you. I have to pee."

"There's a jar back there," says the driver, "it's in the blue bag". The leg presses on me as he strains forward to reach for a bag. I hear fumbling, a jar lid unscrewing, a second or two, then the sound of a steam of piss, followed by a sigh, a jiggle, more jar screwing and a thud. The smell of urine floats past my nose. Gross. The big guy settles back.

"Thanks, Marco."

"No problem. We should be there in two hours. The boss already has Patel. I don't know what he wants with the girl, though."

"Shhh ... no talking. You know the rules. Drive. I'm going back to sleep."

"Sure," says the driver, "whatever," and he turns up the radio. I wait. My legs are aching and I can hardly feel my left foot. I wait so long that I fall asleep and wake up as the van starts down a gravel road. It is very bumpy. I try to adjust my limbs in rhythm with the bumps. I think I'm doing a good job being unnoticed until I hear, "You can get up if you want to. You are not tied up. No need." I look up and the big bouncer-looking guy from the Science Building is looking back down at me. "We are almost there. See!" and he points out the side window. I struggle to get up, my legs are numb and I am cold. I push up on the seat and manage to get my legs under me to boost up. I'm squeezed in the back row of a mini-van. The guy in front of me turns around and looks at me with animosity but the bouncer guy is not fazed. He points again as we head up through a farm to a farmhouse. It looks old but not abandoned. I look out the windows, nothing but cornfields in every direction. I can see low mountains further up. I see a silo off in the distance and some old trucks parked farther up one road, but that's it. I get an icy knot in my stomach. Nobody will ever find me out here. We turn left and head up to the farmhouse. Red curtains shift in the windows and I can see two other cars already parked in the front yard. We pull in alongside an old blue Alero and park. Marco stays in the car while the mean guy gets out first, and the bouncer guy shoos me out in front of him.

This is surreal; it's happening, but I also feel very distanced from it because it has nothing to do with me. I don't know these men. I have no idea what they want (except Patel), and I feel like a bit player in a bad movie. I'm just waiting for it to end, or make sense, or for a commercial to come on so I can change the channel. But I walk across the yard, I mount the stairs, I walk through a kitchen to a set of stairs and am led down into a cellar (of course.) There is a chair, a sandwich, a bottle of water and a toilet with a ragged roll of toilet paper. I sit down. The bouncer guy says, "Wait here."

I turn up to him and say, "What do you want from me?"

"Me?" he replies, "Nothing. My boss ..." he shrugs, "You'll find out soon enough. Eat. Wait." He leaves.

I look around. There's not much to see. I drink some water. I eat half the sandwich. I try to figure out what is going on upstairs, but all I can hear is the squeaking of floorboards and occasional laughter. I use the bathroom. Through a small, murky square of window, I can see the sky is a lighter shade of black. I hope somebody is looking for me, but I kind of doubt it.

༚ ༚ ༚

A few hours pass without me getting any closer to figuring out what to do. It's clear that I am not a priority. I can hear lots of movement above, but no one has come down. I finished my sandwich, but I'm trying to reserve my water, and I've inspected the entire room three times. There is no exit. There is no more food or water. There are no scraps of metal or bits of rope or anything I can use to jerry rig any contraption of any sort. There's just dirt, scraps of old newspaper and rotting wooden bins. I have gone through my options, and none of them are good or seem remotely feasible.

First option: Try to bust out of window and call for help – But the window is too small and low to the ground and there is no one to hear me.

Option two: Try to run – But the door is locked, the men are huge and armed, and there is nothing but cornfields for miles. Where would I go?

Option three: Flood the toilet – Pretty sure I would only be inconveniencing myself.

Crazy option number four: Shift out of here.

The last seems like it has the most potential, which is crazy because I'm not at all sure of what will happen. Meer said I blinked or blipped, but I never disappeared even though I felt like I was gone for hours. What if I jump but then just end up back here a second later?

But still, it's my only feasible option. I'm just scared because I don't really know what I'm doing. The other problem is that I can't recall making any conscious choices today. I did everything as it had already been planned. The date with Meer, class, eat, work, go home. The only possible choice I can think of was choosing to go to work even though I didn't want to go. Ok.

Experiment #1 – choose to go home instead of into work.

I close my eyes and try to summon the roar. I think back to the moment I hesitated in the hallway. I'd felt uneasy. I concentrate on that. I think about choosing to go home instead. I concentrate, I bring the roar, my vision blurs. I close my eyes. I push, I push hard. I sense it. I'm through.

I open my eyes. I'm in the same room. It's the same time of day. My water bottle is empty though and there is an apple core on the table. I am colder, stiffer and I see I have stacked the wooden boxes near the window. Sigh.

Ok, maybe I can think of an earlier choice. Maybe during my date with Meer … no … maybe earlier that day … just worked on scholarship essay … maybe night before … I gasp. Oh, shit. What if I choose to go back to not reading to the kids but going on the date last night? Shit. I bet that would change everything. I think the cops were coming, Meer was getting beat up … oh, I don't want to go back there but it won't really be back there, it'll be now, after that. I have a pang of regret because I know this will probably nix any chance of Meer and I.

I sigh and begin to decide how to fix the choice in my head when I have another idea. What if I decide to go to the basketball game with her after all? Then no drama at the lounge, no ex, no pool sticks, no cops. I grab onto this idea. And I distinctly remember thinking about my decision whether to go with her or get home in time for dinner. I chose to avoid my mother's disapproval rather than hang out with this interesting new chick. I settle in and visualize the street I was standing on while I was talking to Meer. I see her face asking if I want to come along. I think to myself, "yes, I want to come along. I'd love to go. I see myself reaching for the door handle. I summon the roar, I think about getting in the car, I hear the roar louder now, my vision blurs, I push myself into the car, I push hard. I push through.

卐 卐 卐

I open my eyes. Fuck me. I am still in the room. There is some water in my bottle. The sandwich is gone, and the boxes are not stacked. But I am a little different. My body feels loose, and I'm wearing one of Meer's shirts. It smells like her. And I have new memories. Sweet memories.

I went to the game. I watched her play. We went back to her apartment so she could change her clothes. We decided to just eat something there. We listened to music. She likes '70's soul music so we listened to the Spinners and Phoebe Snow, Dionne Warwick and Earth, Wind and Fire. She lit candles and we drank cheap wine. We made out and made love. It was good. So, so good and sweet and good. I slept over. We kissed goodbye for 20 glorious minutes until I tore myself away. I got home just after everyone left for work and school. Then I worked on my scholarship, read and started a paper for Evolution, went to Math class, ate, and went to work. I was in the middle of texting her when they took me.

Ugh. I have got to get out of here! I sit back overwhelmed with my new memories, the old ones fading and I'm just trying to keep my memories straight in my head. I drink the last of my water just as I hear the click of the lock. Finally! I look up and coming down the stairs is Dr. Patel.

Chapter 11

Dr. Patel hesitates, staring at me in disbelief. He looks beat up and tired, but manages some dignity when he turns to bouncer guy behind him and says, "What in God's name is she doing here? She has nothing to do with this. She is just a work-study student helping with plant experiments. Let her go! She should not be here." But there is more fear than indignation in his eyes, and I do not know why.

"Hey Doc, I don't make the rules. The boss will talk to you, and then maybe you will talk to him." The Bouncer guy is holding another chair and two water bottles. I notice he still has his gun tucked into his waistband. He sees me look at it and smiles.

"No trouble from you, right sweetheart?"

I shake my head "no," and turn back to Dr. Patel. He takes the chair from bouncer guy and sits down with a sigh. Bouncer guy puts the waters on the table, takes my empty bottle and the sandwich paper and leaves without a word.

"Well," I say, "Professor? What is going on? Do you owe these guys money or something? And why am I here?" I haven't done anything!"

He lowers his head. "I'm so sorry, Kim. No, you haven't done anything, and you shouldn't even be here. I'm very sorry they got you."

"But got me for what? I don't have anything! I have nothing but a math textbook, a book for bioethics and my notebook. I don't even know what they did with that stuff."

"No, it's me they want. It's me who owes them something. You … you just happened to have the misfortune of working for me. Maybe they think you can tell them something about me. I don't know."

"How long have you been here?" I ask because I don't know what else to ask.

"A few days. They got me … Saturday, while I was on Kelly Drive for a run. My family is probably so worried about me …"

"Professor … you haven't said what they want. What do you owe them? Can you give it to them so we can get out of here?"

"Sorry Kim, I don't think it's going to be so simple." With that, we heard the lock turn and the door open. A thin bespectacled man in a blazer descended the stairs with an air of intellect and authority. All eyes turn to him.

Dr. Patel appears unnerved even when the man approaches him with his hand out. The gesture is friendly, but his eyes are cold. "Good to see you again, Patel. Unfortunate circumstances notwithstanding."" Dr. Patel shakes his hand but backs away when they release their grasp. He inclines his head and says, "Dr. Wasserman, I'm pleased to meet you in person. What a privilege." He glances towards me. I nod as well, and Dr. Wasserman turns to me. "Ahh Kim Thornton. A pleasure to make your acquaintance." I reach to shake his extended hand but instead of shaking my hand, he holds it for a beat before releasing it. I pull it back and shove it in my pants pocket as he turns back to Dr. Patel.

"Now, are you ready to give me the information I want, or do we continue to have a problem?" he says in a very controlled voice.

Patel starts to answer, but he ends up stuttering and stammering and making no sense whatsoever.

"Enough!" demands Wasserman and he slaps Dr. Patel hard across the face. "Give me what is rightfully mine, and I will try to forget that you stole from me, hid from me and then lied to me about it. You used to be such a man of integrity, Arun."

Dr. Patel looks conflicted. He looks at me and says, "Let her go, Wasserman. She has nothing to do with this. She's just a student."

Wasserman stares hard at Dr. Patel. "Is that so? If she has nothing to do with this, then why have you been studying her? What is all this?" He gestures to bouncer guy who, from over his massive shoulder, swings forward and drops a bag of videotapes on the floor.

"You've been recording her work sessions since last year. Why? And I've studied your lab tests. Why does each one include a separate human DNA scan? Her DNA scan? She may be a fool, but I am not. It's clear to me that you have not abandoned the work we began together, the work I funded. I want your research, Patel and I will have it!" At that last, he steps up to Dr. Patel and is scant inches from his face.

Dr. Patel is swallowing hard and looking from Dr. Wasserman to the bouncer to the stairs, his intentions written clear all over his face. The bouncer guy steps over the videotapes towards Patel. "I wouldn't try it if I were you." But it's too late; Patel shoves Dr. Wasserman into the bouncer guy, who stumbles back. He bounds up the steps and slams open the door. I think he gets one step into the kitchen when a hand shoves him back in. Wind milling his arms, he can't catch his balance and tumbles backwards down the steps, cracking his head on the old concrete floor. The sound is horrifying. Throwing a disgusted glance at bouncer guy, Dr. Wasserman walks over to Dr. Patel. He checks his breathing by bending low over him and putting his ear to Patel's mouth. He mutters, "good" and stands up. Giving Patel a swift kick to the ribs, he walks up the stairs. "Take care of him," he commands bouncer guy "… and her … I guess we'll have to keep her. Bring her upstairs, too. We have a lot of work to do."

Bouncer guy looks at me and shrugs. I look at Dr. Patel lying on the floor out cold. Bouncer guy picks him up by the armpits and drags him backward up the stairs. His legs thump, thump, thump. I hear the door lock when they clear it. I walk over to the bag of videotapes. I pick one up. The label, handwritten in black ink, consists of my initials, KT1 and a date. I look through the bag, and it seems that there is a tape for every session I worked in the lab. There are about 100 tapes in the box, each labeled with my initials. My stomach sinks. Maybe he is obsessed with me? Maybe he thought I would steal something? Then I think back – how many times did I pick my nose? Pull out a cranny? Act out scenes with Mabel? And just act weird because I thought I was alone? Ugh. But Wasserman said he did DNA tests on me, why? I quickly understand that it has to do with this thing I can do now. Has to. That would explain the metal walls, the "jumps". I don't know how and I don't know what, but it has to be Patel who did this to me.

I sit down and try to think about getting out of here again. I have to think long term; I have to think a big jump. Maybe before I went to Temple? Then I will never have met Dr. Patel. But I'm not even sure I can do that, and I'm not sure I want to. Besides this ... craziness, I'm happy with my life ... kind of ... I'm on the path I chose. I'm in college and doing well and about to go to MIT, I think ... oh ... I don't know what to do.

I hear the door unlock and bouncer guy comes down. I look for any sense of compassion in him but I see nothing. He has a small tray with food and another bottle of water.

"I'm not coming up yet?" I say, hoping to start a conversation.

"No, we have to prepare your room," he says pronouncing each syllable. "Enjoy your food," he adds as he walks up the stairs. That would have sounded like sympathy if it didn't sound so much like "Enjoy your last meal." Ok. No more equivocating. I have got to get out of here.

❧ ❧ ❧

I spend the next two hours going over in my head all the risks of trying to jump again. The last two were ok, but I didn't end up changing much of anything. I'm trying to remember the moment of a choice from more than two years ago and not too much seems significant. I've been on the same course, my life just following along some assumed trajectory. I'm running out of time. I can feel it. I hear a lot of walking back and forth above me. I hear a lot of grunting like they are lifting things and carrying things and the knot of fear is growing ice cold in my belly. I am starting to panic. I try to think logically but I'm also worried. What if I jump and don't go to Temple, and never meet Patel and then lose the ability to "jump" if I get into a bad situation? What if my "choice" gets me or somebody else hurt? And there's something else I'm not admitting to myself: somewhere in the back of my mind I think I don't want to lose Meer. The memory of last night (was it just last night?) is still fresh and it felt like love and I don't want to let it go. As I'm thinking about her and the way she smiled at me while we danced, I have a flash of a memory that is not a memory. I close my eyes and try to tease it out. I reach towards this *other* memory and pull at a thought. I looked into her eyes on a date (what date?) at a restaurant? (did we have a date?). I jumped and went *back*. I was at a party (I don't remember a party); there were guys I didn't know and that girl, Amber. I remember her. Did she invite me to a party? Yes, but I didn't go but I remember going … and then the guys. Amber was there with the guys, and they tried to get me, but Meer came. And she saved me.

I hear voices just outside the door. It sounds like maybe two or three men making plans for me in thickly accented English. I'm wracking my brain but I don't have any better ideas. I grab for the memory that I don't really have. I try to imagine looking into her eyes and that I pushed but went backward. I hear the click of the lock above me. I snap my eyes shut and summon the roar. It comes, but faintly. I'm afraid. I hear feet on the stairs. I block it out and concentrate on her eyes. I bring the roar and hold the vision of Meer's eyes, but I feel hands on my arms. I stay in my head, but somebody is shaking me. I open my eyes, but my vision is blurred. I smile and close them again. I focus on losing myself in the roar, but hold on to Meer looking at me. I push through hard. Like a diver off a cliff, I feel my body fling itself backwards as I throw myself back into time and towards Meer. The roar is agonizing and I scream from the pain of it.

卍 卍 卍

I am sitting up in my bed. It is dark. I just screamed out. My mother comes down the hall and sits on my bed. She reaches for me and holds me. I cry. I don't know why, but her compassion, my fear and the release of the scream bring me to tears. The memory of what those boys and that girl did to me come back to me, and I cry the same tears but new pain. My mother just holds me, rocks me, and tells me she loves me. I hold on to her as my life now takes shape around me. I am sixteen. I am in high school. I was almost raped. I told a girl I liked her, and she tried to have me raped. I was saved. That was ... how many days ago? I rack my brain. Maybe it was three or four days ago? The weekend has passed. Everyone knows what happened. My mother is here. I have school in the morning. I am humiliated. We are not going to the police since "nothing" happened. The boys don't go to my school but she does. Amber. I am filled with fury, helpless, hopeless fury. My mom said it would go away. She said it like she knew from experience, but I didn't ask any questions. From the hallway, I can hear a whimper turn into a cry. "Mommy". It stretches into a wail. It's my little brother, Walt. He's two years old. He keeps calling. I can feel my mother stiffen. I know she has to go to him.

I let go of her and say, "It's all right. I'm all right. Go get him."

She says, "Are you sure? It's probably nothing." But we hear him again, getting louder, sounding more and more awake.

"Go get him before he wakes Maya," I say.

"Yeah, you're right," she says and starts to get up. She dips down and kisses me on the forehead.

"I'm so sorry sweetheart. But I promise you, it will get better."

"Thanks mom," I say.

She leaves, closing the door behind her. I hear her open my brother's room and start shushing him and comforting him. The sound muffles as she closes that door too. I lie back down in my bed and pull up my comforter. I kind of remember that I was in a basement, that somebody was coming to get me, but none of that makes sense. Maybe it was a dream. But the image of the basement doesn't fade and I remember a man being dragged up the stairs. Thump, thump, thump. I fall asleep to its rhythm.

Chapter 12

It's been two weeks since "the incident" and I am hiding in the bathroom. Why? Amber. I cannot believe I ever, ever, ever liked that girl. She is the worst human being on the planet ever, EVER. Because she is pretty and because she is popular and because she is fucking awful, she has started a campaign against me! As if I did anything to her. She told everyone at school that I tried to kiss her – a lie! And touch her – double lie! And that's why her friends had to do what they did. Of course, I told the truth, and she called me a liar and a dyke molester. This was today at lunch. I don't think anybody believes me except my best friend, Jen, my STEM crew and Meer. But nobody wants to say anything. Nobody wants to get involved. Nobody will say anything to her; they just are waiting to see what happens. She wants to fight me. I want to kick her ass badly, except, I know this will get me kicked out of my STEM clubs, kicked out of the Honor Society and maybe kicked out of school. And I have a meeting today, a genetics experiment with my science club that will count for AP lab credit, and I'm going to miss it if I don't get out of here. But she is out there, somewhere, waiting to jump me. I know she won't come in the bathroom. There are security cameras in here.

I'm holding onto the window grate struggling to distinguish anything through the bleary glass when I hear voices in the hallway. Sounds like a teacher … sounds like Jen … sounds like Amber. The door slams open and in walks Jen with Ms. Feinberg, the school counselor and resident disciplinarian.

"What are you doing in here?" asks Jen. I don't answer. I just look at Ms. Feinberg.

"Kim, is there a problem? Mr. Hawkins called my office to say you were missing, then Jen came in and told me there is a problem between you and some other girls. Is Amber one of those girls? I saw her in the hallway with some other girls."

Ms. Feinberg, crosses her arms and looks at me with raised eyebrows. I look at Jen and shake my head.

"Kim, if there is a problem you can tell me about it, we can go to my office if you like, but you can't stay here in the bathroom."

"Um, there's no problem, Ms. Feinberg, I just got caught up thinking about stuff. I'm just going to go to genetics now." I start to sidle past her, but she puts a hand on my arm.

"Listen Kim, I've heard some rumors and I just want you to know that you can come talk to me. It might help to talk about it, and maybe we can come up with a solution to your problems," she says looking towards the door.

I look at Ms. Feinberg. Despite her bird nose, pursed lips and cold demeanor, she seems sincere, and I am grateful for her kindness, but she has to know that I can't go to her or any teacher. It would just make things worse.

"No thanks," I say and grab Jen. "I'm good, thanks for checking on me, though."

Jen walks out first, then me, then Ms. Feinberg. The halls are quiet now. There are just a few students here and there making their way to after-school clubs. Jen puts her arm around me and walks me to the fourth floor. Even though she couldn't hurt a fly, I feel protected.

After the lab, I decide to leave the school through the back door just in case Amber is out there waiting for me. I go down the back stairs and end up near the gym. The custodian is in the doorway, leaning on a mop, watching someone shoot hoops and counting the made shots. I hear just one person running, dribbling, and jumping. As I walk by, I peek in. It's Meer. I pause and watch. She's sweaty and breathing hard but she looks obstinate and takes one last shot. Swish.

The custodian yells, "Twenty-five! Ok, you gotta go, I have to mop!"

Meer practices a cross-dribble and makes her way over to her pile of stuff on the floor. She pauses just long enough to throw on her coat and backpack and starts dribbling one handed to the door. She looks up to say something to the custodian but she sees me. She breaks out into a huge grin and catches the ball. The custodian snorts and walks past us pushing his bucket and whistling.

"Thanks Sean" she murmurs. To me, she smiles and says, "Hey."

"Hey yourself," I reply.

"What are you doing down here?" she asks.

"Hmm … just leaving … going the long way, I guess."

"Oh yeah. I heard Amber is being an asshole. You hiding from her?"

"More like avoiding trouble. I can't risk being expelled. I'm trying to get a scholarship to go to NASA camp this summer."

"NASA camp? What's that?"

"Space camp. For teens who want to study space travel or be astronauts."

"That's what you want to do? That's crazy! But cool I guess."

"What about you? What do you want to do?"

"Me? Ball. I want to play ball. Maybe overseas, maybe for the WNBA. But basketball is my thing."

The custodian is making a racket as he folds up the bleachers and rolls the carts of balls to the side.

"Hey, let's go. Want to come over to my house? I have some homework to do, maybe you could help me, smarty pants."

"I don't know. I have a lot of homework to do too and most of my books are at home."

"Oh, ok, well I'll just walk you out then, you know, like a bodyguard."

"Ok."

We walk down the hall and out the back exit. It closes with a loud metallic slam behind us. As we walk out through the parking lot, we see a group of girls walking up the street away from us. I think it's Amber and her crew. Meer sees them too and tenses up a bit. I look at Meer and say, "Maybe I will come to your house for a while if that's ok."

"Yup", she smiles. "I have no idea what I'm doing in biology anyway." She puts her arm around me and steers me down the street, the long way to her house, which is just fine by me.

≈ ≈ ≈

Now, I go to Meer's house every day after school for homework. It's worked out well for both of us. She practices basketball, either with her team or by herself, and I get to go to all my afterschool clubs. Sometimes, her brother Quadir and his friends meet up with us, and we all walk home together. I don't know what happened, but he must have said something to somebody because Amber never bothered me again at school. She did troll my Facebook page, though, so I just shut it down. Jen told me she started a new one bashing me called, "stupid molester dykes to watch out for", but Facebook shut it down after a few days.

Meer is nothing like I thought she would be. I thought she would always be loud and bold and audacious. Turns out she can be shy and silly and insecure, especially when it comes to school. We have become a "thing", but it's weird. Quadir is very protective of her, and so are all his friends. None of them say anything to us about our friendship. They just assume we are together and they leave us alone. Even my best friend Jen assumes we are a couple. Since she can't quite wrap her head around it, she doesn't ask for details and gives us plenty of space. My STEM friends are in awe of my association with her since she is so popular and we are so geeky. My mother, so far, is unaware as she is busy with the babies and happy that I am just busy with school. The problem is us.

I had a boyfriend in 7th grade and a better one in 9th grade, Jackson. They were very nice and I liked them a lot. I just wasn't super excited about them or in love or whatever. But I knew what to do, how to act. I knew they were supposed to call me first and ask me out. I knew they were to hold my hand and try to get a kiss. I knew what to expect and what my appropriate response should be. I have watched movies and television and my family my whole life. I know exactly how to be heterosexual. But gay? I am not sure about that at all. Because Meer is athletic and tall and bigger than me, sometimes I act like she is the boy and I am the girl and I giggle and flirt. Sometimes that's good and she comes up to me with that swagger and smile and makes me weak at the knees. But other times, we are just like two girl "friends" and we gossip or tell secrets or confess our complete ignorance of politics or Spanish or whatever. And I feel so close to her, like she is my soul mate and I can be myself, and I feel so free. It's at those times that I find her intensely attractive and sometimes I want to throw her down and kiss her. But I don't. I feel like I shouldn't and I get nervous. I'm not sure how she would react and I don't know if I can go through with it or if I will do it right. So, I wait for her to make the moves, and she sometimes does, but most of the times she doesn't. And then I get frustrated but I don't say why 'cuz it's stupid and we argue. One time I stormed out her house and ran to Jen's house crying.

"What's the matter, Kim?" Jen asked while trying out different hairstyles in the mirror.

I just sat there. I couldn't figure out what to say.

"Did Meer do something?" I shook my head, "no". She thought for a moment, "Amber?" I shook my head "no" again and just laid back on her bed.

"It's nothing. I'm just stupid," I said.

"Well, I doubt if that's it because you are like one of the smartest people I know." She had her hair in two buns on the side of her head, like a black Princess Leia. I laughed.

"What? You don't like it?" She switched to a whisper. "I have a date tomorrow."

I sat up. "With who?" I asked.

"An older guy, someone you don't know. He's a friend of my cousin's. I met him at his 21st birthday party last weekend."

"Jen! He'd better not be out of high school." She was suppressing a smile. "Jen! Seriously, how old?

"Just 22, not that old, and he's sooooo nice and soooo cute! And he has a job selling cars … and my mother met him and got along with him. It's not like he's a criminal or anything."

"If he dates you, he's going to be a criminal!" I say worried for my friend. "I thought your mom said no boyfriends until you are a senior?"

"Kim, I'm going to be 17 in two weeks. I'm practically an adult. I think I know what I'm doing."

"How can you know what you are doing when I don't know what I'm doing?" Jen looked at me.

"Ahhh … Kim, you have always liked challenges and complicated questions, that's why you are the scientist and now you have decided to be gay, so more challenges and complications for you." She said in her most affected voice.

"I did not choose to be gay, for your information, I just came this way."

"You could have chosen to ignore it and not hook up with the biggest lesbian in school, perhaps?"

"True, I could have chosen to be someone else or maybe not to be me. Is that what you think I should have done?"

"Me? No, I think you should do what's right for you. I support you no matter what but this is the harder road, you know?"

"Yeah, I see that. And you think by secretly dating a man you are taking an easier road" Jen stopped her hair styling and looked at me. "No, it's not a road, it's just some fun. And let me show you a picture, he's so sweet and cute and sexy!" She takes out her phone and scrolls through her pictures. When she finds the picture, she squeals and sighs and holds it for me to see. Light-brown skinned, with a mustache and goatee, he is wearing a suit and tie and standing in front of a shiny red car. Oh, he's cute. I shake my head. He looks like trouble with a capital "T" to me but I see what she sees in him.

"Alonso Belafonte Malfis. My future husband." I sigh and hand her back the phone. "Be careful, Jen. Please be careful."

Chapter 13

By the end of my junior year, I am seventeen and getting ready for a big robotics competition. Meer had helped the girls' varsity basketball team to a citywide championship, and Jen is pregnant. Meer and I haven't figured out all of our romantic dynamics, but we know that we love each other and we are happy enough. It is the best of times for me, but the worst of times for Jen. Jen's pregnancy set off a firestorm at her house and at our school. She is the fifth girl in eleventh grade to get pregnant, but it seems worse because it is so unexpected. Jen had never been in any trouble of any sort for the first 17 years of her life. Then she met Alonso and she changed. She met him right before Thanksgiving, and I barely saw her after that. I heard about their first date and their second but after that, I could never get a hold of her. She started cutting school and ditching any kind of school activities. I could tell she was under some kind of stress, but she wore his ring around her neck and always seemed to be swimming in gifts from him. So, I thought it was ok, though a little weird. Still, she kept calling him "my husband" so all seemed well. To be honest, I was too busy with my schoolwork and going to every one of Meer's games to pay too much attention to Jen anyway. Meer and basketball took up a lot of time. Meer tried to get me to be a cheerleader, but I just could not bring myself to do that. Cheering and jumping around was just not my thing, and I was too busy with my academics. The STEM club had quite a few competitions, and I was just about finished fulfilling the requirements for the space camp scholarship though I was competing with everybody else in my club.

One of the last contests we had for the year was to compete at the statewide robotics competition. I was paired up with Savvy Montana, the new girl from Brooklyn. Beautiful and smart, Meer was jealous and wanted me to switch partners. I laughed it off, teasing her and taunting her to "up" her game. Secretly, I was excited and nervous. I tried hard not to be attracted to Savvy, but it was a losing battle so I did my best to keep my distance. I was determined to be neutral and focused on the work. That was my strategy.

We were to be working under the careful eyes of her overprotective parents at her house on the weekends, so I felt pretty comfortable with the situation … until I got there. Turns out, her parents didn't think that I was somebody to worry about, so they put us in a workshop, in a garage, out in their backyard. It was very private.

Savvy knew I was gay. Because of the Amber situation and then my relationship with Meer, everyone knew I was gay. Savvy took it as a personal challenge. Every day we worked on the robot, I worked on being distant and professional, and she worked on me. I tried. I really tried, but she had anticipated my presence and knew my weaknesses. Day after day for a month, she picked my defenses apart until I had none. I was a wet, panting mess by the time she finally kissed me and I lost all self-control under her skillful tongue. By the time we came up for air, the sun had gone down, Meer had texted me five times and I was completely undone. Her parents called her in for dinner, and she left me grinning. I staggered out into the cool spring air trying to gather myself and get my lies straight. I texted Meer that I had to go talk to Jen because she was having a problem. Then I texted Jen to say she was having a problem if Meer called her. I put my phone away and got on the bus to go home. I felt awful for being a cheater, but worse for being a liar, too.

When I get to Jen's house, she is sitting on the steps outside in the middle of a heated phone conversation. I am ready to lay my troubles down at her feet, but she is having her own problems so I sit down and wait. I sit and think about what I did, how Meer will feel if she finds out, how terrible a person I am and how I wish I could take it back. Lost in the detailed remembrances of my own treachery. (I can't help thinking about Savvy and that kiss. That kiss! Oh my god!) I almost don't notice Jen getting up and walking into the house.

"Hey, where are you going? I was waiting for you," I exclaim. Jen stops and turns to me. "I'm just too tired and sad to talk right now, Kim. Maybe another day, ok?" she says. But I just stand up and say, "then we don't have to talk. I'll just sit next to you, ok? We haven't hung out in so long. I've missed you, Jen. Oh, and look at your belly, I can see it! Your bump!" I stand up and walk towards her. She takes my hand and puts it on her small but robust belly. She smiles at me and says, "Ok, come on in. You're right. I miss my girl!" We spend the night eating potato chips and drinking grape soda. I tell her about my cheating ways, and she tells me about what's going on with her.

"He wanted me to have an abortion but I told him it was too late for that. Then he says, he wants me to give the baby up for adoption. I don't know. I know I'm young to have a baby and take care of a baby, but I think we could do it together. I told him I want get married."

I suck in a breath. Wow. "So what did he say?" I ask.

"He laughed, said I was fucking crazy and hung up the phone," she says.

"That was just now?" I ask.

"No, that was a week ago. I was talking to his sister on the phone. He's changed his phone number and won't answer any of my calls or texts." Jen hangs her head down and starts to cry. I walk over to her and put an arm around her. She cries into my shoulder, long, deep, soul crushing sobs and for once, I forget about myself and just try to be there for her. When her sobs subside into shudders and sniffles, I look around for tissues for her. Her phone rings. She jumps up, grabs a tissue out of my hand and wipes her eyes and nose. She answers, "Hello?" Her voice is clear and strong, but her face is falling in disappointment. "Yes, she's here." She turns to me and hands me the phone, mouthing "Meer".

I take the phone and start apologizing for not answering earlier, and for not telling her when I left Savvy's and for not letting her know where I was. I tell her Jen needs me and that I'll call her in a few. She tells me she needs me too and has been waiting all day to talk to me. I ask her what is it, but she wants to tell me in person. It's late and I have to get home as it is. She begs; I already feel guilty so I tell her "yes", and to meet me at my house as soon as she can get there. I hang up and look up at Jen. She waves me off and tells me to go.

"I'm tired anyway, Kim. Tired of crying, and tired of trying to figure out what to do. I'm going to go to bed. Call me tomorrow though, ok?" I nod, give her a big hug and head back out into the night.

Meer is there almost as soon as I get there. She's in her usual black Adidas tracksuit, baseball cap and a white t-shirt. She looks super excited but I make her wait outside while I ask permission for company. My mother is asleep and Big Walt is half way there.

He says, "Its cool as long as she's out by midnight and you guys keep it quiet. And no funny business, ok Kim?" I shrug and look offended, which I am. I usher Meer in, who nods to Big Walt and we head down into the basement "family room". There isn't much there: a TV, a sofa and a gazillion baby toys. We kick those out of the way and sit down.

"Now," I say, "what is so important, Meer?" Her eyes widen and she inhales a deep breath.

"I got a call from Geno Auriemma today."

I'm searching my brain but have no idea who that is.

She looks annoyed at my obvious ignorance. "The head coach for UConn? Only one of the best coaches ever at one of the best schools ever?" He wants to send down one of his assistant coaches to talk to me and watch me play in person!!!" She's grinning from ear to ear and almost bouncing on the couch. I up my energy level and exclaim, "Aww baby! That is great news! UConn, even I have heard of them. I'm so happy for you. I hope it happens for you. I really do. You are such a great player!" She reaches over to give me a big squeeze.

"I've been waiting to tell you all day! Does that robot thing really take that long? Aren't you two finished yet?"

The shame of my cheating hits me full force, and I struggle to maintain my face so she doesn't see it. "Yeah, I reply. "We're just about done. But come here, let's celebrate." I pull her down on top of me and kiss her. It takes a minute but soon we forget everything else except each other. I even manage to stop thinking about Savvy and how I just had her in my arms a few hours ago. Oh, I think, I am going to hell for sure. Then I stop thinking altogether.

Chapter 14

Life got a little more complicated after that night. Meer became obsessed with improving her game and skills before the UConn coach came. She spent most waking moments playing ball. I had to keep on her to keep up with her homework and studying.

"They will only take you if you actually graduate high school", I would say. She scoffed but managed to maintain a C average.

Savvy and I finished our robot the following week, but her parents had to go out and left us with her little brother, Ramon. I was relieved. I didn't want to cheat again but didn't think I had the will power to resist her. She kept looking at me sideways but she kept her distance. Her brother was seven, curious about everything and very observant. After we tested it for the fifth time, I announced that I was going to leave, and she gave me a pouty face. She sent her brother on an errand for food and turned towards me.

"I missed you all week," she said.

"Savvy, last week was … last week …. Look, I really like you but I have a girlfriend and I didn't mean to do what we did," I stammered.

"Hey, I'm not gay. I just had fun with you and I thought about you, that's all. Amira, she's your girlfriend, right?" I nod assent.

"Well," she says, "I could just be your friend and we could just have fun sometimes. You know, science experiments …" She giggles and starts walking towards me, gazing in to my eyes.

"Savvy, I … It's not right …I can't…"

Her brother interrupted our conversation when he came back with three bags of Doritos and handed them out. We crunched our chips while he kept up a steady stream of bragging about what he would do once he's on the Robotics team. After I finished the bag and wiped my hands on my jeans, I got up to leave.

"Thanks for the chips. I'll see you in school on Monday."

"Ok, let me know if you change your mind," she said.

"Ok, I will." And I beat a hasty retreat. As I walked to the bus stop, I felt very proud of myself. I texted Meer that I was done and ready to hang out. She texted me back that she was playing ball with her brother and friends and was probably hanging with them all night. Disappointed, I headed home alone.

At the last minute, I decided to stop at Jen's house. I arrived in the middle of an argument. I stopped outside the front door, but the upstairs window was open and I could hear everything.

"No daughter of mine is going to her prom pregnant! You will look ridiculous, like the whore I always knew you would turn out to be!"

"That's just great Mom! I make one mistake, one mistake and now you hate me!!

"A baby is not a mistake, Jen; a baby is a life, a life that you had no business making and now have no way to support!"

"I will find a way to support my child, mom, with or without Alonso; don't you worry. I won't be a burden to you anymore!"

"Oh, don't try to throw it back on me. I dedicated my life to care for you and support you and protect you. You decided to take all of that and throw it away after some man, some man you hardly know, and now that he got what he wanted he left you. I knew he was no good and I told you to stay away from him! But no! You just had to defy me! Now see what happens when you don't listen to your mother! You are looking for "pregnant prom dresses!"

Jen's mom started bawling, and I could hear her leaving the room and the door closing behind her. Then I could just make out Jen's quiet weeping. I texted her. I told her I was outside and asked if she wanted company or maybe wanted to get out for a while. I sat on the cold cement stoop and waited. A few minutes later, her front door opened and she stepped out.

"You heard everything?" she asked.

I nod.

"Yeah, it's like that just about every night. I don't know how much longer I can deal with this." We started to walk down the street and pass my house.

"I'm really sorry Jen. The whole thing just sucks."

"Yeah, I know. But she's right about one thing, this is my problem, my responsibility."

"So, what are you going to do?" I ask.

"The baby is due in August so I won't be coming back to school. I think I'm going to just get my GED and then I'll be finished with school."

"Not coming back to school? But Jen!" The thought of her dropping out just shocked me. It had never occurred to me that she would quit school. We had been in school together since we learned to talk.

"Yeah, I know Kim but school is not the place for me anymore. It's bad enough going now that I'm showing. How can I go when I have a little baby at home? Who's going to take care of her? I'm already ahead enough in my classes that I can probably pass that GED today. So once I get my GED, I can get a job, maybe something at night. That way I can watch the baby during the day and Mom can watch the baby at night, when she's here anyway."

I'm trying to wrap my head around this new Jen. This Jen who has to think ahead and make plans with her life. I can only nod.

"But that's why I really want to go on this prom. It's my last chance, you know."

"Yeah, I get it. I hadn't even thought about this prom. You know, it would be ... weird."

"Do you want to go with Meer?" she asks.

"I wouldn't go with anyone else but I don't know if I would do that. I think my mother would die of embarrassment and I don't know. People "know" about us but a prom? It might be pushing it, you know?"

"Well, I'm going to be "pushing" it. If you two go, people won't even notice me and my bump!"

"So you want to use me as a decoy? Is that it? That's the love you have for me?" I give her a playful squeeze.

"Hey, what would you wear? A dress, right? But what about Meer? Would she wear a dress or would she wear a tux? Ooh, she would look good in a tux!"

"I have no idea, but you're right, she would look good in a tux. She's been so busy with basketball though, I doubt she would want to go. I don't even think I would want to go."

Jen stops walking and looks at me. "Please. I want to go. I can find a date but I want you to go with me. I always planned on us going to prom on a double date, you know, sharing a limo, going out to IHOP afterwards ... please, for me Kim."

I look at her and think about how she is about to be a mother, a grown-up. She's right, this might be our last chance to hang out and have some fun.

"Ok, I'll go. I'll see if Meer wants to go but I don't make any promises. My mother is going to freak out!"

"Eh, whatever, she can just go get drinks with my mom." She puts her arm around me and kisses my cheek. "Thanks Kim. This is going to be fun!"

Chapter 15

My mom did freak out. She refused to help with buying anything and was adamant that she would not be there to see me off. Then she went to church to go pray on it. Meer refused even listen to the idea until I suggested her brother could go as Jen's date. Even then I still had to beg and plead and promise to go with her to tour UConn … and to tutor her in algebra … and chemistry … and to pay at IHOP afterwards!

Jen and I had everything we needed except dresses and a limo. But we had the internet. I discovered a group call Fairy Godmothers that donated prom dresses to needy girls (which we were) and we found two we liked at their makeshift store. We went to five thrift stores to look for shoes but we finally found them, too. The limo was harder but we got lucky. Jen had a cousin who had a best friend who worked for a funeral home. For $50 bucks and a carton of cigarettes, he agreed to drive us.

Prom night is warm but humid after a week of rain. I pack up my stuff and haul it down to Jen's house to get dressed with her. All those years she subscribed to Teen Vogue finally pay off and we manage to do a decent job putting on each other's makeup. She helps me upbraid my short locks, I help her squeeze into her dress and we both groan inching on the hated pantyhose. My dress is a peach halter-top gown with a low-cut back. Jen's lilac chiffon dress has an empire waist to hide her belly, though it doesn't really.

The limo comes at 7pm, and Meer and Qadir walk up to the door to get us. Meer looks sheepish in a tailored black dress with a tuxedo-like top. Qadir is his usual quiet self in a simple black tux. His earrings, goatee and tattooed neck speak for him. We are all awkward though. Jen and Qadir have only met once before, and Meer and I are super self-conscious being dressed up in dresses together. The only person who comes to see us off is our old friend Kendra and she is more excited than any of us. Although she got sent off to military school and we hardly ever see her anymore, Jen called her to take pictures and she showed up to do just that. After insisting on about 50 different poses, we are more than ready to go and Kendra relents after hugging and kissing each of us goodbye. I spy Jen's mom watching through the window. I wave to her as I get in the limo, but she just wipes away tears.

The prom is pretty fun. Jen, determined to have a last hurrah, dances all night long, keeps everyone laughing with her corny jokes and leads the soul train line three times! Some people stare at Meer and I and whisper, but most don't seem to care. We dance alone a couple of times, but Jen and Qadir are never far away and we all seem to gravitate to each other anyway. The only time I am unsettled is when Savvy comes in with Nate, another STEM kid. He looks on top of the world, and she is stunning as usual. Later in the evening, she corners me at the punch table. I am relieved when a group of kids come over at the same time so I don't have to deal with her alone.

"Having fun?" she asks. "You look just beautiful. I really like your make-up." She leans toward me and whispers, "that lipstick would look good on me." I look up at her as she blows me a quick kiss, spins around and leaves.

I am mad at my hands when they shake a little as I fill the little cups with punch. I walk back to Meer as fast as I dare in my high heels. She looks up at me when I get close and stands up, takes the cups and sets them down on the table. I realize at that moment that I love her.

"What's the matter?" she asks.

"Nothing, I just … I'm just really happy, here with you tonight. You look beautiful and I'm just so happy we came together." I reach for her hands and bring one up to my lips and kiss it. Startled, she laughs long and hard and pulls me to her for a bear hug. When we separate, she gives me a quick kiss on the lips then steers me onto the dance floor. I see Jen watching us as we pass by, smiling but wistful.

On the dance floor, the DJ mixes in a slow song. We hesitate and begin to drift towards the tables but Qadir and Jen swoop in next to us and begin a long elaborate slow drag next to us. We can only laugh and rejoin them in a much more dignified two-step. I glimpse Savvy out of the corner of my eye but she seems engrossed in whatever Nate is saying so I turn my full attention back to Meer. She gazes at me with so much love and affection that I worry my heart will burst with happiness. It's then that I decide that whatever happens, I want to be with her.

Chapter 16

A year later, Meer and I graduate from high school. I am, of course, valedictorian. My dream is to go to MIT. I get in but they only offer me a partial scholarship, not the full ride I need. If I had gotten into the NASA space camp, I might have had a chance, but I didn't get in, Savvy and Nate did. My back up plan is to go to Temple University, live at home and try again next year. But then Meer is offered a basketball scholarship to UConn, which of course, she accepts. She asks me to come with her, and I, because I cannot imagine being without her, say yes.

The day I leave home, my mother is relieved. I can tell in the way her shoulders relax even though she has my little sister on her hip and my little brother running circles around her. She kisses me good-bye on the cheek and hands me $50 for the road. As Big Walt drives me up I-95, I am freer, lighter with every mile between us. She won't have to worry about being embarrassed by me or inconvenienced by me. I won't have to worry about her disapproval and my guilt at being happy despite her. It's better this way.

College is everything I thought it would be and a bit more. Everything is new and exciting – the cafeteria and eating whatever I want all the time, the 24-hour library, the daily parties and the sports culture. That last is quite a shock.

What I think will be a cozy situation on campus between Meer and I is not that at all. Meer has basketball practices every day, sometimes twice a day, and classes and tutoring and media training and "etiquette" training. She tries to find time for me but it is rushed and fleeting. Sometimes I only see her at night … late at night and then we just go to sleep. Meer was told, in no uncertain terms, that players on the girls' basketball teams were not "allowed" to have girlfriends. Of course, many of them did, but they had to be discreet about it. On the other hand, there are groupies, lots of "curious" girls turned on by these very popular goddesses of basketball under a very charismatic coach. Most of them have no hesitation whatsoever when it comes to flirting with the new players on the team. They are all about conquest. Our relationship becomes very lonely for me. Of course, I make friends with my hall mates and other kids in my major. I have a work-study job in a lab. I joined a womanist organization, the African-Americans in Science club and I take a dance class. But I came for Meer and Meer is nowhere to be found.

道道道

For Thanksgiving break, I stay at school to support Meer in a big game against Tennessee. They win a tight game and the team celebrates with a huge meal afterwards that I am able to attend (as her "friend"). That weekend we go to the movies and out to dinner and hang out like old times. The campus is pretty empty for the holiday and at times, it's like we are the only two people in the world, or at least the only two people who matter. I relax in the knowledge that we are getting back to the way we used be. I'm hopeful that everything will finally be alright.

Two weeks later, I am passing by Meer's dorm and decide to stop in to see if she wants to have dinner with me. She's there, but not alone. I walk in and find myself speechless. Straddled on top of my girlfriend, one of the assistant team managers, is topless and rubbing oil onto Meer's back and rubbing her breasts over her as she slides her hands up and down. Meer moans with pleasure. I clear my throat. Adding insult to injury, I have to clear it twice to get their attention. Marie looks up at me with surprise but she doesn't move. Meer opens one eye, sees me then hops up and dumps Marie to the floor.

"Oh baby, it's not what you think …" She comes towards me but I stare at her breasts and look at Marie half-naked on the floor. She follows my gaze and tries to cover up.

"I pulled my back and Marie was trying to …"

"Yeah, I can see what's she's doing. I just can't believe that you are doing it too."

I turn and run out. I can't stop my tears but I hold back my sobs while I run half way across campus to my dorm room. Then I let go and wail for hours. The betrayal, the disappointment, and the demise of my first love is almost too much to bear. The tears eventually run out but the ache in my heart, the hollowness in my stomach, the swirling in my mind … that doesn't go away for a long time. Meer calls and texts and tries to come see me but she is thwarted by her own schedule, my complete devastation and the efforts of my roommate Roxanne who protects me. She is also a science major on scholarship and understands the importance of finals. I don't know why or how but she keeps me focused on school. I burrow myself in our room, eat when necessary, slip out to take my finals and drag myself to the end of the semester.

I return home for the holidays and that helps. I want to stay in my bed and cry all day but I don't. Maya is just starting to talk and Lil' Walt is just starting to understand about Santa Claus and that there were toys coming for him. Their excitement and simple joys keep me out of my head and occupied enough. I try to call Jen but Jen left her baby with her mom in November and nobody knows where she is. Her mom receives cashier's checks from her with no return address. Unwilling to leave the house, I watch Christmas movies nonstop and eat cookies.

And then one night, Meer comes to my door and I fall apart all over again. We walk down to the familiar sofa in my basement and have that painful truth telling talk where she confesses all her transgressions and betrayals and begs for understanding. Yes, she had slept with that girl but only once before they had been caught and then again after, because why not at that point? Yes, some groupies had pursued her since she arrived on campus, and yes, she had flirted with a few. And yes, she still loved me but no, she didn't think she could be or wanted to be monogamous anymore. There was too much pressure on her and she couldn't take the pressure of owing anyone anything else. Like her faithfulness, like her love. She didn't want to owe that to "anyone" and that anyone was me. She cheated on me and broke up with me and blamed it on basketball. Ok.

I cannot begin to give voice to all the accusations, anger, hurt, reminders, blaming, cursing and pain that I have inside. I roil with it. It's stacking up in my chest, but I tamp it down. I will not yell here in my house. I will not scream and cry and rend my clothes in anguish. I feel indignation wrapped up in fury enclosed by sorrow. Regret is closing in on me in my rearview mirror but I can't even look at it yet.

"Ok."

"Ok?"

"Ok, Meer. What else can I say? We've been together so long maybe it was crazy to think that it would last. I don't even think I can cry anymore, I'm too sad for that. I just … I just want to wish you well and I let you go."

"What?" she asks.

I speak louder. "I let you go." I lift my palms up demonstrating that I hold nothing there.

"Kim, I'll always love you, ok?" She reaches for me but I turn her aside.

"Go." I say. She goes. I lie down on the floor and weep. I lay there until my mother comes and walks me upstairs. She gives me a sip of blackberry brandy and strokes my hair until I fall asleep in my bed.

৯ৎ ৯ৎ ৯ৎ

A few days later I get a text about a holiday party hosted by the STEM club at my high school. They are inviting alumni back to share their college experiences. I am not interested in going. I happen to mention it to my mother and she makes me go. It is December 23 and I have not left the house in a week. I have not showered in a week. I have not done anything but play with the babies and when they take naps or go to bed, I watch TV or play Myst on the computer. Sometimes I sneak the brandy. She makes me take a shower, put on some clean clothes, tidy up my locks into a bun and go. She even gives me a tin of cookies to take.

It is so cold outside! I breathe deep and puff out clouds of vapor. The air, sharp and brittle, stings my cheeks into numbness. A gust of icy air blows and sets the neighbor's wind chime to tinkling. I start walking. Up and down the street Christmas lights glow and twinkle. I was going to take the bus, but the walk feels so good that I just keep going. Despite my heartbreak, life goes on; people haul packages; stores play Christmas music; and cars carry trees on top. By the time I reach the school, I am a little sweaty, a little out of breath and my feet are sore but I am lighter on them. I open the door and am greeted by yells of "Kim!" and "Merry Christmas" and "Welcome home stranger!" I smile and make my way around the room, dispensing hugs and hellos to almost everyone there. I am back with my tribe.

I am sipping eggnog and talking with my AP Chemistry teacher about my coursework when the door opens again letting in a cold gust of air and Savvy. She is greeted with yells of "Savvy! And "Merry Christmas" and "Welcome back!" She, too, circles the room giving out hugs and kisses at random. She talks with the students she knows and gets introduced to those she doesn't. I know she knows I am there. I am pretty sure she is saving me for last. I try to concentrate on my conversation, but I am just biding my time and waiting for my turn. When she reaches me and Mr. Conklin, she grasps his hands and kisses his cheek. She turns to me, exclaims, "Kim!" as though she is just seeing me and pulls me into a big bear hug. I squeeze her tight. Turns out I really did miss her and tears come to my eyes. When we pull apart she sees them and steers me into a private corner.

"What's the matter, Kim?" she asks with a frown.

"I really don't want to talk about it here. I'm really just trying to enjoy the evening, you know?"

She looks at me for a minute. "Ok, I won't push it. So, how's UConn?"

"Oh, it's ok. Big campus, lots to do, it keeps me busy."

"MIT is as awesome as I thought it was going to be! I'm trying to get an internship this summer at Boeing where they manufacture some of the parts for the space shuttles. I think I can get into it if my "Interstellar Engineering" professor gives me a good recommendation."

"You have a class called "Interstellar Engineering??" I am awestruck.

"Sure! And the work you and I did on the robots was actually really helpful. I simulated the propulsion system we devised for one of my projects and got an "A" on it." She pauses. "What's the matter, Kim? Don't you like your courses?"

"Yeah, but we don't have anything like that," I say. I am feeling kind of numb.

"You know, I wish you had come to MIT. Don't you? We have a little bit of unfinished business between us."

I take a moment and study her. She is still beautiful but she is not the girl I had fooled around with, she looks like a woman now, more self-assured and … smarter.

"I'm sorry. I shouldn't have said that. That was a long time ago and you're probably still with Meer, right? She still a basketball star?"

"Savvy!" We hear someone yell her name from across the room. She raises her hand and starts towards him. "I'll see you later, alright. Let's get together before we go back to school, ok?"

I nod as she moves away. I watch her for a minute then close my eyes. I am crashed by the wave of regret I had refused to look at, refused to acknowledge earlier. It fills me up, my body trembles with it, my head roars with it. And I allow myself to think the thoughts I had pushed away. I wish I had not gone to UConn. I wish I had not gotten involved with Meer. I wish I had pursued Savvy. I wish I had stuck with my plan. I wish I had left Meer. I wish I had followed Savvy to MIT. My head roars. I can't stop thinking the thoughts, I am drowning under their combined weight and all of the sudden I am simultaneously pushed and pulled. I offer no resistance and go through. All is silent around me.

Chapter 17

I open my eyes and I'm in a bathroom stall … a school bathroom … my old high school bathroom. I wipe and pull up my pants. I walk out in a daze and go to wash my hands. In the mirror above the sink, I see I have on long crystal earrings and red lipstick. My hair looks freshly pressed and curled. I gaze into and past the glasses and into my eyes and feel disoriented. I hear a faint roar and think it's the noisy ventilation system. I shake my head to clear the cobwebs and pull myself together. I'm at the STEM holiday party of course. It's an annual tradition. I came with Savvy because we thought it would look good if two alumnae who attend the same university came together. We wanted to appear unified and like a good support network for anyone who was thinking of attending MIT. But it's all a sham. We are neither good nor supportive, not any more anyway.

I was just fifteen when cool, smart and gorgeous Savvy threw herself at me in her father's garage. I was enraptured. And when she suggested that we could be "special friends", I misunderstood and dropped the sweet and sincere but not as sophisticated girl who I was seeing. I thought Savvy wanted a relationship but soon found out that she just wanted to fool around with me … sometimes. That pretty much sucked, but we did fool around and without meaning to, we became friends. We even went to prom together. She went with Nate, another STEM club member and I went with my ex-boyfriend, Jackson. We all had a good time but what I remember the most was the sneaking off and making out when the boys were preoccupied with some prank. In hindsight, I think Savvy was into the thrill and danger of getting caught. I was just into her, however I could get it.

That summer Savvy went off to space camp, and then on to MIT in the fall so I didn't see her too much that year, but I was determined to follow her lead. We had often sat around and talked about going into space and I missed the friendship.

Much to her chagrin and my delight, I did join Savvy at MIT, but I didn't recognize her when I got there. Her sweet Brooklyn accent with a Dominican lilt was replaced by the drawling Boston accent of her locale. Instead of her normal funky urban vibe, she exuded cool, calculated and controlled collegiate excellence. When I got there, hair locked, lip pierced and ready to bring the noise, she distanced herself until I was willing to come to her conclusions, which she laid out one night in September over very genteel glasses of white wine.

"Listen, Kim, use your brain, not your heart. This science game is owned, O-W-N-E-D by straight white men. And not necessarily good white men, like men with consciences or altruistic tendencies. These are men that want to own things – not the company but the patents, all the patents. These are men that want to run things, not the ships but all the parts that make up the ships and all the people who run the ships. Don't think these scientists don't have ambition. They do, they just don't have to be loud about it. They don't need you if they don't know you. They won't get to know you if you are too far outside their comfort zone."

"I didn't come here to shut up and sit pretty in the back of the classroom. I worked my ass to get here and I'm going to do my damnedest to bust these classes and make my mark at this school."

"I never said shut up and sit pretty. I said be approachable or they will not approach, and they have the money and the networks. Their parents are alumni, and the professors have connections to every science agency in the world. But if you don't suit up and get in the game, you will never get to bat."

"So this is a suit?" I say nodding her way.

"It's a suit, but I'm the same underneath." She poured more wine.

"Oh yeah? Let me see," I say.

She undressed for me that night and we made a slow and delicious re-acquaintance. But at 3am she kicked me out. Apparently, being a lesbian was not in the comfort zone.

I took her advice and decided to "play the game." My mother didn't even try to suppress her joy when I asked her for hair salon money to cut off my locks and get a weave. Taking out my piercings was tough, though. I had grown used to my face punctuated with classic gold adornments. Without them, my face looked so plain. Savvy suggested glasses. I was a little far-sighted so I bought a pair of classic gold-framed reading glasses from the drug store and they did the trick. Then she made me promise to wear lip-gloss and eyeliner every day. I got used to the new look. I didn't look necessarily like me, but I didn't hate it. I soon got caught up under my workload and had no time to think about what I looked like. I was just trying to keep up and do well. The semester flew by and now we were home for Christmas break, vegging out on TV and catching up with our friends from home. We came to this STEM party together but I can tell from the number of times she's laughed at Nate's jokes that she is going home with him. So be it. I'll get the bus.

☙ ☙ ☙

Christmas break dragged on. There was no news about or from Jen. She just sent the baby gifts for Christmas and more money to her mother. Savvy was busy with Nate, and I tried not to be irked by it. I heard that my ex, Meer was a big baller at a community college, but I never ran into her. To be honest, I avoided her, my guilt still tucked away somewhere between my head and my heart. My mother claimed my leisure time as her free babysitting time. Every day, she had some kind of important errand to run and would leave me home to watch the babies. When she wasn't "out" she would trot me out to her friends at church as some kind of trophy. She even invited Jackson, my old boyfriend from 9th grade over for dinner without asking me. I reminded her I was still a lesbian, but she didn't believe me. I had on eyeliner.

Jackson showed up at 6pm sharp dressed in a dinner jacket and jeans. I almost laugh out loud but then I see his face, looking all hopeful and earnest, and I feel guilty all over again. He has grown taller since the prom and his face has a more serious cut to it. His mocha brown skin glows under the Christmas lights. His goatee is neatly trimmed. I just sigh and curse my mother for putting me in this position.

"Hi Jackson! Thanks for coming to dinner."

"Thanks for asking me over." I lead him to the living room while my mom finishes setting the table and generally pulling out all the stops.

"So how's Howard?" I ask.

"Love it!" he answers. "How about MIT?"

"Awesome!" I say, "everything I wanted and more."

"Oh yeah? That great for you Kim! But what happened to your locks? I mean, you look nice, you're still beautiful and all but this is so different for you. And where's your lip ring? Did they make you get rid of it?"

"No, I needed to make a change, so I did. You know, I want to make sure I'm being taken seriously so I cut my hair, no big deal."

"Oh. Anything else changed?" He reaches out to finger my new hair, which is weird since it isn't really my hair. But I get his gist. Ugh! I could kill my mom. I reach up and gently pull his fingers away from my hair and back to the space between us.

"No, nothing else has changed. Just appearances."

He looks confused. My mother calls us to dinner and we proceed to have the most awkward dinner ever. I head back to school as soon as the dorms open up.

✿✿✿

Spring semester brought interesting developments. Greeks had open houses, parties became formals, jockeying for class rank was considered a sport, as well as Quiddich and something called Magic: The Gathering. Despite trying to maintain some kind of social life, I stayed focused on my coursework and keeping up my grades for my scholarship. That is probably why I did not notice that one of the graduate assistants for my quantum theory class was trying to flirt with me. Savvy pointed it out one day at lunch in the cafeteria.

"Oh my God, is he walking by here again! Kim, would you look up and smile at this poor sucker. He's been stalking you this whole time." I look up in time to see Tim glancing my way and lifting his hand in a wave. I wave back.

"That's just Tim, my GA for QT. What are you talking about?" I turn back to my notes.

"Tim has walked by here at least five times, each time looking right at you. Uh oh, wait, now he's coming over! Be nice!" she hisses.

I look up and sure enough, Tim has abandoned his tray and is headed over to our table. I sigh and close my book.

"Hi Kim, Hi Savvy! How's it going?" he asks standing at a polite distance.

"Hi Tim. I'm fine. What about you?" I answer.

"I'm good. Listen do you need any extra tutoring for class. I know the lecture Tuesday was pretty dense …"

"Why would you think I need extra help?" I say, my indignation rising.

He takes a step back and Savvy kicks me under the table.

"Oh, I was just offering it to all the students … you know in case they … wanted to meet or something …" He trailed off and glanced around like he was looking for an escape route or something.

I took pity. "Oh, I see. Hey thanks for offering, but I really enjoyed the lecture actually and have started writing my opinion piece for it. You could help me by looking it over before I turn it in?" I offer as an apology.

"Oh sure, I'd be happy to look it over. I'd love to read it. The thing you said in class the other day, about quarks, I thought that was pretty brilliant."

"Oh thank you," I said, pleased. "I'll email you my first draft when I'm done. Ok?"

"Ok," he said and drifted away from the table.

"Ooohh, he has it bad for you girlfriend. He's not too bad looking either, you know as far as white boys go."

"Very funny, Savvy. You know I'm not interested no matter how "not too bad" looking he is. He is nice though and if he can help me improve my paper, that would be great, I have a B so far in the class and I need an A."

"I'm pretty sure he would be more than happy to help you with your 'grade,'" she snarked. "I had a GA help me my freshman year with my 'grade' and it was with worst sex I ever had."

I snapped my head up and looked at her. "You didn't?"

"I didn't have much of a choice. Josh was my section leader and even though I wasn't having trouble understanding the material, my grades were coming in pretty low. I went to ask him for help, and he offered to help me if I did some extra credit work."

I stared at her.

"What? I needed the grade. My money was in jeopardy."

"He marked all your work?"

"Yes."

"And it was lower than you thought it should be?"

"Yes." The truth dawns on her. I watch her face change as she processes the information, the premeditation involved with her "extra credit". It was sad and scary. I don't think I'd ever seen her look so vulnerable and so hurt.

"That bastard! That bastard, that bastard, that bastard!' Her suffering had transformed into fury.

"I knew he was a bastard, I mean, but to have set me up! And I fell for it! I. Fell. For. It. What the fuck! I'm never stupid, how did I not see…?"

She went quiet. I did not know what to say and was pretty sorry I had said anything at all. Sometimes it's best just to let sleeping dogs lie. I understand the wisdom of that saying now.

"We have to get him back. We have to. He can't get away with this shit. How many girls has he done this to? What if he's doing it to somebody right now? Fuck! How could I have been so stupid?"

She's pissed off and looks like she could rip the head off a bird with her teeth. But she's looking at me for help, for support, for vengeance. I close my notebook and look her square in the eye.

"Ok, I'll help. Of course, I'll help. What do you need me to do?"

We went back to her room and kept the inner door locked. We plotted revenge. It was new for each of us. But we had always been good partners. We balanced each other. Where she could be impetuous, I was methodical. Where I could be divergent, she was laser focused. When we had a plan that we both agreed was do-able, effective, and discreet but would achieve the desired results, we quit for the day. Exhausted, I just held her as she slept, stroking her hair and wondering how I had gotten mixed up in all this.

☙ ☙ ☙

While carrying on our normal college lives, Savvy and I execute our plan. She begins to flirt with Josh, then sleep with him. She gets him to fall in love with her and they become a "couple". It only takes a couple of weeks and I am both impressed and alarmed by the skill of her manipulation. Then she gives me access to all his dissertation files online and his email passwords. I know his writing schedule, his submission schedule and when his feedback is due. I go through his work and make changes to his findings and his arguments for submission, then change them back so he can't detect it. It is hard to make the changes subtle and untraceable, but I am stealthy and rigorous in my work. Savvy is over my shoulder for most of it and is impressed by my skills. We celebrate after a particularly difficult but finely executed edit, and I am able to tank his whole argumentation without him even realizing it.

But then, things begin to change. She celebrates less with me and spends more time with him. I get very busy with midterms and don't notice the shift until she mentions something weird at lunch.

"Josh is going to help me get the Nuclear Forensics Scholarship. His father is on the board of advisors and he said he can help me with my application and recommendation letters."

"Savvy, that's great but don't you think that's going to be a problem when he gets kicked out of school and you dump him?" I ask. She is silent.

"Savvy?"

"Yeah, I guess … yes! I just want this scholarship. I still hate the bastard, though."

"You sure about that?"

"Yeah, I'm sure." She runs her hand up my leg under the table. "There's one more thing left to do, right? Submit for citations and research data. Once we plagiarize and then fudge all his citations, he'll be done for, right?"

"Right. I can probably get to that tomorrow. Will you come and help? It's going to be complicated."

"Ok, but late, because we're going out to dinner with his parents."

"You are kidding me, right?"

"No, they're coming in town and he wants them to meet me. What am I supposed to do?" She shrugs. "But I'll be over when it's done, I promise." When she doesn't come, I just go ahead and do it myself.

༅ ༅ ༅

Standing in front of the Dean of Students, my face is hot with shame and anger. Savvy stands on the other side of the room with Josh, his hand on her shoulder. They have just explained to Dean Smith how the forgery and document tampering had been all my idea. How my jealousy of their relationship had motivated me to try to ruin Josh and make his life a living hell. Josh was angry and indignant, animosity coming off of him in waves. I look at Savvy who will not meet my gaze. She stares straight ahead, making her stand, making her choice and turning her back on me. That bitch. I try to listen to Dean Smith; she is saying something about honor codes and rules of conduct and no choice but to expel me. I stare at Savvy. I have never loathed anybody in my life before. It tastes like hot metal, feels like an anvil and hammer pounding out thunderous clangs of hate, hate, hate.

࿊ ࿊ ࿊

I am sent home in April. I am in shock. My mother doesn't talk to me for three days. On the morning of the fourth day I tell her I didn't do it. I amend that to I did do it but it was Savvy's idea and she just glares at me.

"Kim, I don't even know what to say to you. You threw away your dream of MIT and NASA for a girl? I'm speechless."

"I did not. I was helping a friend," I plead. "I swear it was her idea. She asked me to help her get revenge on him and then she lied!" I am desperate for her to understand. I am drowning.

"Some friend then. You should have stuck with men, Kim. Jackson would never have done that to you. Either way, you were a fool. Now what are you going to do?" With that, she turns and leaves me.

I return to my bed and put Billie Holiday's "Good Morning, Heartache" on repeat. I stare at the ceiling. I stare around my room. I cannot fathom how I ended up back here, in this room, back home, with my mother. Maybe she was right. Maybe I should stay away from women. I cannot believe Savvy did that to me. I cannot believe she played me like that. I cannot believe I got kicked out of school. I was so stupid, so incredibly stupid! Maybe I was blinded by her, focused on being something to her, being important to her. I wanted her to need me. I wanted to matter to her. But I didn't. I did not think another woman could be so selfish and cruel. But what do I know about women? Two school girl crushes, two summer flings and now this. Maybe I am not even a lesbian, or if I am, I'm failing horribly at it. Just like I'm failing horribly at everything. "Good Morning, Heartache" starts over. I turn it up loud. Billie sings and I sob through the whole song. Had I ruined my chance at the stars? Had I wasted everything I had worked for. Who would take me now that I'd been thrown out of MIT for honors violations? I cry and wish I hadn't listened to Savvy, I wish I hadn't followed her to MIT, I wish I hadn't met her, I wish I'd never paid any attention to my wandering desires, I wish I had kept it simple and stayed with Jackson, I wish I had not set my sights on NASA. I wish, I cry, I sink into despair. The music turns to a roar, my eyes close against the daylight, and I wish to just leave, to escape to not be here anymore. Suicide floats through my thoughts but I shake it away and just wish for all this to go away. The roar increases and I push, hard, I push away from my reality and feel myself crash through, tumbling forward, over and over until I land on something hard.

Chapter 18

I am lying face down on the sidewalk. I can hear the murmur of surprised and worried voices. I open my eyes and see the mica sparkling in the concrete. I am surrounded by the sensible pumps and thick stockinged ankles of older women as they gather around. My vision is blurred and I try to sit up, but my hands are trapped under me, cradling my stomach. Hands pull me up to sitting and I gather myself, clearing my head. I look down and see my hands are scraped and bloody. I see my belly is round and taut. Pregnant. I look up into the faces of church ladies and I can hear yelling in the background. "Call 911, she hit her head." "Oh Lord, I hope the baby is ok. "Kim, Kim honey, can you hear me?" "Would someone get Jackson, he's in the sanctuary, I think."

"Kim?" It's my mother. I look up at her. "Are you ok sweetie? You took a nasty fall." She uses a handkerchief and wipes my forehead. I see the blood smear and feel at my cut. I am fuzzy. I shake my head and try to clear it. I am nauseous.

"You probably have a concussion. Take it easy, Kim, the ambulance is on its way," she says. She rubs my back and examines my hands. "Oh dear." One is turning purple.

On the ride to the hospital, Jackson sits next to me holding my good hand. He speaks to me in quiet tones. He's worried that I'm so quiet.

"Kim, you are going to be just fine, probably just a mild concussion and your hand might be broken, but they think the baby will be fine so that's good. You must have fainted or missed a step maybe? Honey do you remember what happened?"

I shake my head. I look at him. Jackson. Familiar, friendly, loving me.

At the hospital, I am admitted and my belly is hooked up to wires. The doctors inform me that if the baby was harmed, there is nothing they can do. At 18 weeks pregnant, the baby wouldn't be viable. But they want to monitor us for 12 hours anyway. My left hand is badly bruised and my wrist is sprained, but it was not broken. They ask me a lot of questions.

"What is your name?"

"Kim, Kim Thornton, Kim Thornton-Brooks" I answer looking at Jackson. He nods his agreement.

"How long have you been married?"

"Um, we got married right after graduation, um so it's been two years?" Jackson nods.

"And what do you do for a living Mrs. Brooks?"

"I search around my brain for the answer. "I'm a teacher!" I'm relieved I find the answer. "I'm a science teacher. I teach high school, Masterman. I teach at Masterman."

Jackson nods and smiles.

"What is your address?"

"We live on Lucretia Lane, 348 Lucretia Lane, in Mount Airy."

"Do you have any children, Mrs. Brooks?"

"No," I smile, "This is my first." I cup my belly and say a silent prayer.

Despite many correct answers, it turns out I do have a concussion, so they dim the lights, no television, no screens of any kind, but I can listen to music. Jackson frowns when I ask for Billie Holiday but says he'll try to find some for me. I lay back and sip water. He leaves for food and music. I close my eyes and try to settle my mind which is still … wavy is the only word I can think of to describe it. I am disjointed. I remember my life but it feels like a movie I'm remembering. I remember the highlights, the big emotions, the gist of it but it feels light and fluffy like a cloud that could be blown away with a big gust of wind.

Jackson returns with an iPod and Billie Holiday but I find I can't even listen to it. It's too much. We sit in silence watching the baby's heart monitor until he falls asleep. I look at him. He's always had a good face, a kind face, the face of a man you could trust. He's been steady and faithful since 9th grade. I wasn't always sure about him, but he was always sure about me. I broke up with him to date a couple of other guys. They were cute but immature and not too bright. I ran back to him and we held steady through high school. He went to Howard, I went to Temple and we dated other people but by senior year, it was clear that we were meant to be together. So, he proposed, I accepted and we married the fall after graduation. He became an accountant at a law firm, I got my teaching certification and we settled into a nice home in a nice middle-class neighborhood the following year. It's been a good life. I love my students, though not the district. My mother cooks us dinner every Sunday, and now the baby is coming. Everything is perfect. Everything is perfect. I hope the baby is ok.

My mother comes to get us at the end of the 12 hours. The baby seems fine but I will have to take it easy for a month to give my brain a rest. I worry about missing work but the following week is spring break so I won't miss too much school. We go home.

Chapter 19

I'm home a week, listening to audio books and cleaning the house, when I get a call from Kendra. Kendra is that crazy friend that everybody has. She's loud, she's reckless, she speaks her mind and she don't take shit from anybody. I've known her most of my life but I haven't seen her since I got married. She's not a big fan of Jackson. When she calls, I don't recognize her voice through the tears. All I can hear is "It's Jen, it's Jen" and my heart drops like a stone. I have not seen Jen in four years. She was/is my best friend but after she became pregnant, she dropped out of high school. Then she just dropped out of sight. A year later she came home for a while and then took off again, leaving her little girl for her mother to raise.

After talking to Kendra, I take an Amtrak train to NYC. I left a message for Jackson on the kitchen counter. I know he will be pissed. I know he will not understand but some friends just trump all of life's routines and all the best doctors' advice. If she needs me, I am there. Period. And according to Kendra, Jen is as close to lost as a person can get without disappearing.

Four hours after our phone call, I find Kendra at a bar on 34th and 6th Avenue. She is nursing a beer and I can see the remains of a sandwich and fries. I walk up to her table and touch her shoulder. "Kendra?"

"Kim!" She hugs me and I can feel the relief in it. Jen and I have been friends from kindergarten but Kendra brought the energy and drama to our little group. Granted, she caused most of the drama but it bonded us together over the years. After we part, she returns to her seat, and I settle down across from her and motion to the waiter.

"I'd like a water, a ginger ale and can I see a menu, please?" He nods and goes off to retrieve my order.

"No drink? Trust me you will need a drink when I tell you this story," Kendra says. I unbutton my coat and thrust out my belly. She gasps.

"I didn't know! Oh, congratulations, Kim! When are you due? How are you feeling? Oh, if I had known, I wouldn't have brought you up here."

I laugh. "Due in August, feel fine except I'm getting over a concussion but that story is for another day. I'm glad you called and I would have come anyway so don't sweat it, ok?"

The waiter brings the menu and my drinks. I take a good long sip. The water is ice cold and good. The baby makes me so thirsty! I quick order a Turkey Rueben and hand the menu back to the waiter. "OK, tell me everything," I say taking another long sip of water.

Kendra sighs. "Ok, she's back with that Alonso character and you will not believe what she is doing ..."

❧ ❧ ❧

We pull up in front of the *Venus Fly Trap* around 10:30pm. Trying not to look quite as conspicuous or as awkward as we feel, we enter behind a small group of men and hope for the best. It is my first time in a strip club, but it looks just like the ones in the movies. There is a bar on one end, the stage on the other is shaped like a runway, with café tables and chairs in between and bordering the stage. The seating area is uncomfortably dark, lit only by the candles on each table. The floor is carpeted and the walls are papered with a matching paisley pattern. I reach out gingerly and touch the velvet accents. The sconces on the wall provide a minimum of light, just enough so you can see your way to the bathroom and private rooms in the back. We take a seat in a corner, not too close to the stage but far away from the lights at the bar. A waitress comes and takes our order as we wait for the show to begin.

A curvy toffee-colored woman comes out in a matching thong and bikini top with thigh high black latex boots. She struts to the pole in the center of the stage and grabs onto it with authority. I see her bicep flex as she stands there waiting for the music. Old school house classic, "French Kiss" comes on and she hoists herself upside down on the pole and grinds while she slides around it. I can feel my eyes widen and my mouth drop open. I hear Kendra say, "Well, damn!" I try to fix my face, sip my drink and be cool but I can't stop watching this performance. It is impressive. It is skillful. It is sexy as hell. I want to get out of here. I feel … exposed. My cheeks feel hot and I try to look away but I can't. I don't see Kendra looking at me until she closes my mouth and wipes at my chin. "Let me get this drool for ya." She laughs. The dance and the dancer are done. She struts across the stage as people throw money at her. She smiles and waves as she walks back through the curtain. As the stage lights dim, a waitress runs up on stage and collects the money. Kendra laughs and pats me on the back. I laugh along with her and comment that she was "good, very athletic." Kendra, I think, is not fooled.

And then Jen came out, clad in a scarlet red cheap Fredrick's of Hollywood outfit with garter belts and fishnet stockings. She looks like a parody of a stripper right down to the fingerless gloves she pulls off with her teeth. It is hard to watch. I have never seen her dressed like this, dance like this, catering to the men in the front row, who throw money at her. She saunters and shimmies and slides around the stage. I try to get a good look at her face but her huge curly wig keeps flipping around, concealing her eyes. After a minute, I knew it had to be intentional. I look around the room and think I recognize Alonso. He is by the bar, wearing a fedora, twirling a toothpick in his mouth, and watching Jen but talking to a man. The other man, a fiftyish looking black businessman is gesturing to Jen, Alonso is shaking his head. I get the distinct impression they are haggling over a price. I look back at Jen. She is walking her legs over her head. I might be imagining it, but I think I see a tear making a crooked trek across her face. Kendra is shaking her head and then drops it down into her hands. The song ends, and Jen stalks around the stage, gathering up the rest of her tips and shaking for more. She reaches us and almost misses us until I reach out with a 20-dollar bill. She spies it and looks up to see who is giving her such a big tip. We lock eyes and I see the shock of recognition. She backs up and tucks the money away. She sashays backstage, only looking back at us once. I'm trying to decide what to do next when just as she reaches the curtain, I see her crook a finger at us and I am relieved.

As the next girl enters, a big-breasted blonde woman in a leather corset, we leave our pay on the table and make our way to the restroom. Kendra takes the lead and sneaks us to an unmarked door past the bathrooms. The light hurts my eyes as we enter into the dressing room. There are three dressing tables on either wall with vanity lights and piles of make-up askew everywhere. And there is Jen, sitting against the wall looking at us.

As I walk over, she sniffs something off a slip of paper. I suck in my breath but she just stares at me with her mouth twisted to the side.

"So, how did you find me?" she asks. I sit in the chair next to her and face her straight on. From behind me, at the door, Kendra answers.

"I found you. Actually, Mark, my brother, found you. He was here for a bachelor party a few weeks ago. He recognized you, but said he doubted if you recognized him."

She looks over at Kendra, then she shifts her gaze to me and in that instant, I see the drugs take effect. Her face flattens out into a mask of blankness, her eyes widen and she lets out a soft sigh. I can do nothing but reach out and hug her. She lets me. She feels soft and weak, pliable, like a baby doll. Her skin is cool to the touch and almost dried out, like a vague memory of its youth. Close up, I can see faint scars scattered over her arms and legs. It breaks my heart. I pull back and she rests against the wall again.

"Jen, I don't know what you are doing here or why but it's time to come home. Your mom misses you. Your daughter misses you. I miss you. Please come with us, ok?"

Kendra adds, "I've got my car down the block. You can just walk out of here with us. We got you."

Jen just shakes her head. "No, I can't go. I'm sorry but this … I can't leave." She sniffs and closes her eyes for a few seconds. When she opens them, she seems to be seeing me again for the first time.

"Kim, it's so good to see you! I missed you. Come give me a hug."

I reach out and hug her again. She feels hollow, like a plastic replica of Jen. A door opens behind me and Kendra cries out, "Hey!"

"What's going on in here? Jen, Bill is waiting for you in room two." I turn and see Alonso. I remember him. He's taller than I recall, with the broad shoulders and thick neck of a guy who spends a lot of time checking himself out at the gym. He's still fine in that typical high cheekbones, full lips, wavy hair kinda way but the mustache makes him look like a smarmy salesman. "Do I know you?" he asks and tilts his head, stroking his goatee.

"I'm Kim, Jen's friend from Philly. Behind you is Kendra, also Jen's friend from Philly."

"Uh huh. And what can I do you two for this evening?" he asks with an eye on Jen and an eye on his watch.

"We've come to take Jen home. I don't know what you've done to her but this is not Jen, this is … this is wrong!" exclaims Kendra.

Alonso laughs. "Jen doesn't want to leave, do you Jen? We have a fine life here, don't we babe?"

He walks over to her, edging me out the way. He lifts her chin with his hand and kisses her on the lips. She closes her eyes in pleasure. When he pulls away she groans with yearning. Kendra and I were wrong. We thought the problem was a coke or heroin addiction but it's not, at least it's not the biggest problem. It's him. He is her drug and he knows it.

He puts his arm around her and says, "Jen and I want to thank you for coming to visit. It sure was nice to see folks from home, wasn't it Jen?" She nods and does not look up. "Now," he continues, "we have to get back to work. You two are welcome to enjoy the rest of the show, Jen has another number at one am."

He ushers her to her feet and steers her out the door. She stops to give a hug to Kendra and turns and waves good-bye to me. I lift my hand but they are out the door. Kendra and I look at each other. She walks over and sits down. We stare at ourselves in the mirrors. Never in a million years did I ever think that Jen could be in this situation. Stunned and speechless, we sit and stare in the mirrors. A dancer comes in and stops when she sees us. We apologize and take our leave.

Outside the club, we watch the men going in. Jen is in there. We walk to Kendra's car and get in. She turns on the radio and Teddy Pendergrass croons to us.

Before I know what I'm going to say, I say, "I'm gonna stay here in New York."

"What? Where?" she asks.

"I dunno."

"Can you? Aren't you a teacher?"

"It's spring break and I have a two-week medical leave … the concussion I was telling you about … and I just can't leave her here. I have to keep trying. I mean … look at this … this is unreal."

"Yeah, I didn't believe my brother at all when he told me. I don't know why but he made me come down here and see. I only came so I could prove his dumbass wrong but when we got here and I saw her …

"Yeah … I wish I had known … I should have tried to find her before but I just got caught up …".

"…In your own life. We all did Kim. Don't feel bad about this. She chose to leave that baby for a reason. Maybe she knew something about herself that we didn't."

"Maybe. But I'm not giving up on her, not yet." I pull out my cell phone and call Jackson. He's also stunned by the news. He's known her since high school, too. My decision to stay does not go over too well. He's worried about my health, the baby, my safety, the cost, etc. All valid concerns but I'm staying anyway. Kendra calls her brother and asks if he knows anybody who will put me up for a week. While we wait for him to call back, Kendra asks me if Jackson will let me stay.

"What do you mean 'let me'?" I ask.

"Oh I just thought, being a 'man of God' and all that that he would be all kind of "my wife needs to ask permission' kind of stuff."

"No, he's not like that at all. Don't you remember him from high school?"

"No, not really."

"He's really a very nice guy. He's smart, understanding, kind, funny."

"Oh," she says, squinting at me.

"What?"

"I just didn't think you were that into him. I thought … didn't you … oh never mind … so you and Jackson are about to have a baby. That's so exciting Kim. I'm really happy for you."

"What about you, Kendra? Are you still married?"

"Yes and no. Rob and I are separated, but we have kept our businesses up and running. We still have some real estate investments and co-own three gym franchises."

"Oh wow, that's great. Where do you live then?

"That's the tricky part. Technically I live in Miami and keep an apartment in Philly that my sister sublets but I stay with my new boyfriend here in the city."

"Oh, wow, sounds like a very exciting life you have Kendra."

"It does, doesn't it? I would ask if you could stay with him but it's a tiny studio. He's a personal trainer at one of our gyms. And I'm flying back to Miami tomorrow and won't be back for about a month. He's going through a divorce too …"

Her phone rings. Mark found an ex-girlfriend in Brooklyn whose roommate is away for a few weeks and could use some extra cash. Grateful, I let out a sigh. Kendra gets the address and drives me to a big brownstone on a tidy residential street. She wishes me luck and hugs me goodbye. I promise to keep her updated. As I get out of the car, I begin to have second thoughts about this decision. What am I doing? Staying with a stranger when I just had that fall … and something was weird about it … but I can't get the empty feeling of Jen's body out of my mind, so I pray I'm doing the right thing, climb the front steps and ring the bell for #3. I hear a loud buzz, push open the heavy door and wave goodbye to Kendra.

My hostess's name is Lacey. Mid-thirties and efficient, she greets me and shows me to the back bedroom. She is just finishing up changing the sheets and attempts to straighten up but it is the just a token gesture. Whoever lives in the room is a collector of everything and there is not one surface that doesn't display, hold or contain some item of contemplation. Even the empty tea light holders look arranged just so. It's not dirty, just cluttered beyond all reason. I thank Lacey and we exchange cell phone numbers. She gives me a key and a little speech about personal space and respecting other people's property. I'm not even offended. She's taking a big risk too. We are both wary but hopeful that we haven't just made a big mistake. We say goodnight and she clips down the hall to her bedroom. It's late, almost one am and I'm tired. I use the bathroom, swish water in my mouth, send Jackson a text and go to bed.

In the morning, I get up at 10am and Lacey is gone. She left a note saying I could help myself to one bagel, two eggs and coffee. I do just that and feeling refreshed, I explore the little apartment. I adore all the artwork and books and music. I have only lived at my mother's house and then I moved in with Jackson. I wish that I had had my own apartment. Would it have looked like this? There are flyers to events and old Village Voices in stacks. Somebody is into South American folk art, maybe the same one who bought all the abstract art as well. I go back into the bathroom to shower (black soap!) and get dressed. Something in Kendra's voice made me bring an overnight bag but I will need to get some clothes, at least underwear if I am staying the week. Back in "my" bedroom, I sit on the bed and try to make sense of the room. Colorful posters cover the walls, incense holders, pictures of women everywhere, books, magazines, a corkboard covered with buttons and posters. I begin to notice a theme. I wonder if I'm in a gay woman's room. I pick up one of the books, yup, it's lesbian ... erotica. I put it down fast. My heartbeat speeds up. I put my hands on my belly and sit down on the bed. Oh, this is crazy, calm down Kim. One crush does not mean anything ... everybody has crushes, ok two crushes if you count Meer, maybe three because there was that girl Savvy ... ok whatever. That's all in the past. I'm married and pregnant and I'd better get some clothes. I hop up, grab my coat and purse and head out to look for a Conway's to get some cheap gear.

I wander around Brooklyn and enjoy the freedom of having nothing to do. I buy the little bit of clothes I can afford, I hang out in a bookstore, and I grab a bite to eat. I'm back at the apartment by 3pm and am tired. I take a nap and wake up around 5pm. I have five hours to kill before the club opens and I have no idea what I'm going to do with it. I call Jackson and we talk until I can sense that he's getting bored. I say good-bye and try to come up with a plan for Jen. I got nothing except to try and talk sense to her. I'll tell her about her daughter who is almost 7 years old. I also know from the ladies at church that her mother is not doing well. So I have those two cards to play as well as my own pregnancy and hopefully, our friendship.

Lacey gets home around 7pm. She's startled to see me. I think she forgot I was staying there. We chat but I don't want to intrude, so I retreat to the bedroom. I call for take-out and try to relax until it arrives. They don't have cable but they have internet, so I check emails and Facebook until my chicken arrives and I eat alone in the kitchen. It sounds lonely, but I love the casualness of eating when I want, where I want by myself, listening to a jazz station on Pandora. Jackson and I usually eat around 6pm and we eat together at the dining table. It's a nice routine but it feels like freedom to change it up a little. By 9pm, I'm ready to get rolling. I catch the A train and head to the Venus Fly Trap. It's just 10:00pm when I get there.

I pay my admission and head to the back table Kendra and I sat at the other day. I order a Ginger ale. The waitress looks pissed but I thrust out my belly and she just shrugs and walks away. At least she won't be hounding me. I'll be lucky if she ever comes by here again. The music begins, the curtain opens, a caramel colored woman comes out and performs a slow balletic number on the pole. She's graceful and I marvel at her sheer strength. Her thigh muscles are so well defined, and her shoulders … I shake myself and look around the room. I see Alonso and he has seen me. He casually raises and tilts his drink toward me. I nod and turn back to the stage. As the dancer is finishing her routine she glides my way and I gaze up at her. She smiles down at me. I am so embarrassed. I fish in my purse and pull out a couple of ones. I hold them up to her, she shakes her head and extends her gartered leg towards me. I tuck the dollars in and swallow hard. She does a slow split in front of me and then slides across the stage to the next table. I am sweating a little and drink my ginger ale too fast. I choke on it. Someone pats me on the back until I gather myself. Alonso. He sinks into the chair next to me. I hadn't planned on talking to him and am caught off-guard.

"I'm surprised to see you here again. Unless, of course you came to see the ladies." He gestures to the dancer walking off the stage.

"No, I came to see Jen. I'm in town for a few days, so I just wanted to spend some time with my old friend." I turn to him. "You know we've been best friends since pre-K?"

"Really?" he says with a smirk. "No, she didn't mention that or you, ever. So you can understand why I'm confused, right? I mean, I don't know you at all and now you are stalking my woman? It makes me a little suspicious, a little jumpy you know?"

"Alonso, I was with her as she was dressing for your first date, so whether she has mentioned me or not, we have always been friends, *best* friends."

"If you are so close, then where have you been for the past, I don't know five, six years? " I open my mouth to answer but Jen enters the stage and locks eyes with Alonso. She dances for him until she notices me next to him. She falters and almost loses her balance. I smile at her. She looks away and starts dancing for the crowd, face mired in thought. Alonso sucks his teeth and leaves the table without another word to me. Jen finishes her set but instead of leaving the stage, she hops off and sits down next to me.

"You're here."

"Yup. I'm here."

"I wasn't sure yesterday. I thought you were here but I wasn't sure, it just seemed too crazy." She pauses and looks at me. I gaze back.

"Was Kendra here too?"

"Yup, but not today. Today you only get me."

"Oh. It's good to see you Kim, but what are you doing here?"

I take a moment. I want to tell her to just come with me but I think a subtler approach might be better.

I open my mouth to deliver my speech "I'm having a baby, Jen and I'm scared and I want my best friend to talk to. I miss you and I need to talk to you."

But the next dancer is already coming out to "Turn Down for What" and it's loud as hell. Jen doesn't hear a word.

She yells over the music, "We can't talk here!"

"Ok," I yell back, "Can we meet up tomorrow? Have dinner or coffee? Where do you live?" She starts to look around. I'm sure she is looking for Alonso but mercifully, he is nowhere in sight.

She looks unsure but says, "Sure, let's have dinner. Can we eat somewhere near here?" I nod and she stands up. "There's a Chinese/Mexican place on the corner. Let's meet there. How about 7pm? That'll give me time to ..." She stops talking abruptly. "Ok, I'll see you tomorrow, right? I have to get back to work, they're calling me."

I turn my head and see Alonso and a young heavy-set guy waving her over. She goes to them and the guy grabs her ass and squeezes it hard. She jumps a little but doesn't move. I look away. I had planned on staying until they closed at 3am but as the dancer starts to make her way toward me, I get up and leave.

సహసహసహ

The next morning, I awake hungry. I venture out and find a diner serving up huge stacks of silver dollar pancakes. I order too much but I am lonely and feeling unsure of my every move and I need the comfort. Afterwards my belly feels big and itchy and I am heavy with food and burdened with dire decisions. I decide to walk. I walk through Brooklyn, over the bridge and into Chinatown. The walk tires me out but clears my mind. I spy and claim a park bench near Houston to people watch for a bit. I call Kendra and she picks up on the first ring. I can hear the roar of the ocean behind her. I tell her about last night and ask for her advice. I have no idea what to do about Alonso. Kendra suggests kidnapping. I laugh and we get off the phone but I am no closer to a plan.

I spend the rest of the day in a public library. I skim through books about drug addiction and co-dependent relationships and sex workers. Depressed but educated, I leave the cozy library when it closes at 7pm and walk to Koreatown. By the time I get to the restaurant I am famished but

131

motivated. I am much more confident armed with a better understanding of what and whom I am dealing. I decide to offer Jen the only thing that nobody else could or would, forgiveness and friendship.

I go ahead and order veggie dumplings and a chicken and cheese burrito with yellow rice and beans. The baby must be having a growth spurt because I eat it all and contemplate ordering more. I drink water and wait… and wait… and wait. She comes in 45 minutes later, flustered and disheveled.

"Oh, you are here. I wasn't entirely sure if this was the restaurant or time … I just … anyway . . . hi!" To the man behind the counter she says, "Jae, the veggie burrito and just plain rice this time. Thanks babe!" She sits down across from me and I see her eyes are dilated and she is fidgety. She keeps checking her face in the mirror on the wall next to us. She touches her cheek and I think I see a bit of redness, a slight swelling but I can't be sure. She looks at me, the remains of my dinner and smiles.

"You are putting on some weight, Kim, maybe you shouldn't eat quite so much! Was that two dinners?" She laughs.

I reach for her hand and look into her eyes, "Jen, I'm not getting fat, I'm going to have a baby." I lean back, letting go of her hand and poke out my belly. "See!" I rub it.

She stares uncomprehendingly at first but then she opens her mouth in surprise and covers it with her hand. She bursts into a fit of giggles. "Kim!!! You are going to have a baby! Oh that's wonderful! I can't believe it. Oh Kim!"

I'm trying to figure out why she is so surprised and delighted by my news but then it occurs to me that she hasn't seen me since she left town. I was 17 at the time, and focused on going to college. She doesn't know I'm married. I hold up my left hand with my wedding band and make sure I look her straight in the eyes.

"Jen, I married Jackson. Two years ago. We bought a house in Mount Airy."

"What? You married Jackson? Why? I thought you were just hanging out with him until … something better came along."

"What? Something better like what? I fell in love with *him* and I married *him* after we graduated from college. Why would you even say that?"

"I just thought you were going to be onto other things, like MIT and NASA. Why would you marry some guy from your mama's church?" she says exasperated.

I try to keep my voice low but I'm pissed. "What the hell Jen! Are you seriously judging me? Last I saw you were up on a stage, half naked, shaking your tits for money." She glared at me.

"Fuck you Kim. You don't know my life."

"No, I don't and whose fault is that? One day you're home with the baby and the next day you are gone. You don't call me, you don't text me, you don't write me, you just leave me with nothing for years!"

Tears are welling up behind my eyes and I realize how long I have been holding on to this hurt and how deep I buried it. I mean, who was going to understand or be sympathetic? My oldest and closest friend abandoned me but she also left her family – her mom, even her baby girl so how could I complain? I put my head in my hands and press the tears away with my palms.

"I'm sorry. I'm not here to accuse or criticize you Jen. I was just so happy Kendra found you but honestly, I don't understand what happened to you or how you ended up on that stage."

Jen looks away. Jae had delivered her food sometime during our argument but she hasn't touched it. She takes a few bites. I assume she is getting her thoughts together to tell me about Alonso or the drugs, or money or something but instead she says, "You are still going to NASA and still going work on spaceships, right?"

"No, probably not." I swallow and take a breath before I define my life, "I decided to stay at Temple and get my BA in Education. I teach science at a middle school."

"You teach … at a school? But Kim, you are so super smart. You should be working on rocket ships, not teaching snotty nosed kids. Come on!" Her disgust is pretty shocking to me.

"There's nothing wrong with teaching. I like teaching."

"Kim, you have got to be kidding me! You should be writing the textbooks. You should be in the textbooks. I can't believe you just let that go. You've always wanted to fly into space, since we were in third grade. Do you remember that trip to the Franklin Institute?"

"The planetarium."

"Yes, the planetarium and then they had a real astronaut come and talk to us."

"Guy Buford."

"Yes, see you remember. And from that day, nothing but NASA from you."

"Yeah, I know Jen, but we all grow up. Sometimes things change. You should know that better than anybody." I try to infuse it with love and compassion but she flinches anyway.

"I was ok with my 'change' but I thought at least you were going to get what you wanted. I thought least one of us …"

"Jen, why are you here? And please don't tell me it's for love. Please don't tell me that you are stripping and God knows what else for him."

"Alonso? I do love him, oh I love him so much but I started dancing for the money. I needed money and nothing else pays as much at least for a person without any training. I danced at Delilah's in Philly until my mom found out and kicked me out."

"Oh. I didn't know that." I shook my head. I could imagine that scene at her house. "Why didn't you come to me? Why didn't you tell me?"

"I didn't want you to know, Kim. I was embarrassed, ok?"

"If you're embarrassed Jen, then why are you doing it? Why does he let you do it? I'm sorry. I'm trying to understand but I don't understand. I just don't. You could be doing a million different things and if he's your man, he should be supporting you. I don't get it!"

"At first, I did it for the money of course. When I got kicked out, I had nowhere to go so I tracked down Alonso and he let me stay with him. Then he lost his job, and we almost lost the apartment... so ... "

"So, you went back to dancing."

"Yes and Alonso, well he has some ... other ... business stuff ..."

"Jen, you have got to do something else. I don't care what it is but there has got to be something else. Come with me. I'll help you find it. We have two extra bedrooms you can stay with me and Jackson. Please. I can't bear to think about you wasting your life, dancing for strangers." Her jaw tightened.

"That's funny because I can't bear to think of you wasting your life, teaching little kids."

"Touché."

"I'm not leaving Alonso. I love him and I ... owe him."

"He's pimping you Jen."

"He keeps me safe, Kim."

"You wouldn't need to be kept safe if you weren't in this business." She pushes her plate to the side and leans over the table to talk six inches from my face.

"This business pays for my mother's mortgage, her medical bills, my daughters clothes and toys and pre-school. Alonso takes care of our bills."

I shut up. I'm losing this argument. I get up to use the bathroom. When I come back, she is gone. I pay the bill, take the local train back to Brooklyn and go to sleep, exhausted.

彥 彥 彥

I wake up in the middle of the night, it is dark and still. I lay in bed for a long time thinking about what she said, what I learned and how presumptuous I have been. Who have I become that I have no comeback to "it pays the bills"? I used to be so sure of my beliefs, and now I am faltering and precarious. Maybe it's the hormones I try to console myself. Maybe it's the shock of seeing her laid so low. But who am I to pass judgment? She's just as disgusted to see me a schoolteacher rather than the hotshot scientist I had promised to become. But I made my own choices and I'm not ... unhappy. I just thought she was the one who needed saving until she held up a mirror.

I don't like this feeling at all. I try to go back to sleep but I'm agitated. I want to escape my thoughts. I look around and reach for a book. I pick up Shay Youngblood's *Soul Kiss*. I start to read and lose myself in the story. I love the way her words roll off the tongue in my brain. After a few chapters, I drift into sleep.

In the morning, I check my phone. There are seven texts from Jackson. I had forgotten to touch base with him yesterday. I hope he understands, but just in case, I call him before I even brush my teeth.

"Hey babe. I'm so sorry I didn't get back to you yesterday. I was so busy in the library and then I met with Jen for dinner and it was intense."

"Yeah, I was worried when I didn't hear from you yesterday. Is everything ok? How does your head feel? I hope you are staying away from screens like the doctors said."

"Yeah, my head feels ok, better. I was starving yesterday so I think the baby is fine too, my belly feels bigger."

"Can't wait to see it. When are you coming home?"

"Soon. I don't know if I can convince her to come with me though. I think I have to make a long-range plan, you know?"

"I guess. I hope she changes her mind soon. I miss you. The house is empty without you."

"It'll be soon. I just have to figure a few things out, ok?"

"Ok, I gotta go. I have a meeting in five minutes. Love ya."

"Love you too," I say. It feels more like a reflex than a declaration.

I leave the room and head to the bathroom. Lacey is on her way out the door.

"Oh hey, I was hoping to catch you – you are pretty hard to catch by the way! My roommate might be home a little early, like tonight or tomorrow so I think we are going to have to finish up our little arrangement. If she's back tonight, do you mind taking the couch?"

"Oh, no, that's fine. I think I'm almost ready to go. I just need one more night. I'll take off tomorrow, ok?"

"Ok," she says and waves good-bye as she closes the door behind her.

I shower, brush my teeth and get dressed. Then I call Kendra and tell her everything that happened last night. She clucks her tongue.

"Hmm. I guess she's not as out of it as we thought. Did you ask her about the drugs?"

"No, but she was clear–headed when I saw her. Maybe she takes it just for work, you know? Anyway, I have to leave tomorrow so tonight is my last shot. Any last-minute advice?"

"Yeah, she's right. What the hell are you doing being a teacher? Go back to school and become the astronaut you always said you would be. That's my advice."

"Seriously Kendra? You too?"

"Yeah, me too. I got nothing against teachers but *you*: married, pregnant and a schoolteacher? It's not right, sorry to say, but you are not where you are supposed to be."

"Fine, you've expressed your opinion. Any advice for getting Jen home?"

"Make a deal with her. Tell her you'll go to MIT if she stays off the pole. She would keep her word if you kept yours."

"Very funny Kendra. Are you coming back to the city anytime soon?" I ask.

"Yup. Coming back next week. If she's still there, I'll go and give her the hairy eyeball for you and an ass whipping from me."

"Ok, I'll talk to you tomorrow." I hang up with her and go out to eat something. I grab *Soul Kiss* on my way out the door.

爽 爽 爽

Since it's going to be my last full day, I decide to go into Manhattan. I take the B train up to 81st Street and walk into Central Park. I grab a breakfast burrito from a truck and pretend I don't know where I'm going as The Rose Center for Earth and Space looms ahead of me. I finish off my breakfast and go in. Along the Cosmic Pathways, I wend my way through bunches of color coordinated school kids and find my way through the Scales of the Universe and into the Planetarium. The first show starts in 10 minutes. It's just enough time for me to find the perfect seat, put on some vintage Esperanza Spalding, pop in my earbuds and look up. The lights dim and I sigh with satisfaction. The lights turn off and I am transported. I can hear the announcer walking the audience through the sights and sounds of the universe, fact and speculation alike. I listen with one ear but hear Esperanza's heavenly lilt in the other. Vast and mysterious, the sky is like home to me. I search its corners and find my old friends, Leo and The Big Dipper constellations; I find the Swan Nebula, the planets Sirius and Vega, The Butterfly Nebula and the much-misunderstood Pluto (glad to have you back fella!). After the show, I stroll through the Halls of Planet Earth and the Universe. I sit and read the plaques on the wall. I watch as group after group of school kids listen to a lecture on the history of rockets. I think about my old dream and wonder when it became some unreachable goal. When did I let it go? The aging tour guide passes around a small meteor rock and most of the kids look bored but not one little boy. He holds it and strokes it and sees millions of years of travel in its shiny surface. I hang out there all day until they close at 7pm.

As the sun is setting, the windows and cars on Columbus Avenue begin to reflect an orangey-pinkish glow. I am surprised that even this big dirty city can be washed in the magic light of sunset. Everybody I pass looks transformed. I stumble into the first decent restaurant I see and order a shrimp salad. As I stare out the windows at the passers-by, a beautiful mahogany skinned woman catches my eye and smiles right at me. I turn to watch her stroll down the street and fade into the distance, my tiny happy thoughts tumbling behind her. After dinner, I get on the C train and take it back to the little Mexican/Chinese café. I order tea and a churro, and read as I wait for the club to open.

I steal into the club a few minutes after 10pm and take my seat in the back. My plan is to read until Jen comes out, but I catch myself watching the dancers over the pages of the book. I remember being intrigued by other women as a young girl but fear held me back from pursuing any answers. Fear of rejection from my mother and her new boyfriend, fear of losing friendships, and the fear of being different kept me silent. I distinctly remember taking that curiosity, balling it up and putting it away one Sunday morning when I was thirteen. But now here it was, everything I had been scared to look at, scared to contemplate for more than a few seconds. It was here and it wasn't leaving. Desire. I find myself intoxicated by the fierce power of the pole dancer with the toffee-colored skin and mesmerized by the voluptuous curves of this blonde. I am not supposed to be looking at these women like this. I am supposed to be rescuing Jen from this life. But I can't help myself. It's wrong. It's objectifying. It's base and crass and exploitative. I know all these things but I find myself lustful just the same. Maybe it's the hormones. Got to be the hormones.

Jen comes on stage and that tamps down my desire. She's like a sister to me and I only see the history of our long friendship when I look at her. We make eye contact and I can tell that she is not high. She is alert, maybe too alert. Her dancing is a little stiff and awkward. Her audience is a little restless. I smile at her and blow her a kiss. She laughs and loosens up a bit. She finishes, collects her money and steps off the stage to give me hug.

"Hi Kim. I'm glad you came back. I was worried you wouldn't," she says.

"You can't scare me off that easy Jen. But I have to go back home tomorrow. I wish you were coming with me."

"I wish you would stay."

"Suddenly I'm feeling like we are in E.T." We laugh. "So, I talked to Kendra," I say.

"Oh yeah, and what does Miss Kendra have to say?"

"She thinks I should offer you a deal and I am considering it."

"A deal? What deal would that be?" she asks.

"If I go back to being a scientist, you find another line of work."

"And why would I accept that deal?"

"Because you really want to do something else, you're just too scared to try."

"And you?" I hesitate.

"Same, I guess."

"Would you stop teaching? Would you try to get back to NASA?"

In that instant, I commit to the idea. "Yes, I would try to get back to NASA. Maybe I'd have to go for a PH.D or something first."

"And you would do that?"

"Yes, I will do that if you promise to find another line of work, too." She takes a moment, giving me a hard, searching look. Her mouth twitches from side to side. I have a flashback to our long afternoons playing Uno as kids, then Spades as teens. She always took forever to decide which card to play.

"OK, I accept the deal."

"You do! You promise?!?" I reach out to hug her, and she hugs me back hard. We are interrupted by loud throat clearing. We separate.

Alonso says, "What the hell is going on here?"

Kim says, "Just saying good-bye to an old friend, honey." She stands up and leans into him.

"You're leaving? Good. Take care, Kim."

"Jen! Don't forget to check the papers, ok?" She smiles at me. "Ok, Kim. I will. Good-bye."

"Bye." And with that, Alonso steers her off to the bar and gives her two shots. She downs them and then turns to the man next to her and starts chatting. I tuck away my book and head to the bathroom. In high school, we had codes for passing notes and rumors. I knew she would remember. In the first stall, next to the toilet paper holder I write my phone number, bookended by my initials. Then I do my business and leave the Venus Flytrap feeling lighter and happier then I have in weeks. I splurge and take a cab back to Brooklyn as a light rain begins to fall. I think of that old movie Taxi Driver and peep my driver but he is an older Sikh and I feel pretty safe. I sit back and think about the promise I have just made. It brings a smile to my face and I fall asleep easily that night.

The next morning, I shower, pack up my stuff, and have a cup of coffee while I count out $200 cash and write a thank you note. I put the money and note under Lacey's pillow as we agreed and get ready to go. Just as I am walking to the door, I hear keys in the lock and a tall, chocolate brown woman in jeans and a red poncho walks in. Her long turquoise and silver earrings chime as she struggles through the door with her bags. She looks up and gives a little yelp to see me there. I apologize, as she stands frozen by the door. I quickly explain the situation and that I am just leaving. She relaxes and puts down her bags.

I stick out my hand, "I'm Kim, by the way. Sorry we didn't have a chance to talk but I enjoyed staying in your room. So thank you."

She shakes my hand and something electric passes between us. She lingers over the contact and looks at me but I, butterflies in the belly returning, let go and look away.

"It was nice meeting you too, Kim. If you need a place to stay again, we could probably work something out. Just give us a call, ok?"

"Ok", I say as I shuffle past her and out the door. My heart beating fast and palms sweating, I shout, "good-bye" as I scoot out the door and it closes behind me. I can hear her soft laughter and the tinkle of her earrings. Whew.

Chapter 20

Two months later, on a warm and sunny morning in June, I have a meeting at Temple University with the new alumni advisor, Professor Willis. As I enter the science building, a group of seven students are walking towards me. Unlike most college students, they are subdued and walking in an uncertain line. I look in their faces as each one passes by and their expressions range from confused to worried to frightened. I'm trying to figure out if they are on academic probation, or maybe some kind of hazing line when an older man trots up to accompany them. He takes the lead and looks to be suppressing excitement. He is also the only one smiling. He looks up and nods at me, arms behind his back. When our eyes meet, the name "Patel" comes unbidden to my mind and a jolt of fear thrums through my body and my vision blurs. I stop walking, but they continue and I turn around to watch them exit the building and cross the campus green. One of the students turns back and catches my eye. She mouths a word. "Help?" But she keeps walking. My head is buzzing with alarm; goose bumps raise all over my body. I watch as they move away unsure of what to do, something is wrong, very wrong, but what?

I turn to start down the hallway and pass a room marked 'Professor Patel' and I stop and stare at the sign. Was that the same man I just passed? How did I know his name? I continue on down the hall looking for Room #135. I pass a series of labs, dark except for the plant lights shining on sweet potato vines. One, two, … six, seven labs. The hallway is dark and quiet except for my footsteps. I turn the corner and see a group of students at the end of the hall. I hear music and see open doors and the vibe has done a 180-degree turn. I examine the signs besides the doors and come upon #135. The door is ajar but I knock as a courtesy.

"Professor Willis?"

"Yes? Oh, come in, come in."

"Hi, I'm Kim Thornton-Brooks… we have a 5:30pm meeting?

He stands up and grasps my hand. "Pleased to meet you, Kim. Have a seat. What can I do for you again?"

"I graduated two years ago with a dual major in biology and education. Now I'd like to go to graduate school for biomedical engineering. I need a recommendation from you to do so."

"Right!" he says and starts rifling through folders on his desk. After a 20-minute conversation about my time at Temple and my future plans, he agrees to write my recommendation.

I stand up, extend my hand and say, "Thank you Professor Willis. Thank you very much. You won't regret it."

"You're very welcome, Ms. Thornton-Brooks. I hope you enjoy MIT and knock their socks off! And please let me know if there is anything else I can do for you."

I start to turn to leave but I remember the students from earlier. "I have a question. As I was coming in, I saw Professor Patel, I think, with a group of students. It seemed very odd to me. Does he have a science club or a study group or something?"

"Oh that must have been his work study students. He has his own system of choosing them for his experiments, and they usually stick around for their whole four years. They get to be a pretty close knit group, I hear."

"Hmmm… interesting. And what kind of research does he do?"

"Mostly botanical. They measure the physical and chemical reactions plants have to insect and environmental stimuli."

"Oh, ok, I was just curious. Thanks again Professor Willis."

"No problem. Have a great day, Kim."

I am careful to control my reaction in the office (I need that recommendation letter) but once I get outside, I start to tremble. Patel, plant reactions, work-study, it all feels so familiar but I have no idea why. I retrace my steps back down the hallways to the exit. I stop at Lab #19 and stand there. It means something to me but I don't know what. I look in at the plant. Somewhere in my brain, a voice says, "Mabel". I don't know how long I stand there, but after a while I shake myself out of my reverie and go home.

🌀🌀🌀

Jackson greets me with roasted chicken, potatoes and asparagus for dinner. He is playing the Isley Brothers and has already set the table. I kiss him hello and tell him my good news about Willis. Applying to graduate school is still a point of contention between us. He assumed I was done with that NASA business and liked being a teacher. I told him I wanted more. The problem would be the upending of our comfortable life and the logistics of how it would or could work. I had to concede that point. However, I plan to be a rocket scientist so I should be able to figure that out, right?

We sit down to eat, my belly starting to rest in my lap.

"I did see something weird today," I say between bites of chicken. "I saw a bunch of students with a professor, but they seemed like they were hazing or something. But they were science students, and who hazes science students?"

He looks thoughtful, "Maybe it's some kind of secret society or honors program."

"Willis said they were all work-study students. I don't know, something about the way they were so quiet, it was just weird."

"Hmm … why don't you just ask one of them or ask the professor, he probably knows. But Kim, what difference does it make? You've graduated, you just need the recommendation, right?"

"Right."

☙ ☙ ☙

A day later and I cannot stop thinking about the girl. I replay it it over and over again and I'm sure she looked directly at me and asked for my help. During my prep time, I decide to do some research on Professor Patel. I look him up on Temple's website and as soon as his face pops up, I have a hard time catching my breath. I sit back in my chair and try to relax. I read his biography, which I find to be quite interesting. He's a biology professor but majored in physics at Harvard and worked for the John Hopkins Applied Physics Laboratory in Maryland. He left there after 5 years and got a PH.D in biomechanics at Princeton. Then he went straight to Temple University to teach. Interesting. I decide to scroll through his list of publications. It is a very extensive list, but I found the gap during his years at APL curious. Maybe his work there was considered their property and not his work. I am just about to open up their site when the bell rings for the next period to begin.

I teach my lesson on cell structure but I am not even listening to myself. In the back of my mind, I am running over Patel's biography. During breaks in the discussion, I relive the memory of the girl and "help" coming from the oval of her mouth. Somehow, I am able to carry on with the lesson, to say the words, to teach the concepts and to keep up the actions of the "teacher". The day ends, and before I'm done saying goodbye to the last of my seventh graders, I sit down at my laptop. As I start to go back to my page on Patel, I get a great idea and log into the Temple portal as an alum. I go to the student portal and select directory, turn on photographic view, filter for science majors and voile. Ten pages of students, their pictures, names, class and major information appear. I increase the screen size and scroll through. I find the girl halfway down the first page. Amy Archeletta. She's smiling in the picture, carefree and eager looking, with her brown hair waving around her face. Her freckles are visible even in the black and white photo. I switch tabs and go to Temple's email portal. I send her a quick cryptic email.

Dear Amy,
We saw each other on Tuesday. I was going in and you were going out of the Science Building. I am an alumna and would like to learn more about what the Science Department is doing lately. Let's meet for coffee so we can talk.

Best,

K. Thornton-Brooks

I hit "send" and cross my fingers. There was no immediate reply so I log off of everything and pack up for the day. My car ride home is a blur as I rack my brain thinking about Patel and what that group could have been up to. Jackson is not home from work when I get there so I sit down at the dining room table and try to mark papers. I get halfway through my second class when I notice I have a message in my Temple email account. My heart starts to beat faster. I click the window open.

Dear Kim,
If I remember correctly, you had your hair in a bun and wore glasses. I almost didn't recognize you. If that is you, I'd love to have coffee and tell you all about the Science Department. How about 10:00pm tomorrow night? I have a place in mind. Here

*is my phone number, text me at 9:30pm and I will send you
the address.*

Amy
215-555-2358

I reply.

Amy,
Thanks for your reply. That was me with the bun and glasses.
I'll text you tomorrow at 9:30pm. My number is 215-555-
1321.

K.

Thursday night? Ugh. At first all I can think about is how
tired I will be Friday morning. I re-read the message. Two
things. How does she know my name? What does she mean
"recognize me"? Just then Jackson comes through the door
with two bags of Indian food from Tiffin. I shut my laptop
and jump up to help him. The smell of curry makes my
stomach growl and we both laugh. I kiss him hello but I tell
him nothing.

Chapter 21

At 9pm on Thursday night, I lie to Jackson.

"Oh babe, I just got a text from Kendra. She's in town and wants to talk about Jen. I'm going to meet her downtown, ok?" Jackson sits up from the couch where he has been groaning over the Sixers game.

"Now? It's nine o'clock at night! Why doesn't she just come over here?" he asks.

"Oh you know Kendra, she likes to be fancy. She's at some kind of tapas bar or something. I won't be long. You know I'm already tired."

"Ok," he responds, eyes drifting back to the game. "Do you want me to drive you?"

"No." I blurt out but he's watching free throws so he doesn't notice. I hurry on my coat and kiss him good-bye. "Good-luck with the Sixers."

"Yeah, sure" he says. "Be careful!" he yells after me.

"Ok," I yell as I close the door. Whew.

Ok, step two: drive to Temple, park and wait. It's a cold night and my car doesn't warm up until I'm almost there. I turn onto Diamond Street and pull over next to fire hydrant. Even at this time of night, there is no parking. I lock my doors, turn up the music and wait another seven minutes before I hit send on my text at 9:30pm on the dot. She responds with "lol that was quick! Meet me at Tiny Bubbles, next to Robin's Bookstore on Thirteenth Street." I text back, "ok".

Driving down 12th Street, I start to feel excited and nervous about this meeting. I have butterflies in my stomach. It's not until I'm crossing Vine Street that I realize it's the baby. I swerve to the curb and turn off the car. I sit still and wait even though it's getting colder. From somewhere I can't quite pinpoint, there is a flutter, then another. I hold my belly, though it's my heart that is expanding. Wow. I want to call Jackson and tell him. But I can't. He'll want me to come home. Another flutter. I am alone with my baby and he or she is moving, alive inside me. Wow. I breathe. I wait. No more flutters.

"I hear you, little one. I feel you. Can you hear me too?" No flutters in response. I start the car and pull back into the driving lane. I feel both blessed and burdened like Moses at the burning bush. Nobody else knows, nobody else can hear. My conversation with my baby is secret and private and special. I will share it with Jackson tomorrow. He'll still be happy then, right?

After a few trips around the block, I find a space and park the car. I hurry down the street, past the bookstore with a dozen half-naked men on a half dozen book covers and enter Tiny Bubbles. I don't see anybody who could be Amy so I order and pay for a Pumpkin Spice Muffin with green tea at the counter and take a seat by the window. At the table next to me are two women, one African-American and one Latina, having a friendly argument about the lack of feminism in superhero tropes. I listen and enjoy the points they make about the costumes and lack of technology employed by women superheroes – Wonder Woman her bracelets and her rope, Storm and her "mother nature" talents … it gets me to thinking. I hardly notice when a thin white woman sits down on the stool next to me and clears her throat.

"Kim?" she says not too confidently. I turn startled.

"Oh, oh hi … Amy, right?"

"Yes." At that moment, my hot tea and muffin arrives. I thank the waitress and she flashes her freckled dimples at me. I turn back to Amy who is waiting patiently.

"Not this time," she says.

"What?" I say.

"Never mind. I'm so glad you contacted me, Kim. I wasn't sure you would."

I take a deep breath. "Amy, are you in some kind of trouble? When I saw the group of you at the Science Center, it just didn't feel right to me and then I thought I saw you ask for help."

"I did."

"What's going on? Was that some kind of secret club or hazing?"

She looks away. "I guess it is but it's so much more than that. The problem is … we are in over our heads and need help … it's so hard to explain."

She stops and looks at me.

"Are you happy, Kim?"

I choke on my muffin. "Am I happy? What kind of question is that? I thought you needed the help."

"I do, we do … but it's going to change things for you."

"What are you talking about?"

"I just would feel bad if you are really happy … Are you happy? I mean, you are pregnant now, right?"

I look down at my belly, instinctively covering it with my hand. "Yes, I'm pregnant but what does that have to do with you?"

She sighs and opens her mouth to reply but closes it as the two women next to us got up to leave. They walk past us, smiling and nodding as they do so. I can't help but feel like I have seen them somewhere before, have had a conversation with them before, but I shrug it off as the familiarity that comes with eavesdropping on someone else's conversation. Amy is watching me as I watch them pass by the café window. Talking and laughing, they stroll out of the streetlight and into the darkness, I am left seeing myself in the window's reflection. At first I don't even recognize myself and run my hand over my hair. Then I do and turn back to Amy. She is watching me.

"I think you are the only person who can help us, Kim. I don't want to tell you much more than that, but I want you to know that by helping us, helping all of us, your life will change. We need you but I couldn't live with myself if you weren't clear on the consequences of doing so." She breaks off a piece of muffin and plops it into her mouth.

"Your life, as you know it, *will* change." She looks down at my belly and back into my eyes. "I don't know how it will all end up, most of that will be up to you, but I want you to be sure."

"Well what this is all about? Why do you need help? You seem fine now."

"If I told you anything, it will already change everything."

"How could I make a decision without all the facts? And if this is so dangerous, why don't you call the police? Or the FBI or something?"

She just looks at me and shakes her head.

"I don't know what you are asking of me." I lean back in my seat and wait. She looks conflicted but she just bites her lip and doesn't reply. I lose my patience.

"Look, I'm sorry for whatever trouble you are in, but this is just too crazy and I ... I already have a lot on my plate. I think I should just go." I pull out a couple of ones for the waitress.

"Kim, I know this seems crazy and maybe I should just tell you everything right now, but I can't, I won't. I will tell you this. You are caught up in this already and I don't know if you can be unknotted from this tangle." I stare at Amy for a moment, certain that she is sincere but certain that I don't want to hear anymore. I look away and try to catch the waitress' eye. Amy leans forward and lowers her voice so that only I hear what she says next.

"Have you ever felt like this life, your life is not exactly right? Like you are not exactly doing what you should be doing right now? Like maybe you should or could change it? Professor Patel ..." My stomach flips and my head starts to feel fuzzy.

I cut her off. "Amy, enough. I cannot deal with all these riddles. It's getting late. Tell me or don't tell me, but I can't deal in crazy. I have a baby coming and I'm applying for grad school and I have to teach in the morning. I'm tired. I'm going. Good luck." And with that, I get up, stumble out of my chair, out of Tiny Bubbles, and somehow make it back to my car. I fall in to the seat and shut the door. The silence helps. I close my eyes and exhale as I try to still my shaking hands. Batting off thoughts and questions like gnats on a hot summer evening, I fumble with my keys and seat belt, but manage to start driving through downtown streets, looking for the right one-way street to get me on my way back home. My mind is buzzing but I refuse to let the thoughts gain purchase. I pass a group of college students waiting on a corner staring across the street. As I pass them, I notice another running across the street to join them. Through my rear-view mirror, I can see it is Amy arguing with someone. HONK!!!!!!

I slam on my brakes halfway through a red light, my heart racing. Some man is yelling at me through his windshield. I mouth an apology and reverse my car. He curses me all the way through the light. I don't blame him at all. I try to slow my breathing down and concentrate on the road. Think. Slow down. Pay attention. Breathe. I turn on the classical music station and try to settle myself. Drive. Don't think, just drive.

At home, Jackson is asleep, the news watching him. I get undressed and into bed. I kiss him on his cheek, turn off the TV and snuggle against him. He grunts and reaches a hand back to rest on my hip.

Safe and warm in my bed, I hold my belly, snuggle my husband and know it all for a lie. How did I get to this life? What am I doing here? I touch my straightened hair and turn on my bedside light. I squint at my reading glasses on top of *What to Expect When You're Expecting* on the nightstand. I look around the room and remember but don't really remember decorating it. Who picked out that print? Was that me? It was, I think. Did I choose this comforter because it's beige? I don't think I like beige. Or do I? Didn't I pick it because it went with everything and we weren't sure what color the walls were going to be so we went neutral, right? Oh, this is my bed and I'm lying in it. I laugh but when I close my eyes, I see ghosts. I review what happened, meeting Amy at that cute café and how I knew exactly what to order, the waitress was familiar and pretty (what are you saying Kim!?!?), the two women talking felt like old friends and Amy said 'My life but not exactly right'. That's what it feels like. Or like I'm living someone else's life. Everything will change. But what about my baby? I felt her today.

I turn out the light and fall into a troubled sleep, half-waking up sometimes to call out strange names. Who is Mabel? I get up to pee early in the morning and open the closet door instead of the bathroom. Jackson hears me get back in to bed and he turns to me. My back is to him but that doesn't slow down his ardor. He reaches around and holds my breasts, fingering my nipples. He kisses the back of my neck. He lowers his boxers and nudges himself between my legs. As I lift my nightgown and open my legs to fit him inside me, I let out a sigh. He takes his time stroking inside me, there is no rush. He squeezes my nipples until I moan. It feels good. I forget my confusion of last night and lose myself in feeling. He moans and calls my name. I reach back and pull him tight to me as he reaches climax. He holds me tight afterward kissing my neck and cheek. I grab onto his arms and pull them tighter around me. I am safe here. I am loved here. I'm not sure I want to change this. Even as I think that, even as I revel in his embrace, I'm watching the clock, counting the minutes until his alarm will go off and I will be free to go.

Chapter 22

After marking my last papers of the day, I text Amy what I have been thinking (not thinking) all day, "I want to know more." She texts back an address in North Philly and a time, 7pm. I sit in my car and text Jen to call me right away. It takes five long minutes but she calls me back. She sounds very rushed and out of breath.

"What is it? Did you get in?"

"Huh? Oh, MIT. I won't know for a couple of months."

"Oh, then what's so urgent?"

"I just wanted to tell you that something crazy has come up and I ... I can't tell you what, don't exactly know what to say ... but ..."

"You're leaving Jackson!"

"What? No! Well, maybe but why would you say that?"

"I knew it! Honey, Jackson is as nice as they come but he don't light your fire. I have never seen you be anything ..."

"Jen, I don't want to talk about Jackson right now. He's fine. I wanted to tell you that something else, something important but weird has come up and I'm not sure what's going to happen but I love you and I want you to come back home."

"Kim, first, what are you babbling about? Second, we have a deal. You go to MIT and I will go to beauty school in Philly. While dancing of course ..."

"Wait, what? You're supposed to give up dancing!"

"Well, how will I pay for it nitwit? Listen, that's the deal. I will stop dancing when I graduate and get a job. By then, you should be on your way to NASA."

"Fine! That's not what I called you for anyway."

"Yes, you love me and want me to come home. I already know that. Love you too honey!"

"I felt the baby move."

"Oh, that's wonderful. I remember how that felt." She goes quiet. "I have to go now Kim. Congrats on the baby. Good luck with whatever new thing you are talking about and let me know about Jackson, ok. Be careful, ok?"

"Ok. Jen. You too!"

"Ok, bye!"

"Bye."

I hang up and look out the window. I text Jackson and tell him I'm going to visit my parents. He responds that he'll pick up some Chinese for us and will see me at home. I start the car.

৯৯৯

As I pull up to my parent's house, I can see my little brother coming out the house with a couple of friends. He's twelve now and thinks he's so grown up with his iPhone and Jordans. I park and get out, happy to have found a space.

I wave him over, and he gives me an embarrassed hug but a genuine smile, so I'm satisfied with that as he saunters off down the street. My mother answers the door, gives me a one-arm hug and rubs my belly at the same time. After I kiss her hello, she bends down and starts crooning to the baby. Then she waves over my sister Maya, now ten, to look at my belly. Maya is shy but she glows when my mother reminds her that she is going to be an auntie. She runs off to draw a picture for the baby. Satisfied, my mom heads into the kitchen and starts bustling about, straightening up things and bringing out dishes.

"So, you staying for dinner honey? Walter should be home soon with steak sandwiches for the family, but I'll share mine with you." You saw Lil' Walt, right? Ain't he a trip, out there by himself with his friends? I told him he has a half hour until dinner. Let's see if he can mind his mother. How are you feeling baby? Heavy yet? Or still feeling pretty good?" She pauses wiping the table and looks at me.

"I'm fine, Mom. I'm doing just fine. And Jackson is just fine too. Everything is good. Oh, guess what? I felt the baby move yesterday!"

"You did!" she squeals. "Ooh! That's my grandbaby, a high achiever. She's going to be smart just like you!"

"Thanks Mom." I smile to see her so happy.

"I've always wanted you to be married and happy, and now you're having a baby. I couldn't have asked for more. You have the perfect life, Kim. I hope you know that." I try not to let my smile waver. I try not to let her see my disappointment. As a kid, all I wanted was to work on spaceships. I wanted to travel into outer space, to explore strange new worlds, to build robots, and to learn about the universe. I wonder if she remembers any of that. I wonder if she ever noticed. She goes back to bustling around the kitchen while Maya comes in with her picture – she and I and the baby in a grassy field with flowers.

"It's beautiful, Maya. A beautiful picture," says my mom. Maya beams under her approval. I thank her and tuck the picture under my arm. I hug them both good-bye just as Walt comes through the door with Lil' Walter behind him begging for some video game. I hug and kiss the guys on my way out, closing the door behind me. I start to walk to my car then turn back to look at the house. I should have said something. I should have told them that I love them. I should have given them something of mine. But I can see their silhouettes through the curtains sitting down to their Friday night meal and hear laughter through the stone walls. They will be fine. I get out my phone. It's 6:30pm. Time to get moving.

Chapter 23

I pull up to the address and check the number on my phone again. The building is an old stone and brick warehouse with an ancient wooden loading dock. There is a faded sign on the front that I can't quite make it out, but it might say Starkly's or Sharky's or something like that. It's dark and there is not another car in sight. The streetlights are dim and the only movement on the street is an old stray cat wandering down the sidewalk. I'm a few minutes early. I decide to wait in the car. Click. With the doors locked.

After a minute, I see a person walking down the street towards the building, then another coming down from the opposite end. A dark car pulls up, and lets out three people who walk to the building, and then takes off around the corner. I'm trying to determine if these are the students from Temple when a loud rapping on my car window startles me. It's Amy. She waves me out the car but puts her finger to her mouth to indicate that I should be quiet. I get out and press the door closed behind me, but even that sounds loud out here and everyone turns to look at me. I shrug and follow Amy to the front stoop where everyone else has gathered. A short guy pulls out a key and opens the creaky front door, everyone slips inside with one person running up behind us. She shuts the door behind us and you can hear everyone exhale at the same time. They all head straight to the back of the building and enter an inner room with no windows. I follow. Someone flicks on the lights and we all blink from the glare of it. There are a few murmured greetings but most are subdued as they take off their backpacks and stow them away in various corners. As I become adjusted to the light, I can see several couches and chairs, a few tables, a file cabinet and crates and crates of notebooks. There is also a retro grey boom box, a small refrigerator and stacks of water bottles. Everyone relaxes into a seat, someone turns on the radio to an indie rock station and most grab a bottle of water. They all end up looking at me. Most are smiling.

"I knew you would come, Kim. I always had faith in you," says the guy who opened the door. He is Asian, maybe Korean, with a punk haircut and an easy smile. I learn later that his name is Mun-Hee but he goes by the moniker, Manny.

"Do I know you?" I ask. He laughs.

"You did and you will again." A hear someone suck their teeth in the corner.

"Stop sucking up to her, Manny. You are so pathetic!" An Indian woman with a short asymmetrical bob and an intense stare crosses the room and extends her hand to me. "I'm Sujatha. I wasn't so sure you would come but I'm glad you did. We need you." I return her firm hand shake and look around at the others.

"I'm at a clear disadvantage here. It seems like everyone knows who I am, but besides being Temple students, I don't know you." One by one, they raise their hands and state their names. Amy takes the lead, then Manny who is looking pretty smug. Then there is Marcus, an African American with an intentional nerd look – glasses, braces, polka-dotted, no… those are planets, bow tie. He is sitting with a Latino guy who looks familiar to me but it isn't until he says his name, Ramon Montana, that I know him as Savvy's little brother. Small world. The last two students are huddled over the stacks of crates, looking through the notebooks. The first, short, white and prematurely balding raises his hand, grins and introduces himself as Liam, the other looks over his glasses and grunts something like "Grayson". He is skinny, tall and pale with a raggedy looking beard. I recognize him as the one who was yelling at Amy last night. I guess he hasn't gotten over it yet.

"And you know me, I'm Sujatha, can we get on with this now?" I like her bluntness, I think.

"Indeed. Why don't you tell me what the hell is going on and why I am here?" We sit down, Amy hands me a water bottle and Sujatha begins to explain.

"You are a scientist, right? At least a teacher, so you should be able to understand even if you can't believe it right away. Professor Patel has made the most wonderful (someone snorts), the most game changing discovery in the history of mankind."

Marcus pipes up, "I'm not so sure about that Sujatha; I consider the discovery of dark matter to be..." Manny interrupts, "No, no I tell you, the invention of heating/cooling has changed the entire evolution of our ..."

"Would you guys shut up! I am trying to talk to Kim! *The* Kim!" Sujatha yells. They quiet down, some taking out their phones or laptops to occupy their thoughts.

"As I was saying, Professor Patel has made one hell of a discovery, and, while it may revolutionize the way we live in the future, right now, we are worried that it is being used to change things that should not be changed. It is becoming dangerous, and we think they have plans to ... and I am aware that it sounds dramatic ... to control the world."

I stare at her trying to determine if she's crazy, if I'm on a hidden camera, if they are about to hurt me or if this is the beginning of cult indoctrination. I decide to remain quiet.

"Ok, let me back up. Do you know what quantum mechanics says about the many worlds theory? Every time a decision is made and an action taken, the opposing possibility or decision also pops into existence in a parallel but occasionally interacting universe. It's controversial and not many scientists believe it because there was just no way to prove or disprove it. Until now. Professor Patel has found a way to allow people to jump dimensions. You can do it. We all can do it."

"I can do what now?" I quip.

"You can jump into parallel universes. You have ... many times actually."

I scan the room for a camera crew, or juice or satanic symbols, but I see nothing. So I say, "How do you know? How could you even know if I'm jumping universes if you are staying in your universe?" I ask trying to humor them.

"We know you from the other realities. You are different there. You are you but you are definitely different."

"What do you mean? Different?" I wonder why I am even asking this question.

Sujatha looks around for help. Ramon sits up. "I don't remember you from this time, but from 24XB, you were friends with my sister, Savvy. Good friends I think." He shrugs.

Amy nods, "We meet in the future 29XH. You have these long beautiful locks, with blondish highlights and cowrie shells. You are working at NASA building their robotic arms for space junk retrieval. And true, you are friends with Savvy Montana. I think she is your supervisor."

Manny says, "Kim, you are my mentor when I enter Temple in 17BG. You were a senior and I was a freshman and you taught me the ropes. You were very kind to me and honest. I appreciated that. Now, thank god, neither of us stayed in that timeline because ... uh, it was just too painful but we got out, so that's good..."

"Wait, what ... what was painful? I don't get it. So I've met you all before? Or I will? Maybe?"

Sujatha puts a hand on my arm. "Yeah, the thing is this. We jump a lot. We go on missions for Patel and Wasserman, so we jump a lot. Sometimes we stay for a while, sometimes we're just there for a few hours, it depends on the mission, but we run into the same people a lot but under different conditions. Grayson, can you bring the map?"

Grayson comes over with a "map" on graph paper but it looks like a big colorful tree to me. Every line has a different color: some run with each other then branch off; some have dotted lines; some have wavy lines; some are numbered; and some are blank or have question marks. Then I notice that the map is made of separate but overlapping sheaves of thin tissue paper. The X-axis marks years starting from 1775 to 2398. The Y-axis is labeled 10 to 100. I try to comprehend what I'm looking at but I can't even fathom it. The top sheet is labeled Sujatha; the line color is deep maroon. She has at least 20 lines, under her is Marcus who is navy blue and has at least 30 or 40 lines. I look up at him. He meets my gaze.

"I'm better at quick jumps. I figure out the problem, solve it, and jump back to wherever they tell me too."

I turn the page and see Amy's page, her line color is gold but she only has 5 lines and they are all close together. I look at her. "They like me for special long term assignments. And sometimes I forget to come back right away. Sometimes I just like where I am, you know?" I nod at her and flip through the other pages. Grayson's lines go deep into the 1700's and I think I understand the gruffness of his manner. He's been roughing it. The jumps must be so jarring. I smooth the papers down and look at the totality looking for a pattern or a clue. I see a point where all the lines intersect and guess this is where and when they met each other and Professor Patel. I point and look up. "Yup, that's when it started." I follow and see just a few lines foray into the future but they look to me like search patterns, probes looking for something and most are forest green, Ramon.

"You are searching for something?" I ask him. He nods but doesn't respond.

I turn to Sujatha. "Do I have a page like this?"

"We tried to draw one but it's only off our chance encounters so it doesn't make much sense."

"Can I see it?" Sujatha gestures to Grayson who hands it to Liam who brings it over gingerly. My line color is brown, but they are right, my three lines are very close together and don't really go anywhere. I lay mine on top and notice one of my lines runs smack dab next to the one where they all met, and it ends right before the intersection.

"I wonder what happened here. What is that four years ago?" I say to myself. Amy clears her throat.

"Funny you should notice that," she says. "We think that's where you need to go back."

"What? Why?"

"We think that is the tipping point. Where this all can be stopped, never started actually."

I place the papers down on the table and take a deep breath. I take a sip of water. My phone chimes and startles all of us. It's a text from Jackson. My dinner is getting cold. I put my phone away without answering.

"What is this place?"

Marcus steps forward. "You gave us the idea for this. We found your journal with your experiments, but you don't remember that now. Anyway, we started keeping notebooks, records of our jumps and what we did, but we didn't want Patel or Wasserman to find them. So, Grayson went back and bought this building in what was it? 1883? So whenever we are and wherever we are, we can come here and leave our notes and mark our lines for the others to see. It's unusual that we are all here at the same time. We communicate by leaving messages." He gestures to the chalkboard covered in gibberish. "It's a safe haven."

I look at the stacks of notebooks, the water, the tea kettle, the much-used couches.

"I suppose that's some sort of code?" I say pointing to the chalkboard.

"Of course." Marcus sits down next to me. "We've gotten together in this time because we thought we should all be here to meet with you. One of us might seem, you know, crazy. But seven of us … well, we still could be crazy, but I think you know more than you know, right? Your abilities are not as refined as ours, and you haven't had the practice, but from

Nikki Harmon

what I've studied about your brain waves, you have more natural affinity for jumping than most."

My head hurts and I want to run out of here and back home to my nice warm cozy sofa with some General Tso's chicken and a spring roll and watch good old movies and snuggle with my husband who loves me. Instead, I ask for more water and ask to see my notebooks. Grayson brings them to me. I open them and see my handwriting. I see my doodles, my misspellings, my tendency to bail on the last two letters of a word. I don't remember writing these notes but I feel like I did. Apparently, I experimented with jumping and after a few attempts I did it. I changed the color of the walls in my bedroom. And there's stuff in there about Patel and the room, Lab #19. My stomach drops as I read about the metal walls and Mabel ... Mabel ... I was just thinking that name. It's a plant? I laugh out loud. It stops after a mention of a guy with a thick accent. I leaf through the book but there is no more. Amy comes over.

"The notebook is from this time line." She points to the brown line on the paper that ends abruptly. "The one that stops. We call it 23AK."

"23AK" I repeat. I'm hovering between believing and not believing. No, that's not true. I believe and disbelieve at the same time. I look at the people around me who all seem so sincere but I'm looking at their "evidence" and I can envision how a deranged mind could have made up the whole thing. I hear a noise in the back of my head, a growling growing in the back of my brain. My vision starts to double and blur. I have two choices. I want to leave and be free of this mess, this burden, this insanity. I could just walk right out that door. I tilt my head right and can almost see myself standing up, holding my belly, feigning some kind of distress and walking out the door. I tilt my head left and I see me sitting down, drinking water and listening to Marcus. I shake my head to clear it and I notice Grayson watching me. He recognizes the choices floating in front of me and though his face remains stony, his eyes are wild with desperate fear. It frightens me but it sobers me up enough to make my choice. I sit down and grab my bottle of water. My vision stabilizes, my brain settles and I exhale with relief at having made a decision. Marcus comes and sits across from me. He reaches for my knee.

"Listen there are some things you have to know about before we get started," he mumbles.

"Get started doing what?" I ask.

"You have to finish your conditioning and then you have to train."

"What conditioning? What training?"

"Kim, you have the talent, we can all see that, but Patel never got to finish your radiation blasts, your dosing and you never even had basic training."

"I have no idea what you are talking about."

"In 23AK, you were the first person, that we know about, that Patel began conditioning. You thought you were doing experiments on plant communication but really Patel was blasting your molecules with gamma rays while you were dousing yourself with various combinations of LSD and Salvia divinorum."

"He did what?"

"Disrupted your atomic structure and altered your brain chemistry so that you could achieve the sensitivity necessary to perceive the parallel universes and the flexibility to move into them. At least that's how we think it works."

I sit there gaping.

"With a little more dosing and some focus training you should be able to jump at will, with intention.

"You guys have had all that stuff?

"Yeah."

"Did you know about it or did he experiment without your knowledge?"

"Well, because of you or Joan, he didn't have to experiment on us, he just conditioned us and trained us to work for him."

"Joan? Who is Joan?"

Grayson brings over a crate with two notebooks in it. I open up the top notebook. In very neat, block handwriting a young woman describes her concern, then confusion, then suspicions about Dr. Patel. I flip through the book and see records of her experiments, her successes, her failures.

"I don't get it. It seems just like what I wrote in my notebooks." As I say the words, I realize that I am affirming belief in them and their assertions. It feels odd but then it doesn't anymore; it feels right.

"Look at the dates," says Amy.

I compare the dates in her notebook with the dates in mine. They coincide.

"She's from a couple of other timelines, ones when you did not go to Temple or if you did, you did not major in science, like this one."

"Oh."

"She was the recipient of the Mendel Honors Science Scholarship when you didn't take it."

"Oh. But I didn't get that … I didn't even try for it." Amy shrugs at me. "You got it in other timelines, Kim, just not this one."

I turn back to Marcus. "OK, so where is she now?"

"She's dead," says Ramon. "They found her body halfway to the Poconos in a cornfield."

"How did she die?" I ask.

"The police report said she was shot in the back. No suspects."

"How long ago was that?"

"About four years, now. Nobody was ever charged with her murder, but we know it was Wasserman or someone working for him," says Sujatha.

"How do you know who it was?"

"After Joan died, Patel gave up all his research to Wasserman and we were recruited. You and Joan were just work-study students for Patel. We go on missions for Wasserman under the guise of work-study for Patel, of course."

I'm quiet. I need a minute. A woman is dead. A woman who could have been me, I guess. I'm shuffling through all these facts, which make sense only if you believe the basic craziness that all assembled can jump into other possible universes. So, I look around again, close my eyes and pray. I pray for God's protection and grace. I pray for wisdom and I pray for my family who, in my heart of heart's I know I am leaving behind. I pray for their forgiveness. When I open my eyes, everyone is looking at me.

"Were you just napping?" Sujatha demands incredulously. I laugh.

"No, I prayed." Marcus nods his head.

"Glad you are here to help us Kim. We need you."

"Ok", I say, "well, let's get to work."

Chapter 24

To say I was not prepared for what came next would be an understatement. After I assented to help them, nothing more specific was said about how I would do that, but all the discussion turned to what appears to be an old and well-worn argument among them – how to complete my training and conditioning and who would be in charge of it. As there is 10% of me that is holding on to the idea that these people are crazy and I was unwittingly joining a cult, the theatrics that ensue do nothing to quell my suspicions. Half of the group is emphatic about me going to the labs at Temple in the "old 19" so I could receive virtually the same dosage and have the same environment as my previous training. The other half insists that I get the new and improved conditioning that they are familiar with and can replicate here in the safe house. I just listen.

Then the argument turns to the trainer – who can be spared, who can slip away out of their life to jump, who has the least to lose and the most to give. I thought Manny would win out; he seems very fond of me, but in the end, it is Amy who will be missed the least from this timeline and who, I suspect, the others would like to get in some practice making quick jumps. I like Amy and find her the bravest and most rational so I am happy about the decision. I do feel bad that she won't be missed though. I hope I would be. At that moment, at that thought, the baby moves. A subtle rolling that feels like gas but it isn't. It is life. I gulp.

I am ok to leave my life behind, I can already feel myself sloughing it off like so much dead skin, but what will happen to this baby I already love? My baby. Will he or she cease to exist? I watch the group so sure and passionate. They are making plans, swapping stories, figuring out logistics to problems I cannot begin to fathom. I take a step back away from them. What will "dosing" do to this baby? What about the radiation, the pheromones? I take another step back. What kind of woman would put her baby at risk like that? Is that who I am/will be? I eyeball the door that leads to the hallway. There is nobody between the door and me, but Manny could reach me if he sees me. If I jump into another timeline, will she just disappear? Will I be killing her? Erasing her existence? How can I do that to my own child? I turn towards the door, intent on saving our two souls when I feel a hand on my shoulder.

"Wait." It's Amy. "I know that you are worried about the baby and I might have a plan."

I turn towards her like in a dream and breathe a sigh of relief. The room is suddenly quiet. I belatedly realize that the roar had already started. As my vision sharpens, I stare hard at Amy.

"I hope you have something good because I don't know if I can leave the baby behind. I'm its mother."

"I know. I've been working on a plan since we found you here."

"You have?" exclaims Sujatha from across the room. "Why?"

"Really? Do you really think it wouldn't mean anything to her?"

Sujatha shrugs. "I don't know, she doesn't have children in any of the other threads."

"I'm standing right here you know." I interject.

"Right. Sorry. We're used to talking about you. I guess we'll have to get used to talking to you."

I turn to Sujatha. "No children at all?" She shakes her head. Any prospects? Husbands? Boyfriends?" Sujatha looks at Amy. Amy coughs into her hand.

"Yeah, it's weird to see you with a husband. In all your other threads … you only dated women."

I look from Amy to the rest of the group watching us. They are all nodding and smirking. Ramon grins.

"Oh. Sorry? I don't know what to say. I'm gay in every other thread? Geez…" I sit down. Amy rushes over.

"It's not a big deal to any of us, Kim. Manny's gay and Sujatha is constantly staring at my boobs …"

A shoe flies from across the room. "I am not, you simpleton!"

The whole group laughs. Amy waves them off and they all turn back to their former discussions.

I sit there, my mind racing though all of my thoughts are too fast and too slippery for me to hold on to. I can feel Amy feeling bad for me and I don't want her pity. What I want is some space. Or the blue pill. Or to wake up from this crazy-ass dream. What I get is her offering to make me some tea. I accept. It will have to do. She leaves my side and ambles across the room to the little kitchenette area. I sit feeling stupid and embarrassed and overwhelmed. A tiny little bit of a secret that I just (re)discovered about myself is apparently common knowledge to everyone else … well, not in this timeline but still … The more I think about it, the more I'm not surprised. I am very curious about what I've been doing but here comes Amy with the tea. It is hot and sweet and good. Ahhh.

"I will not risk the life of my baby."

"I know, I wouldn't either", she says. "I know this is hard to digest, but if you jump into another timeline, this "you" continues and this … you will stay with your husband and have the baby. But you and I will have to leave this here and now to finish the conditioning and training."

"You make it sound so easy."

"Well, it's not easy but it's not so hard for me. What will be hard will be taking you with me. I've never jumped with another person before, but we have to end up in the same timeline to do the work."

"And what happens to me here?"

"You have a bit of disorientation and some memory loss but not complete. You will remember some of tonight and our earlier meeting, but it'll be like a dream you had or some late-night TV show you watched half asleep. That's why we have to do it soon."

"Why?"

"You don't want to build up a lot of memories about this, us, you. It'll be harder to shake and harder to go on with your normal life."

"So, tonight then."

"Yeah, tonight."

"What about them? Will I see them in the next … timeline?"

"Maybe but not on purpose. I'll set up another meeting time and we'll all meet back here at this house, maybe in a month. I think we can be done in a month if I push it."

"How can you choose which timeline to jump to?"

"I'll teach you that later. But we have to pick the right one. Where you and I can both exist, living our normal lives in Philly."

"Not 23AK, though right?"

"Oh my God, no, that's where we will end up sooner or later but that's the crux of the whole problem. No, we have to find a good timeline, one without an impending crisis."

We walk over to the map and the whole gang tries to help us pick. I suggest 29XH, the time when we meet in the future but everyone shakes their head no, that could jeopardize the future's outcome, which already happened. I nod not really understanding. We look through Amy's five lines trying to determine if there is one she would risk changing but she is resistant. We look at my lines, I can't remember what happened in them and they can't be sure. We decide that if I jumped out of them, perhaps there was something traumatic that should not be revisited. We think about creating a new timeline but no one can assure me that I will not carry my pregnancy into it. I have to co-create the line and no one thinks I can jump back or forth along the time line.

After much debate, we decide to do a blind jump. I will concentrate on the one thing that I know to be different about me in the other timelines, and on the one person I believe I was involved with, Savvy. If I try to focus on deciding to be gay and being with her, maybe Amy can push us into a timeline where that is the reality. Craziest plan ever. But I can't deny that I'm a little intrigued.

With our next meeting date set, I say my goodbyes to my new co-conspirator's. Did Sujatha's hug seem extra-long? (Did I actually just think that?) Amy and I leave the safe house and steal to my car parked across the street. I hold my breath the entire way.

"Let's drive to your block so you will get home ok," she says.

I nod and start driving. I try not to think the obvious things. I'm leaving my husband, my mom and dad and brother and sister. I'm leaving my home and my job, my students … ahhhh…my students. I'm leaving my baby behind. And Jen … what will happen to Jen? I'm walking out for what? This crazy chick beside me? I glance at Amy. She looks sane but what if we try this thing and nothing happens? Then I'll know myself for a woman who would leave it all behind and where will that leave me? I'm starting to panic. I'm driving slower as we get closer to my neighborhood. Amy reaches out to touch my hand. I glance down a small street and see two figures playing basketball. I think one's a girl. I see locks or braids swinging. I suddenly think of Meer from high school. I don't know why but it sends a shiver down my spine. Meer. I haven't thought about her in ages but now I can't stop repeating her name in my head. There are no thoughts or memories, just the name, like a pickaxe banging out a rhythm. A block from home, I pull over and turn off the radio. I didn't even realize that it had been on the whole time. The sudden silence does not affect the mantra of Meer. It continues on in the background. I try to clear my head and focus. Amy sits patiently besides me.

My block is quiet. Porch lights are on but most of the houselights are off. There are a few second-floor windows glowing blue but most are not. A four-minute walk puts me home, in my bed, under my covers. Amy finally breaks the silence.

"You do have a choice to make now, Kim. You can stay here and resume your life and there is nothing anyone else can do about that. Or you can take this jump with me. I'm not sure where we will end up but I promise to do my best to keep you safe and prepare you for the challenge we have in front of us. It's your choice." She reaches out again and this time entwines her fingers with mine.

I look down the street towards home, then turn to see Amy's anxious face. The clock reads 11:58pm. I think I can faintly hear the thumping of a basketball. Meer again? The roar begins dully in the back of my brain but intensifies. My eyes blur and Amy's face blurs. I squint, she's saying "Make a choice, Kim. Choose Savvy". She holds my hand even tighter. I envision Savvy from high school, smart, beautiful and intimidating. I imagine my husband, warm and cozy in bed. I think of space, I was/am/will be working at NASA? And Meer resurfaces again. Why am I thinking about her? Focus, Kim, focus. The roar is deafening. Tilt left and I can see me getting out the car. Tilt right and I can see me driving off. My hair looks different. I think I shout, "now!" And I am shoved sideways. I turn to protest but no one is there.

༄ ༄ ༄

I shake my head to clear it. Why did I pull over here? This isn't even on my way. Weird. I take a sip from my Wendy's cup. Mmm …. Ice cold Coke! That clears away the cobwebs. I look around and find my container of fries has a few fries left, and still warm. I look in my rearview, turn up the radio and pull off. I head down Greene Street. I can cross the drive and jump on Washington Lane. I can get home from there.

Chapter 25

Squinting against the morning light, I am cozy and warm in my old bed. I can smell pancakes and bacon. I can hear my mother bustling about in the kitchen. Aahhh… I had forgotten how nice it is to have somebody cook for you. I stretch out slow and lazy like my old cat Chuckles, who is a warm unmovable lump beside me. I have two whole weeks to do nothing. Spring semester is over and I am relieved and happy to have finished my second year of this doctorate program. Next year starts the good stuff … more field research, flying to the Tesla headquarters for my co-op orientation, and beginning work on my dissertation. Well, not actual work, but researching to write the proposal and to get funding. There will be so much to do, but not today. Today, I sleep, eat, chat, read and hang out with my brother and sister who I hardly know anymore. In June, I head back down to Huntsville, Alabama and my NASA summer fellowship. All is right in the world. Well, my world anyway.

The rest of this shitty world is going to hell in a hand basket, but that's ok because by the time it does, I'll be on Mars. That sounds messed up but it's true. The economic collapse of Europe is cascading over here and all hell will soon break loose. I'm no economist, but I have friends who do statistics for fun and, at first, they were enthralled and amused by the rollicking fluctuations of the world economy. Then, they started to pull their money out of banks and put it in home safes with their newly purchased gold coins. But I didn't worry too much until they all bought bikes, mobile hydroponic gardens and solar chargeable everything. I'm getting a bike as soon as I get to 'Bama. Europe seems to be slipping back into feudalism. Independent African countries are dissolving borders, raising up dictators, and laying down human rights. Asian countries are consolidating under China's economic umbrella as "associated territories". South and Central America are prospering as the Middle East did decades ago through the drug trade, which has quadrupled as people are determined not to witness their own society's decline. But I digress. Yes, the world's economy is collapsing but my mama is cooking pancakes and bacon and that is my current drug of choice.

"Well, here you are! I thought I would have to send Maya in to check your pulse. Did you know she's decided to be a nurse? I'm so proud of her. Nurses will always work. People are always sick!" I have brushed my teeth and thrown on a robe for my family. It's so weird being in a house with people. I have gotten quite used to being alone.

I sit down to eat and listen as they discuss their plans for the day. My mother is taking Maya to meet friends at the library for a Mommy and Me book club. Walt Jr. is headed to basketball practice and a game, and my step-dad has a honey-do list the length of my arm, his first stop being Home Depot. They each invite me along but I don't want to intrude on my siblings' social activities and Home Depot on a Saturday? Nope.

I decide to try to connect with some old friends. I can't remember the last time I've gone out for drinks. I call Jen at her mother's house. I knew she wouldn't be there and I was right. She hasn't been home for a year. I talk to her mom for a while but learn nothing new. Jen still sends money and gifts but keeps changing her phone number so there's no way to contact her. We end the call because there is no way to comfort each other. We both miss her. We both have regrets.

Disheartened, I call Kendra. She is very busy today but can definitely do drinks tonight. That brightens my mood somewhat.

I jump in the shower. The water is hot, and the water pressure is much harder than the one in my apartment back at MIT. While I'm in there, relaxing and rinsing my hair, a memory tugs at me. The sound of the water, the thrumming of it on the hard plastic is making me feel kind of woozy. I'm forgetting something. I start running through my academics. Wrote my papers, turned them in. I'm sure of it. Completed my paperwork for this summer, turned off my lights and shut off my cable at my apartment, answered my professors .... What am I missing? Something is nagging me, like a small child is tugging at my hand trying to get me to go somewhere. I rinse off and step out. Turning off the water helps. The bathroom is steamy and the house is quiet as I dry off. I look in the mirror. I'm just a gauzy blur. I wipe my hand across it and I let out a little yelp. I see a woman looking back but she doesn't look like me, or not the me I thought I looked like. Her face is thinner, her mouth is harder, her hair, my hair is in a short 'fro. I blink and stare until ... of course, of course that's me. I cut my hair last year because I started swimming and it just made it easier to take care of. One less thing to worry about. I remember being worried about it being too dykey or too black or too different from my classmates. Turned out that it didn't matter. I was already too dykey, too black and too different. Locks or fro, it made no difference. Anyway, with a scarf, earrings and lipstick, I reclaimed all my identities and focused on what was important. Astrophysics and whether or not I would be able to get in to space. The mirror steamed back up. I wiped it again but this time was not shocked or surprised to see my own determined face. Now ... I have the whole day to myself... Netflix binge? Sleep? I look out the window and see the new green leaves not yet at their full length on the dogwood tree. Maybe I'll take a walk on the drive. I love Kelly Drive in the spring.

❀ ❀ ❀

I had forgotten about the many regattas in the spring. As I am being detoured around the drive, I cross Diamond Street and decide to take the ten-minute drive down to see my alma mater. Maybe I'll stop in and see if any of my old professors are around. I wonder if the same food trucks are there – I miss those crispy dumplings! Maybe I'll see if that the chick, Bennie, still works at the library on Saturdays. We flirted for two years straight. I don't know why I never asked her out. Busy, I guess.

I get to the campus feeling happy and nostalgic but am soon disenchanted. There are just a few random students wandering here and there, a couple of grimy food trucks but not the ones I like and Bennie is off today. My attempt at nostalgia just makes me feel pathetic, like an old chick hanging out at the bar trying to look cool just in case somebody is looking. I never want to be that woman. But here I am, haunting old haunts, wondering if anybody still knows me. I've already parked, might as well complete the tour and see if Patel is around. I take a turn to go to the science building, pull open the heavy front door and am struck by the familiar odor. It smells the same – like chemicals and cleaner and something designed to mask them both. It's a weird non-smell smell, like something trying to be nothing at all. A woman is coming down the hall. She looks familiar. I start to lift my hand in greeting but I realize I don't know her. That's why I am startled when she walks right up to me and hugs me.

"Kim! Where have you been? That didn't go as expected, right? Weird. I don't think we are where we are supposed to be."

I look at her and try to think. I must know her right? She knows me but what the hell is she talking about?

"Hi…. I'm sorry, do I know you? Maybe you are confusing me with a different Kim?"

She studies me.

"You don't remember me? Amy?" she says.

"No, sorry. I just came to see an old professor. I used to go here."

"Yeah, I know. You didn't come to see Professor Patel, did you?"

"As a matter of fact, I did. Did we take a class together?"

"Oh God," she says, "This is a mess." She rubs her temples with her fingertips but doesn't stop looking at me.

"Ok, sorry you are having a bad day but I have to get going. Nice meeting you, Amy? Take care." I sidestep to the right of her and start to walk down the hall to Patel's office when I feel a thump on the back of my neck and I drop to the floor.

☙ ☙ ☙

"Kim? Kim? I'm so sorry. I just didn't know what to do … thank God it's Saturday. How much do you weigh? I don't remember you ever being this heavy," Amy babbles. I am lying on my back, looking at fluorescent lights and a white drop ceiling. Something seems familiar. I turn my head towards Amy's voice. My heads pounds and my neck muscles pull taut, but I can see plants and lab tables and desks all around me. It all seems familiar, maybe I'm in an old lab room? I try to sit up but realize my wrists are bound to the table. What the hell!!!

"Amy? What is going on here? Take these things off my wrists! I want to sit up."

"Sorry Kim, but if you don't know me then we are not in the right place. Trouble is, I need you to understand before we can do something about this, and you won't understand unless you listen to me."

So I try to pay attention but I'm pretty pissed off and only half listen. Most of it makes no sense at all until she starts talking about Joan.

I met Joan when I started Temple as a sophomore. Joan was already everything I wanted to be. She had the best scholarship, she had the best work-study, she was smart and kind and we studied together for advanced org chem class. And that's when something strange happened that I tried to forget about. We were in the library, heading to our favorite nook in the corner of the second floor, near the window. It had two loveseats and a table with outlets. We would plug in our laptops, phone chargers and each take a couch. We got up there one evening just as the sun was setting and we saw a couple making out on our couch. Now, we didn't own the couches, but that didn't matter. We were pissed because we wanted the seats and who the heck was there getting busy in our personal studying space? In the moment of our hesitation, when we were deciding what to do, I had the weirdest daydream. I saw Joan do two things – she tapped the couple and asked them to leave and she turned around and asked me where I wanted to go. She did those two things at the same exact time. For that brief moment, I saw two of her. I heard two of her. Nauseous and panicky, I turned away and walked towards the wall. Then I felt her touch my shoulder and ask if I was all right. I shook off the vision. I pushed it way, way back because it was so unnerving and made myself forget about it. Months later, when Joan was found dead way up in Lancaster, I thought back to that weird moment, but then again, I pushed it away because why? What would that figment of my imagination have to do with the fact that my friend was dead? I missed her. By junior year though, she was just a memory. Her absence was just another challenge to overcome in my busy college life which was moving full steam ahead, so I pushed her and her mysterious death back, way, way back while I moved forward.

Now this girl, Amy, is asking me to trust her. She brings in a vine, the name "Mable" pops in my mind, no idea why, she brings in spray bottles, which are labeled with all kinds of pheromone names. She asks if any of these look familiar. They don't. She asks me if I have ever changed my mind about anything important. I can't recall anything. She asks me what was the last decision I made today. I can't remember any.

She's getting exasperated and keeps looking at her watch. I have to pee.

She picks up the bottles and pumps a couple of sprays from each. The mist drifts down on my face. Some make me sneeze, some smell very pleasant, some irritate my eyes. I'm starting to get scared and ask her to stop. She tells me to wait one more minute and walks out the room. My gut tightens with fear. That woman looks harmless, but she has sprayed me with chemicals and left me here tied up on this table. I should be more afraid. I should be more panicked but I am calm. I strain my neck and try to read the labels on the bottles. I try to taste my mouth. What if she drugged me? Why am I so passive? Just as I have that thought, a blast of light/electricity/cold ripples through me. I don't know what it is or where it came from, but my body, which had felt relaxed and solid, feels looser. My body parts have expanded, my physical form unmoored from its center, drifts ever so slightly out, then like a gentle wave, crests back onto itself and settles. Now, I am panicking. My body, back together, ripples in the wake of whatever the hell that was. My head, my brain, my thoughts … still expanding and Amy's crazy talk is creeping back from where I pushed it and starting to make sense. Parallel universes, jumping timelines. I close my eyes in desperation. I hear the door open and close. Somehow, I can smell her. She smells different than everything else in this room. I reach to touch her and she takes my hand.

"I'm so sorry. I realized you don't remember this because you weren't here for so much of this, but we came here for a purpose. We have to get to it."

"What purpose?" I manage to slide out of my mouth. I'm not sure of my be-ingness.

Amy sighed. "Short-term, our purpose is to get you able to jump at will. Long-term, our purpose … is kind of to save the world, or at least the world as we know it." She shrugs and unties my wrists. She helps me sit up and gives me an orange Gatorade to drink.

I want to say things and deny things and go back and away but I don't. I am sure, in this moment, that I am right where I am supposed to be. Amy pulls out a granola bar.

"Sorry," she says, "it's all I have on me." I ravish it and feel better afterwards.

"Can you walk?"

"I don't know. I'll try." I struggle to upright myself and find the ground under my feet feels harder than I expected. Amy restores all the bottles back to their cabinets, carries Mable, the vine, back to her perch, and then turns to me. She puts her arm around my waist and walks me out of the room. Walking feels a little like falling, like when you miss a step and step down hard enough to rattle your teeth. But I adjust. I think we are leaving, but she steers me to an elevator. The ascent is slow and noisy, but it disorients me and I'm grateful when we get off at the 5th Floor. We go left and then right and end up in a lounge room near a vending machine and the ladies' bathroom. The vending machine lights capture my attention and we stop so I can dig in my bag and find just enough change for Caramel Creams. They might be fifteen years old, but with my tongue, I push out that cool chalky center and chaw on the sticky, chewy ring left behind. I am seven years old again. Amy indulges the first two caramels but then steers me into the lounge and closes the door.

I look around. It's empty and looks like it hasn't been used in years. The couches are old and plaid with wide wooden armrests. The seats are caved in; the backs are worn and frayed. The carpet is threadbare and all the edges are covered in a thick layer of dust. The view out the window, however, is spectacular. It faces south and looks out over Broad Street towards the Philly skyline. It's not as impressive as some cities, but when the sun hits it going up or down, like now, it looks beautiful. God what time is it? I grab at my bag and search for my phone. It's 6:00pm! I look up at Amy.

"Yeah, we lost quite a bit of time but we have to start now, Kim."

"Start what?"

"Training. Sorry about the room but I can almost guarantee that we won't be interrupted. I think maintenance has forgotten this room exists."

"I'm sorry, did you say 'training'? I'm supposed to meet my friend Kendra for drinks in a couple of hours."

"That probably won't be a problem." I look at her. I pop another caramel.

"Ok. So, what do you want me to do?" I ask between chews. Amy looks around and closes the door behind us. She reaches in to her purse and pulls out a notebook and two pens, one black and one purple. She puts all three on the table with the pens on either side of the notebook about ten inches in toward the center. She motions for me to sit and I do. She opens the notebook to a blank page.

"I want you to think of a phrase or sentence, it can be real simple, then imagine writing it down. Then I want you to think about which pen to use, and give it serious consideration, then pick one and write down your sentence."

I look at Amy and decide to just humor her. Maybe it will all make sense, maybe not and I can go home and forget about today. I look at the page, the sentence comes easy then I consider the pens. Purple is pretty but black makes a statement. I look at both pens, then grab the black one and write in the book, 'What the hell is going on!?!?' Amy laughs.

"Ok, now look at the page and change your mind. Decide that it was really the purple one you wanted to pick. Visualize the purple pen, visualize you are grabbing it and writing with it and see the words on the paper, the purple words."

I look up at her. She nods at me and stares at the page. Ok. I close my eyes and tell myself I prefer the purple pen, the ink is more soothing, the color more like spring, I visualize my arm reaching across my body for the purple pen. I pick it up with two fingers, I bring it back across to the page. As I reach, a sound starts, a low growl turns into a roar, the back of my head buzzes. My visualization changes from fantasy to memory, I remember myself reaching, I remember myself liking the purple, I remember drawing the letters like swirls on the page, 'What the hell is going on?'. I feel a tiny jerk, like someone bumped my chair. I open my eyes as I hear Amy gasp behind me. I shake myself to full consciousness and look at her to see if she bumped me. She is a few feet back but she's grinning at me and pointing at the page. Purple ink, swirly letters wondering what the hell is going on. I jump out of my seat and back away from the table. But I remember choosing black and writing it in black, but I also remember choosing purple and writing it in purple. I look at Amy.

"Is this what you are talking about?" She nods.

"But bigger jumps, bigger decisions, bigger consequences."

"What did I just do?"

"You created two possible timelines and jumped between them."

"I did? You didn't do anything?"

"No, not here. I did dose you though."

"Dosed me with what?" I ask.

"A combination of chemicals that loosen molecular bonds, heighten electrical sensitivity and a little PCP and then I hit you with some gamma rays." Oh, is that all? I close my eyes. I don't know whether to hit this girl, run out of here screaming or ask for the formula. From behind my eyelids I hear Amy.

"Kim? Are you trying to make a decision right now?"

"Yes, actually, why?"

"I can see you pulsating a little. The air around you, I don't know but the light is altered."

"I'm trying to decide whether to kick your ass or not."

"I'm an Aikido Black Belt so you won't get far but come on Kim, we have work to do. You saw what you can do and that was just peanuts though I'm impressed you did it on the first try."

I look at the purple writing on the page and shake my head.

"Ok, what's next?"

"Go back and pick the black pen." I sit back down. It's easier this time. I focus, I see it, the roar, I flick myself to it and there it is. 'What the hell is going on?' written in black, and not swirly letters but angry lines. I smile up at her.

"Good," she says. "Now I need you to think. You must have made some decision earlier today, some choice, something." I think about it and remember the detour.

"Well, I was going to go for a walk on Kelly Drive but was detoured by the regatta. That was not a choice but in the midst of trying to decide what to do, I saw the sign for Diamond Street and decided to visit Temple. See where that got me …"

"What would you have done otherwise?"

"Hmm… not sure, probably complete the detour, end up back on the drive, maybe ride up Fairmount Avenue and look for a coffee shop? Maybe park on the Parkway and walk anyway? Nah, probably find a coffee shop with outdoor seating and call someone."

"Who?"

"Maybe Kendra to see if she could meet earlier. Or maybe this old friend of mine I was thinking about, Skylar. We used to hang out when I went to Temple. I'm not sure what she's doing now."

"OK, that's good. I want you to sit down. Then try to visualize that whole scene. Go back to when you saw the detour, remember taking it but think about seeing Diamond Street and deciding not to go. It's a beautiful day, you want to be outside or whatever. Just decide not to drive down Diamond or towards Temple. But listen I have to do two things first and you are not going to like them."

"As though I have liked all the rest of this?"

"I'm going to give you another spray. I need you to be a little more receptive." I open my mouth to protest but she squirts me right in the mouth with a tube of what looks like Binaca but tastes like corn chips. I want to spit it out but she grabs my jaw and shakes her head. I swallow glaring at her. Too late I see her glance at my hairline and quick as a snake she reaches up and yanks a hair from my head and jumps back three feet. I rub my head, biting my tongue and trying to control my need to strangle her.

"I'm so sorry Kim but we don't have a lot of time. I need a DNA sample and I don't have time to go back to the safe house."

"You could have just asked me!" I am pissed off.

"I'm sorry, you're right. I'm just a little stressed out here. I will always ask from now on, ok. I'm sorry." I roll my eyes at her.

"Listen carefully. I need you to remember to come to Temple tomorrow. I will meet you back here. I am going to try and find you on Fairmount Avenue but if you don't go there, I need a failsafe. COME BACK HERE TOMORROW." The last sentence she says in a firm and loud tone of voice, shifting her voice to contain more bass. It feels like it penetrates into my skull. I don't just hear it; it vibrates my bones. Weird.

"Ok, sorry again but are you ready? Close your eyes. Let's go back to the detour. Feel the car you are sitting in, see the sign, feel the frustration, and concentrate Kim."

Despite being pissed off that she jumped and bamboozled me like that, I do as I'm told. I go all in and find it not too hard to take myself back there, to imagine the drive through the cones and up the small street into the park. There is a rumble in my brain as I see the Diamond Street sign and I want to turn there but I shift my thinking to the sun and warmth and desire to relax. The roar increases and I am drifting back and then nudged sideways.

৵৵৵

I don't turn onto Diamond Street. Eh, maybe I'll go back to Temple next week. I complete the detour. It's a perfect spring day but so crowded down here on the drive. Maybe I'll just go up Fairmount Avenue. I heard that with all the gentrification, there are some cool little coffee shops.

I'm in luck, right across from the Penitentiary; there is a cute little shop with café tables out front. It's crowded but I'll be able to get a seat. I find parking and get out my car. It's a beautiful sunny day. I parked in front of a sports bar. I look up at the sign and read it aloud.

"The Tumble-Down Lounge? Stupid name." I try to remember why it sounds familiar to me but I can't. I shake it off and cross the street to the Shameless Café.

Inside, it's bustling with people. There are the determined workers who, even on this warm brilliant day have committed themselves to their laptop and chair with view of the world going past. There are the young parents who are doing right by their kids by taking them out for a walk but first, they have to accessorize themselves with their cool coffee cups to go. There are the dog walkers, the older newspaper readers, the angsty teenagers who should not be drinking coffee but it's ok because it'll go good with the cigarette they are going to have later. And there is that couple, who after a long night of lovemaking, woke up to only two teaspoons of coffee grounds and nothing much to say to each other so they came to the coffee shop. And me. Not sure of my plans but sure some coffee will go good with whatever I decide. I get my large caramel latte and snag a seat outside. It's a little cool but the sun feels good on my face. I feel a little "off". The coffee will help.

I text Kendra to see if she can meet me earlier. She can't. I run through the names of the other people in Philly, who I might want to hang out with. Skylar is in Zanzibar on assignment. Jen is gone. Meer. I don't want to think about her but I do. It was so long ago. Four years since we broke up. Four years since she broke me. But I managed to survive. I had never understood the analogy about the ostrich with his head buried in the sand until I had to finish out that year at UConn. I became that ostrich. I buried my head so far under my books I didn't hear nor read nor know anything about her basketball season that year. I didn't know about how she came off the bench and became a star, I didn't know anything about her injury during the first round of March Madness, I didn't know anything about them losing to Tennessee in the Championship. I found out all that after I transferred, when I was miles and miles away. The last I heard, she graduated UConn and went overseas to play ball. I guess that's where she is now. I try to think about something else, because the thought of Meer takes me back into a world of hurt and regret. If I dwell too long, my bones ache for her.

Lost in my reverie I don't notice a slight white woman in a beat-up Chevy honking at me. She's waving at me. I don't think I know her. Then I hear her call my name. I can't believe that bass came from that skinny little chick, but as soon as I hear it, something clicks and I remember her … Amy. I wave back. She sighs, indicates that she is going to park and she pulls off around the corner.

I close my eyes and sip my latte. I sense Amy and open my eyes to see her speed walking up the street. I search my brain trying to remember how I know her. She must have seen my confusion because she sat down with a huff and spat out, "Patel! Jumping! Save the World!" And like the ball in a pinball machine, my brain rolled around hitting bumpers and the memories snapped back, one by one. Temple, dirty room, purple ink, Patel, Joan, Mabel. My smile fades. I know my relaxed afternoon sipping lattes and warming my face in the sun was just an illusion. That small bliss slips away as I watch Amy order something to eat, then come right back to the table.

"Ok, so that's good. You made a deliberate small jump. Let's see if you can jump along this timeline. Do you want to try past or future first?"

"Which is easier?"

"The past, although there is the danger that you will make a different decision and then alter the timeline."

"I'll go with the future then. I want to see what I end up doing."

"Ok. If you are done your drink, we should probably go somewhere a bit more private."

I down the rest of my coffee while Amy goes back to the counter to pick up her food. I glance at a newspaper on the table next to me. The headline reads, "City of Philadelphia

Declares Bankruptcy. Martial Law Possible." I sigh and walk with Amy back to her car, the sunshine is still bright but is no longer keeping me warm.

Chapt**e**r 26

Amy drives down Fairmount Avenue and makes a left up 13th Street. She talks non-stop about traffic and cars and sun glare. I sense her nervousness and it's not helping me at all. I decide to think about when in the future I would like to go. To my graduation? To my first job? None of these feel right. What event can I visualize hard enough to get there? The car stops in front of an old warehouse on an abandoned block in industrial North Philly. There could have been factories and stores here, but everything looks like it's been demolished. Everything but this weathered stone building surrounded by weeds and faded trash. Amy pulls an enormous set of keys out of her bag. Some of the keys are skeleton keys, made for ancient locks, some look like regular keys and a few are like a grayish hard plastic (graphite?) and smooth with no notches whatsoever. She clinks through the ring, finds the one she wants and says, "Ok, let's go."

We look around as we walk up to the door, but it seems no one is around for blocks. I have an immediate sense of dread. I think I know this place but its isolation is unnerving.

Amy opens the door and we enter. She turns on the hall lights and I follow her to a large room in the back. We are alone in this place but my mind is conjuring up snippets of conversations and laughter and nervous energy. She turns on the radio and Donna Summer blasts into the room singing "Bad Girls". We both laugh.

"The radio always helps," she says. I breathe a sigh of relief. I hadn't realized how long I had been holding my breath. Amy opens up the little refrigerator in the corner and offers me a bottle of water.

"We should have stopped to pick up more food," she says. "I think we, or at least I will be here for a few days. " I nod and head over to the stacks of tissue thin paper on the desk.

"Oh yeah, we're going to need to start a new line. That's something I can do while you're gone."

"Gone?"

"Yeah. Look we might as well get started. Do you remember this place? It's our safe house. We own it and this is where we meet when we need to talk privately."

I nod, it makes sense but something else is tugging at me.

"Do you remember the others? Sujatha, Ramon, Manny, Marcus, Grayson?"

"No … kinda…maybe."

"Kim, what's wrong? I know this is a little overwhelming but you are safe here."

"I don't know, I just feel a sense of loss. Like I had something but I've lost it."

"Oh," she looks away. "… well let's just move on, OK? We have a lot to do and though we can continue to go back in time, the threads are starting to coalesce and shift."

I sit down at the worn wooden kitchen table. She sits across from me and slides my water to me. She opens her bag and pulls out a bunch of sprays, chewing gum, a calculator, three cell phones, a plastic box, a portable scanner of some sort, a pad of paper, pencils and a roll of candy buttons that I suspect are not actually candy.

"You can't pick a specific year but you can focus your emotions and try to visualize a specific event that will happen in the future. For example, when I want to travel, sometimes I just focus on an election – they are inevitable and if you pay attention, you can guess who is going to be in it. Sometimes I focus on a holiday like Christmas if I'm trying to find family, sometimes the Olympics are good for jumping because they are planned so far into the future. The trick is to anchor yourself so you can get back to when you came from."

"How do I do that?"

"We have to provide an event in this "when" for you to recall and focus on."

"And that would be ....?"

Amy grabs the plastic box and pops it open. Inside are needles, gloves, a small pot of ink, witch hazel, Band-Aids, gauze and small squares of paper with designs on them.

"I'm gonna give you a little tattoo."

"What! Here?"

"Sure, don't worry, this is the best way to make an anchor. You'll see it, you'll remember, you can focus on when I gave it to you and come back. Piece of cake!"

I already have a bunch of piercings and a few tattoos but NASA does not like that kind of thing so I was in the process of letting most of the former close up and the latter fade away.

"OK," I say, "but we have to pick a spot that's not going to interfere with me getting my gig at NASA. Because if I don't get that, I don't know where I will end up in the future … probably homeless or insane."

"Ok, but we have to put it somewhere you will see it so it can't be on your back or under your boob or anything like that.

"How about my upper thigh? I'll see it when I use the bathroom. Or you know, when I'm with somebody …"

Amy gives me the side eye. "Kim, you are not supposed to stay that long. We are just practicing your skills. Getting you comfortable and able to jump whenever and to whatever timeline you are needed."

"Fine, fine I was just joking, relax. So, where are we going to do this?"

"I usually just use this table …"

"Right here? There's no place more sterile?"

Amy gets up and walks over to a cabinet. She pulls out a paper white medical sheet. Smiling at me she lays it out on the table, then goes to the sink to wash her hands.

"Now, take off your pants and lay down. This won't hurt a bit!'

I look through the box and pick out a pretty little stencil of a teardrop shaped mandala. Then I sip my water, pull down my pants, fold them on the chair and lay down as told. I'm only able to maintain my sense of humor and self-respect because I am wearing new Wonder Woman panties given to me by my little sister. Amy laughs when she sees them but then gets straight to business. She appears to have done this many times before. The first few pokes hurt but then I relax into it.

"Now Kim, pay attention to how it feels, how it looks right now, how you feel laying on this table … in your Wonder Woman underwear … focus on touch, feel, smell, look at me and hear my voice. You will need all this to get you back. Ok?"

I try to pay attention with all my senses. I watch her as she moves around my thigh, concentrating on her work, I have to tamp down my smoldering arousal. Getting tattoos always make me a little horny. I make myself focus on a breathing meditation instead and before I know it, she's done. Sweaty and stretching from the effort, she looks satisfied. I have a sore but beautiful design right on top of my thigh.

"Nice job, Amy. Did you learn that in the joint?"

"Funny. No, it's just a little hobby of mine. Comes in pretty handy though."

"Does everyone have a tattoo?"

She looks thoughtful. "I think everyone except Grayson. He goes to the past. And Sujatha … she has a few. I think she just likes getting them though. Not sure if that last one was really necessary."

Amy reaches into the box and pulls out a little jar of salve and puts it under my nose. It smells of cocoa butter and camphor. Not pleasant at all but when she rubs it on, all the tenderness around the tattoo evaporates.

"Wow!"

"Yeah I learned about it a few years ago. It's from the future. Only thing I've ever brought back here."

"You brought that jar back?" I ask incredulous.

"No, I brought the recipe back but I keep it to myself just in case."

"In case of what? I bet it could help a lot of people."

"Yeah, but it could also change that timeline, or direct attention my way, and we don't want either of those things. So that reminds me. You have to be careful about asking too many questions or bringing up anything from the past. Try not to talk too much. Just listen and figure out your way back. Ok?

"Ok. I got it. Can I get up now?'

"Oh sorry, yes! I'm going to put a bandage on it for now though."

I get up after she applies the bandage and get dressed. Amy cleans up the area and we sit back down at the table.

"Ok Kim, let's try a small jump into the future first. Something simple. Breakfast tomorrow morning? Or … didn't you say that you were meeting a friend for drinks tonight? Just a couple of hours and then come back once you remember. "

Amy is sweet, but I know when I want to go and what I want to see. I say, "Ok, I'll try drinks tonight with Kendra at Champagnes."

"Good luck, Kim." Amy looks at me with so much worry in her face I reach out and grab her hand. "Don't worry Amy. I can do this and I'll be back."

"I'm not worried about that; I'm worried that we need to get this right. Things are beginning to unravel and I feel just terrible about it. We have to fix it! Swallow this and hold the spoon until I take it out, Ok Kim?"

"Ok." She sticks a spoonful of bitter liquid in my mouth and I gulp it down it lest I spit it out. I suck on the spoon, which seems to lessen the taste. I close my eyes and think about the one thing I really want to see in the future. I picture it in my mind, trace the course, review schematics and throw myself forward.

Chapt**e**r 27

Tight. Taut. Chilly. Moving but not moving. Lying down but feeling upright. Breathing but not sure that it is air I'm running through my lungs. I open my eyes. It's dark. My vision is blurred. I'm focused too close. I see my own eyes staring back at me. Clear, brown, scared. I don't know where I am, who I am. I am trapped. I begin to panic. My heart starts thumping in my ears. I catch myself, close my eyes and breathe. Launching into decades of practiced breathing techniques, I breathe and *Om* myself back to stillness and peace. Now, think Kim. I open my eyes and see my reflection again, but I try to focus further. I see small glowing lights on gray or pale blue panels. I see a monitor to the left of my vision, black with a white wavy line humping at regular intervals. Below the white line is a red one, also peaking and dropping. I try to turn my head but I cannot. I try to lift my arms, hands, legs and feet but cannot. I'm feeling trapped. I watch the red line peaking faster and faster, the white one holds steady. I know where I am. The drugs are beginning to lift but I'm wondering if they are lifting too soon. I am supposed to stay sedated until we reach the orbit of Phobos, one of the Martian moons.

I experiment with my voice. I can't get my mouth to move; my lips feel sealed shut. It takes me a minute to wiggle them apart using my tongue, which tires from the effort. I try to hum. As I make a sound that is muted to my own ears but audible to the computer I'm attached to, a puff of moist oxygen is pumped into my helmet. I sense the moisture on my dry face, I inhale it up my nostrils, it lights upon my lips. A subtle warmth envelops my body. My suit is heating up, the puffs of air continue, the fog is lifting. I unseal my jaw and mouth to sigh. I am alive. Although my tongue feels thick and dry, I try to make a sound with my voice. "Uh, uh…" is all that comes out before I cough. It's a slight cough but it leaves me breathless and fatigued. I decide to rest and close my eyes.

卍 卍 卍

I hear something. Not quite a sound but more like a vibration in my bones. Happy, I know what that is. It's the aft thrusters slowing down the ship. We must be close to Phobos. Opening my eyes, I see my own eyes reflected back at me. Hi Kim. They smile at me. I run my tongue around my mouth. I look past my eyes and see more lights on the panels. The ship is also waking up. I try my voice. "Uh .. Uh.. A, B, C, E, F, G, H, I, J, K …" I'm tired but the talking activates the drinking tube and it pops up right in front of my mouth. With my tongue, I pull it into my mouth and wait. A tiny squirt of liquid comes out, minty and lukewarm but I swish it around as best I can and swallow it. I give the tube two quick sucks and a mouthful of fresh water comes out. I want to do it again but I know I have to wait. I don't want cramps. I push the tube out and try to turn my head to the right where my co-pilot is ensconced. I can see a dim light and guess that he is doing the same things I am. I try to move my arms to push my food button but I know it's too soon. I'm just relieved to be able to move at all. I rest again.

卍 卍 卍

Thirsty. I stick my tongue out and find the tube. Two quick sucks, water. I shake off the sleep. I wiggle my fingers and manage to push the food button. A swallow of nutrient rich liquid pumps into my mouth and I devour it. I push the button one more time and get another swallow. I can feel my body waking up. I am more energetic and antsy. I wiggle my feet and legs. I lift my arms out in front of me. I can just see my fingertips. I wiggle them to make sure they are mine then my arms collapse in fatigue. Six months of sleep will do that. I lift them one more time just to get a good workout. I think I see Ray's leg lift up but I can't be sure. Two more days and we'll be able to detach ourselves and get to work. Until then, sipping and wiggling is the best we can do. I try to locate another switch with my left hand. It's a recorder pre-loaded with instructions about what to do and the order in which to do it, classical music, messages from home, updates from NASA, reminders of how to be patient with the body as it awakens, meditations, and two short stories in case I get bored. I find the switch and flip on the music first, I jerk at first to hear something so loud and close to my ear but I get used to it and acclimate myself again to sound.

※ ※ ※

I had my first urination today. It went well. The diaper worked and I don't feel a thing. As much as I practiced peeing in this diaper, apart from being blown up, my biggest fear was feeling wet all day. Ray is trying to signal me with his feet. I rotate my body to the right as much as possible with this tether. He smiles at me. I wave and smile back. He gives me the thumbs up and I give it right back. He's ready. Tomorrow, we get unhooked. I take another suck of food. I can't wait.

※ ※ ※

Swimming through the ship, listening to vintage Janelle Monae, checking and double-checking calculations and diagnostics. Out the window I can see Phobos, Mars is set to appear starboard in 3.5 hours. I want to be done all our checks so I can just watch it. It's hard to describe my brain. I vacillate between calculating and attending to every little detail needed for my survival to being freaked out because I am in space, only 20,000 miles from Mars, closer than any human has ever been before, except Ray. I share the honor with Ray, which I don't mind. Ray and I have trained together for 5 years. Our cohort started out as a group of 37, then 22, then 14. I am one of the oldest at 45 and had to fight to get on this mission. It was my last chance. There is another pair set to join us in a couple of years, but the real prize mission is in the planning stage and those ten are going to Mars' surface, once we have it ready for them. Today we establish our baseline of operations, tomorrow we fire up the 3-D printer, the hydroponics and the meteorological monitoring satellite. Today is a day for poetry and wonder.

I glide over to my bunk. I store the few personal items I have in my compartment and I tether myself there to sleep. I glance at the picture of my wife and son. She made me leave a video for my son before I left "just in case". He'll be sixteen in a few weeks, but I left advice for his wedding night and for dealing with a pregnant wife and a new baby. Just in case. I have ample experience with that. When Meer said she wanted to have a baby, no one was more surprised than me. All her life, she'd been an athlete and a butchy one at that. But I was not going to risk my career with a pregnancy. Her retirement from basketball left her a little lost, her clock started ticking and a baby seemed the perfect next adventure. She also said she wanted to keep a little bit of me if I ever got off planet. Just in case. So we had Barack. Tall, bold and tender, insightful and pragmatic. I love him so much my heart aches. And Meer. I've always loved Meer, even when she broke my heart in college. Even after not hearing from her for years. Even when she called me out the blue from Russia and I cursed her out. Even when she sent me five-dozen red roses from Serbia. Every one of them had thorns and I bled from them trying not to call her. Even when she sent me a plane ticket to Turkey. And I went, scowling the whole flight. But when I saw her. Ah, my heart sank and rose with her very breath and I fell right back in love with her. There was no one who compared to her, and I stayed with her until they kicked me out of the country.

Despite the space program and all the progress we have made, I am worried for my country and the world itself. The Soviet Union has started issuing tariffs on all oil consuming countries. Their stronghold on the Middle East and Africa has tightened with every year since their conquest of the region. Though they promised to be fair and rule lightly from afar, it has proven a lie. One after the other, they have stripped the power and the wealth from each sovereignty, carving them up and selling them, reducing them to no more than corporate landholdings. Employees are more like serfs, supervisors maintain their status by abusing the poor souls they ride into exhaustion. Every industry serves the oil and as it is used up, the land is ravaged by more and bigger drills. As the world community watches, civilization has reversed itself and we are back to the Industrial Age. But some of us want out. And so, the scientific community, along with wealthy innovators pushed for Mars. So here we are, having paid a king's ransom to the Soviets for their oil, hoping that perspective will bring some kind of humanity. But I worry that it won't mean a thing.

I kiss the picture of my family, say a silent prayer for us all and tether down for the night.

卐 卐 卐

I awake to Ray singing, "Signed, Sealed, Delivered, I'm Yours". When I float over to him, he smiles and informs me that before we get to work, we are to take "showers". It's been a week. I agree to go first, even though I know the water will be stale and smell horrible. I head into the shower room, review the procedure posted on the wall and begin to disrobe. It feels weird. I'm already lacking any heft in zero G, and with each item I take off, I feel more and more insubstantial. The bright lights and white walls reflect on my skin, which has lost its richness. I knew this would happen but six months with no lotion, little humidity and no sunlight has left my skin flat and grayish and papery. I rub my hands over my body to remind it of human touch and maybe wake up the life inside my skin, which seems to be asleep. I reach down to squeeze my thighs and notice my tattoo. I keep pinching and rolling my muscles but I can't stop looking at the intricate design on my leg. I've had it for so long but now something is nagging me … it's supposed to mean something. My hands move down to my calves, but the tattoo has me transfixed, like it's whispering to me, not demanding attention but pleading for it. I'm rubbing my feet and toes when it hits. "KIM!" I'm supposed to go. I'm not supposed to be here. No, I'm supposed to be here but I'm not supposed to stay. Amy gave me this tattoo… on a table… in a warehouse … "KIM!" Oh, but I don't want to go. I want to see Mars rise again. I've been trying to get here my whole life. I'm not leaving. I don't care. I don't care. I rub my legs and thighs, I shake my bottom, I cup my breasts. We are here in space orbiting Mars! I'm not leaving! I massage my shoulders, wiggle my fingers, and twist my hands. I reach for the soap foam and sponge and scrub myself. It feels so good. I watch the dead skin flakes float off of me and get sucked into the vent by my side. I take my time and get clean. I'm beginning to feel like my old self, my skin is waking up and the brown is less gray. I wash my face, closing my eyes against the foam. I see Barack and Meer behind my eyelids and I remember that I have to help them. Help us all. I have to go back. I slap at the tattoo, angry at it. I remember now that I chose it. And Amy did it by hand. I want desperately to finish my mission. I trained so hard for it! I gave up so much for it! Fuck! I make myself a promise, a vow that, no matter what, I will get back here. I take a deep breath and glare at the tattoo but nothing happens. I gather myself and think back to getting the tattoo, how I laid on the table, Amy's (stupid) face and the joy she seemed to take in poking me. I force myself to concentrate on the remembered pain, the design of the stencil, the teardrop, who I was then, another mission I had to complete. I focus and bring forward the rumbling in the back of my head. I close my eyes and submit to the blurring, the roar and push, no, fling myself back and inward to Amy and the table.

Chapter 28

"You're back!!!" Amy squeezes me though I am still lying on the table. I sit up and begin to sob.

"What's the matter? What's wrong?" Amy comes close to hug me again but I shrug her off.

"I was orbiting Phobos."

"What!?"

"I was on a spaceship, orbiting Phobos, Mar's moon? I was there! And now I'm here. In this ... warehouse... with you!" I wipe up my tears on the back of my hand.

"Oh ..." she says, "But I thought we agreed that you were going to do a small jump. I thought you were just going out for drinks ..."

I jump up from the table and walk away from her. I'm remembering myself on the ship, the feel of weightlessness, the sounds of the computers, Ray singing in my headset, the view of Mar rising. It's starting to fade and I am desperate to hold on to it. After a minute, I turn back to her and say, "I know. I wanted to know if ... never mind," I say, shaking off any guilt, "Ok, I can jump forward and back if I have a trigger."

"How long were you there?"

"I was in hibernation in the beginning, so I'm not sure. I didn't see the tattoo until I had been awake about a week. It was my first shower."

"Oh, but as soon as you saw the tattoo, it reminded you?"

"Yeah, it reminded me. It felt like I could hear your voice calling my name." Amy smiles.

"Good, I embedded the energy pattern of my yell into the tattoo."

"You did what?"

"One other little thing I picked up from the future but, please don't tell. I wasn't sure you would come back and we really need to move this along."

"Wow. Ok, well, it worked. I'm here."

"Yes, you are." She reaches to hug me again. This time I let her.

"Phobos?"

"Yeah", I sigh, "fucking Phobos."

"That's pretty awesome…"

"Tell me about it."

I start to pull on my clothes. I feel weird to myself, heavier, meatier, moist. I don't want to lose my space flight but the memory is slipping away. I grab at a notebook and try to write down my thoughts but each sentence I start, I cannot finish and the result is like looking a collage too closely. All disjointed images but you can't perceive what whole is supposed to be. But I remember Meer and Barack, even as they disintegrate I blurt out, "I was married to Meer!"

Amy whips her head around. "What?"

"We had a son, his name was .. um, his name was… I can't remember but we had a son, a boy. Meer." I shake my head trying to force my brain to fish for the threads and connect the dots but it's too late. I look down at the notebook, at the words on the page, and I clutch it to my chest. Phobos.

༄ ༄ ༄

After eating a quiet, luke-warm meal of Pad Thai, Amy and I agree to just get on with it. She was kind of pissed that I jumped so far. I was kind of pissed to come back. But I have questions.

"Amy? I can't say that I understand how I'm able to do what I did but moving along a timeline seems more plausible then jumping from timeline to timeline. How do you, how do we do that? How do you remember the "you" from the other timeline? How are you able to pick and choose, come back and still know who you are?"

Amy looks at me and sighs a big sigh. "Well, you are about to find out because that's next." Amy walks over to a big bookshelf and pulls out books on Voodoo, Buddhism and the Bible and pushes them across the table in front of me.

"Do you know what all of these have in common?"

"They are books about religion."

"Yup, and they all assume and rely on the notion of a soul, a "self" that is intact enough to take to heaven, or to another body or to move aside while a god rides your body."

"What?

"Every religion teaches that we have a spirit or soul, separate from the body, distinct in this lifetime or another."

"And you are saying ...?"

"They are correct."

I sit and stare at her. "Ok."

"Most of the time, unless you are praying, you don't think about it, it's tethered to your body and hotwired to your brain. Jumping back in time requires access to your brain and the memories it stores. But jumping forward and across timelines while being conscious of it, requires a little more."

"But I jumped before, right?"

"Yes, but you don't remember much and didn't stay conscious. You lost consciousness as your soul reached off."

"Wait, what?"

"Your soul is like a wave, stretching across all timelines, in all universes, connecting all the yous and possible yous that exist. But it is one entity, one pulse of energy, capable of extending into infinity. You have to learn to acknowledge and connect consciously with it. When you learn to stay conscious within it, even as you move along it, then you can travel anywhere, anytime and not get lost."

I sat back and looked at her, again weighing my options, while judging her sanity and mine. "How do I know this is not just the drugs talking? How do I know that all this is real? I just, even though I was there, I know I was there, I just … it's so hard to believe. My soul? Fuck Amy…"

"What did you think it was? And does the name matter? You are traveling through time and across dimensions … soul, energy, essential you, what any culture, religion or scientist calls it is irrelevant. Call it a rose, but it exists."

"My soul travels?"

"More like your consciousness travels along the pulse of your soul. You access your soul in the dimensions it reaches."

I try to wrap my head around it. "So I, Kim can travel to any dimension or time where I, Kim, exist?"

"Yes, with training and help."

"But I can't go where Kim is not?"

"Exactly, not yet at least."

"So if I have died in another thread?"

"You could access the past, but not the time after the death."

"What happened to my soul then?"

"Nothing. It continues in its other threads."

"And when I die in all my threads?"

"Depends on what you believe I guess or maybe not, I don't know. Just try not to die, ok?" I sit with that for a minute.

"Is there anything to drink?" I ask, thinking about how good some liquor would taste right now.

"Sure, check the fridge."

"No, scotch or anything?"

"Oh, um, yeah, I think there is some bourbon."

"Perfect." Amy opens a cabinet and takes out an old dusty bottle of Wild Turkey and two equally dusty highball glasses. As she washes them off in the sink, I watch her for signs of crazy but she looks calm and rational as she sets up the drinks.

"How can you be so matter-of-fact about all this? You know this is crazy, right?"

"I've had a while to get used to it. And I've done it. And once you do it, you know it and you don't doubt it again." I reach for the glass closest to me and gently sniff the clear brown liquid. Sharp and warm and sweet. I take a swallow and it burns all the way down but settles my nerves. I can feel the tingling suffuse along my limbs. It's been a while since I've had something this strong to drink but it gives me the courage to ask, "So, how do I become aware of my soul?"

Kim downs her small glass of bourbon and nods at me as she shakes off the sting. She walks to the small refrigerator and takes out a small white bag from the back. I can hear a slight tinkling as she closes the door firmly. She holds out the bag out me and I take it. Inside there are six small vials of clear liquid and a tiny silver teaspoon. I'm guessing it's LSD again.

"A small sip with a guided meditation is how we start. It's not that hard if you've ever prayed before," Amy says.

I think back to my many years sitting in the pew at my mother's church, listening to the pastor yell about this and that, smattering bible verses as punctuation to his sermons about sins and transgressions. In the beginning of the service we would pray, at the end we recite the Lord's Prayer, our voices a rumbling drone of memory but not conviction. Have I prayed? When I was little, my mother used to sit by my bedside and I would repeat that horrid little verse, "If I die before I wake, I pray the Lord my soul to take." I try to think back to a time when I spoke to God and was not just following the lead of whoever was standing at the pulpit, or my mother squatting by my side. And then I remember. I was thirteen, maybe fourteen and I prayed to God to make me normal. I prayed so hard, tears squeezed out from under my lashes and my jaw hurt from tensing it so hard. I don't think God listened to me though. I was still gay the next day.

"I don't know that I've ever really prayed," I confess to Amy, "Church was always an obligation, not something I believed in." Amy nodded. "Meditation?" she inquired.

"No, Amy. I'm a scientist. I believe in known quantities and chemicals and data. And I already know how to breathe." Amy scratched her head and pulled her hair back into a tighter bun. "Have you ever danced until you forgot yourself?"

"Well, yes."

"Ok then, same thing." She placed the bag down, attached her cell phone to the stereo and flicked at her screen until she found what she was looking for. The sound of flutes filled the room. I just looked at her and smirked.

"Really? Flutes?" She smiled back at me and said, "Don't knock it until you've tried it. Now have a seat, get comfortable, we might be here a while, relatively speaking of course."

As I sat in the least uncomfortable looking chair, she walked to the light switch and dimmed the lights. I pulled up another chair put my feet up and she had lit a candle and put it on the table in front of me.

"Ready?"

"I suppose so. But I have to tell you, I don't like all these drugs in my system."

"That's cute. You think you are not already altered?" She snorted for emphasis then poured a few drops of liquid from one of the vials onto the spoon.

"Hold the whole spoon in your mouth for 15 seconds. Make sure you swallow all of it." Then she fed me like a baby and I counted while I watched her put the vial back in the bag, pull up a chair next to me and look me in the eyes.

"Done?" I nodded and took out the spoon. She washed it, returned it to the bag and put the bag back in the fridge. I noted her every movement, the precise way she turned the spigot on and off, the 90-degree bend at the waist to push the bag to the very back of the little fridge, the firmness of her closing and rotate around to look at me and slow (at least to me) walk towards me and sit down.

"Look at the candle, Kim. And listen to the flutes." I did both wanting my ability to follow directions to be noted as "I tried" even though none of this would have an effect on me. No sooner had that thought finished creating itself when I realize how completely mistaken I am. I can literally feel my soul trying to separate from my physical body so it can fly free. Only looking at Amy reminds me of where I am and what we are about.

"Do you feel it?" she asks. I can only nod as I struggle to stay attached to the head that nodded.

"Don't let go. That's not what we want. I want you to go inside and explore it, if that makes sense. Your soul is a fixed entity that's not fixed in this universe but it is a complete thing anyway. Does that make sense? You are not to separate, just get a feel for it as separate from your body, a thing that could go free, but that could be dying if you are not careful. You must obey me this time, Kim."

I nod again and resist the urge. I close the eyes and turn my attention to understanding the breadth and composition of this thing that I am but never acknowledged before. I could not describe it. There are no words created yet to circumscribe a thing/energy that exists outside, through and beyond current human knowledge. The poets have not arrived yet and I can only say as a scientist, that it is far more advanced and mysterious and ancient than anything I ever learned or encountered. Akin to dark matter in the universe, it is dark DNA – unique to me but too enigmatic for me to comprehend. Yet and still, I attempt to grapple with its existence even as it is me, defines me, encompasses all that is and will ever be me. It is overwhelming and I can feel my heart rate speeding up, my breathing with it. In the background, I hear Amy crooning to me.

"Flutes, Kim, hear the flutes? Listen to the flutes, slow down, it's ok, you are almost there, I think you got it, I think you understand, flutes, shhhhh, ok, listen, listen you are you are you are you. When you travel, you go first into you, this you, then make the jump, but you can't be scared or unsure. This you is you, stay in it and move the universes through, focus on the one you want and bring it to you, go to it, but stay in the you. You understand me Kim?"

I nod the head but am not sure I understand. I listen to the flutes. I can observe the sound waves as they move through the room.

"Kim, do you want to try a jump? A small jump. A small decision. Something easy." I think back to the morning, which seems like a lifetime ago. This morning I had a lot of choices … Home Depot, the library, a basketball game. I could have done any of those things. Now, I will. I nod the head and mumble, "How do I get back here, to you, this?" I ask, feebly gesturing with the arm.

"You just have to remember your choice to go to the park instead right? And the detour put you back at Temple, right?" I nod it. "Remember you chose to be alone and walk in the park, but were detoured. Don't get caught where you are though, remember that you are just visiting, passing through, hold tight to the soul energy. Hold it with both hands." I cock the head at her. "Metaphorically speaking, of course. It is literally your life line. Don't let go." I blink the eyes and close them. I think with the brain and recall the memories of the morning, the smell of the pancakes, the warmth of the kitchen, my mother's face and I think I hear myself mumble the words "I'd love to go to the library. The same one we used to go to Mom?" There is an echo. I know it to be caused by the distance of the sound waves from when they form in the brain, exit the mouth, reach the ears and register again in the brain. I know the pattern of the delay. I imagine my mother nodding and saying, "good". Shorter echo, three points of contact. I see so much. I choose library and am aware of a path that was always there. It is both inside and leading off. I feel pressure and then a roar in my head but I don't shut down, I move towards the path, to a pinpoint of light.

శ్రీ శ్రీ శ్రీ

I am at home, my mother's home, in my bed. Something has woken me up. It's my mother on the phone. She's crying. No, she's hysterical. Big Walter is trying to calm her down. I can hear whimpering in the hallway. I slide out of bed. I remember that I am a visitor, just visiting, I remember the path and the pinpoint but I have to know what's wrong. I grab my robe and throw it on. I can hear drawers opening and slamming shut. I come out my old bedroom and find them in the hallway holding Maya. My mother looks up at me with tears streaming down her face.

"Kim, I'm so glad you are here. Stay with Maya, stay with Maya, keep her safe."

"Ma, what happened? What's wrong?" But my mother can't answer. She breaks down into sobs again. Walter answers for her.

"It's Little Walter. After the basketball game, he went to a friend's house and they got into something and they were arrested."

"What!?! But he's only 12? What could they have done so bad at 12?!"

"Kim. They just called and said he had a medical emergency. We are on our way to the hospital. Watch Maya. I will call you when I know something but have to go."

My mouth agape, Maya clinging to me, I know myself a visitor and I just want out of here. I search for and find the edges of mySELF and yank up memories of earlier in the day, of Walter and a project from Home Depot. I become aware of the path that was always there and I rush for the pinpoint.

࿐ ࿐ ࿐

I find myself in the hallway with Maya clinging to me. I hear my parents bustling in the foyer, then shutting the door behind them. The only thing different about me is the soreness of my back and a bandage on my thumb. Maya is looking at me, scared and confused. I give her a hug.

"How about a little TV to calm our nerves?" I lead her to our parents' bedroom and we climb in their tussled bed and snuggle. I search the onscreen cable guide, find an old black and white movie and try to give myself a moment to think. I know I am just visiting. I am here and yet separate from it. I don't know what to do. I don't want to leave Maya, though I know I won't be. I know I should travel on to another. What if I go with Walter to the game? Maybe my presence would have stopped him from going out with friends ... the path becomes available but I hesitate. I'm scared to go. I'm scared to see. I kiss Maya on the forehead and give her a squeeze. I pull up and into my SELF and I head to the light.

෯ ෯ ෯

Now, I understand. The memories of what happened all come rushing at me and I struggle to absorb it all. The hospital smell, the beeping of the machines, the flickering fluorescent lights, the multitude of silent TV's flashing blue lights in every dark room up and down the hall, little Walter lying on the ground. I am watching my parents rush towards me. Walter was tased, Walter is in a coma. I was there. I saw it happen. They are distraught. I am defeated.

"Kim, what happened?" What happened? What happened?" My mother wails over and over again. She is addressing me but she rushes past me and into the room where Walter lies silent. Eyes closed, breathing regulated by the machine next to him, narrow chest rising up and down with it. I watch the scene and am crushed by my mother's pain. She grabs his lifeless hand and weeps onto it. She caresses it and prays on it and presses it to her cheek. Out of the corner of my vision I see a shimmer I try to turn to look at it but it evades my observation. I know it is there and it starts to dawn on me that it is Walter, not quite in his body but bobbing around it in confusion. I look down at my feet and I can just distinguish it at the edges of my peripheral vision. It frightens me and I back away down the hall. My mother does not notice. I can hardly breathe. I stare at the elevator doors and my distorted reflection in them to calm myself. I see myself, silvery, striated and smeared with unknown fingerprints. The park, the park, I went to the park, it was a beautiful day. I was so proud watching him play, stepping into his own self. And then … As I step into the open elevator, I pull up away from here and into mySELF. I see the dull gray warehouse walls in the pinprick just above and rush towards it.

卐 卐 卐

Flutes. Stiff leather chair beneath me. Amy is sitting across from me, eyes closed. It reminds me of Walter. I gasp and jump up out of the chair. I rush to my purse and fumble at my phone. Two missed calls and one stark text. "Walter is hurt in the hospital. Will text more details later. Pray."

Amy walks up to me. "Kim, I'm so sorry. I read it when it came in." I turn towards her. "I did it Amy. I traveled. I traveled on purpose. I can do that. I tried to stop this though", I shake the phone her way, "but I couldn't. I went to three different timelines but they all ended the same. Even when I went with him to try and prevent it, it still happened. I just saw it happen. The boys wanted sodas so they stopped at the corner store and got sodas. Next thing, we are walking back to Eric's house and cop cars come out of nowhere. Like six of them and they just scooped up the boys and Walter … Walter resisted. I tried to get the boys home fast, I tried to speak to the cops, I tried to tell Walter to shut his fucking mouth but …". I slam my hand down on the table over and over again.

"I'm so sorry," murmurs Amy as she guides me to a chair.

"But why?" I demand. "Why couldn't I change it? Isn't that the whole point of this travelling? Isn't that what this training is for? So we can change the terrible things that are happening?"

Behind me a door clangs open and scares me half to death. I turn and see Sujatha and Manny walking towards me. Amy calls out, "That was quick!" Sujatha looks straight at Amy. "Well, can she do it? Did she?" She looks at me with apprehension. Amy replies, "yeah, she can do it but something has come up. Something personal." Manny smiles at me, "No offense but personal shit always comes up. Grayson found something, he texted me last week but now I can't find him. He thinks he knows what the Russian plans to do or rather, plans to have us do. I can't be sure but I feel like things are shifting. We have to get moving."

Chapter 29

A shot of bourbon and Earth, Wind and Fire calms my nerves as I call my mother back and get the details. Another shot stopped the crying. A third and I was again resigned to saving this messed up world. Manny left after studying a book left on an otherwise empty shelf, I walked over to see the title. The book was tattered and faded and bloated with water damage but tilted the right way I was able to make it out ... *The Anarchist Handbook*. Great. I throw it back on the shelf.

Sujatha was asking Amy about Grayson. "When's the last time you talked to him?"

"Um.... Actually, I haven't seen him in a couple of weeks." While they talk, I look up from the rings my empty glass makes on the table to look at Sujatha. Her big brown eyes are looking from me to Amy. Her skin is a warm cinnamon color that seems to glow from within. Her nose ring is miniscule but it catches the light and flashes every time she turns her head. Her heavy black hair hangs in a tousled braid over her shoulder. I watch her talk, and though her lips stay twisted in impatience they are full and perfectly drawn with deep burgundy lipstick. I guess I never noticed before. She waves a hand in front of my face. She snaps and I break my stare.

"What the hell is wrong with you?"

"Sorry", I reply "but you gave me the bourbon, remember?" I look away from her towards Amy who is watching us with a raised eyebrow.

"What?!" I fling at her. "Oh nothing," she answers and turns to Sujatha. "So, did you check other timelines?"

"Yeah, but I think he is stuck back there. I got worried. I even went back to the warehouse and checked his lines …" Sujatha pulls out her phone.

"Look, I took a picture." She opens her pictures and zooms in on the screen. "There is his line on this timeline … see … it stops here … now." Amy takes the phone and studies it. I peer over her shoulder. Then she clicks it off and puts the phone face down on the table.

"You think he is gone?"

"I think he went too far back and something happened. Maybe too far back this time."

"Hey," I say, "let me see that phone again." Sujatha opens it up for me. I look at the picture and look at the dates. "I don't understand. How can he go back before he was born? That doesn't make sense with what you told me, Amy. I thought if we weren't there, we couldn't go there." Amy looked at Sujatha who nodded in my direction. "Tell her. She can handle it."

Amy looks at me and sighs. "So, as you noticed, Grayson's lines extend way back before his birth?'

I think back to the lines and the graphs. "Yeah, it didn't dawn on me at the time but his went back, way back. I remember thinking that maybe that was why he looked so rough around the edges but now, I don't get it."

"Grayson claims that he can access his past lives and he travels back through them, the people he used to be."

I look from Amy to Sujatha and back. "Past lives? Are you kidding me?" They shrug and nod back at me.

"Well, what about you two? Do you have past lives? Do you believe in that?"

Sujatha smiles at me. "I'm Hindu honey, of course I believe in past lives."

Amy interjects, "Kim, I didn't believe in past lives, I grew up Presbyterian but you have to admit, considering what we can do, it's not as far-fetched as it used to seem."

I turn to Sujatha. "Have you gone back to another lifetime?" She laughs. "No, Kim, I'm pretty sure I was a cat in a previous life and have no intention of catching rats for the Russian."

I roll my eyes at her. "Seriously," she continues, "I observed Grayson and I decided that it didn't seem worth the risk. You have to double the dosing to crossover, he says, and when he comes back, he is bedridden for days and sometimes can't get his language back; once it was his eyesight. Took him two weeks, right Amy? That was kind of scary for all of us. In any event, I think he's gone back again, way back and I'm worried."

"Let me see the text," sighs Amy. Sujatha hands her phone to Amy then walks over and sits next to me. "Do you want some water? Maybe something to eat? You shouldn't drink on an empty stomach." She smells good, like oranges and coconut.

"I would like another shot, if you don't mind."

"Sorry but we need you sober. Amy?"

"Hmm?"

"Let's go out to eat. Even superheroes need to eat, and I haven't had a decent meal in ages."

"Ok. This place is depressing. We can talk over dinner. Casual or fancy?"

"Let's go fancy. Could be our last meal."

"That's really fucking funny," I reply.

"I wish I was fucking kidding," Sujatha replies as she gets up.

I think back to my brother, lying in a hospital bed, unconscious. "I don't know if I can eat. I should probably go to the hospital."

"You can go after. We have to make plans and you will probably be in the middle of it all, right Amy?"

"Yeah, enough talking, let's go."

꽃꽃꽃

We enter Dharmama under-dressed and without reservations but manage to get a table anyway. By the time we sit on the plush chairs and I am handed a menu, I can feel my stomach rumbling in anticipation. It might have been the warm glow of all the candles, the light piano being played just over my left shoulder or the smells of the Thai fusion, but I am grateful we came. It feels so ordinary. I look at the other patrons, eating, drinking, laughing and whispering secrets and just breathed in the normalcy of it all. I must have sighed a thousand times, the last I tear up with relief. So much had been so crazy, I hadn't realized how tense my shoulders were, how shallow my breathing, how tight my tenuous grip on sanity. Sujatha smiles and takes my hand.

"It's ok. It is crazy. But we are in it together. You will feel better after you eat. This place has the best Indian food in Philly. And you can have one glass of wine, ok?"

She slides her hand away and immediately I ache for it. I slip my hand down into my lap and quickly look away, tears welling up again. Amy leans over and starts pointing out various dishes on the menu, distracting me with their whimsical names and elaborate descriptions. She pretends not to notice my discomfiture. I am thankful.

꽃꽃꽃

Bellies full, wine relaxed, we begin to make our plans. We decide that the simplest course of action would be to sabotage Patel's research on me. But we decide against it because if I am the key, and it doesn't work, then we have no back-up plan. Sujatha suggests killing Patel, but that leaves Wasserman with his research and with thousands of other unknown scientists eager for funding; he could probably still complete the research and get the technology. We also have no idea of when they met, how, why or what their communication was like. Killing Wasserman is probably not a good plan. He has goons. We laugh, but none of us can think of a better word. "Goons" is pretty apt. And we know little about him nor how to get to him. Amy and Sujatha discuss trying to go back to their "missions" and undoing what they did.

"Why did you guys agree to do the missions anyway? I mean, how did you even get in this position?" Amy looks embarrassed and nods towards Sujatha.

"Fine. I'll tell her. Originally it was a just like any regular "study" they conduct on campus. Come for a few days, earn $300 dollars for taking some experimental but safe narcotics and you know, being monitored. I came for the money; but I know some came for the drugs. We started out with a cohort of 30 people. Some of the students became ill and some ran off in the middle of the night. Then they ran a second session and 15 came back – the ones who enjoyed the high or needed the money. Again a few got sick. And this time they added some weird personality tests. The third time they ran the experiment only a select few were invited back and they were offered a lot more money."

"Were you jumping the whole time?"

"Oh no, that didn't happen until the third session when we had to sign a non-disclosure contract and several waivers."

"And you weren't suspicious?"

"No, by that time, we were familiar with the scientists and each other. The first time I jumped though ... I'll never forget it. It was stupid but incredible at the same time."

"What did you do?"

"They set up limited scenarios like changing your shirt and picking pepperoni pizza over vegetarian but it was so freaky! I could still taste the mushrooms and garlic as I was biting into pepperoni. It was ... just a singular experience."

"You liked it?"

"I liked it a lot. And then I got good at it and it was fun."

"Fun?"

"Yeah. When I jumped for me, it was exciting. We had to come back and report. We did little experiments. I mean, we are all scientists, so who wouldn't want to pursue this new discovery. It's fucking amazing! When I realized I was being used …"

Amy, who had been nodding the whole time turned somber. "When he first asked me to convince my parents to invest in Macintosh, I thought he was being generous and smart but when it worked, when it actually worked, I realized how dangerous this could be."

"But it was too late," adds Sujatha.

"Why don't you just stop then?" I ask. "Why don't you just leave this dimension and never see them again?"

"We tried that," answers Sujatha.

"They just got another group of students . . . And they started to train their … goons."

We all laugh. "It took months to go back and fix that mistake. We all had to go back individually and undo what we undid … honestly that was exhausting to keep track of."

"Yeah, the problem is once the technique gets solidified, it's probably too late."

I ask the obvious but I need to hear it anyway. "When did it solidify?"

"Kim, you already know, on 23AK, when you get captured by the Russian. Before that, Wasserman doesn't know what Patel has accomplished because Patel doesn't know what you can do. It's still hypothetical at that point."

"I have to go back there?"

"Yes. But …" Sujatha hesitates.

"But what?" My buzz has worn off and I am just tired now. Tired and full and feeling the weight of this murky responsibility.

"We have a few things we could try first and you should get a little more practice before you go back. When you go back, you go alone." Turning to Amy, Sujatha says, "Let's head back to the warehouse. I'm ready to have some fun."

※ ※ ※

Sujatha guides me into the car and we make the drive back to the warehouse. The sun is setting and the buildings take on a brilliant orange glow, even on the oldest, most decrepit of walls. The sky has begun its subtle shading down for the night. Bright blue on top, hinting towards coral near the horizon, dark shadows on the ground. We are soon back at the warehouse. I want to stand in the waning sunlight and watch the sky but Amy reminds me that our safety lies in our discretion and I duck into the cold gray walls of the warehouse.

Amy makes mint tea and we bring our chairs close, cupping our mugs for warmth.

"Maybe Joan is the key?" I offer. "She's like me, right? The one who gets the experiment first right? Maybe I can convince her there is something fishy going on and get her to destroy the lab or something?"

Sujatha sighs. "It's worth a try. But I think Amy should go with you just to be safe and to make sure you get back. You ok with that Amy?

"Of course. Joan is on this timeline … we have to go back then. What like five years? I was 17 … ugh… Let me think, what was my trigger then ...?"

"I transferred from UConn to Temple my sophomore year and met her that August."

"You said you were friends with her right?"

"Yup, she was my TA and helped me study."

"Let's pick a time to meet. How about homecoming of that year?"

"I was new. I don't think I would have gone to any of that stuff."

"Of course not! Let's meet in the science lounge, sometime during the football game, ok?"

"Ok."

Sujatha gets up and goes to the fridge. She hands Amy and I cold silver spoons and drops 3 drops of the ice-cold LSD on them. We guide the spoons into our mouths and swallow the liquid. The metallic taste of the spoon makes me want to gag, but I know I need the minor chemical reaction that sets off to get the full effect. Instead of a candle I look into Amy's eyes until she closes them. She hands her spoon to Sujatha and lounges back in the chair. She faded and shimmers into a mirage, there and not there. Sujatha retrieves the spoon from my mouth and pushes me backwards. I close my eyes and focus on that first fall at Temple, the bitter heartbreak always in the back of my mind like a stone. I ride this wave and find myself standing in line at a food truck. Aware of mySELF but hungry in this body, I am relieved when it is my turn to order. I order the taco chicken cheesesteak with extra jalapeno sauce and fries. The guy who takes my order looks at me.

"Something different about you today Kim."

"Oh?"

"Yeah .. you seem stressed. Here, take some Peanut Chews. It's on me."

"Thanks ... Zo." It took me a second to pull up his name, but then I remember the drugs, and something else ... the lounge, the science lounge ... Amy. Feeling like a visitor in my own body, I take my food and turn my feet to the Science Building. It seems like everyone else is walking the opposite way and I can hear the roar of the crowd in the far distance. Homecoming ... yeah, that's right. The air is crisp, but the sun is warm as I shuffle through the newly fallen leaves. I open the door to the building and head to the back of the building. The lounge is empty. I sit at a table speckled cherry and white, open up my sandwich and take a huge bite. So. Good.

Ten minutes later, a young Amy comes through the door just as I'm popping the last of my sandwich in my mouth.

"Damn, it smells good in here. What was that?"

"Cheesesteak but I dogged it. You can have the fries though," I say pushing the thin white bag towards her. She sits and starts pulling them out one by one.

"So, we did it. *You* did it Kim. You chose, you jumped and we met up."

"Yeah, I guess we did do it."

"I believe you have completed my course in dimension jumping and time manipulation."

"What no final exam?"

"This was it and you passed."

We stare out the window while she finishes the fries.

"Anything to drink?"

"No."

"Weird."

"Sorry but my friend at the truck gave me some Peanut Chews."

"Sweet! But I'm stuffed, save them. Let's go find Joan."

卍 卍 卍

We find her deep in the library, by the window looking out towards the football field and the crowds streaming towards it. She turns and smiles when she sees me in the reflection.

"Kim! What are you doing in here? Why aren't you at homecoming?"

"You know that's not my thing. I'm so behind in my classes! I thought I would come and study."

"Oh", she said looking at me strangely. "Well, where are your books?"

Amy, wearing her book bag, steps up to us and Joan looks at her. "Oh. Hi?"

"Joan, this is my friend Amy. Amy, this is Joan." Amy leans down to shake Joan's hand which she takes hesitantly.

"Amy? Are you in the department too?"

"No," says Amy, "I'm just a senior in high school. Kim is showing me around."

"Oh, ok." I sigh, bored with all this pretense and pussyfooting around.

I pull up and chair and roll it close to Joan. Amy takes a seat on a bench behind me.

"Joan, I need to talk you about Professor Patel."

"OK".

And then I just went for it. I asked her about her work-study, I told her about the experiment, I didn't mention all the dimensions, just the other one when I got the scholarship instead of her. That's when I lost her.

"Kim, I'm willing to admit that Patel is a little strange and I could even be convinced that his experiment is two-fold but parallel dimensions – come on, nothing like that has even been close to being proven; it's impossible physics."

"Joan, I know it's hard to believe but I'm telling the truth and you are in danger."

"Listen, I really did come here to get some work done. Please let me work."

"It doesn't matter what work you get done today if you don't get yourself out of that work-study situation."

"You know I depend on that for money. Are you after my scholarship? Is that what this is about?"

"No, I couldn't care less about that!"

"I'm leaving." Joan grabbed her books and shoved them in her bag. "I don't know what's going on with you but maybe you should get some help. Take the window seat, I'm leaving."

"Joan, please." But Joan kept walking and we let her go. I watched her walk stiffly down the hall and turn the corner towards the stairs. We could hear her steps echo all the way down. Amy turned to me.

"Trying to steal her scholarship?" Amy smirked. I ignored her.

"Maybe we should sabotage the lab. Try to skew his results?"

"He has cameras, remember? We would get caught."

"There's something else, Amy. I didn't get the sense that anything was happening with her. By this time in the year, I was already experiencing weird vision. She didn't seem to connect with anything strange or out of the ordinary."

'Hmmm ... do you think the experiment is not working on her?"

"Maybe Patel is using a different formula, or maybe she's just not receptive to the treatments."

"Maybe she's not conducting the experiments according to protocol." We go back to staring out the window, crafting and tossing out ideas in our silence.

"I got it!" I blurt out. "I'll leave her a letter. I'll write a letter, leave it under Mabel and tell her what to look for. There's no way she will be able to sit there for 6 hours and not be tempted to look." Amy looks at me skeptically. "Got any better ideas?"

"Not really," she replies.

We leave the library and head to the crowded bookstore. Surrounded by nostalgic alums, excited freshmen and encouraging parents, we stand in line for 40 minutes just to buy a notepad, envelopes and a pen. I write the letter and we head over to the Science Building. I make my way to the lab and find Mabel green and healthy under a sunlamp. The rest of the room is dark but I can see a sliver of metal in the corner. I draw an arrow on the front of the envelope and hope she gets it. I scurry back to Amy who is waiting for me in the lounge.

"Ready?"

"Ready. I have to go back home though I doubt anyone even noticed I was gone."

"Really? The dramatic teenage thing?"

"Whatever." Amy tosses her hair and flings her book bag up on her back.

"Just kidding Amy. Sheesh! I'll see you in a few, Ok?"

"Ok. See ya." Teenage Amy leaves and I sit and enjoy the quiet.

I shake my head at the craziness of this whole thing. I am riding the subconscious of my own subconscious in another dimension. I think about praying but I'm not sure what I would ask. That this whole situation is not real? Then that makes me crazy. I don't want to be crazy. I can't pray for that. I lay back in my chair and retreat inward to return to the warehouse and Sujatha. The roar begins and I ride out on it.

Chapter **30**

I lift out of the fog to see Sujatha sifting through the timelines, Amy is not back, she sits there but not there. Molecules tenuous, her breathing steady and slow. I watch Sujatha frowning and then she turns back to look at me and sees I am awake.

"Well, any luck?" She brings me a bottle of Orange Crush. I shake my head no and take a long sip. Amy shimmers in my peripheral vision and by the time I turn my head, she is solid and awake. Sujatha hands her a soda from off the table.

"I was going to ask you the same thing. She thought we were crazy but we left a note in the lab about what she should investigate. But I don't think.... Wait ..." I search my memory.

Amy murmurs something. "Didn't Joan disappear ... before?" I ask and look around. Sujatha nods and puts her head in her hands.

"She didn't die. I remember. She didn't die, she just ..."

"... transferred to USC or something."

"Right!" I exclaim. "She transferred and ..."

"I got the Mendel scholarship." Amy sighed. "I got it. My freshman year, I did the work-study for Patel."

Sujatha and I both turn and look at Amy who looks like she's about to throw up.

"It's ok, Amy." I say.

Sujatha walks over to her and puts a hand on her shoulder. "Did the Russians get you? Did you go the farmhouse?" Amy shakes her head. "No, I think, I think I made it easier for them." She tears up a little.

"Why, what did you do Amy?" I ask feeling my heart speed up in my chest.

"I'm so sorry. I posted some … some videos up on YouTube."

"What!?!" Sujatha yelled.

"I'm sorry, I didn't know but I knew something was happening and I videotaped myself doing small jumps, changing clothes, hairstyles, that sort of thing … I had an old YouTube channel from high school. I had a decent amount of followers but most people thought I was just good at special effects, you know … ugh… that was so stupid."

"Patel never said anything to you? Did you ever make the connection?"

"No, not then, not until later. I just thought I was …special." She looks overwhelmed as she tries to absorb and make sense of all these new memories. I know the feeling.

"Oh, and my channel was shut down too, but I didn't think much of it at the time."

"And then the study came along?" Sujatha asks.

"Yes, then the study, and we all trained together. And the missions began."

Sujatha and Amy stare at each other for a minute.

"At least Joan got away," I say and take a sip of my soda.

Amy jerks forward and throws up all over the floor. "Sorry," she says and starts to cry. Sujatha runs to her and hands her a tissue then walks her into the other room. "Come on Amy. It's not your fault. You should lie down. A lot has changed, you should rest. You have a lot to process."

I listen to Sujatha's soothing as I look around for something to clean up Amy's vomit. She comes back just as I finish up with a roll of paper towels. I gag over the smell though. As I'm washing my hands in the sink, I hear a match being lit. I turn to see Sujatha holding a stick of incense in the flame. She blows it out leaving the fire red tip and a coil of smoke. She looks at me and raises her eyebrows. I look away and dry my hands on my shirt.

"Well, that was kind of a bust," she says.

"I hope she'll be alright," I say gesturing towards the open door. Sujatha steps towards it and closes it with a whisper.

"Yeah, she fell asleep almost as soon as she laid down. I'm not sure what is happening with her but she is very shook up over this."

"What should we do now?" I ask.

"We have to find a way to distract Wasserman, maybe we can get him interested in something else, some other business venture ...

"Maybe something personal ...

"Maybe a problem? What do we know about him anyway?"

"Nothing much ... ok, let's start there. Maybe he is the key."

"I don't know anything about his past, maybe we can find him in the future. Wanna try?"

"I'm game."

卐 卐 卐

With Amy snoring in the next room, Sujatha and I made our plan. It was going to be a little more complicated but I had a hunch of where we should go. She had a hunch of when. Somehow, a tape of Prince's Graffiti Bridge had been left in the old tape recorder by the bookshelf and we needed a trigger. We listened to the tape and decided on The Symbol used by Prince as his name for the tattoo. It meant both woman/man and god, though I thought the arrow could also stand for "go home". It was specific enough and nostalgic enough to remind us of this time and place.

We played "Still Would Stand All Time" over and over while she tapped on my wrist. Dip and tap, dip and tap, dip and tap. She held my hand still. I mulled over our plan as I watched her work.

"Your turn," she said as she finished.

"I'll try but you know I've never done this before."

"You'll be fine, draw it first, then just follow the line." I did as I was told and only messed up when I looked up at her. Her eyes were closed as she hummed along with the music. I thought of kissing her. Stupid mistake. My heart raced, my hand shook and her arrow got a slight curve. When she opened her eyes and looked, she raised her eyebrow at me and laughed.

"Well, that should remind me of you." I withdrew my hand and blushed, embarrassed. "Ready?" she asked, swabbing her new tattoo with disinfectant. I nodded and turned to put the kit away.

"Hey," I felt a hand on my shoulder. "Don't worry about that, it's fine, ok?"

"Oh, I'm not worried about that. I just … I just wish this wasn't. I just want to go back to my life. I want things to go back to normal."

"What? Tired of me already?" she teased.

"No, not you. But I'd rather get to know you, you know, under different circumstances."

"Yeah …. you never know, maybe we will. March 22, right?" I nodded. We held our silver spoons in our mouths, closed our eyes and leaned back. "Still Would Stand All Time" was still playing, my wrist pulsed with its fresh wound and I reached for the wave of my SELFsoul, focusing on my 30th birthday. She grabbed my hand at the last minute, I felt HER as a vibration – faster, lighter in some way and I knew I would be all right.

Chapter **31**

Red, blue, white, dark, purple, red, blue, white, dark, white, dark, white. Thump, thump, thump. Police siren. A face, another, faces, faces in the crowd, eyes closed, faces crunched up, lips pursed, or mouths open in ecstasy. I'm moving, dancing, gyrating my hips along the beat, dip, bounce, turn to see a face, looking at me. Oh, she's cute! Ok. I smile, she smiles back. Asymmetrical blonde fro, dark shiny skin, is that glitter? Big feather earrings floating a half beat behind the music. She dances up close to me and I get lost for a minute in the music, in the invitation behind her eyes.

"Kim!!!" I feel a hand on my shoulder. I turn and see Kendra.

"Come on girl, I have the shots lined up!"

I turn back to the woman I'd been dancing with, she makes a sad face then turns to dance with another woman on her left. Giving her one last look, I dance off the floor following Kendra's bright blue locks. They reach down to the back of her knees. I am pretty sure it's a weave. At the bar is Jen and her boyfriend, Darryl. He looks kind of uncomfortable. It's his first time at Ellen's Last Stand, named after the comedian Ellen, who was killed a couple years ago. A stab of regret goes through me. Kendra is cozied up to a very well dressed man, who, I have a feeling did not start out that way. I turn to the drinks, then to Kendra.

"They are Flaming Lemon Drops. Don't worry you will love them!"

"Vodka again? You are going to kill me with this stuff Kendra!"

"That's what friends are for!" She smooches me on the cheek and hands out the glasses. "To Kim! Thirty, dirty and I heard she was squirty!"

"Ewwww... Kendra!"

"Drink up pussies!" Everyone toasts and takes their shot. It burns, then twists but ends up sweet from the sugar rim. I shake my head from the intensity but that just makes me a little dizzy. Kendra gives me a huge hug. "You still hot girl!" Then she waltzes off to the dance floor with her fine friend. Jen looks happy but sleepy and then I remember why.

"How's the baby?"

"Oh he's fine. He's with my mom and Brittany. Hopefully he's asleep by now. She looks at Darryl who indulges her with a smile. "I don't think we are going to stay out too late, Kim. We'll both be up early tomorrow."

"I'm so glad you are back in school, Jen."

"Well, I had to do something else, right?" She shrugs and I think back on all she's been through – the dancing, the addiction, the abuse that got Alonso arrested and the accident that brought her home. "Let's dance. Can you dance yet?"

"Yeah, not quite the same but I still have some moves."

Jen and I head out to the dance floor. They are playing some old M.I.A. song mixed with neo-reggaeton, and it is on fire. We bump into Kendra, and for a few blissful minutes, lose ourselves in the music, the liquor and the comfort of familiarity.

Then the siren blares. Another raid. Another invasion of privacy implemented under this neo-fascist regime. The music stops abruptly as people find the people they came with and stand in groups. We begin digging through our wallets to pull out our citizenship cards. Covered in black body armor but guns holstered, they walk in. Arrogant and efficient, they sweep through the room, scanning cards with the finger lasers built in to their suits, eyeballing each person through their infra-red eyepiece. They are looking for dissent, looking for a reason to yank somebody out as a show of force. And they find one. A young woman is huddling in the bathroom. She doesn't have her card. She doesn't speak English though she's dressed like a patron, not a worker. They whisk her out of the club as she weeps. Nobody steps forward to help her. She doesn't ask for it either. They leave. The door closes behind them with a loud rusty clang. There is a moment of silence as we all exhale. Then the DJ plays a huge fart noise. We all laugh and put away our wallets. The lights dim, the music ramps back up but it is hard to get back in the mood. We should be used to it by now, but the fear and strain persist. Like the proverbial elephant in the room, it is massive, imposing and capable of crushing any and all of us at a moment's notice. Jen comes over.

"I think we're going to go now," She smiles crookedly. "My hip is killing me and ... you know." She shrugs our collective resignation. I hug her tight and kiss her cheek.

"Thanks for coming out Jen".

"Happy Birthday Kim! Love you so much, bestie. Have fun and please, keep an eye on Kendra. She has been out of control since her divorce."

"I know. I'm on it." Darryl hugs me good-bye and I squeeze his hand hoping he knows I mean for him to take care of my best friend. Our eyes meet and he nods. Thank God. I look around for Kendra. She is slow dancing with her friend in a corner, no matter that the music is a frenetic electronic rendition of "Fight The Power". The DJ is determined to scrub away the past few minutes, the dancers consent to the tactic by whirling around me like Dervishes. Kendra, however, has always danced to her own beat. I am on way to check in with her but something catches my eye at the bar. It's the golden-haired glitter girl. She smiles at me, then beckons me to the bar. I decide that Kendra is fine and head over to the bar.

"Hi" I say smiling and edging my way through the crowd.

"Can I buy you a drink?" she asks.

"Yes, please."

"What are you drinking?"

"Vodka, I guess."

"What's wrong with vodka? It always does the trick." She sips her pale drink for emphasis.

"I guess so, but I've always had a gut feeling that brown liquor was better for you. You know that old saying ... the darker the berry ..."

"The sweeter the juice?" She laughs at my corny line but leans in to kiss me anyway. It is tender and as predicted, sweet.

"You just proved my point," I say staring into her beautiful brown eyes. Her expression changes in that instant from playful desire to bemusement as she looks over my shoulder. I turn to see what she is looking at. A gorgeous Indian woman, dressed head to toe in black leather, eyes lined with kohl, lips a bruised shade of purple, stands with hand on hip, shaking her head at me. It feels like I just got caught cheating, but I don't think I know this woman. The glittery girl slides from her seat and whispers as she passes.

"Catchya later cutie. You look like you already have more than you can handle."

I open my mouth to reply, but the woman in black raises her eyebrows and sighs.

"Kim... Sujatha." She extends her hand to shake, and, as I unthinkingly reach to shake it, I see her wrist tattoo as a mirror of my own. Memories flood through me crowding out the linear history of this timeline, cutting through my buzz and reminding me of who I am and what I'm about. Holding her hand, I pull her to me and to the bar.

"I would have never pegged you for a black leather type."

"You think you know me that well?"

"No, I don't think I know you at all. How did you find me?"

"This is my fourth club. I figured a thirty-year-old would probably pick a club to celebrate. I was right."

"Ugh, I hate being so predictable."

"In this case, it worked to our advantage." She smiled as she looked around the bar. "So this is a gay club, huh?"

"First time?"

"Yes. Despite the clothes, I'm not really a club kind of a girl."

"The clothes give it away", I say, "Nobody would come to dance in leather."

"Oh" she said, suddenly looking unsure.

"No, they might come in leather to impress the ladies, but you would sweat your ass off in that outfit."

"But I look good right?"

"Yeah, you look good... Would you like a drink?" I ask trying to reign in my attraction to her.

"Oh, how about a cognac, neat?" I smile and order her drink and get myself another Lemon Drop. We toast when they arrive.

"Happy Birthday," she says. "Listen, I know we have a mission to find Savvy, but let's just enjoy your birthday tonight, ok?"

"Savvy ... right, right..." I pull out my phone and scroll through my messages.

"We don't have to find her. She's in Washington. I have her contact info."

"You do?" I hand her my phone and she reads through the logs.

I sip my drink. "D.C. is just down the road. She's been working on this project for almost a year. I never pictured her working as a lobbyist but she says the pay is through the fucking roof."

"I bet. Well, we can't travel at night anyway. So DC tomorrow then?"

"Should we take my car or should we go on your bike?"

"I don't have a ..."

"Kidding!"

Someone bumps me on my other side and I turn to see Kendra and her friend sweaty, smiley and ordering more shots. Kendra looks happier than I've seen her in a long time.

"Did Jen leave?"

"Yeah, after the card check."

"Card check my ass! Illegal search and seizure is what it is!"

"Yeah, well after that, she said her hip was hurting so she and Darryl went home."

"I hope he's the real deal. That girl has been through enough."

"Yeah, so speaking of girls, whatcha doing over there?" I nod my head to her friend.

"Oh Jay? I'm just having some fun. He's fine though right?"

"Yes, but are you sure he's your type?"

"He's my type tonight. And who's that?" She smiles over my shoulder at Sujatha.

"That's an old friend from Temple."

"Is that right? She's beautiful. I suggest you hit that. ... or maybe she'll be my type tonight too ..." Kendra leaned around me and stuck her hand out to Sujatha.

"Hi, I'm Kendra. I see Kim's taste in women has improved."

I gasp and turn to Sujatha. "I didn't say anything like that ..." But she is just laughing and smiling at me. She kisses Kendra's hand and says, "Charmed. I'm sure." I look back and forth at them flirting and I step in between them.

"Hey, let's not forget whose birthday it is!" The bartender returns with four shots and we each grab one. Jay winks at me. I just laugh and down the spicy sweet lemony goodness. Sujatha grabs my elbow.

"I might sweat but let's dance anyway, ok?"

The four of us jump up and head to the middle of the dance floor where, in our minds, we own it for the next hour.

卐 卐 卐

Though I had every intention of trying to make out with Sujatha, by the time we got back to Kendra's house, I was so tired and drunk I passed out on the couch. Sujatha, dehydrated and exhausted from her long night in leather, found her way into one of the many guest rooms in the mini-mansion. Only Kendra and Jay managed to finish the evening as they started it – all over each other.

☙☙☙

Morning found us late and cotton-mouthed but satisfied. We ate in silence, downing aspirin with our coffee. It was Friday so Sujatha and I left right after we ate to try and beat the Beltway rush hour. Kendra and Jay, not quite out of bed, looked like they were happy for us to go.

The ride to DC was quiet since both of us were hung over, but we chatted about inconsequential stuff like how cars have gotten larger and slower as more people use them for housing. We passed several of the new mobi sites set up along I-95. It started as a fad for the young entrepreneur but now, after the last recession and the tornado clusters that tore up the northeast, this was home for hundreds of thousands of people across the US. Whole new economies sprung up around the communities so now they are being targeted for regulations, permits, fees and taxes like all the cool new stuff. RIP World Wide Web. I also learned that Sujatha had quite the foul mouth and a weird obsession with Mozart. Under duress, I confessed my fear of public bathrooms. Of course, we ran straight into the DC Friday afternoon traffic. We listened to the news while I patiently inched the car forward and Sujatha cursed a blue streak. The global news was not good, as usual, but we were used to that and tried to plan our lives around the various impending disasters.

I made arrangements to meet Savvy at her office on 16th Street. She sounded busy but intrigued. We haven't seen each other since competing for the same summer internship at SpaceX. I was bitter about that until I realized they had been hijacked by the Russian equivalent – SPUTNIK21. That's who she lobbies for now – the new privatized space program, SpaceX International Associates.

❀ ❀ ❀

Savvy meets us in the lobby. She says it is to get us through security faster, but I think she wants a chance to figure out what I want first. She hugs me like she means it and treats us both like old beloved friends. I am suspicious. She hasn't changed much. She is still stunning, but now she is also sophisticated, her youth weighed down a bit by her import. Having known her for 15 years, I am not fooled by her poise and casual elevator chit-chat. I know just who she bribed to get that internship and how much she paid. Sujatha is both warm and cool to her, a feat I admire. I struggle to keep my eyes from rolling with every neutral, polite phrase she utters.

When we walk into Savvy's office, I am struck by the stark lighting and absolute quiet of the room. I conclude that the walls are not only sound-proof but that the room is probably under constant visual surveillance. There is a huge map of the known galaxy on the wall behind her desk. But she faces an artful arrangement of black-framed photos of her posing with various important world figures on the opposite wall. These are interspersed with her multiple gold-framed degrees announcing her undeniable qualifications. Sitting down, I realize that from my vantage point, she stands between me and the rest of the universe; from hers I am just another in a long line of accomplishments. The lack of subtlety seems very …. Russian, hell, maybe it's just political. Either way, it seems like a clear and probably very accurate message to whoever comes through her doors.

After a quick visit to the ladies' room, we sit and get down to business.

"So, Kim. While it is always a pleasure to see you, I'm sure you and Sujatha have come for some purpose."

"Yeah, we have. Savvy, we have a long history and you have never known me to be anything but honest and forthcoming, right?"

"Well, I can think of one time I thought you could have been more forthcoming …" She laughs and glances at Sujatha who just looked confused. "Sorry," she continues, "Honestly, I just haven't seen anybody from home is such a long time. Whatever this is, it is good to see your face Kim."

"Thanks Savvy. I get it. This is going to sound bizarre but I'm looking for some information on a scientist, a Russian scientist who, I think, might be capable of causing a great deal of harm to this country, possibly to many countries."

She leans toward me. "What kind of damage?"

"I can't say because I'm not sure yet. And honestly, I don't want you to know too much in case it's not safe. I just need to know more about him."

She sits back and looks at me. "This is some bullshit story, Kim. Who sent you here?"

"Nobody sent me here. I'm here because I ... I got caught up in something, unintentionally, you understand, and I have to help undo the damage that I did."

"Ahh ... so you are the bad guy. For a minute, it sounded like you were on some superhero ego trip."

"Nah, I just need to know a little something about a scientist."

"Are you going to kill him? Because I cannot be involved in anything like that."

"Kill him? No, I just need to know where he's from, where he lives, where he studied maybe."

"Why don't you just go through the university databases? He's sure to be in one of them."

"I don't think he's affiliated with any institution."

"Rogue scientist? With no funding? Well, then I do think I know where to look but what's in it for me?"

I stare at her furious with myself. Of course, I should have known she would want something. And then it comes to me. Phobos.

"OK, I may have some information you can use but you can't ask me how I know. I want the scientist first."

"Kim, I'm kind of tired of playing games. I have a late dinner date and I have a report to finish up first..."

"Ok, ok .. I know something about the first human trip to Mars ... I know some of the specific formulas you will need to fuel the mission and hibernate the crew. I will give them to you for this scientist. You will be a hero and maybe you can leave all this bullshit behind and get back to science."

I hit a nerve.

"What makes you think that I want to give up all of this?!?! Especially to go back to some smelly, sterile lab?"

"Savvy, you can dress this up all you want, but you are a paper pusher here. A very well-paid one but nevertheless, what do you do besides have meetings and charm the people your bosses want you to charm?"

"I beg your fucking pardon!? I influence the ENTIRETY of the space exploration budget across the globe! I write the fucking policies and line items and ensure that we will get what is required to fund our mission."

"Your body and beauty are being used and your brain is being wasted. Sure, you write policy, so what? How many lobbyists are there up here on M street? A few thousand? But you, you Savvy, have always been smarter than all of your teachers. You should be writing equations, not line items. This is beneath you and you know it." I sit back and stare at her, waiting for her to continue to lay down some bullshit.

"Fuck you Kim."

"Fuck you Savvy. You stole my internship for this? To be a puppet? Maldita sea la madre que te parió y te pujó!" Savvy jumps up from her chair and comes around to stand in front of me. Sujatha slides out of her chair and stands behind me, but I don't get up. I don't have to.

"You bitch! I should have you thrown out of here for this."

"You are being an idiot!" I look up at her, "Don't miss this chance to be the hero of Mars. You know I don't bullshit around. If I say I have it, I have it." She turns and grabs a notepad off her desk and shoves it at me.

"Write down what you know about this scientist and what you want to know." I take it and scribble some notes. I show it to Sujatha, she adds a line and makes a correction then hands it back to Savvy. She tears off the paper, folds it and tucks it in to her bra with a wry smile. Then she writes an address and a time on the notepad, tears off a few pages with it and hands it to me. I tuck it into my bra and smile back at her.

"You better not be fucking with me Kim. You know I know people." I laugh and give her a quick hug.

"Thank you and trust me, we will all be better off." I step aside as Sujatha extends her hand and politely adds, "It was a pleasure to meet you, Miss Montana."

Savvy shakes her hand but looks at me. Sujatha and I turn and leave. In the elevator, she just stares at me. "I hope you know what you are doing."

"I do." But I don't. I am not at all sure I can come up with the equations I've promised.

❦ ❦ ❦

A couple of hours later, Sujatha and I leave the weed bar and I have my answers. It was a lot simpler than I imagined. I pulled up flutes on my phone, smoked and concentrated. I didn't have to make a jump so much as I had to remember the future. Two meals, 1 gallon of water, two hours of flirting and a slow-motion make-out session later, I was able to remember the engine formula needed to get a ship into Phobos' orbit as well as the precise amounts of Propofol and Hydrogen Sulfide gas needed to slow down the human bio processes.

We sober up by taking a walk on the Mall. Though surrounded by see-through concrete security walls, the Capitol, Monument and White House retain their nobility in person. Too bad nobody works there anymore. Politicians meet in cyberspace now, coming together only for formal affairs of state. They don't do much anyway, just signing off on whatever their official sponsors want. But the disintegration of our democracy doesn't bother me as much as the quiet shrug of acceptance from the citizenry. Tonight, though, some of those citizens are out and about taking in the majesty of the buildings gleaming white in their spotlights. History buffs already wax nostalgic about those empty beacons in the darkness. But I look up for my true north. Beyond the moon, beyond the sun, space is where I want to be. Politics doesn't matter up there, money doesn't matter up there. Just discovery and survival and the ability to solve problems before they become predicaments. I feel a tap on my shoulder.

"Still high I see," Sujatha comments.

"Yeah, maybe a little. I was just thinking about …"

"Phobos?"

"Yeah … it was incredible."

"You'll get back there. It was this timeline, right?"

"Yeah, and others I hope. What if finding this Russian and somehow reversing this ability messes up my chances? What if anything we do, has larger ramifications than we intend? Are we just going to spend our lives jumping around trying to fix the course of this ... this… human trajectory? Maybe this is what is supposed to happen, maybe we are supposed to learn this and this is how we end. Implosion."

"High taking a dark turn is it?" Sujatha laughs.

"I'm serious, still high, but I know what I'm saying. What if our messing around changes too much and we end up blowing us up, or blowing our chance to hit rock bottom and then rise up again? What if stagnation is what ends up killing us?"

"Ok, Kim. I believe this is all about you and Phobos, but hypothetically, if Patel and Wasserman were supposed to make and exploit this techno-ability, then why does 23AK exist if not to give us another chance? Why did we students individually and collectively decide to stop helping them? It seems to me that they are interfering with the natural course of civilization, for better or worse. They are trying to skewer it to benefit the few. We are just trying to let it fall on its own sword, in due time."

I stare at her. "So, you think our civilization is doomed? Then why are we even trying?" She shrugs.

"Every living thing must die, Kim. We all know it is coming. It is what you do with the life you have that is important. Like go to Mars. Humans should go to Mars because we can. We should go for the joy of it, the excitement of a new discovery, the possibilities of another place to live. We should not go to own it and its resources. That's what SpaceX and Sputnik21 are about – owning the transportation, owning the habitats, owning the right to restock and provide necessities. It's sickening."

"You think we can change that?"

"I do. And it's worth trying. I don't much like the idea of giving up on the whole human race. That's just too ... pussy."

"Sujatha, I swear I had no idea ..."

"Don't be a pussy Kim. Is it time to see your friend yet? I'm getting a little hungry."

I pull out the paper. It reads "midnight. Busboys and Poets, Underground.

"What time is it?"

"It's almost eleven."

"Close enough, let's head over to the Underground."

"The what?"

"It used to be a subway, then it was a mall, then it was a bomb shelter, then a homeless shelter, now it's collection of performance spaces and cafes. It's kind of cool. At least it was."

Despite the plethora of little Uber Coopers hovering about, we hail a taxi. They are the best way to get around off the grid. The driver doesn't bother looking at us. He just grunts when I state our destination, starts the meter and puts on the complimentary Comflix. My high finally wearing off, I stare out the window instead and note the changes. Sujatha pulled up some old Bollywood.

"I used to love these movies when I was a kid."

She shimmies her shoulders and leans back recalling the moves from a long forgotten dance routine.

"There was so much joy back then!"

"It was fake joy."

"Yes, but it was joy nevertheless."

I turn back to my window and wonder about Savvy. Sujatha continues her dance down memory lane until we get to our stop way out in South East DC. I pay the man cash, which he also grunts at and we step out. It's quiet for a Friday night. We head to the gate and the bouncer, show our IDs and head inside looking for the right café.

I'm surprised when it's the first one to the left. I was expecting to find it tucked away in the back, under an eave with a locked door and secret knock. But no, it is a well-lit, bustling café and bookshop with a tiny stage on the left side. Tonight, there is just one scruffy white guy strumming an acoustic guitar and cooing into the mike. It is strangely comforting. We head straight to the counter, order a couple of sandwiches and drinks (I eyeball the pumpkin muffin and laugh to myself) and we head to the furthest table in the back.

After eating, I use the store bag to make a neater copy of the equations I remember from the future. I tuck the original away for safekeeping. I carefully fold up the bag and tuck it in my back pocket. Sujatha seems hypnotized by the crooner; I leave her to it and wander the book aisles. It feels indulgent but I open some books and read the first few pages. I contemplate buying the latest Stephen King but then I remember when I am. Even so, I think at least I will remember reading it later …? I put the book down. Too complicated. When I look up, there is Savvy looking right at me. I can't decipher the look on her face, only that it makes me worry for her. I catch her eye and walk back to our table. She joins us there.

"I'm glad you came, Kim. After you left I started to wonder if I had hallucinated the whole thing."

"You? Hallucinate? Dream about me, maybe".

She laughs. "You wish. I can't stay long, I'm already pushing it but I think this is what you want." She pulls a small manila packing envelope from her bag and pulls out a small picture.

"Is this the guy you are looking for?"

I have to stare at the face for a while before I can recall it. Sujatha squints and nods.

"I believe that's him," I reply.

"Are you sure Kim, because, this information is classified and I don't want an innocent scientist in trouble because of me."

"Oh trust me. This guy is not innocent." She shrugs and hands over the envelope.

I retrieve the bag from my pocket and unfold it on the table. Pointing to each of the equations, I try to seem more confident than I am. "Fuel to orbit Phobos – but check this particular calculation and take off has to be perfectly timed – don't even try it if you are not 100% sure of the timing. Ok?" Savvy frowns studying the numbers. "This one is for hibersleep. It's simple enough but preparing the bodies is crucial – eating and storing lots of fats and simple amino acids help with muscular degeneration. The relevant research came mostly from polar bears and those 17 year locusts, you know what I'm talking about?"

Savvy slides the bag into her purse and nods at me, but her gears are already spinning.

"Savvy? Thank you. And listen, you should backend your research so these look like they came from you ok? Don't speak my name at all, not even once."

"Don't worry. I'm very good at this kind of thing. You should know that."

"True."

"You be careful with this guy ok? He seems well connected, but clean. It's weird."

"I'll be fine. I hope that works out for you."

"Thanks." Savvy smiles one more time at me, nods at Sujatha then leaves, not sparing a single glance at the singer on stage.

"I'm tired," Sujatha says resting her head on her palm.

"I'm tired too. You ready to go back?"

Sujatha nods. "We have to get your car back to Philly though, and us."

"There's no way we can just make that happen? You know like twitch our noses or something?"

"I wish it worked that way. Let's get a taxi back to the car." We haul ourselves up and out of the cozy café and into the brisk night.

🌀🌀🌀

After an uneventful taxi ride back to the car, we survive the excruciatingly boring ride up I-95 back to Philly by reading the papers Savvy gave us. We have to memorize the information to take with us. Some of it is in Russian so we have to download a translator and try to interpret the information. Most of it is standard biographical information – educational history, awards won, a brief resume, a scant mention of family. We search for something we can use as leverage, or blackmail, or influence but it is all pretty tame. We repeat it and repeat it and repeat it so that we can carry it across with us. Our only break from the monotony is a delightful rest stop at Chesapeake House where they had just cooked a fresh batch of Cinnabons for the early morning truckers.

I drop Sujatha off at her parents' home in South Philly, then drive myself to my parent's house where I fall asleep as soon as I hit the bed.

Before I awake I can hear my sister complaining to my mom about her curfew. The house smells of coffee, bacon and pancakes, and I want to stay here, in this moment, listening to my mom and sister have the same argument they have had fifty times before. But duty calls or rather, my hand itches. Half asleep, I scratch it but it keeps itching. I look at it, and the tattoo brings me right back to the mission. I think of Savvy's face last night and pray the information she gave me is correct.

I get up and stuff the envelope in my bedroom closet, under boxes of old report cards and certificates. I don't think I'll ever need it, but if I do, maybe I'll be able to find it again. I repeat the biography one more time and try to visualize the words on the page. Then I take a big breath, close my eyes, press my thumb into my tattoo and seek out mySELF. Resting on that wave I send myself back and back and back to the warehouse.

Chapt**e**r **3**2

Sujatha is already back. Her chair is empty and I hear her talking with Amy in the next room. On a whiteboard across the room, she has written the information we memorized. I walk up to it, correct a couple of things, add a line she missed and stare at her translation of his family history. It isn't quite what I remember, so I write my version underneath. I step back … everything else seems fine. Over my shoulder, I can see Amy and Sujatha come in the room.

"Well," says Sujatha, "What do you think?" Amy reads over the board.

"It's great except it tells us nothing except where he came from. There's nothing else that we can leverage, at least as far as I can see. What do you think, Kim?"

"I think we need to go to Russia, the Sverdlovsk Oblast to be exact. Should we get ready?" I look at Sujatha who smiles back at me.

"No," Amy steps forward, "I should go with you. I know some Russian. I used to be obsessed with Pussy Riot. You know them?" I shake my head no, annoyed at my disappointment. "I'll play you some on the plane. They were very radical back in the day. Marched topless, spoke out on women's rights, artists' rights, gay rights."

"And then what happened?" I ask.

"They disappeared, one by one. They never found the bodies though. Anyway, I want to go. I'm pretty good at detective work and … I will probably blend in better." Sujatha and I exchange a look, both of us too brown to blend. She had a point.

My mother called me the next morning to tell me that Lil' Walter was out of the coma and recovering. She sounded so exhausted that I didn't bother to tell her where I was going, only that I was with friends. That sufficed.

🌿 🌿 🌿

Two days later, Amy and I are on a plane, eating turkey and stuffing and practicing Russian phrases with a language app. The plane is filled with mostly Russian businessmen in suits and American students with long beards and duffle bags. There are few other women – mostly older, well-heeled and meticulously well-mannered – but the men outnumber them at least five to one. Together, Amy and I stick out like sore thumbs, but I get the most stares. I realize they think I am either a singer or a basketball player. I'm kind of short but I try to look sporty anyway. It would be way too easy to call my bluff as a singer. Amy had done her research and made sure that she is wearing the popular style, which is basically feminine but very conservative. She looks like the librarian from "It's a Wonderful Life", glasses, long skirt, frilled white blouse, and sensible heels. I am relaxing in my comfy lounge pants, Old Navy sweatshirt and sneakers. But it all works out in the end.

When we finally get through the long line at Customs, I am accosted at baggage claim by a couple of young men asking me if I am going to join the Ekaterinburg UMMC team. I try to play it off by saying I'm tired and nothing is certain but one of them is persistent and asks for an autograph. He shoves a team picture in front of me. I am trying to give it back to him when a familiar face catches my eye. Meer. Disbelieving, I pull it closer and read the names underneath

… Amira Clarke, forward. I smile at him, trying to mask my reaction to this new information, sign the picture and give it back to him. He thanks me and the two bounce away to find their party.

Amy is looking at me, amusement all over her face.

"Really? We are supposed to be keeping a low profile and here you are signing autographs! Are you serious?"

"You are never going to believe who is here right now."

☙ ☙ ☙

Though we tried to pick non-descript, mid-range accommodations, our hotel is luxurious. The linens, the towels, the carpeting, the cleanliness, and the service are so indulgent that I keep asking Amy to show me the rates again and again. But as we drive through the city I can see that the standard of living is the same all over. It is a big metropolitan city but there is no dirt, no trash, no graffiti, and no homeless people. In fact, the city is so sterile and well-kept that I become suspicious. Where are the poor people? It reminds me of apartheid South Africa when Sun City was the jewel of Africa. But that distinction came at the price of the poor, the colored, and the immigrants who were all cordoned off and kept out. Stuck in slums outside the city, they suffered so that the "city" could appear flawless. Looking out onto Yekaterinburg's streets, I keep looking into the negative spaces and wondering where? Where? Where? Once I run in to a cleaning person who, though tidy and mannerly, cowers and scurries and refuses to speak in more than a whisper. The dullness of her skin and hair make me think of a hospital patient, one who hasn't been outside in months.

Amy, secure in her disguise and fledgling Russian, ventures out into the cold every morning to research Wasserman's life. She finds and tours Wasserman's old schools and past addresses trying to find some link or connection that we can exploit. I stay inside trying to get in touch with Meer. It turns out that all basketball players, even the female basketball players are treated like A-list celebrities in Russia. They have personal assistants and press people and bodyguards and are hounded by the paparazzi. Nobody believes me when I say I know Meer from high school. Apparently, I am not the first to use that line. After three days of getting nowhere, I come up with a rather obvious plan.

※ ※ ※

The arena is small but packed with fervent fans. Meer is a rookie on the local team. She backs up the aging but still very popular Australian 6'9 superstar, Jane Smith. They are playing a team whose fervent fans tend to follow them to every game, so half the crowd is dressed in the Ekaterina gold and black, while the other half wears bright green and purple. It is quite dizzying and we are lucky to get a seat. Amy is not a basketball fan but is happy for the distraction. I spend the whole first quarter studying the security, which is incredibly tight. I spend the next quarter focusing my non-existent psychic powers to make Meer look at me while Amy munches away on popcorn. The game is pretty good but "our" team is down and the coach is apoplectic. I remember her from Meer's college basketball scouting sessions. She coached for Baylor but was let go after some well-guarded scandal. As the half winds down, I watch fans approach the tunnel to the locker rooms. The guards stay close but they let the fans, mostly young girls, get close enough to get autographs. The bench players, which include Meer, enter the tunnel first while the stars linger to give quick autographs and interviews.

After using the restroom (also scrupulously clean), Amy and I take the long way back to our seats and luck into the one bar selling alcohol. We are sitting at a high-top table, grinning at each other and toasting our good fortune when Amy freezes. She ducks her head and swears under her breath.

"What?" I ask, too nervous to look for myself.

"Sshhhhh! Drink your drink, laugh, act natural," she whispers.

I sip my cocktail and conjure up my best fake laugh and Amy responds in kind. She flips her hair down and pretends to rummage in her purse as a couple of men pass us heading back to the game.

"That was him!" she says.

"You are kidding me. Wasserman?"

She downs her drink and shakes away the sting of it.

"Shouldn't have done that. Uh … Anyway, yes. I can't be sure if he would know me or my face. I didn't want to take the chance though."

"What do you think he's doing here?"

"I don't know. It probably depends on who that other guy was." The buzzer sounds signaling the beginning of the second half. We leave a tip, hope it was adequate and hurry back to our seats.

Meer gets some good playing time at the top of the half – she scores 6 points and steals a ball to the delight of the crowd. I watch her and try not to fall back in love. It was so long ago but watching her play brings it all back. I allow a tiny part of myself to be proud of her. Who knew she would have the courage to come to Russia to follow her passion? I really didn't think about what she would do after college basketball. While I contemplate Meer's life, Amy spends her time scouring the crowd until she finds Wasserman sitting behind the visiting teams bench. He is sitting with two little girls and an older boy. Amy is thrilled.

"Gotcha."

A second later the Jumbotron features the smiling face of the other guy. The announcer says something in Russian, of course, I pick out the word spasibo … thank you. The guy smiles and waves and sits down.

"I think that's the owner of the other team," said Amy.

"I think you're right. What does he have to do with Wasserman?"

"I don't know, but most of these teams are owned by big businessmen looking for good publicity."

"Hmm … I'm going to try and follow him."

"The owner?"

"No Kim, Wasserman! We've been here three days and nothing. I'm not going to let this opportunity get away from me."

"I don't think it's safe, Amy."

"No, but he has his kids with him, so I'm betting that he's going home and I'm hoping if he does see me, he wouldn't do anything in front of them."

"Seems very risky to me, Amy."

"Do you have any better ideas?" she asks. I didn't.

"I'm just going to try and tail him in a cab. I want to know where he lives so I can do better snooping, ok?"

"Ok."

"What's your plan?"

"I plan on getting my program signed. Hopefully they let me up there. I thought I might try to get going when there's about ten minutes left in the game."

"Ok, so we'll leave at the same time."

Fifteen minutes later we hug goodbye and head through the concession tunnel in opposite directions. I head down towards the tunnels, trying to guess the right entrance back into the arena. I find it with only a minute to spare. The score is close but our team pulls it out at the end with a dunk from Smith in the last five seconds. I position myself behind a group of pre-teens in team sweatshirts. They seem like they would be naturals to get some attention. I am only about five feet from the exit route. After the obligatory team high-five line, the teams start towards the tunnel. My heart rate speeds up when I spot Meer. The girls start waving their pens and paper and I realize that I am about to be lost in the sea of arms. I move to the left, and squeeze in between the girls' team and a young man with a Hornets baseball cap. The team is walking too fast and Meer is busy talking and joking with one of her teammates. I yell out.

"Meer!!!" She disappears under the overhang and I think I blew it until I see her sneak back along the wall against the current of players and coaches.

"Kim?" Eyes locked, a million memories fly between us. She starts to walk towards me but a security guard steps in and shakes his head. She speaks to him in halting Russian and points at me but he just shakes his head again. She holds up a finger signaling me to wait. I nod, find a seat and wait. A scant fifteen minutes later, the crowd has thinned, the reporters are packing up their laptops, the crew coil their cables and the maintenance people begin their night shift. I'm trying to figure out what to say when I hear a throat clear behind me.

"Kim?" Startled, I turn to see a silver-haired man in a neat black suit.

"Yes?"

"I am Sergey, Meer's driver. She said to fetch you and have you wait in the car for her. She will be out shortly." I sit there for a minute trying to be sure I understand him through his thick accent. He clears his throat then begins to repeat himself but this time with hand gestures.

"I am Sergey. I drive Meer, your friend, yes? She plays basketball, yes?" He makes dribbling moves with his hands. "You will wait with me …"

"… in the car." I complete the sentence for him. "Yes. I'm sorry. I understand. I'm just … surprised. Thank you so much." I stand up. He nods and motions for me to follow him. Meer has a driver?!?!

☙ ☙ ☙

Twenty minutes in the warmed butter leather seats of the car is enough time for me to realize that I need to come up with a plausible excuse for being in Russia. Luckily, Sergey helps me. As soon as we get in the car, he begins to chat about the game, the traffic, the weather and all the English that Meer is teaching him. Then he asks me why I came to Yekaterina. I open my mouth to make a bathroom excuse when he answers his own question.

"You look very smart. I bet you are here to study, am I right? You have a very serious face, like a scholar. I had a scholar in here once. I forget what he said ... fullback, fulfill scholar or something like that. Very serious fellow, that one. He made me nervous, actually, to tell the truth. Ahh, here she is, Amira, love that name, don't you? The way it rolls off the tongue ..." Before I can answer, he jumps out and opens the car door for her. She slides in grinning.

"You really are here. Hot damn!"

"I am." She throws her duffle bag on the floor and reaches over to give me a quick awkward hug. Sergey jumps back in the driver seat and pulls into traffic.

"Ms. Amira, where would you like to go? Home or would you like to go to restaurant, get something for your friend to eat?"

She turns to me. "You hungry?" Eyebrow raised, she waits for my answer. I bite my lip, ignoring the flutters in my stomach.

"A little I guess, but I know you're tired. We can relax ..." I realize that besides finding her, I have no plan at all.

"How about we pick up a little take out? Some fine Russian cuisine? How about Puccini's, Sergey?"

"That place again? Amira, you really should eat better, you're an athlete, and your friend, she should have some good food, she needs to study!"

"Study?" Meer turns towards me. "Of course! What are you studying here in Russia, Kim?"

"Um actually, I was thinking of applying for a Fulbright here in Russia. I'm here to do a little research and then I saw you on a flyer."

"You saw me? What one of those promo flyers? I look so stupid."

"Yes, and I didn't think you looked stupid, I thought you looked good. Anyway, that's how I found out you were here."

"Happy coincidence."

"Yeah, just a lucky coincidence."

"So, you hungry?"

"Take-out is fine with me."

"Good," Meer replies. "Sergey, my guest would like the finest pizza in Yekaterina."

"Fine," Sergey growls. "Puccini's it is." He reaches in the glove compartment, pulls out a menu and thrusts it at us, grumbling under his breath. We spend some time deciding what to eat. The menu is in Russian but the pictures are clear enough. Meer decides to order a pasta dish for herself. I order a cheese pizza and Pelmeni on the side (Sergey insisted). Sergey orders something too. I have no idea what it is but when we pick up the food, it smells like sauerkraut.

During the ride we keep the conversation pretty casual. We talk about the game, her team, her crazy life in Russia, the cold, cold weather and she tries to teach me a few Russian words to no avail. Sergey drops us off in front of her building and we bid a hasty goodbye with the wind stinging our faces. Inside, Meer nods to the doorman, the receptionist at the front desk and we whisk ourselves into an open elevator. It is black and gold and mirrored. I turn to tell her I am sorry for just showing up but she raises a hand and a finger to her lips.

"Not here, Kim." I hold my tongue and look at her in the reflection. She just shakes her head. We get off on the 12th floor and walk down a long, dim hallway. It is quiet, conservative, tasteful. I am getting claustrophobic. At last she stops and sticks a key in a door while pressing her thumb to a pad on the right of the keyhole. The latch clicks and we step into a large and airy living area. There is a large chocolate brown leather sofa facing an even larger television screen with a scattering of DVDs and game disks in front of it. From the entrance, I can see the kitchen area, set off by a bar and large island with tall barstools. But the light coming in through the large windows catches me off guard after the darkness of the hallway. Meer steps over to a far wall and pushes a button. Privacy blinds descend from the ceiling leaving most of the light but obscuring the view of the city glowing in the late afternoon sun.

She walks back to me and takes the food and my purse and sets them down on a table behind me. I open my mouth to speak but nothing comes out. She steps in close and places her finger under my chin to tilt my lips up to meet hers. They are still cool from the outside, stiff in their unfamiliarity, their uncertainty. But all that soon melts away. When my lips touch hers, I almost weep with the gratification of homecoming. I have missed her so and I fall into kissing her like a prayer. She tastes the same, her lips soft but not weak, her mouth molding to mine as it has so many times. Her hand is on my back holding me close, the other entwines in the hair at the nape of my neck. I reach up and touch her cheek, her mouth, her delicate ear, remembering the shape of her face, the arch of her eyebrow. I touch a tear and wipe it away. With my other hand I reach to her waist and follow the curve of her lower back opening to the swell of her ass. I am so lost in her, I don't notice the passing of time until I hear her stomach growl. She laughs in my mouth and I swallow it like communion.

"Hungry?" I whisper.

"In so many ways," she whispers back. She lifts her head to gaze into my eyes.

"God, I did not know how much I missed you, Kim. I can't believe you're actually here."

"Meer ... I don't want to talk." She laughs, but I lift her shirt and cup her breast, her nipple hardening in my palm. She leans down to kiss me again, this time with growing passion. She takes my hand from under her shirt and pulls me into the bedroom behind her. There we kiss and undress each other. She pushes a button and Marvin Gaye's "Let's Get it On" spills out into the room. I laugh and she takes that moment to push me gently back on to the bed while she kneels over me and kisses me from my lips, down my neck, and lingers over my left breast. I swear my heartbeat speeds up just to match the rhythm of her breath. Her kisses resume, igniting small fires on my skin as they travel down to my hips. She takes her time unbuttoning my pants and pushes them down to my knees. I look down at her locks trailing along my skin, and my long suppressed love for her nearly bursts my heart. As much as my clitoris is aching for her mouth, I want to feel all of her on me. The solidness, the realness of her is what my soul needs, so I pull her up and kiss her while I finish undressing the both of us. We sit naked for a minute, remembering and then we lay down and make love face to face, skin to skin, beating heart to breast, hips rocking a slow rhythm that I ride to an achingly sweet oblivion. At the moment of my orgasm, my closed eyes see Meer in a hundred universes, making love to me. At that moment, mySELF expands into herSELF and somehow they rise and crash in the same wave and I feel her orgasm as my own and there is something more. When mySELF … ourSELVES expand and shoot up and out we touch/ride/connect what I can only describe as a GODwave. It is electric and keen and full of raw power. It is the briefest of moments but time itself pauses to take note then we hurtle back down into ourselves and the wave crests and crashes and we float back into our separate selves. We lay still in each other's arms. Slowing our breathing, slowing our hearts, staying quiet, not wanting to leave that sacred space.

"My God Kim," she murmurs. I kiss her, breathe her in. Her stomach grumbles. We both chuckle. I open my eyes and remember where I am. She pulls a thick down comforter on top of us and I nestle into her body.

"Kim? I don't even know what to say about … did you…"

"Shhhhh…." I cut her off. "Not yet, not yet, not yet." And then I fall asleep.

卐 卐 卐

Meer got up early in the morning and went to practice. I remember her kissing me on my forehead and promising to be back in a couple of hours. I try to fall back to sleep but the sound of her heavy front door closing and locking startles me and triggers a vigilance that I can't shake. So I get up and play pretend. I take a 30-minute shower then put on some of her clothes and wash out my underwear in the sink. I eat some grapes and cereal. I play a video game. I stretch. I walk around the apartment and inspect her stuff. There is a picture of a woman I don't know on her fridge. She's cute, I guess. On her wall are some vacation pictures but all the people in the photos look like teammates. She has a laptop on a small corner desk but I don't open it. I have some self-respect. I glance in her closets, they are full of work-out gear of course, along with fifteen pairs of sneakers and 2 pairs of winter boots. I look out the window and wonder what I will say when she comes home. Just after noon she returns with bags of take-out. She seems surprised and relieved to see me.

I get up from the couch and hug her tightly. Until she came back through the door, I wasn't sure if she would. I am feeling a bit unglued. It is disorienting to shift through dimensions and travel back and forth in time but to be back in the same room with your ex, after years of getting over her ... well that is a most disconcerting feeling. I cannot forget what she did to me. The betrayal and the abandonment have cut too deep but I still love her. She pulls away from me.

"I'm sorry, really sorry for what I did to you and to us, Kim. I know I can't change any of that now but I am. Being over here, I didn't think I'd ever see you again. But now that you are here, I want you to know that I am really sorry and I hope you can forgive me." She let out a big breath.

"You practiced?" I ask.

"I wanted to get it right."

"I accept your apology. I'm sorry too."

"But you didn't do anything."

"No, not to you. I'm sorry I followed you to Connecticut. Not because I didn't love you. I did. I just should have loved myself more and pursued my dream, not yours." Now, I exhale. I'd been practicing that speech since I finally figured it out. She absorbs that truth and nods.

"I hadn't thought about that."

"Well, I have. And your cheating put me back on track, so thank you for that ... I guess." She leans back on the counter and crosses her arms.

"So are you a rocket scientist yet?"

"Yes and no and almost. I'm at MIT but trying to get a fellowship at NASA ... oh, and if that doesn't work, a Fulbright to study ... here, in Russia."

"Ahhh. Ok, well do I get a vote?"

"No, not in the least." She laughs.

"Fair enough. How long are you here for?"

"Not long ... a few more days. I'm here with a friend who is also doing ... research but we should be going back soon."

"You don't have a ticket yet?"

"Its kind of flexible ... it's hard to explain."

"Oh, ok. But you'll be here tonight, right? Can you stay at least one more night? I got food." She waves her hands towards the bags on the counter.

"Yeah, I'm definitely staying at least one more night with you." Her smile lights up the room and makes my heart flutter.

After lunch, we play a couple of video games and talk. Meer leans back with her controller.

"We have an away game tomorrow with Alapayevsk. The bus will pick me up at 2, but if you want to come, I can have Sergey drive you there and then we can drive back together."

"Isn't that the same team you played yesterday?" I asked.

"Yeah, it's a small league and we play a lot of back to backs. They are like mini-series. Gets the crowd more hype to see who will win two out of three, you know?"

"Yeah. I was wondering about the owners. It's so weird not have a team named after a city or a state."

"Yeah, takes some getting used to but it's no big deal. We are owned by this guy who owns a lot of mines .. isn't that crazy? And the team we are playing is owned by some kind of oil tycoon."

"Really? I thought I saw him last night, thanking the crowd or something?"

"Yeah, he donated some money to a local orphanage or something."

"Oh, interesting ... do you know his name?"

"Something Yeltsneft. Yeltsneft Oil, you know."

"Never heard of it but ok."

"He's a big deal but all these old Russian guys are, you know. They are stinky fucking rich. Don't even know what to do with all their money so they buy teams just to have something else to put their names on."

"How do you like playing for them?"

"My pocket likes it very much. But it can get lonely, you know." I sneak a peek at her. I never thought about her being lonely. Both our characters run out of health and die. Game over. I put my controller down and stand up to stretch.

"I should probably check on my friend. I don't even know if my cell phone works here."

"Probably not. At least not in this building ..." She leans in to me. "I'm pretty sure this building is monitored all the time." I stare back at her. "The government is no joke here. I think some politicians live in this building and they have it tapped. I'm not paranoid but I'm just saying ... I try to be careful about my phone conversations, you know?"

I decide to send a quick text instead ...

I'm hanging with my pal. Will be back in the morning. Amy doesn't respond but service has been spotty since we arrived so I'm not too concerned.

Meer and I decide to watch an old Eddie Murphy comedy and laugh our asses off. I am like a thief ...stealing time, stealing someone else's life. I tell her I'm leaving in the morning. I say I have a meeting with someone from the Fulbright organization. She accepts my excuse and I have a feeling even she knows that this honeymoon is borrowed. There isn't anything else to talk about so we put on Funkadelic, light some incense, drink cognac and have sex. Lots of it. And it is good. We make the most of it ... warding off the ending even as we are in the middle of it. Every orgasm flaring up into distant galaxies then drifting back to earth with a sigh. In the morning, we manage the mundane tasks of bathing, tooth brushing and fixing our hair side by side in the bathroom mirror. She turns to me and asks if I am ok.

"I will be. I do have some heavy stuff to take care of, but I can and I will. You know me, I can handle it." She seems like she is considering asking more but then decides against it. She has her life, her contract and her season to think about. And I have my "stuff".

"If you have time, come back, ok? I put my number in your phone. I have my schedule but when I'm not playing or practicing, I'm here, ok?"

"Ok. I'll call you if we stay longer. I promise."

Sergey seems surprised to see me when we get in the car but Meer plays it cool. They drop me off at my hotel and then drive off through a light snowfall. I am stirred by a vague memory of our wedding. I think there will be snow. I shake it off and turn toward the hotel hoping to find Amy asleep in bed.

柊 柊 柊

I am disappointed to see the room unchanged from when we left it to go to the basketball game. I inspect the bathroom, the luggage and the refrigerator and don't see any evidence of Amy. I check with reception to see if I have any messages. I do not. And there is nothing coming through on my phone. I sit down and try to think through the possibilities. The next day finds me in the same chair staring out the window and wondering what I should do and how long I should wait. I have the name of the oil tycoon and the village where Wasserman lives and debate going there to look for her. I send her a text every few hours in the hopes that one will reach her. Meer sends me a goodnight text, loneliness writ in every word. I ache for her, I do but I have bigger fish to fry. Where is Amy?

Another day and no Amy. My concern is turning to panic as I scour the newspapers looking at the pictures. No calls, no texts, no emails. I look out the window onto the street below, hoping to see her pseudo-librarian guise. I'm tempted to distract myself with a visit to Meer. The last text made some intriguing promises … but I can't stop thinking about Amy and what might have happened to her. The hotel sends a bill on the day we are supposed to check out. I extend our stay. I watch the weird state run television stations for news of some sort. I eat a little but not enough. My stomach is permanently clenched, my heart like a drum beating out warning. What should I do if she doesn't come back? It's been five days since I've seen her. I wish Sujatha was here. I fall into an uneasy sleep.

At first, I think I am dreaming when I hear the door latch open then close. I open my eyes but don't move. It is dark and I can't be sure who's in the room. They go to the kitchenette, opening and closing the small fridge. Then I hear tiny tapping and a swoosh. Then a snap and the room lights up. I turn my head and see it is her, awash in blue. I gasp and she looks up and into the bedroom to see me jumping up and running towards her. She shuts the laptop and jumps up to hug me.

"Amy! Oh my God, I'm so glad you're ok. I was so worried!"

She hugs me hard and once I calm down I pull back and ask her, "Where the hell have you been? Are you ok? What happened?" She plops down on the sofa and says, "It's a long story Kim. You sure you want to hear it now? It's late and I'm tired."

"Oh, I want to hear it." She sighs and takes a big gulp of water.

"Ok. After the game, Wasserman and the bigwig he was with got in a car with the kids. I grabbed a cab and followed them. Wasserman and the kids got dropped off at the train station. So I followed them onto a train. I was lucky to be able to buy a ticket on the train. We ended up going almost to the end of the line, got off at a town called Alapayevsk. By now, it was late so I kept my distance, but they got into a car parked at the station and left. There were no cabs. So I slept at the station."

"What, like on a bench?" I am mortified.

"Yup … I didn't sleep much and it was freezing but what else could I do? It was like one in the morning, no cabs and I had no idea where I was."

"You should have called me."

"Why? I didn't want to leave. Anyway, in the morning the workers came, the station opened and I was able to figure out my next step. I walked to the main street and found a café, then I found a library, then, after a couple of days, I found Wasserman. Turns out he's a scientist who works for an oil company."

"Yeltsneft Oil?" I ask. She furrows her brows at me.

"Yes, Yeltsneft Oil. He works at the company's administrative offices in the town. He lives with his wife, kids and his parents in the poor section of the town. But here's the funny thing. It took me so long to get all this information because he goes by a different name. Moshe Aleichem is his real name. Wasserman is his wife's maiden name!"

"That's weird. Why would he change his name? Maybe he's running from a crime or something?"

"Maybe, but here is Russia, there is still a lot of anti-Semitism. I think he was running from being Jewish."

"That makes sense. Also, didn't Savvy's notes say he was from a wealthy, notable family or something like that?"

"Yeah, that's what his official bio said but that is not true, at least it isn't today, you know what I mean?"

"Can we use that as blackmail? It sounds terrible I know, but if he wants to keep his Jewish identity hidden, can we use it as blackmail?"

"I don't know. I don't know if it's enough."

"Can we use it to get him killed?" Amy gawks at me.

"I'm just asking Amy! Otherwise, what are we doing here? We are trying to stop the world from being destroyed, right? If he is the key, then he is a sacrifice."

Amy replied, "I'm pretty sure that he is not the key." I swallow hard.

"So what? I am? I should be sacrificed? Is that what you are saying?" I stand up, heart racing and feeling very suspicious of her all of the sudden.

"No, calm down, Kim, that's not what I'm saying. I'm saying that he is one scientist, one scientist of many working for this Yelsneft guy. I don't think killing him will change anything. There will always be another scientist."

"Kill Yelsneft, then?" Amy rolls her eyes at me.

"What is wrong with you Kim? Even if we were those kind of people … This guy is crazy rich. He has bodyguards with guns, *big* guns. What could you or I do about him?"

"So what, we just give up? We just go back home?"

"I think so. That was my best shot and I really didn't learn anything except where Wasserman works. Yelsneft could be calling the shots, bankrolling the research from behind the scenes but I don't see a way to stop it from here and now."

"Maybe we could go after a younger Yelsneft or his company?"

"We could but what if it doesn't matter in the long run? And if it's not him, it'll be some other rich guy who wants to get richer. I'm sorry but this was a complete waste of time." Amy props her head on her hand and sighs.

"Well," I say grinning, "not a complete waste of time …" Her face searches mine.

"Did you hook up with Meer?"

"I did!" And then I tell her the whole story.

卍 卍 卍

Though I want to see Meer again, I know it is not our time, so I don't. I can't lie though; we did sext the night Amy went to the airport and bought our plane tickets. We fly home on a Sunday, get there on a Tuesday and I sleep until Thursday.

Chapter **33**

Amy is gone when I wake up. Sujatha is reading a book in the corner of the room and I am sore all over. I sit up and clear my throat. Sujatha glances at me over the top of her glasses.

"Hi" is all I can manage. My nose is stuffed up, my throat burns and I am exhausted.

"Hello. Seems like you brought back a souvenir from Russia."

I groan. "Where's Amy?"

"I was going to ask you the same thing. I went out for food and when I came back she was gone. Really gone, not shifted, at least not here anyway." I groan again and rub my neck.

"Oh dear. I'll go check for medicine." She gets up and begins rifling around the rooms. I start to get out of bed but I am dizzy and lay back down.

"Did she tell you what happened?" I try to talk loud enough so she will hear me but it comes out a crackly whisper. Sujatha returns with two bottles.

"All we seem to have is ibuprofen and a sleep aid. Sorry. I'll go and get you some cold medicine, ok?" She turns to go.

"Wait! Please." She turns back. "What did Amy tell you, Sujatha?"

"All she said was that you didn't find anything usable. She said it was a dead-end."

"Did she tell you Wasserman was Jewish?" Sujatha nods and shrugs. "Did she tell you about Meer?"

"She mentioned that you ran into her. How was that?" She puts her hand on her hip. I clear my throat again.

"It was … nostalgic."

"Hmmm … well, I'm going out before it gets dark. You should rest. You don't look good." I watch her walk away and hear the heavy door slam shut. I am shivering and miserable. I grab my phone from the table next to the bed and tuck myself back in. My battery is on 8%. I look through my texts and read the ones from Meer. I hope Sujatha hasn't seen them. I delete them. Best to let it lie for now. Where the hell is Amy? I look through my pictures … nothing new. I scroll through my email … nothing but the usual junk mail. The only thing that catches my eye is a new app. It just has a small red "j" in the center of an olive-green button. I tap it open and it closes in the blink of an eye. I tap it again and the same thing happens. I want to ask Sujatha about it but I fall asleep as my battery slips down to 2%.

When I awake, Sujatha is back in her chair, this time watching something on a screen with headphones. It takes a lot of hand flapping to get her attention. She slides the headphones off her ears. ….

"I'm bored."

"Sorry," I croak. I close my eyes and hear a big sigh as I fall back to sleep. Sometime later I open my eyes to see Sujatha talking on the phone. Sometime after that someone gave me a pill and when I awake again I am a lot better. Sujatha and Amy are across the room talking.

"Ok, but we need to have a meeting. We need all of us. Have you received any new messages?" Amy shakes her head and Sujatha sucks her teeth in disgust. She looks over at me and I lift my hand in greeting. Smiling, she walks out the room. Amy sits down next to me.

"How are you feeling?"

"Better. I don't know what I got but I got it bad."

"Yeah." She picks up my phone and looks at it.

"It's dead. I'll plug it in for you." I notice she has a freshly inked tattoo on her left wrist, a tiny flower with seven red petals. I'm about to ask her about it when Sujatha returns with steaming chicken noodle soup for me.

Amy gets up to make room and takes my phone with her. I'm about to ask her about the strange app but Sujatha sticks a spoonful of soup in my mouth instead. Distracted by Sujatha's uncharacteristic nurturing, I forget all about my questions.

Chapter 34

It takes two days to track down and get messages to the rest of the group. Ramon was on mission for Patel and returns nervous as hell. When we ask him what he had to do, he is vague and deflective. The others seem to understand. I am annoyed but he won't meet my eyes and I leave it alone. Grayson is still missing, but Manny is confident that he is ok.

When everyone is seated and finished chit-chatting, we get down to business. Amy, Sujatha and I report our failed attempts to find anything to change the situation. Marcus and Liam both had been going back to reverse some of their missions but were also unable to change anything significant. We are back to square one, and the consensus is that I have to go back to the farmhouse. It is a moment of reckoning. If I go back and destroy the techniques and evidence of Patel's research, what will happen to our abilities? What will happen to the group, their lives, their relationships? Will we remember any of it? I realize that what I have been thinking of as my sacrifice would be a sacrifice for everybody. We all have to agree to give up our superpower, the one thing that makes us special and different from anybody else in the world.

There is a lot of debate and some begin to try and find other alternatives. Marcus and Ramon argue that we should all travel back to our births and just live our lives again. What are the odds we will make all the same choices? I am surprised to hear Sujatha in a passionate argument with Manny about trying to find Grayson and getting him to wipe out Patel and Wasserman's ancestors. I think of all of us, she enjoys the freedom of jumping the most. Others are resigned to jump to their favorite timelines and hope that it will be all they remember. Amy is sitting in a corner, watching the discussions and looking thoughtful. I walk over to her and sit at her feet.

"I already know that I will try to get back to this timeline. I know Phobos is ahead for me. Phobos and Meer. Whatever happens, I will try to get back here." Amy tilts her head quizzically.

"You'll be the only one left with the ability to jump."

"I guess, but when I go back, I don't know if I'll remember how."

"But you might."

"I might."

"Lucky you." She sits back in her seat and crosses her arms. I stand up.

"Lucky? I have no idea what will happen. I might not be able to jump out at all and I'll be stuck in a building with Russians who want to kill me. You call that lucky?"

"You'll get away. I know you will."

"What are you getting at Amy? This isn't about me. Isn't this what we *have* to do? Isn't this what we *all* decided?" The various conversations come to an abrupt end and everyone is looking at us. She stands up to look me in the eye. She studies me for a moment. I hold her gaze, desperate to find an explanation for this sudden change in attitude.

"I didn't mean anything by it Kim. I'm just a little freaked out and I'm going to miss you, all of you." She looks around the room. "But yes, it has to be done, we all know that. I was just making an observation. I'm sorry." She reaches out to hug me and I embrace her firmly. I want her to know how much she means to me. She lets go first and withdraws into a corner of the room. I let her go. I'm tired.

In the end, we have to move forward. Sujatha volunteers to set the bombs. Between Google maps, my spotty memory and Manny finding a news article on Joan's murder site, we are able to come up with an address for the farmhouse. We zoom in and I am confident that we have it right. The plan is simple. In 23AK, I am the only one with the ability to jump, but even Patel is not sure about it. The tapes, Patel, Wasserman and I are all there. One thing we are not sure of is what information is stored on Patel's computers, but Sujatha says she will take care of that, too. After I get abducted, she'll destroy Lab 19 and Patel's office. Sujatha seems gleeful when she begins to teach me about the bombs, where she will place them and how I am to set them off. I am getting nervous about the whole course of action, especially the explosion part.

As the plan takes shape, exhaustion, and maybe melancholy, takes over and one by one, we drift off to find a place to sleep.

卐 卐 卐

I am in a deep sleep on the couch when I feel someone shaking my shoulder. I open my eyes but it is pitch black.

"Kim," Sujatha whispers, "I have a brilliant idea." I try to sit up but can only get as far as my elbow.

"What time is it?" I ask.

"Who cares? Listen, why don't we take a little vacation? We don't know what's going to happen with all this so how about one more trip with me? There's something I want to show you. I promise you will like it."

"A vacation? We can do that?"

"Sure! We'll pop out and pop back. Easy. And I have the perfect timeline. It's very strange though. I ran across it by accident when I was on a mission for Patel."

"Ok, but what about the others? What if they think we bailed on the plan?"

"We'll leave a note, but we won't be gone long. I promise you will love it."

"Ok. Let's do it." She gets up and leads me into the "jumping room". I don't know how she can see so well in the dark. I find my way to a lounger while she opens the fridge and pulls out the vials.

"I was supposed to be following up on some climate regulations... I followed this rogue Senator from the 1960's, a real asshole, who refused and denied every piece of climate change legislation. I found a very thin thread where he gained the support, well, he blackmailed and got the support of his party who then got control of the government ... anyway, it's kind of complicated but there was this tiny, tiny thread that I found stretching through him ... the world if he got his way and all environmental regulations were banned."

"What happened?"

"Oh you have to see it, it's amazing."

"Amazing good or amazing bad? And how can you be sure that I'm there?"

"Now that is the good part ... I remember you from there. We were actually working together in a lab. I was working on making genetic modifications to human DNA to support survival on Earth, and you were working on the creating transportation systems needed for evacuating humans up to space stations."

"Sounds lovely".

"I think you will find it very interesting. Now, it's a thin thread, you have to stay close to me. Do you mind if I lay with you? Sometimes that helps."

"Be my guest."

"Here's your vial." I drink it as she throws back hers and squeezes into the chair with me. She spoons me and I relax into her embrace. Our hands entwine, and she whispers into my ear.

"Let's go now, Kim. Feel me, follow me, stay close."

꩜ ꩜ ꩜

I close my eyes and mySELF takes over. I feel Sujatha'sSELF pulling and guiding me. I let mySELF be steered and ride the gentle wave of me. It seems we are drifting for quite a while, flashes of brightness, snippets of sound play in my peripheral senses. For a dizzying moment, I am upside down and pulling left and up, then I look to the right and see a sliver of green opening itself to me. There is no resistance, so I move toward it and sense an anchoring that jolts me out of my reverie. I am lying on a beach blanket looking up at palm trees, bright sun rising just over the ocean at my feet. I sit up. The sun's warmth is beginning to burn and I start at the voice behind me.

"Hey babe. Let me put some more block on you." I turn to see Sujatha in a white tank top and blue bikini bottom. I remember falling asleep out here after making love to her. We are on a two-day vacation from the lab trying to clear our minds and feel like people again. We are staying in a bungalow on an island in the Arctic ... one of the few places where people can breathe outside without respirators or the new oxysuits. The island is small and exclusive, only the heads of states and the scientists who serve them can get time on it. There are 50 of these artificial islands up here, thanks to the Chinese who barter them for foodstuffs. I remember all of this as much as I remember strategizing with the group in a North Philly warehouse. As my brain wraps itself around, Sujatha's hands are on my back, soft and warm, slathering on the sunblock that will turn my skin temporarily blue. I take a big breath and inhale the coconut scent of it. The ocean, despite its impending death, smells salty. The air thick with humidity manages to conjure up occasional cool breezes. I turn, tilt my head up and kiss her.

"Why didn't you tell me about this?"

"I like to keep some secrets. And honestly, who would believe this anyway? But here we are ... also trying to save the world, well at least the people. My first trip here, we had just come back from this vacation, and I was so confused by our relationship. But then when I met you again at the warehouse, I understood. .... So, how do you like the beach?"

"Well, I can't say I like it. I mean this world is pretty fucking terrible, but I like this ... being here alone with you." She raises her eyebrows.

"Alone? Who said, we were alone?" She claps her hands and a young man in a Hawaiian shirt comes out of the trees behind us.

"James, could we have two frozen lime margaritas, a plate of fresh fruit and a couple's massage?" James bows.

"Of course, Madam Chaudury." He turns and proceeds quickly and smoothly across the sand and through hibiscus bushes where a small path is barely visible. I realize that he is a robo-waiter. Only the top half is animatronic and appears human. The bottom half is a pole that travels on a track. We look at each other and laugh.

恋恋恋

Later, after a candlelit dinner of fish, mangos and honey wine, we relax at the table. The breeze is soft and the night is quiet. I remember the two mass extinction events and sigh over the loss of so much. I miss the birdsong.

"So, should we talk about here or there?"

"I don't think there is much to talk about here. I checked, this thread fades in about twenty years. I don't think anyone gets off-planet and I don't think people survive for too long after we lose that hope."

"So I fail? Well, that sucks."

"No, we all fail. There aren't enough resources, and we can't get to them anyway. Let's talk about there. Amy was weird when she came back, quieter than usual. Did something happen?"

"We spent a couple of days fishing around until we found Wasserman. She was gone for a few days following him but the only dirt she came back with was that he was born Jewish and poor and he tried to hide that. Not much of a smoking gun," I shrug and don't mention Meer.

"Gone for a few days ... that's interesting, so what do you think?"

"I think I have to go back, I think we have to follow the plan. Unless someone else comes up with another answer, I think it has to be me."

She reaches over and grabs my hand. "You are going to have to blow that whole place the fuck to pieces."

"Do you think I can survive?"

"I don't know, I hope you can jump out of there in time. But I really don't know, Kim."

"Ok, enough talk. Is there more wine? Let's get drunk ... I haven't been drunk in a while ... and then let's have some fun, ok?" Sujatha stands up and walks around to my seat at the table. She sits on my lap, cups my breast with her hand and kisses my neck. She murmurs, "Can we just skip to the fun part?" I nod and we do.

❦ ❦ ❦

Two days later, as the helicopter is landing at the lab, we jump back. We open our eyes to find Amy staring at us.

"Seriously?" she says with no small amount of disgust. I clear my throat.

"Sujatha suggested a vacation jump. What's the big deal?" She scoffs at us as we disentangle.

"Well, while you two were doing whatever you were doing, Turkey was annexed by Russia with Iran and Iraq next in line."

Sujatha scoots off the chair. "What?!"

Amy is quiet. I wonder if she is jealous. Maybe she had a thing for Sujatha. I start to walk over to talk to her, but she gets up and starts making tea and scrambled eggs for everybody. I retreat back towards Sujatha. I don't know what would happen with our friendship. We might never meet at all. I try to recall the details of the jump, they are fading but I remember the feeling of Sujatha under me, the sun over me, and the deepening blue of the sky. I am embarrassed by my failure and burdened by the knowledge of how fragile our life on Earth.

卐 卐 卐

Amy awakens everybody and feeds them as she shares the news about Turkey. The mood is friendly despite the gravitas of our situation. After breakfast is cleaned up, we begin to make our final plans. I think half of the group is worried that I won't succeed, the other half worries that I will. As awkward as it now seems, I decide to focus on Meer as my trigger. In 23AK, I never had a relationship with her, but I need to get back to this timeline, 2A2, when she cheats on me and I end up back at Temple to complete my degree. I have to get to Phobos.

Sujatha is the first to leave. She hugs everybody goodbye, making jokes and teasing them as their faces began to fall. I stand back and wait my turn. We go into the hallway for privacy.

"It's been an honor," she says bowing to me.

"That's not funny," I reply, voice quivering. "Thank you."

"For what?"

"For risking your life for this, for me, I guess." She sighs.

"Kim ... all of this has been a most interesting adventure, the parts with you particularly exciting I'd say, but I have been waiting all my life to be a hero. And now, I get to set bombs to kill the bad guys and save the world!?! It's going to be so much fun! I only wonder what will happen to my memories ... I'm going to try and record them if I have the time." And it was true, the rest of us are anxious but Sujatha is energized. I am heartened.

"Ok, then, maybe I'll see you on the other side."

"I hope so." She raises my hand and kisses the Prince tattoo. It leaves a warm buzz there. "Now, I have a lot to do and remember so I'm going."

"Do you want me to sit with you?" She laughs.

"No dear. No distractions." She pecks me on the lips and slides into the room with the tiny fridge and comfy chairs. She closes the door without looking back. I turn back to see the others turn away. I walk down the hall to the bathroom alone.

❦ ❦ ❦

Each person has their favorite timeline and one by one, they leave to go and jump from another location. By 3pm, only Amy and I are left. We decide to delay my jump for a day to watch the threads and see if anything seems off. We binge watch the original Heroes TV show and eat Thai food and popcorn. In the morning, everything seems the same and there is nothing left to do or say.

"So, are you going to stay here?" I ask her.

"Yeah, this timeline is as good as any others. At least I will have the best chance of remembering from here."

"And I'm coming back here. Do you think you'll remember me?" Amy shrugs.

"I have no idea of what will happen once the ability to jump disappears. This warehouse might just become a warehouse, or maybe it's gone, demolished or turned into condos."

"I'd better jump from somewhere else then, right? Maybe Temple?"

"Yeah, that's what I was thinking. You ready to go?"

"I don't want to leave Sujatha there."

"She is where she wants to be. Don't worry Kim." We gather up our important stuff: the notebooks, thread sheets, PCP. At the last minute, we decide to clean the dishes and wipe down the furniture and door knobs with bleach wipes, just in case. No fingerprints … We leave Sujatha behind the closed door. I can hardly see her in the chair but I know she is there, but not there.

The evening is chilly, the sky deep blue and clear promising a night full of stars. Amy drives. I am heavy with the responsibility and the guilt. I am about to close off and shut down this science. I mean, this was a whole new field of inquiry and a whole new branch of existence in this universe that I am going to destroy. It is antithetical to everything I believe and learned as a scientist. But I look at the people we drive by, the mothers, the kids, the young guys hanging out trying to look cool and I know. Humans are not ready for this. Those who get it would exploit it and deny it to others. Some would never know anything about it, only that their lives are getting progressively worse. It is too dangerous and we, as a people, are not evolved enough to handle it. I sigh a deep sigh and we are at Temple's main campus.

"Are you coming with me?"

"No. Whatever happens, happens. I think I'm gonna go home, see if my dad is around, maybe catch some TV with him." I look at her and notice how anxious and distracted she seems. Maybe it was the all the jumps, maybe just the strain of it all but she looks years older than the night we met at the café. It seems 100 years ago but it was only a few months in this thread. This is where she first trained me.

"Amy? Thanks for everything … you taught me everything I know."

"I know and I'm sorry about all of this. I didn't have much choice but I'm sorry I brought you here and got you involved in all of this."

"Yeah … this part sucks but the rest of it was pretty awesome. I'd never been to Russia before." She smiles at me. "Are you ok? You look … stressed out."

"I'm just tired, it's been a long haul. Go on, Kim. Do what you have to do. I'm going to go … and do what I have to do." She reaches over to hug me. I give her a squeeze then get out of the car, dragging one of the backpacks with me. It has the tape player and the PCP vials. I can hear them clinking around.

"Be careful," she calls out, waving through the window. I watch as she pulls off into traffic. I am alone. I trudge up the walkway to the Science Center. The campus is still bustling even at 6pm. I enter the Science Center as a student is leaving and he politely holds the door for me. I take the elevator up to that grungy old lounge and find it as abandoned as it was before. The view is still amazing though and I position my chair to enjoy the city lights. I plug in the tape player and turn the flutes on low. This is my first time going it alone; I want to make sure I do it right. I put a book on my lap so it will look like I have fallen asleep reading if anybody comes in. I pull out my spoon, sip the PCP, then tuck it away before it takes effect. I sit back and think about Phobos and Meer. I try to envision Mable and the lab and Patel and me, younger and happier. I feel ME grow and expand and mySELF begin to bob and disconnect from the here. I focus on younger me and Patel and Mable and Lab 19. I look for us on the horizon as I grow and expand. I am listing right and then falling back, and back and back.

Chapt**e**r **35**

I'm in the lab. I've fallen asleep reading bioethics, again. I will never pass this class at this rate. I check my phone, 9:56pm. Time to pack up and head home. I look around the room warily again. I remember that something strange is going on. I'm turning off the light and closing the door because that is what I always do. I take another look at Mabel; something is nagging at me, but I shut the door and lock it anyway. As I leave the Science Center, another student is entering. She smiles at me. She's cute and seems familiar, but I can't place her. I mumble, "hi" and keep going. When I look back, she's looking at me through the glass. Weird.

I can see the subway station when a hand yanks me from behind and another covers my mouth. The accent is thick and Russian. "Don't even think about trying to fight. You are nothing to me and I will kill you like nothing if you give me any trouble. Get in and you might not get killed." He shoves me into a green van and I tumble in. As he covers my mouth and nose, I have déjà vu. I remember this. I remember this. That's my last thought before I lose consciousness.

I wake up cold and hungry and nauseous. I am lying on a floor … of a van. It's moving. I open my eyes but don't see anything but the floor rug and the feet of the person in the seat in front of me. I try not to move. I try to keep my breathing even. I am groggy but I keep thinking, 'I remember this'. Over and over again until I vomit a little on the floor.

"Hey, she's awake. Asshole just threw up all over the floor."

I felt a kick in my ribs.

"I just cleaned this fucking van, you cunt."

"Sorry." I try to get up but my balance is off. The road is bumpy and I don't feel like my head is clear. The phrase keeps repeating in the background of my brain while I try to work out what is going on.

"Are we almost there?" asks the man who abducted me in his thick, slow speech.

"What are you, my kids?" retorts the driver. He also has an accent, but it is not as thick as the big guy. He sounds smaller, nasally and quick. The big guy grunts, "Fuck you. I have to pee."

Another big bump and my head bangs on the floor. I close my eyes. The van rumbles, the men talk, I smell urine. Gross. The driver turns up the radio. We drive for hours on a highway until the van veers right and slows down. I try to sit up again and feel a little stronger this time. I look out the window. We pass a slight figure on the side of the road bent over a pack or something. I stare as we go by straining to see who and why someone would be out here in the middle of the night. The figure looks up just as we turn a bend, but the pale face is a blur and the figure seems to fade away. I look ahead and see we are approaching a farmhouse. It is dark outside but the windows are glowing with light. Somebody is out front waiting for us. We park and the sound of the gravel gives me pause. As I am guided out the van and into the house, the déjà vu returns but even stronger. I remember this. I look around the house. I tune into the voices. Yes, I remember. I'm supposed to do something here. As we walk down into the cellar, my mission comes back to me. I'm supposed to blow this shit up! I stumble on the stairs. There is a chair, a sandwich, a bottle of water and a toilet with a ragged roll of toilet paper. I sit down. The bouncer guy says, "Wait here."

I turn up to him and say, "For what?"

He shrugs, "You'll find out soon enough. Eat. Wait." He leaves. I remember this all now. I eat the whole sandwich for strength. I drink the water. I pee and use all the toilet paper. I won't be here long. I look around, not sure if there are cameras, so I try to look random and desperate. I see etched in wood, just above the sink, the Prince sign. I smile, she was here. Thank God. OK. I try the doors and windows just for effect, I stamp my foot for good measure but I see the bomb under the stairs, just two little wires sticking out from the dust bunnies and frayed blankets. OK. I continue my pseudo-inspection around the room, but I've already seen the matches; they are taped underneath the chair, and a backup is taped under the windowsill. I slip that one in my hand and into my pocket. I try to be patient. I am nervous. I look at myself in the blackening mirror and try to find courage there. I don't. The Prince sign helps though. She was here. Sujatha was here and she did what she was supposed to do. The cute girl at the Science Center! Yes, Sujatha, OK. She is supposed to wait until night to destroy the lab and Patel's office. Less collateral damage that way. I just have to wait until Patel and Wasserman are here.

When the sky begins to lighten, when I hear the first chirp of the morning (birdsong!). I pull the blue wire out with my foot to start the timer. That puts the bomb in standby mode. I have six hours until it goes off or I can pull the red wire to set it off manually. I should have plenty of time. I remember they came in the morning. I stand by the window and imagine the sunrise to come. I breathe deep and try to relax. I want to be sharp and focused. I imagine what is going on upstairs. I exhale. Then I hear tick... tick... tick ... click coming from under the stairs ... it dawns on me what is happening ... and just as the room explodes around me I throw myself up, out and back with all my might.

I awake with a jump, like from a bad dream. Head on a book, heart beating triple time, hands shaking. It takes a minute to calm myself and gather my thoughts. What happened, what happened? That was like six minutes, not six hours. I pick up my phone, which I must have dropped on the floor. It's 9:57pm. I try to catch my breath, what to do, what to do? I don't want to go back there. I can't. Sujatha. I look around. I remember the cameras. I gather my things. I turn out the light. I wait in the hallway outside the door. I see the outside door open and someone is looking around. A moment later I hear her before I see her come down the hall.

"Psst!" She startles and rushes over to me.

"Kim? What are you doing? You are supposed to be getting abducted right now!"

"I did. I did go back but the bombs went off too early. It went off on me when I was alone!"

"What?!? I triple checked those timers, they were perfect. I swear it Kim."

"Are you sure? Because I almost got killed. Well, I will, I guess. Oh, God, I don't want to die like that."

"I'm so sorry. I'm sure the bombs were perfect when I left them."

"Maybe the timers were defective?"

"No. I'm telling you I checked them. Maybe somebody messed with them."

"Who would mess with them and still leave them there?"

"I don't know." She looks thoughtful. "Everybody agreed to the plan but maybe somebody sabotaged it."

"You think it was one of us?" I am thunderstruck.

"Well, who else could it be? Who else knew where it was? And how it worked? It had to be one of us. … it wasn't me though Kim. I swear." I think back to the warehouse. I can't imagine any of them trying to kill me. I just can't. But then I recall the figure by the side of the road and I know who it was. My heart sinks. Amy? I don't share my suspicions with Sujatha. I don't want her to tell me I'm crazy but more than that, I don't want her to tell me I'm right.

"Ok, what now? I have two more live bombs in my backpack for the lab and Patel's office."

I close my eyes and run through all possible scenarios until I have my solution.

"Ok, place the bombs in his office to go off six hours from now. I'm going back in."

"Into the lab? For what?"

"I'm going back in this timeline and I'm going to mess up his experiment. I won't let it succeed at all."

"Ahh."

"The bombs are just a backup, Ok?"

"Ok. But what does that mean for jumping into another thread?"

"It probably means I won't be able to. But you will. Set the bombs and then go, go wherever you like." Sujatha looks at me.

"And you'll be stuck here."

"Yeah. I'll be stuck here. I don't see any other way to be sure."

"What about Phobos?"

"If I can get to it in 2A2, I can get to it here. I'll be fine." She leans in to kiss me and I lose myself in it until she pulls away.

"So, you really are the hero then huh?" I smirk. She shrugs on her backpack and gives me a mock salute.

"I hope I see you again Kim."

"I hope so too!" I reply with a grin. She turns and rounds the corner to the elevators. I turn and put my key back in the lock to open the door to lab 19.

I switch on the light and close the door behind me. I sit down and work out my plan. My main concern is that I won't remember. What reminder can I give myself in the past? I dig through my book bag and find my calculator. I turn it off and then on again. It blinks the date 1 1 01 and the time 12:00am. It just blinks and blinks. I remember deciding not to set the date and time because that was just a waste of time. I mean who would set the date and time on a calculator? The same

Nikki Harmon

person who would use the alarm on a calculator. If I make that little change, I could set the alarm, maybe. It was worth trying. The alarm could go off every night, just after midnight, I bet that would remind me if I didn't crush it out of annoyance first. I set the time and the alarm for 12:19, then I think back to that moment of not setting and I choose to set it. I see myself sigh in great annoyance and resignation because ... what if I needed it one day and I watched/felt/decided to set the date and time. I hear the roar back in the back of my head, my eyes blur and the date appears on the calculator. I check the alarm; it is still on. I hope for the best and stuff it in my backpack. As I am dropping it back to the ground, I have another idea. I grab a small notepad, make a few notes, rip off the page and jam it into one of the inner pockets of my backpack. Satisfied, I shove it away.

Then I settle into my chair and try to remember the first time I came into this lab. This job seemed so cool. I remember giving Mabel her name, the first thing I sprayed on her was seawater, which I could tell she did not like, she seemed to turn a little brown and limpy. The rest were kind of hard to discern, they were mostly clear without much smell. Of course, now I know why but then I just thought they were too diluted. I look around and think I will be able to substitute the bottles easily. I say a quick prayer. Me, virtually an atheist, prayed. I'm all about covering my bases. I am confident that I won't need any drugs to go back and I don't. I close my eyes, think about giving the plant her the name Mabel, think about how cool my first work-study job was and throw myself back there. I hear the roar, fall backwards and land right where I was.

❧ ❧ ❧

I spray Mabel one last time and check my phone, it is 9:59pm. I pack up, turn out the lights and head out to the subway to get home. I am feeling pretty good about this semester.

Classes are manageable, professors are interesting and challenging, and I just started a new cushy work-study assignment, which pays for all of my books with a little left over for food. I am feeling pretty satisfied with life.

That night I go to bed at 11:45pm only to be awakened by a tiny beeping sound. I can't figure out where it's coming from and I decide to go back to sleep.

The next night, I go to bed at 11:05pm, and am jolted awake again by a tiny beeping sound. I remember it from the night before but am not getting up out of my bed. I put my covers over my head and go back to sleep.

The following night I am watching the *Star Trek* movie marathon when I hear the tiny beeping again. At the commercial, I get up to investigate. It isn't in the den; it isn't in the bathroom where I stop to pee and it isn't in the kitchen, where I stop to pick up a couple more cookies. The noise stops and I go back to Star Trek and forget about it.

The next night I am up studying for a test and I hear the tiny beeping noise again. This time it is by my foot. I looked in my book bag and pull out my calculator. It's flashing "12:19am" and beeping. I am annoyed but relieved to have solved the mystery. As I enter the menu of the calculator to turn it off, I have déjà vu. I remember going into this menu, I remember setting the alarm but not for midnight, for 19... Lab 19. Mabel. Patel. The Spray. The Room. Jump? Jump. Choices. Changes. Sujatha. A bomb. Amy. Wasserman. Russia? Meer? It all comes rushing back in a torrent of words and images and sounds and smells. The last and most intense thought is sabotage. Someone had sabotaged the plan. And I ... I need to sabotage the experiment. I can't comprehend all the ideas that were floating through my brain so I grab onto the one thing that seems imperative. Sabotage. It reverberated over and over again until I wrote it down on a piece of paper. Sabotage. I am scheduled to work tomorrow but I have this test first thing in the morning. Sabotage, ok, I tuck that away and go back to studying for my test. I need an A for my scholarship and nothing is going to mess with that. Nothing.

卍 卍 卍

After the test, I sit down on a bench just outside the Science Center and breathe. I am exhausted from pushing away thoughts of sabotage so I could focus on my test but I had done it. I am a beast at academics; I assure myself. But now, sabotage.

I close my eyes and try to let myself remember but the images are overwhelming. I pull out paper and pen instead, and I write. I learned stream of consciousness writing my senior year in high school. My English teacher made us do it every day for five minutes before we even said "Good Morning." I do it now and think of him. Fifteen minutes later, I stop and look back at what I wrote. It is like some crazy acid-fueled poem. I had written with a multicolored pen and changed colors as I wrote. It scares me a little. I don't quite believe it but on some level, I do. I was part of some kind of rebellion. I was on a mission and I had to destroy the experiment, the death star. Or Khan. And no one could know. Ridiculous and yet…

I'm not religious or a poet or a mystic. I believe in science. She is my God. Challenging and reassuring, she chooses when to hide or reveal great mysteries. She is at once unfathomable and yet transparent, and I am her faithful follower. I decide to trust that I am not crazy and that I have glimpsed the future and am needed to preserve it. I decide to believe myself and that what I have written is the truth. I am many things, but I am not prone to flights of fancy. So, I gather up my faith, buy a cheesesteak from Zo on the corner and go to my job in Lab 19.

As soon as I enter, I see the cameras and I peek the metal. I swap out some of the liquid in the vials with hydrogen peroxide and set it aside to be tested at a lab in Delaware. It takes two weeks to come back, but there was LSD in one and PCP in the other. After that confirmation, I swap out the liquids each and every time. I am very careful about the camera. I pretend to conduct the experiments and complete the required paperwork. I even give Patel the cheek swab he asks for with no questions asked. I feign apathy. I do this for the entire semester. I lose the stream of consciousness papers. I think they went out in a moment of overzealous recycling.

Regular life continues. I enjoy my other classes, I make a few new friends, I hook-up with a girl at Bryn Mawr, and I get a few new tattoos. I run into an old friend from high school and we start hanging out. She's not my type, but, there's something about her I like.

卍 卍 卍

When I come back to school in the fall, I get the same work-study assignment with Dr. Patel in Lab 19. He seems anxious when we meet to review the protocols but I smile and nod and when he leaves, continue my sabotage. I can hardly remember how or why I started but I know I must continue.

Then one night, after I leave work, there is a terrible fire in the Science Building. I see it on the news as soon as I get home that night. It was some kind of explosion they say. The next day, I am called in to talk to the police with all the rest of the work-study students. The lab is destroyed along with Patel's office and all the offices and labs on the east side of the building. Professor Patel is so shaken up, he takes an immediate leave of absence and my work-study is re-assigned to the Science Library next door. Every day, I go to class and watch them demolish the building. The next semester, I watch as they rebuild it. And I have dreams. Crazy dreams of being pregnant, an old warehouse, color lines on tissue thin paper, sex on a blazing hot beach, and frosted Russian spires.

卍 卍 卍

I receive the NASA fellowship I've always wanted for two glorious summers in a row and I do my best to make the most of it. Then I apply to MIT for graduate school and am accepted. I get a scholarship for a full ride from The Amy Archeletta Foundation. The name sounds vaguely familiar but I can't place it. Apparently, the CEO is a young but ultra-rich heiress with millions to donate, mostly to women in the sciences. The application came in the mail and I filled it out on a whim. Three months later, when the award letter arrived, it is very brief and on very expensive stationary. I am fascinated by the Foundation's logo because it doesn't seem very scientific or even businesslike. It is a flower with seven red petals, and each petal is a tear-drop mandala. I stare at it for a long time until my eyes wander to the amount of the award. Then that is all I can think about and I cry for joy as I run down the hall to show my mom.

She is sitting on the edge of her bed, combing out my sister's hair while they both try to figure out the clues on *Wheel of Fortune*. I stop at the threshold of the room. I remember doing this exact same thing on the exact same edge of the exact same bed with my mom. Is that what we looked like? Me, annoyed at the pulling of hair but distracted enough and wise enough to keep my mouth shut. My mother going about the job of it, detangling and smoothing and braiding and twisting on the barrette without even looking. The ease of their companionship makes me ache with regret. That was me, that was us, before. My mother hears my sigh and looks up to see the tears in my eyes.

"What's the matter? You miss getting your hair done?" she teases. I kinda do but I don't tell her that. I just hold out the award letter. She nudges Maya to hold the end of her braid while she takes the paper and reads it. Her mouth slowly drops open then I see her close her eyes tight. I know she is thanking God. She gently moves Maya out the way and stands up to face me.

"Kim. This is such a blessing. I'm so happy for you and proud of you. I really am. You done good. Real good for yourself." And then she opens her arms to hug me and I fall into the embrace and sob. I feel Maya's skinny arms reach around my waist while my mother just holds me.

"What happened? Why are you crying, Kim?" she asks. I can't speak.

"Your sister is on her way to the moon, Maya, straight to the moon and she is so happy she can't do nothing else but cry about it."

I laugh and think to myself, 'Mars, Mom, I'm on my way to Mars'. I wipe my tears, we disentangle, and Mom and Maya resume their positions on the edge of the bed. I sit cross-legged behind them, determined to guess the clues first. My mom can't stop smiling, neither can I.

卐 卐 卐

Graduation is hot, long and mostly boring but actually feels like a beginning rather than the end. Afterwards in the chaos of families trying to find their graduates, I'm standing up on a step, scanning the crowd for my mother when someone speaks in my ear.

"Hey big shot! You looked pretty good up there." I turn, gasp with happiness and just grab her.

"Jen! Oh, I'm so glad to see you." She laughs and hugs me back. We rock side to side until I pull away and look at her.

"Where have you been? I miss you! How did you get here? Were you here the whole time?" I pull her back in a hug.

"Ok, ok already, you are pulling my hair out!" She laughs, takes a step back and hands me a small wrapped box. I unwrap it and remove the lid. It's a silver necklace with a star shaped pendant. The center of the pendant is a small dark gray bulbous rock. I look up at her.

"Is this a meteorite?" She nods, I laugh and give her another hug and kiss on the cheek.

"Congratulations Kim! I am so happy for you. Your mom told me you were going to on MIT. I just wanted you to keep your dream close to you, always in sight."

"Thank you so much. It's perfect."

"Jen!" My mother, Walter, Maya and Lil' Walt weave through the crowd. My mom gives Jen a hug.

"It's so good to see you. We've really missed you. Brittney is growing up so nice, though."

Jen steps back, her smile falters a bit.

"It's good to see you, too." She turns to me and says, "I know you all have plans. I'm gonna go. I just really wanted to see you graduate."

"Come to lunch with us, there's plenty of room in the car."

"No, I can't. Thank you, but I have to go back to New York ..." She starts to back up and wave her hands in a good-bye. But I can't let her go. I step down and in between, blocking out my family. I speak in low tones so only Jen will hear me.

"You are my family as much as any of them. If you don't want to come to lunch, that's fine but I don't want to lose touch with you, again. Give me your phone...please?" She reluctantly hands it to me. I look at the password protection and type in the word, "Beyonce". It opens. I look up at her shaking my head.

"Still? Really? So predictable ... sad ... pathetic, really."

"What!? I love her!"

I type in my contact information, then hit dial. My phone rings. It's the Star Trek anthem. She laughs and I hand her back her phone. "Now, I'll call you later. There are a bunch of parties tonight, ok?" She's quiet. "I don't want to go alone. Stay for one night. Come on. It'll be fun. Like old times, I promise. I'll see if I can find Kendra, too. Maybe she's still in town." She looks around, then back at me and sighs.

"Ok. Call me." She waves good-bye and walks into the crowd. I turn to look at my family who are all grinning at me.

"Where are we going to eat? I'm starving."

శ్రీ శ్రీ శ్రీ

For graduation, my mother and Walter bought me a new laptop/briefcase. It is expensive, beautiful and perfect. I empty out my old backpack, finding old pens and paper clips, grimy coins and hard, forgotten pieces of gum. I also find a small sheet of notebook paper. It is covered with a few variations of a strange chemical equation involving gamma waves and PCP and silver. The handwriting is mine though I don't remember writing it. I am just about to crumple it up and toss it when I notice a word squeezed in at the very bottom. Phobos. I stop and stare at the word, something in me buzzing. I refold the note and tuck it into my wallet. I bet I can figure this out when I get to MIT.

✦ THE END ✦

Made in the USA
Lexington, KY
16 September 2019

Acknowledgements

I would like to thank NaNoWriMo again for givin
assignment and a deadline and helping me get this
of my head and onto a laptop. That was the fun part
harder parts, I was helped by my real-life frie
colleagues who gave me the most precious gift in th
world – their time.

Thank you, Loretta Brown, for editing the first
the book. Your detailed insights and grammar no
invaluable. Thank you to my beta readers, Teresa Mi
Iatarola, Carla Fisher and Kelly Ward for reading and
your thoughts and feedback with me. It really h
improve the story and I'm ever so grateful. Thank
Aishah Shahidah Simmons and for helping me to
with other authors I would never have been able t
Thank you to Kristal Sotomayor and Eric Hunter, w
been wonderful teammates in my quest to get this n
into the world.

Finally, I want to acknowledge my partner, Kelly
and our children who remain a constant source c
support and humility as I try to do this whole author th

❧❧❧